ENDINGS

ENDINGS

A Novel
by

Barbara Bergin

SANTA FE

book design by Vicki Ahl

Sunstone books may be purchased for educational, business, or sales promotional use.
For information please write: Special Markets Department, Sunstone Press,
P.O. Box 2321, Santa Fe, New Mexico 87504-2321.

Library of Congress Cataloging-in-Publication Data

Bergin, Barbara, 1954-
  Endings : a novel / by Barbara Bergin.
    p. cm.
  ISBN 978-0-86534-519-5 (alk. paper)
  1. Loss (Psychology)–Fiction. 2. Women surgeons–Fiction.
  3. Ranch life–Texas–Fiction. I. Title.

PS3602.E7549E53 2007
813'.6–dc22
                            2007006431

WWW.SUNSTONEPRESS.COM
SUNSTONE PRESS / POST OFFICE BOX 2321 / SANTA FE, NM 87504-2321 /USA
(505) 988-4418 / ORDERS ONLY (800) 243-5644 / FAX (505) 988-1025

To Matt—
We got to keep you.

1

*L*eft hand tightly grasping the steering wheel, the thumb hyperextended, like a hitchhiker. The right hand more relaxed, but placed firmly in the two o'clock position. It's one of the only things she does the same every time, especially now. Now that she tries to do nothing like before.

But her hands are driven to rest in the familiar pose and it triggers unwanted memories. She looks in the rear view mirror, imagines the reflection of matching car seats. Keeping her left hand on the steering wheel, her right hand became an experienced proboscis which could retrieve fallen pacifiers or bottles. When they were little the objects fell accidentally. When they were twelve months old, they dropped them to get attention.

"Mommy! Tell him to get off my side!"

But there was nothing in the mirror. Only spidery black etchings of water streamed down the back window. Black on black. The road from Brownwood dropped imperceptibly away.

Stop now. Pinching her cheeks to the point of pain. Do something to force the images out of her mind. She focused on the raindrops which moved to the beat of little second hand timers, coalescing into larger drops that slid down the windshield to end up on the highway. Leslie quickly moved her hands from ten and two, to eleven and one. Focus on the car in front of her.

But it wasn't a car at all. It was the back of a horse trailer. She hadn't been paying attention. Gradually slowing down. Someone hauling a trailer had to go around her. It was raining hard. The windshield wipers were slashing frantically side to side and still, seeing in front of her was difficult.

Where had the past twenty miles gone? A sign up ahead, color green for locations in Texas, listed several cities along with their distances. Rising Star, Cross Plains, then Abilene, sixty-six miles. She was tired and knew she should pull over. Only another hour. She could do it. She'd done it lots of times.

She focused on the trailer. Someone once told her if she got behind something that took longer to stop than she did, it would be safer because there would be plenty of time to stop, even if they slammed on their brakes. She dropped back a little. The water on the road was deep and every once in a while she could feel her wheels hydroplane on the low parts of the highway. It made her heart skip. Why did she care? The important time to feel scared and prepared had passed three years ago. She had failed then. Her sympathetic nervous system should be numb. Should be rock solid now. But when she felt the deep water in the road and the transient loss of control, her heart sped up, her stomach tightened and she knew her pupils dilated.

She remembered that time when the kids were riding bikes in the neighborhood and Vic had an accident. They were about six or seven. They had been out riding at dusk. Victor had crossed the street without paying attention and had carelessly run into a parked car. He was not wearing his helmet and had sustained quite a bump on the head. The neighbors called EMS and Leslie was contacted by the emergency room physician. When it was certain that he was okay, she and her husband discussed the lessons to be learned. Should he be grounded from use of the bicycle? Must he always come and do a "helmet check" before going out to ride. Should there be rules regarding careless mistakes? The rules that would help him become a responsible adult. But what if he didn't live to become an adult?

The trailer spewed up rain clouds, swirling on either side. Where was a horse trailer going in this weather, this fast? Leslie had grown up with horses and was somewhat of a hand at one time. In another life. She couldn't recall any truck that could pull any trailer at that speed when she was growing up. Her daddy used an old diesel truck to pull their two-horse trailer. He could shift gears without pushing in the clutch.

As they drove into each curve she could see this wasn't some old truck. In New York she never saw trucks. People just didn't drive trucks as a rule. No space for parking, gas prices too high, politically incorrect. But when she passed from Louisiana into Texas, trucks became the rule. Big trucks, jacked up trucks, off road tires, bright colors, four doors and lots of ranching accoutrements like tool boxes, wenches, and deer guards.

From what she could see, this was a matched set. The trailer, white and polished aluminum with red and black trim. She could see wide dual fenders peeking out from in front of the trailer. The truck was white. Dad's truck had been brown and mustard yellow. His trailer was primer red, mostly rust. They were proud of that rig, especially when there was livestock in it.

The trailer slid on the wet pavement as it took the curves and when it did she knew to get ready for the hydroplane. She was becoming more comfortable with the conditions now and settled into her space behind the trailer, not noticing that they were going seventy on a two lane highway in the middle of a thunderstorm. Leslie was mentally and physically locked in behind the trailer. They were alone, moving in tandem. Going into a turn, the capsule shaped tail-lights suddenly became bright red and the trailer slowed down. Then she could see the truck in full to the left of the trailer. Odd, because she could never see more than the fenders on any other turn. The truck had a black brush guard. Why could she see it? Then it was gone and the trailer started sliding, sliding until she was looking squarely at its broadside. It was a gooseneck trailer and she was facing the back of the truck underneath the gooseneck. She was confused. Was she just a spectator in a truck and trailer dream?

Suddenly startled, she slammed on her brakes. She forgot the rule about turning into the spin. Instinctively she turned the other way and crashed sideways into the back of the truck. The trailer was behind her, also sliding sideways. In slow motion it began to swing back behind the truck, crashing into the little Ford Taurus. Leslie began to give up. Why not? Why had she put her seat belt on? Was she screaming? Screaming like she did when she saw her husband and her children facing her in the opposite lane when they had been going her way only one second before. Screaming like when the eighteen-wheeler hit their mid-sized sedan sideways and it began to spin like those carnival pictures made with paint squeezed onto a piece of cardboard on a centrifuge. Screaming didn't do a damn bit of good then. It never does. It just comes out.

As the trailer righted itself there was no room for her Taurus. It shoved her toward the shoulder and she slammed into the guard rail with her right front fender. The Taurus began to go to work to save her. The airbag deployed. For a split second she saw the truck and trailer moving away, pulling over. Now a crash into the guardrail on her left front fender was followed by one from behind. The car came to rest. She was facing the guardrail.

She was alive. She felt a sense of elation. Natural instinct. The inherent struggle to live. Now the doctor in her began to go to work, second nature, learned behavior, but after almost twenty years of combined education and practical experience it was fairly intuitive. There was pain in her left shoulder. A broken clavicle? Not uncommon when the seat belt is in place. She reached up and pressed. No crepitus, no fracture. There was pain in the right ankle. Please, no open ankle fracture. With the advent of airbags, people traded life for bad ankle fractures, but sometimes after the agony of trying to heal those fractures, one might rather have taken the airbagless route. She wiggled the ankle up and down. She couldn't reach it because of the airbag. No crunching. Some pain and she could feel the swollen flesh starting to press up against her hiking boot. Hopefully, just a sprain.

She looked out of the window and through the cracked safety glass she saw a man running toward her. "Hey, you okay?" he yelled. She could see the trailer behind him, emergency lights flashing.

"I think so," she mumbled to herself.

He pulled on the door and when it wouldn't budge, ran back to his truck and returned with a crowbar. He pried the door open. She felt his hand on her shoulder. "Are you okay?"

"Yes. Can you give me a hand with this seatbelt?"

"Yes ma'am," he said, with a slight Texas drawl. Not the kind they made fun of in New York. Pleasant. Concerned. She couldn't remember the last time someone called her ma'am.

He reached in to help her out of the seat. "Easy now." Like she was a horse or something. Like she would start flaring her nostrils and snorting, paw at the ground. She stood and followed his directions. First step on the right foot and it hurt like hell. She stumbled forward and he grabbed her.

"Okay, le'me give you a hand here." He-er, a slight two syllable sound.

"I think I just sprained my ankle."

"Let's get out of the rain and we'll take a look. Think you can make it to my truck?" A little flag went up about getting into cars with strangers, but they didn't ever say that there was anything wrong with strangers who had horses and it was probably okay when it was raining really hard.

He was holding her up on the right side, like a human crutch. He opened the door and the passenger seat was instantly drenched with water which beaded up on the leather seats.

The smell of a new car, new leather. Like her BMW, when she cared about that smell. Like Chris's Volvo before the kids stunk it up with food and juice.

Chris never cared. Within a year of getting the car it smelled like a kindergarten classroom. Not the Beemer. No food or juice was the rule. Clear liquids only. As if they were in the recovery room or something. They needed to learn to take care of nice things. Not like Chris' car. That would only lead to a lifetime of sloppy cars. There was always syrupy goo around his cup holders.

She would let them eat a whole fucking Happy Meal in her car now if they wanted to. They could eat all of the stinky foods, like Cheetos and Cornuts if they wanted to. They could leave the half empty bags in her car. Leslie remembered the hash brown potato bags in Chris' car in the junkyard. Silent sentinels of carefree eating. They weren't among the valuables collected and given to her by a clerk at the police station. Who defines "valuables" anyway?

The truck had a step on the side and she had to climb up on the seat. He helped her in, shut the door and ran around the front to the other side. The truck was warm. The engine had been running. Diesel fuel. Dad always said it was cheaper to keep a diesel truck running rather than turn it off and on. Was that true or just diesel folklore? The engine was loud, but not like dad's. More like a deep, smooth rumbling. White noise. She felt warm and comfortable.

The door opened, letting in a rush of rain and noise, the engine, the wind. He hoisted himself into the seat and slammed the door. "Man, can you believe this rain? Your car is bad. I can't believe you only sprained your ankle. Are you sure we don't need to get you to the emergency room?"

She smiled. "No, I'm fine, really. That was so weird. What happened? What happened with your trailer?"

"Well, I'm not sure, but, maybe I was going a little fast into that turn, and when I applied the brakes, well, it's kinda hard to explain, but the dually with those tires, they just don't have the same kind of traction as regular tires and they locked up on me. Then here comes the trailer. It can't go over me, so it just starts to swing out to the side and since the road was wet, it just went sideways. It may have looked weird to you, but I'm looking out my side window at the mirror, and here comes my trailer. Well you know you're supposed to turn in to a spin so that's what I did. Fortunately, no cars were coming in the other lane, or we'd've been dead. That was pure luck for you. As soon as I started turning in to the spin, the trailer began to come around. Then, I swung back straight and figure I'm home free, except for you're in that spot, and you know the rest better than me. You've been behind me a while and I didn't really realize just how close you were. God, I'm sorry. I should have been paying more attention, with the rain and all. I've got my horses back there too. I'm sure they're going, 'damn.' "

"Damn" was a melodic two syllable word.

As he was talking, Leslie began to relax. She felt safe, and a familiar sound and sensation filled the cab. Horses, in a trailer, attached to a truck. They move, stomp and shift their weight. That movement is transmitted to the truck. It's a good feeling. A sign that they're there, and okay. Some horses get anxious standing still. They think it's time to unload. They might kick the side of the trailer, just like one was doing now.

"That's Gomez. He can't stand to be stopped. I keep sayin' I'm gonna have to hobble him in the trailer, but I just can't do it. Imagine if he'd been hobbled tonight! I need to check 'em out. Be right back." He lowered his head and looked at her as one would look over the top of glasses. "Sure you're okay?" He hesitated briefly for an answer and hearing none he continued, "Listen, I already called nine-one-one, and they're sending a tow truck, but it'll be a little while."

The door opened and he jumped out, letting in another blast

of diesel noise and rain. She looked around. Looked for hints of life. No hash brown potato bags. A black felt hat turned upside down on the back seat. Some kind of access sticker on the driver's side of the windshield under the inspection sticker. She felt the slight shift in weight as he stepped up into the trailer. Very slight. Two hundred pounds compared to thirty-five hundred, if he had three horses. The horses began shifting. They think they're unloading. Where were they going? There were two starched shirts hanging on the hook in the back and a canvas duffle bag on the floorboard. Standard issue key chain. Everything was clean. Spartan.

He was back. "Horses okay?"

"They're fine. Listen, I'm Regan. Regan Wakeman." And he put out his hand to shake hers.

She handed him hers. He had a firm handshake and she returned it. He smiled, "and you are...?"

She sighed. "I'm sorry. Leslie Cohen. Pleased to meet you, although maybe not under the circumstances. This is so strange. I can't believe we've had this big wreck and we're just sitting here, uninjured."

"You got that right. For a second, I thought about giving up. I figured the worst was going to happen anyway. It was like slow motion. Me and my horses were going to die. That's rich. Me and my horses. Like a cowboy's way to go."

"So you're a cowboy?"

In the distance lights were flashing, coming toward them. Reflecting off raindrops on the windshield, there were lots of tiny yellow sparkles. She could hear a siren. Now a police car with its red, white and blue lights flashing. Her question went unanswered.

"Here we go." Regan reached down and flashed his lights. "We should exchange insurance information." He reached in his glove compartment and handed Leslie a neatly laminated insurance card. "I guess I kind of lost control of my vehicle. You can copy this stuff down while you're waiting and I'll help them get your car situated. Paper and pen's in there."

She reached forward to open the glove compartment again.

"Is your insurance card in the car?"

She nodded.

"You stay put. I'll go get it after I talk to this guy."

"Listen, I'm probably at fault since I'm the one who ran into the back of your truck."

"Well, I lost control of my rig." He looked straight ahead, then turned to Leslie. "It all happened so fast." He shrugged his shoulders. "Hey, that's what insurance companies and the police are for. We'll tell them the story. One of us will probably get a ticket. The important thing is, we're alive. It could've been a lot worse."

The police car and the tow truck were pulling up. The police stopped in front of them and the tow truck went around back. The siren was turned off in mid-bleep, making a bloop sound instead. Just diesel engine and rain noise again. Regan jumped out of the cab and into the rain. He had taken control of the situation. Leslie wasn't sure she liked it, but right now she didn't have the energy to do much about it. So what was she going to say? "Now, let's just hold on here Mr. Wakeman and don't put the cart before the horse." That would be putting things in his terms, wouldn't it?

She watched him through the rain. He was a big guy, but not heavy. Maybe a defensive end in high school. She laughed at her habit of describing a man's phenotype based on high school football player body types. Chris had taught her to identify football players by their build. They had loved to talk football. Especially after Vic started playing pee wee ball. So did Regan have a big gut? Offensive lineman? Hard to tell because he was wearing one of those gold canvas jackets with the brown corduroy collars that she had seen a couple of times in rural areas. She couldn't tell if he had a beer gut or not. He had on starched blue jeans. They were wet and bunched up down at his boots. He shook hands with the policeman, pointed toward the car, then toward the back of the truck. He shoved his hands in the coat pockets and hunched his shoulders forward to shelter himself from the rain and wind. As if that would make a damn bit of difference.

Regan stood with his legs apart. They looked thick and strong. Defensive end. He had short hair but she couldn't tell much about it because he had on a baseball cap. The bill was curved, hand curved, like Vic used to lovingly shape his caps. And hers. "Mom, you don't wear ball caps flat like that. It's gay." Then he would bend the bill to the desired curve of stylishness.

Leslie thought to herself, he's probably giving the policeman his version of me smashing into the back of his truck and I'm going to get the ticket. Insurance companies and policemen, my ass. Try good ol' boys. Oh, well, that's what insurance is for. It struck her funny because in the past, every other time she rented her cars, she initialed the part indicating she wanted the full coverage thing. Not every time. Just every other time. It was a rip off, really, she thought, but it was just something she started doing and this was one of the times she had signed for it. "Yyeess."

The policeman turned to get in his car. Regan walked to her side of the truck and signaled to her to roll down her window by scrolling his finger. She did as she was told. They had sign language now.

"Is there anything you need out of your car?" He was bouncing on the balls of both feet as though he might be trying to dodge raindrops and it was definitely cute. He was definitely cute. Simply making an observation.

"Just the insurance papers in my purse. Front passenger seat I think. Could you grab the rental car papers there too?" He looked at her quizzically for a second. People probably don't rent cars around Abilene as a rule. She was used to getting those kinds of looks because people associated rented cars with tourist areas, not small towns in the middle of nowhere, which was often where she ended up.

He soon climbed back in the driver's seat, handing her the papers and her purse. They were soaking wet. "Window's broken. Everything got wet. Sorry."

"Don't worry about it. It's not your fault, really."

"Hey, that's what I told the officer." He paused and looked her straight in the eyes. Very serious look on his face. Then he smiled." Just kidding." She gave him a mad look and they both laughed. She felt like laughing right now. Things were already too serious. She looked down at her lap and then got busy with the purse. She jotted down her insurance information for him, both insurance companies. Thank you very much, she thought.

"Now, where did you say you were from and what are you doing out here...in a rent car?" There was a knock on the window.

"I didn't say..." He was rolling down the window. Asked the trooper if he wanted to get in the truck.

"No sir." He looked down the road. Maybe thinking about it. "But thank you anyway, sir. I'll just need both of your proofs of insurance and drivers licenses." They complied and he returned to his car. Regan didn't repeat his question. She was glad. No need for small talk. There was no point in it. He put his seat back a little and she stared straight ahead, focused on the raindrops and the police car lights.

The officer returned and went to the driver's side again, handing Regan all of the papers. The licenses were stuck into a slot on the top of his small metal clipboard in the universal ticket writing position.

"Unless you object, I'm not going to give either of you a citation. Both of you may have failed to maintain control of your vehicles, and the weather certainly played a part. Do either of you have any objections?"

They looked at each other, as if to ask, "Do you?" Then, "No" from both of them.

He handed Regan his license. "Mr. Wakeman." Next he handed Leslie hers. "Miss Cohen?"

"Mrs." She took her license from his hand.

Regan looked at her left hand as she reached for the card. There was no ring. She was sure he noticed. She stopped wearing the rings on her finger about a year ago. They made people ask questions. "Where is your husband? Do you have children? How do you live away from your family for so long?" Answers led to more questions, curiosity and the worst, sympathy. It was easier not to wear the rings but they hung, always, on a strong gold chain around her neck. They were safe that way and it was convenient. She had to remove them frequently anyway to scrub her hands for surgery. She used to pin them to her scrubs but on more than one occasion had lost them in the laundry. She had to dig through bloody scrubs to find them.

"They're going to tow the car to Abilene. Do you care where they take it?" She shook her head. "Then, if you're ready, Mrs. Cohen, I'll take you to town so you can check into a hotel or wherever you were headed."

Regan looked at her like, "and you were headed where?"

"Actually, I already have a reservation." There was an awkward moment, when she thought Regan might offer to drive her, and in a way she might have expected it. She quickly added, "Regan, I'm really sorry we had this accident but it was nice to meet you anyway, and thanks for helping me out."

"Hey, no problem. Same here, I mean, glad to meet you too. Can I help y'all with her bags or something?"

"No, sir, that won't be necessary. The tow service will take care of that in the morning when they get her trunk open." He turned to Leslie. "Ma'am, if you're ready." She smiled at Regan and shook his hand. Again, a strong handshake and as she squeezed back he held it for a split second longer. Their eyes met. She saw brown eyes, smile wrinkles on the sides, a small vertical wrinkle in between soft eyebrows. He smiled, and there was something else in the smile. Regret? Did she want regret? The trooper was doing the hopping thing outside the window. Was that a Texas guy thing? Cute.

She got out and pain shot through the ankle. She tried not to flinch and held her ground. Pain is just pain. It can't hurt you. She didn't want Regan to come around and do the human crutch thing again. She stiffened up her foot and ankle and stepped with a respectable limp.

"Do you need help there, ma'am?"

"No, I'm fine." And she was.

The tow truck, purple with black and gold lacey decals, itself a work of art, pulled out and for the first time she saw her rented Taurus on the flat bed. Its condition was shocking. It was totaled. It was crushed on the three sides she could see. She wondered about the damage to Regan's truck. Thank goodness she had not run into the horse trailer. She pictured their delicate legs getting knocked out from under them. Innocent animals, they were never meant to ride in an aluminum box. The truck labored up to speed, straightened out and headed toward Abilene.

Now Regan. Left hand signal light flashing, the truck slowly pulled up and over the ledge of asphalt on the shoulder, each tire rolling over it sent a lurch through the truck and trailer until all ten wheels were on the highway. The engine noise grinding to a higher and higher pitch until it slipped into the next gear automatically. The goose neck compartment over the truck slowly swung into place and the whole rig moved past like a ship. She turned to look at the capsule shaped tail-lights through the raindrops on her window.

Voices came across the police radio, scratchy, incomplete. Does the technology of police and taxi radio dispatching ever improve? She couldn't make it all out but soon the officer responded with their location and his plan to take her to the hotel.

"Where're you staying, by the way...chk, schk, chk, the irritating hen scratch from the two way...No I'm trying to get that information right now, hold on. Mrs. Cohen, your hotel?"

"Holiday Inn Express."

"Holiday Inn Express, on Interstate twenty. No one's hurt. She has denied emergency treatment so we're on our way."

"Mrs. Cohen, you're gonna need to contact your insurance carrier in the morning. We'll take care of the accident report."

She was starting to feel sorry for herself and she hated herself for it. Tears began welling up in her eyes and there was that familiar tingling in the nose and under the eyes that preceded them. She was not going to let a tear roll down her cheek or sniff one up her nose. She started blinking. One single tear filled the corner of her right eye, stayed suspended there for a second, then fell over the edge. It rolled down the side of her nose and lost momentum when it reached her lip. She tilted her head back and forced the feeling out of her mind. Think of a funny thing or an angry thing. The tears that were marching to freedom, through a combination of will power and pressure from repeated blinking, were forced back into the tear duct to wait until later when they, and hundreds more like them, could flow freely as always.

The officer looked straight ahead and put the car into drive. He recognized the signs of a woman thinking about crying and did not want to help it along by asking if she was okay. Didn't want to go there. No way. No how. It was never as simple as "Wrecking my car makes me want to cry." He let her be and didn't look over until they got to the hotel.

"Here we are. Abilene's finest. The restaurant out front here's pretty good. When the tow truck gets your trunk open tomorrow they'll deliver your stuff here. I'll make sure they know where you're staying." He handed her a wet business card. "Here's their card if you wanna call them. They're good guys. My brother-in-law's one of the drivers. Anyway, I guess that's about it. Anything else you can think of?"

She pulled the handle on the door and stepped out, the ankle still there. "Thanks for your help. G'night." The car pulled away and she stood alone in the portico of the hotel.

Abilene, Texas. There was a wonderful smell in the air. Clean, west Texas air after a rainstorm. Some combination of ozone and miles of dusty roads soaking up the long awaited rain. She breathed it in deep.

That smell was something her mom defined for her when she was a kid. When it would start to rain they would go outside to smell the air. If they were driving, they would open the vents to let it fill the car. She, in turn taught her kids to love it too. "Turn on the vent, mom! Let's smell the rain!" The longer the drought, the better the smell. The air from the vent would be steamy and fog up the window. She took a big breath and was smiling when the automatic doors opened and she walked into the lobby.

2

"Mrs. Cohen, right?" A thin, very dark, East Indian man was standing behind the counter.

"Yes, how did you know?"

"We do not have many people checking in tonight. You are the only woman, so I figured it was you." He smiled and said in a pleasant lilting accent, "You're going to be with us for a very long time, I see. You know your account has been covered and the only thing you will be responsible for is your long distance calls, laundry and any movies you might order. Is this your understanding?"

"Uh huh," she replied absently. She handed him her credit card, he struck a copy and filed it.

"How many keys you will need?"

"One."

He put a plastic card into the magnet, then slid it into a little envelope.

"You are in room two twenty-five, up the elevator, to the right. Continental breakfast is served every morning at six o'clock. There is coffee available twenty-four hours a day in the dining area. Will there be anything else?"

"Do you have a few things like a toothbrush and toothpaste? I was in an accident and my stuff is stuck in the trunk of my car."

"Oh, my goodness! I'm so sorry! Is everything okay?"

"Yes, thank you. Everything is fine."

"Of course, of course, we have some necessary things." He handed her a simple blue toothbrush in a plastic package, the kind you can't buy in a store anymore. Just dentist's offices and hotels. There were a couple of aluminum packets of toothpaste, a small deodorant roller and a little brush. "Here you go."

"Thank you. Goodnight."

"Goodnight Mrs. Cohen. If there is anything I can do for you, please call. My name is Raghu Ramaswamy and my wife, Kala, is here during the day." The soft voice was pleasing and familiar to her Northeastern ear. How did they end up in Abilene? He probably wondered the same about her.

She walked down the hall to the elevator. Mirrors with fake gold marbling covered the wall of the elevator and she tried not to look at herself, but she did. She looked like shit. Her curly hair was frizzing like a halo around her head. She had been nervously twirling it with her fingers so the strands by the sides of her face were clumped together and she looked...really...stupid. She made a squirrel face and squirrel sound into the mirror. The elevator door opened because she had forgotten to push a floor and an older couple got on. They probably didn't see her squirrel face but she was pretty sure they heard the squirrel noise she made with her front teeth on her lower lip. She pushed two, they pushed three, the door closed and she leaned back into the corner, the naughty schoolgirl.

Her room was clean and as expected. She liked staying in cities where she could find a newer chain of hotels, the kind with inside hallway doors. She could barely hear the highway sounds, eighteen wheelers heading east and west, making time at night. She felt connected, in her own way, with those night drivers. Faceless, driving behind tinted windows.

Now she would go through the litany of thoughts which would bring back the tear soldiers. And come they did. It had been three years since the accident. She had put miles and months behind her but the intensity of her feelings never seemed to diminish. Big tears fell. She threw herself on the bed and lay there, face up. They rolled out the corners of her eyes, down into her hair, into her ears. Her nose became stuffed up.

When she was a kid she had stayed up one night and watched *Twilight Zone*. Hiding behind a chair, she was unseen by her parents. Years later this one episode became both a nightmare and a symbol of total loneliness. In fact she had described the episode to Chris and it had become their catch phrase for being physically or psychologically alone. "Whoa, *Twilight Zone!*" Never in her dreams did she imagine she would live in it.

A group of space explorers had traveled to some Mars-like planet with four suns and no nightfall. Somehow their means of getting back to Earth had failed and they were marooned. Out of necessity they developed their own social structure and government. A person who had previously been a lower level worker on the spaceship became a despotic leader on this desolate planet. Many years later a rescue mission materialized and a ship came for the stranded explorers. Everyone was to assemble for the return and there was a specific lift-off time. Their leader was upset for the obvious reasons. He would be forced to resume his lowly position on Earth. He tried to convince people to stay, but they would have none of it. In fine *Twilight Zone* fashion he stayed behind, only to realize too late the mistake he had made. He ran screaming toward the space ship taking off in the distance. He then returned to the deserted settlement. The sunlight, heat and desolation seemed oppressive.

Leslie had been terrified by this episode despite the absence of monsters. She was sure the show had been in black and white, but in her mind's eye the stage was red. The four suns intensely yellow. And now, she lived there too.

3

*L*eslie was the only child of elderly parents. They had passed away a couple of years apart, while she was in school. Her husband tried to fill the gap. Life went on. She was as prepared for her parents' death as any child could be. They had both lived long, happy lives. After her dad died, her mom became despondent and was never herself again. She lived for a while with Leslie and Chris. When she started needing constant supervision, Leslie had to place her in a nursing home. Wasn't long before mom joined dad but she lived to see her daughter graduate from medical school even if she didn't know it.

After her mom died Leslie took a year off from school and during that year she got pregnant with the twins.

After the accident, she was alone. *Twilight Zone* alone. More to it than just being lonely. Sometimes when she cried she called for mom and dad, sometimes Chris, Vic and Vivi. Now she was having trouble remembering their faces, except for the last time she saw them. Pictures at a carnival.

She lay there in the dark, staring at the ceiling. Little pieces of foam stuck forever in an endless landscape of acoustic white. Light from the parking lot bled into the room from behind the plastic curtain along with the waxing and waning sounds of trucks and cars on the highway. This was to be her home for the next month or so. Its similarity to all her other homes was a slight comfort. The king-sized bed, microwave oven, mini-fridge and coffeemaker were all she required right now. Tomorrow she would repeat a ritual of purchasing the necessities. They would be left behind when she departed. She would eat meals at the hospital.

The flow of tears slowed, all played out. She began to focus on the foam pieces on the ceiling. A form of self-hypnosis. She could search for the patterns, lose them and find them again. In time the tears dried against her temples, plastering strands of hair into their crystalline rivulets. Slowly she began to lose focus on the patterns and finally fell asleep, deep sleep, which she needed. Her mind took care of her in that way. She had important work to do each day and when the opportunity presented itself, sleep would come. Once she had read that ship captains learned to sleep deeply during the short interludes between watches and action. Their bodies and minds were forced to adjust to the rigors of life and war at sea. Sleeping was the only time Leslie's mind was not fighting the memories. She appreciated her brain's offer of that luxury. Deep sleep and no dreams. She had friends who would see their parents or others from the past in disturbing dreams. It would seem real to them, almost like a visit. She could thank her brain for that deficiency as well.

Over the past three years she had come to appreciate her brain. She had good reason to be depressed, clinically depressed, and she supposed that she probably was. She was tearful, a lot. Her appetite had diminished. She didn't even have a desire to taste good food. Initially she lost sleep. Of all the signs of depression, this one could have been the most devastating. Her work required her full attention, attention to every detail. Sleep deprivation could be a killer. Sometime after she finished her residency, they made some new rules about the number of hours residents and medical students could work because studies showed there was a direct correlation between hours worked and patient complications. She didn't really buy that because when you're in the heat of battle, surgery or ships, you're wide awake, energized. And if you're not, then pick another field, dermatology or something. Of course, if you're a ship captain, you're dead.

Six months after the accident, she finally started to sleep. No need to take pills, not for sleep and not for depression. She owed Chris and the kids her depression and she carried it with her like a backpack. But the sleep helped. There were a few times when she felt like taking her own life, but her brain said no, so she couldn't do it. Couldn't find the way to do it. Couldn't get the energy to do it. Another sign of depression. No energy to commit suicide. Sometimes really depressed people start taking anti-depressants and then, just when everyone is feeling good about the change in behavior...*voilà*...they find a rope and end it. When they're really depressed, they can't find the rope. Leslie had plenty of energy now but she was way past looking for ropes.

The wheat must be taken with the chafe. That's the way it works. The good with the bad. Good brain lets her sleep. Bad brain serves up the memories with amazing efficiency. When it's ready to do so, there's no stopping it. Leslie's brain was a good one for the most part and she had to forgive it for the memories because it also gave her the ability to memorize the Krebs cycle, and so many facts, both useful and useless, which enabled her to get into medical school and ultimately become an orthopedic surgeon.

Her wonderful brain has an area called the *cingulate gyrus*. It's a little comma-shaped area nestled deep inside that links sensations with memories and emotions. It's conveniently placed so it gets first dibs on the sensations coming in from the outside. Things like smell, taste and feel. They're shuttled into the *cingulate gyrus* just like into other parts of the brain that enable one to move or decide or scream or operate. But in the *cingulate gyrus*, a smell or a sighting hooks right up to some old visceral feeling, good or bad. The smell of certain cologne might remind her of an old boyfriend. The smell of a baking cake, a wonderful day she had with her mom when she was six years old, and she might be able to see that day and whatever was important in her mind. The color of a table cloth. The taste of ice, chipped from the freezer. Licking the icing from the little cagey stainless steel beaters, a precious offering from her mom. Working her tongue in between them to get every possible ounce of icing. Just from the smell of a baking cake. Boom. Before *Twilight Zone*, it could really be a wonderful feeling. A link to her past, usually pleasant in every regard. Warm memories of a terrific childhood, free of struggles.

Now every possible visual, oral, or auditory stimulus with even a remote connection was taking the B-line to the *cingulate gyrus* and shuttling it right to the stream of consciousness, wherever that was. Focusing on work, her next assignment, or foam particles on the ceiling was the only way to keep the brain confused, get it off track. Otherwise, in idle moments, sensations came in and opened the photo album. Sometimes they were good memories, a vacation. Sometimes bad. A cut or a bad grade. But now they were surely unwanted, and she worked hard to keep them away.

Leslie slept.

Out on the wet highway passing trucks were fewer and farther between. And out off County Road 605, between Abilene and Rowden, Regan Wakeman was lying in bed wide awake, still thinking about the events of this evening. How had it started? He had never had a wreck, even when he was just starting to drive and having an accident, for most of his peers, was just another rite of passage. Tonight he had almost caused, or been part of an accident that could have been catastrophic for him, that lady and the horses.

After leaving the accident and, "What was her name? Leslie. C something," he had continued north on 36, then to his place. He unloaded the horses, fed and watered them. That was a chore in the rain. He disconnected the trailer, only after he had completely detached the tailgate by its hinge. The Taurus had smashed in the bumper, which had in turn come up and smashed the tailgate, which in turn disrupted the locking mechanism. After a shower he tried to read in bed but was too keyed up to fall asleep. What a lapse of attention on his part. He felt a surge of nausea. Besides the fact that a person could have died, just a small injury to a horse could be devastating, requiring euthanasia on the spot. He had friends who had to shoot horses with broken legs just to put them out of their pain and keep them from flailing about or trying to get up. He went over and over the scene in his mind until the sky over the flat plains outside of Abilene started to turn pink.

4

*T*he phone rang at eight o'clock sharp as planned. Leslie answered it after the first ring. She was instantly wide awake. Answering the phone quickly was a habit. Calls at night were usually emergencies and required thoughtful attention. She always felt that she had to sound as if she were not asleep when she answered. Responding quickly made it seem as if she were sitting by the phone, waiting for the call. And extra rings usually woke up everyone in the house, even though it didn't matter now.

"Hello." Expectant voice, with only a touch of morning scratchiness.

"Dr. Cohen?"

"Yes." Now the voice was tested, and adjustments made to erase all remnants of sleep.

"Hey, Terryl Wells here. We weren't sure you were going to make it in last night, with the rain and all! Did you have a good trip over from Louisiana?"

"Do you want to know the truth or would just a 'yeah, no problems,' do?"

"Wait a minute, you weren't by any chance involved in that truck and trailer deal out on thirty-six last night, were you?"

"Okay, so you want the truth. How did you know about it?"

"Well, the emergency room folks got a whiff of it through EMS, even though nothing materialized, in terms of, you know, ER admits. This is a small community and word gets around. Man, I can't believe it was you. What happened?"

"I'll tell you what. Aren't we supposed to get together today to go over things at the hospital?"

"We are."

"So, why don't we talk about it over coffee?"

"Sure, sure, sorry. How much time you need?"

"Give me forty-five minutes. I'll need a ride."

"No problem."

"And actually, we better make it an hour so I can call the rental company and get them started on delivering another car."

"An hour for a lady to get dressed, after having a wreck and just waking up. Can you talk to my wife?"

"I was already awake." She lied unnecessarily.

"Uh huh. Well, I tell you what. Why don't we meet at that restaurant out front of your hotel? It's pretty good. Good breakfast. That way, if you're running a little late, I'll just wait for you."

"Sounds good. See you in an hour." She hung up and looked at the clock. 8:10. How did that happen? She overslept. Not that she cared. It's just that her inner clock always woke her up at about six o'clock in the morning. She must have been tired. Setting an alarm was something she almost never did anymore.

Leslie swung her feet over the side of the bed and it hit her. That delayed soreness after an accident. It's the same soreness some accident victims can't ever shake off and just attribute to getting tossed around. Nothing's broken. It'll get better. As Leslie stretched, she smiled, thinking about the tendency to call an attorney versus a doctor.

"Bet there's the phone number of one conveniently located on the shiny back page of my telephone book." It was the universal back page of every phone book, in almost any community she'd been to. "What the hell do they do in places where they don't have trial lawyers? Go to a doctor? Hey, that's a good idea. How about just wait and see if it gets better on its own."

She picked up the phone book to look up the local rental car agency. Couldn't resist the urge to confirm her theory. Sure enough. If a town can support an orthopedic surgeon, it can support a trial lawyer. Ed Sayers. Specializing in negligence of all sorts. Nursing homes, accidents, medical, workman's comp.

Thumbing from back to front, auto sales, repair, rentals. Hertz. Out of the Abilene Regional Airport. She called the number and made arrangements for a new Taurus to be delivered. Gave them the information on the accident. No big deal. Too easy. She remembered that guy's comment. "Let the insurance companies handle it."

She got up and headed to the bathroom. Only had thirty minutes. No time to spare. She got in the shower letting the warm water hit her very sore traps and neck. The ankle was swollen. There was a little bruising along the outside. Maybe she would try to find a brace today. That shouldn't be a problem. Being an orthopedic surgeon was handy.

Shower, shave. Towel dry her hair, massage in the anti-frizz product *du jour*, get dressed and go. Life with curly hair meant a never ending search for the right products and stay the hell away from blow dryers. She put on some basic black wool pants, a pullover sweater, practical shoes. Ready to go meet the Taylor County Regional Hospital administrator for breakfast at the twice recommended restaurant out front of the hotel. Does it even have a name? She walked through the door, looking at her watch. Only two minutes late, thank you very much, she thought to herself.

Terryl was four minutes early and was already working on the first of four cups of coffee, served in the little brown crock coffee cups typical of just about all country restaurants. If you could call a restaurant out front of a brand new Holiday Inn Express in Abilene, Texas, a country restaurant. He stood up and yelled to her across the dining room.

"Dr. Cohen, over here!" Just about everyone in the place turned to look at her. She was embarrassed. She didn't like to call attention to her degree in public. People have preconceived notions regarding doctors, good or bad, and she preferred anonymity. Still, in places like Abilene, people generally respected and liked doctors. As she walked between the tables toward Mr. Wells, people smiled, tilted their heads in greeting. One old fellow touched his index finger knuckle to his ball cap bill, a salute, in his day, to the noble profession. Most likely, a doctor had saved the life of someone dear to him. Just the administration of penicillin, perhaps, no more.

"Hey, you weren't kidding when you said you'd be ready in an hour! Terryl Wells, doc, nice to meet ya."

"Same here."

"You hungry?" He looked across the restaurant and signaled a waitress before Leslie had a chance to respond. A young woman came over to the table.

"Coffee, ma'am?" Now that was the second time she had been

called ma'am on this assignment. She was going to have to get used to it all over again.

"Please." There was already a little stainless steel pot of cream on the table and a box of blue and pink stuff. She was set, breakfast or no. Terryl was drinking his black and he watched her fix hers. Tons of half and half along with one blue and one pink.

"Whoa doc, have a little coffee with your cream. Okay, so tell me about this accident. Are you all right? Do you need to have a consultation with Doc Hawley before he goes under the knife?" Terryl laughed at his own joke. "Now, wouldn't that be rich? You come here to take over his practice while he has his cancer surgery, but instead you have an accident and he has to take care of you!"

"You don't know how close it came to being just that." She told him the details of the accident.

"Did you wreck into a local?"

"Yes. Some guy named Regan Wakeman."

"You're kidding! Regan Wakeman? Big guy? Terryl held his hand about four inches above his head. "Taller than me?"

"You know him?"

"Sure, everyone around here knows Regan. Comes from an old Abilene family. Went to school here. Abilene Christian College. Played high school ball, you know, just a guy everyone knows. Good guy. Has a place about ten, fifteen miles south of here. Runs a big construction company. Can't believe you had a wreck with him. Well anyway, I'm glad you're okay."

"Thanks. So what's the deal with Doctor Hawley? The agency didn't give me much detail. They just tell me when and where to show up for the most part. Usually it's just a week or so, while someone takes a vacation or something."

"Well, this is a little different. Doc Hawley, and that's what everyone around here calls him, just so you know. Anyway, Doc's come down with some kind of colon cancer. Okay, now he's taking it real good. Keeps practicing, because it's what he does. His patients just will not let him quit, and he's not about to quit. Hawley's like Wakeman. Born and raised here. Went to as much school as he could in Abilene, and then took off to medical school and residency. Came back after he was done and set up his practice. He's real popular. His practice is huge. There's other guys in town, but he's definitely *numero uno*. He's got a couple of nurses that work with him," Terryl turned his palms up and shrugged his shoulders, "but they can't take over his practice while he's out."

"Does he have partners?"

"Nope. He's pretty much a loner. Doesn't even share call with the other guys in town."

"Really." Not in the tone of a question or doubt, just amazement that a busy orthopod could do it on his own. Never having a weekend off. Even when she had two partners, every third night on call had been rigorous.

Doc Hawley had been practicing for about twenty-five years, getting *locum tenens* doctors like Leslie, to cover him for extended vacations and asking the local guys to cover him for shorter periods of time. He got along well with his peers in town and they respected him. There was plenty of business to go around. No one felt threatened by his success because they were all eating too. He just didn't want to deal with partners and their needs. His wife ran his business and did a good job of it, according to Wells. While Doc was out, she was going to keep things going from that end.

He had a general orthopedic practice, as did most of the surgeons in Abilene. There weren't a lot of specialists in this community. He did a smattering of sports medicine, knee scopes, anterior cruciate reconstructions and so on. He did the bulk of total knee and hip replacements in town. All the athletes he took care of in the beginning were now coming back to him to get their joints replaced, bringing their wives and children with them. These were the signs of a long standing referral base which also included his extended family and all the people who called themselves his friends. He worked long hours and weekends. If you wanted to see Doc Hawley, you could. Once his son went off to school, there was nothing to keep him and Brenda from working hard. He did back surgery and trauma, two things a lot of guys just didn't want to do. Too much risk of being sued. No one ever sued Doc Hawley. Probably wouldn't unless they were planning on leaving town. Doc Hawley was an old fashioned "saw bones." Definitely a dying breed. Leslie pictured a gracefully graying, elegant man in a seersucker suit.

"So Brenda talked Doc into getting his first colonoscopy a few years ago and they found some polyps or something like that. He was supposed to get a follow-up regularly but put it off. Then the next go around they found the cancer. Now he's got to have surgery and chemo. You know better than me." She didn't. Not her line of work, but nodded her head in the affirmative. "He wants to get back to work ASAP, but they're saying at least two to four weeks, and even then, who knows? I guess we've got you on line for a month or so.

"Right."

It didn't really matter to her one way or the other. Some places she went for a weekend, some for a week, depending on the circumstances. There were still a number of guys out there trying to hang on to solo practices. When they went on vacation, they needed someone to cover them. There were some guys in small communities who just couldn't get partners or other orthopedists to take care of their patients while they were out. More recently, there was a growing need for orthopedic surgeons to cover emergency room call in larger cities where the local docs couldn't tolerate the load on their practices or just didn't want the liability. The hospitals were forced to try to recruit surgeons to come build a practice in their community, basically paying them to use the hospital and cover call in the ER. When that failed, hire a *locum tenens* doc. Agencies had developed to provide these doctors. It worked for Leslie. No commitments. No extended stays. No relationships.

This assignment was a little different. A month was a long time for her. Can't let things get too complicated. This was enough time to get complicated if she wasn't careful. Get to know people and they ask you for email addresses. They want something from you. They want to give you something. Extended weekend assignments were the best.

"So basically you'll be taking over his practice and let me tell you Ozzy Osbourne could be taking over his practice and the patients would go for it. Whatever is good with Doc Hawley is good with them. Occasionally some will see the other orthopods in town, but not many. It never makes a dent in his business."

"But he's never been out like this before."

"Sure, but nobody's gonna leave him now, not with the cancer and all. Besides Brenda is still there and she's part of the deal. Knows all his patients. Probably could treat them herself if it were legal. Doc's plan is to come to the office whenever he can, even if it's just to sit around."

"That'll be interesting."

"Well, that's pretty much it in a nutshell. Probably more than you want to know, but it's kind of an odd case. You probably thought someone was just going on an African safari or something."

"Yeah, something like that." Leslie signaled the waitress for a refill on her coffee.

"So what's the schedule?"

"Okay, so Doc is doing cases this week and trust me, they're lining up like there's no tomorrow. And they know you'll be following them, taking out their stitches and stuff. He's going to spend the rest of this week getting you up to speed and then next Monday, he's having his own surgery in Lubbock."

"Surely there are guys here in town that can do his surgery."

"Yea, but Doc doesn't want anyone here messing with his hind end business." Terryl nodded his head up and down. "So, then you're on your own."

She laughed, thinking about Doc Hawley's hind end business, but also remembering YOYO, you're-on-your-own. When she was a resident, one of her chief residents would say YOYO when walking out of a difficult patient's room. That was followed by the development of a litany of acronyms such as AMF (adios mother fucker), saved for only the most egregious of patients, and BYE, which simply meant – bye. That kind of irreverent disrespect was left behind in residency, where sick humor was sometimes the only way to make the hard work tolerable. Of course, no patient was ever witness to these outbursts. A good laugh went a long way in the middle of the night. And what better source of sick humor than the human condition. She hadn't thought of YOYO in a long time.

"Yeah, it's kind of funny, but it's typical Doc Hawley. So after he recovers in Lubbock he'll be back to help you out, even if just in spirit. I think you'll be fine and probably enjoy it. Doc's got a great staff. Efficient, nice to patients, they know all the rules, and they'll do all the coding and paperwork for you."

"Nice." Coding and paperwork she could definitely do without.

They ordered. She got a western omelet, the edges of which were slightly crispy. It came with grits and salsa, two biscuits. They talked about hospital policies, the status of her hospital privileges, orthopedic emergency room call. She put real butter on a biscuit. It melted in her mouth. Terryl Wells' southern accent and affability were appealing. He finally finished his fourth cup of coffee, she, her second, and they were ready to go.

"Are you ready to go tour the hospital, or do you want to wait until tomorrow? Doc is operating all day today. I wanted you to get a chance to meet him before we get together tonight, but if you've got stuff to do..."

"I really need to get this accident stuff in order. I've got to contact my insurance company and wait for my new rental. It should be here this afternoon."

"Why don't you call me after you get all that taken care of and we'll go see if we can catch up with Doc." He handed her his card. She saw he was the CEO of the hospital. In a place like this, he might do just about everything there was to do at the Taylor County Regional Hospital. Hiring, firing, coordinating peer review and making sure there was toilet paper stocked in the restrooms.

"Then I guess tonight Brenda's invited you to dinner, if you feel up to going. My wife, Selma, and I will be coming. Brenda can coo-ook." A two syllable word meant it must be good. "You know, in all the time I've been here, they've never sent us a female *locums*. Ought to be interesting."

She thought of a female *locums*. She wondered if it had eight legs and an exoskeleton, and a pussy. Shi-it.

"Okay, I'll call you. Then you can tell me where to meet you." They shook hands. Terryl paid the bill and she walked back to the hotel.

Behind the desk was a tiny Indian woman wearing a bright pink, Americanized version of the sari. Kala.

"Good morning, Dr. Cohen. Was everything good in your room last night?"

"Just fine thank you...Kala?"

"Yes, Doctor."

"Kala, I'm expecting delivery of a rental car this afternoon. I'll be in my room if they call."

"Very good, thank you."

Leslie finished her calls regarding the accident. There were no surprises. Apparently her account of the accident was in line with Regan's story and so there were no glitches. No need for further investigation. No tickets given. She had always wondered if the extra insurance she signed up for every other time would really pay off and indeed it had. Her agent said she was totally covered and thanked her for it. Leslie thought, so now you know.

The new rental, a light blue Ford Taurus, was delivered that afternoon and she was in business. She did not like accepting rides from people. Too much time for talking without distractions. No way to leave. She didn't like to depend on people. Leslie scanned the outside of the Taurus, then signed the form that said everything was okay and the car had a full tank of gas. She always rented the basic mid-sized car, usually a Taurus. She found that any other car was associated with some kind of preconceived notion about her personality, whether it be sporty, well-to-do or family plan depending on if she rented SUVs, foreign cars or vans. Renting a Taurus was neutral, no preconceptions. Just a rented car. No Jaguars or Hummers even when there was a promotional rental price on them. She didn't want people to know she had lots of money.

Leslie had a successful orthopedic practice in New York prior to the accident. Chris had stock options from his company and a large pension. They owned a big house in New Paltz and a desirable bungalow on the coast in Maine. After the accident, she made her plans and sold everything. Even had an estate sale at the house and all their things were sold off to strangers and antique dealers. Anything that didn't sell was given to the Salvation Army. She kept her rings and the two little silver boxes containing her children's first cut locks of hair. She put all her photo albums, film, letters and mementos in a temperature controlled storage unit on the outskirts of New Paltz. She left town. An automatic draw from her bank paid for the storage forever, or at least for the rest of her life. After that, who cared?

Then there was the life insurance policy. Something she never thought about receiving. The policies were supposed to be for the kids, not for themselves. There was a lot of money. She wouldn't have to work another day in her life if she didn't want to. But a life of leisure was not for Leslie. She was trying to decide between joining the armed services or some volunteer organization like Doctors Without Walls or the Peace Corps, when the idea of *locum tenens* work came up and she realized that in doing temporary work she could live anonymously and never again establish roots.

Leslie found an agency and went to work. They kept her very busy. *Locum tenens* docs were in big demand. She went from one job to another, flying or driving, depending on the accessibility of each location to an airport and the amount of time between jobs. She stayed in the local hotels with inside corridors and rented mid-sized cars. She stocked the mini-fridge with Diet A & W root beer, yogurt and baby carrots. She did her job, got paid, moved on. There was always work, and in fact Dr. Cohen was in big demand. She may have made more than she had as a physician in private practice and there were less hassles. *Locum tenens* work was inconsistent with a normal family life. The people who did it were usually single or retired and didn't have kids to look after. There were also guys out there who just couldn't handle working in a practice with all the relationships and commitments that came along with it. *Locums* work was ideal for that sort.

Leslie fit in there somewhere. She was single and couldn't handle private practice any more. She sent letters to all her patients. She turned her practice over to her partners after she had, for the most part, finished caring for all of her post-operative patients. That had taken about four months.

The whole process of divesting herself of everything she and Chris had taken fifteen years to build took all of about six months. Done. She left the storage room and the five urns containing the ashes of her mom and dad, Chris, Victor and Vivian Cohen in a New Paltz mausoleum. Then she headed off to her first assignment in Bolivar, Missouri where a local orthopod needed a well deserved vacation with his family after two years of working without a break.

5

*L*eslie thought about calling Brenda Hawley and making up some excuse to get out of going to dinner. She avoided personal engagements, period. Personal engagements meant personal questions without exception. No one ever talked about the weather or the job. They wanted something. They wanted a history. She remembered some song from the sixties. *"What's your name...Who's your daddy?"* One question always led to another and eventually she had to lie. The truth was too painful to tell. But more than that, it was too painful to hear. People couldn't bare the truth. All conversation stopped as people pondered her situation, and then the significance of their own lives. She learned that it was easier for everyone if she just lied. Vic and Vivi ceased to exist and she was just a widow. There were a lot of widows and widowers out there. They can relate. It was too bad, but she was still young. Life goes on. But then they start to try to match her up with someone. Soon, the lie extended to time. The date of the accident ceased to exist. If it's only been a year, no one tries to play matchmaker. They don't even think about it. She was still in mourning. Not proper. She hated to lie, but it was easy and it worked.

Of course she was going to have to go to dinner. Doc Hawley and his wife/office manager wanted to check her out and give her the lay of the land. To them, this was more than just covering random emergency room patients and rounding on patients in the hospital. It was taking over their practice for a while. She was also certain they wanted to see what a female *locum* looked like. There was no doubt in her mind that ol' Doc Hawley never came within spitting distance of a female orthopedic surgeon in his training and maybe in his entire career. When dealing with the *locum* agencies a physician usually had to take what was available. Clients were always happy with the job Leslie did and so the agency didn't have any problems convincing subsequent clients to use the female orthopod.

Terryl called with directions. He had been held up with some hospital business and would have to give her the tour tomorrow. Hospital business. She remembered the time she had gotten caught in her hospital restroom without toilet paper. She had to walk out into the sink area with her pants down around her knees to grab some paper towels out of the canister on the wall. Fortunately no one was in there at the time. She finished her business with as much dignity as she could muster. She washed her hands and went straight to the administrator's office where she chewed him out and was assured that it would never happen again. And it didn't. Hospital business.

Terryl apologized. Leslie really didn't mind missing the tour today. She didn't change her clothes. Watched a little TV before it was time to go.

Raghu was back tonight. "Goodnight, Dr. Cohen. See you later."

She gave a short wave as she walked past his desk. Outside it was windy and cold. The two sets of automatic doors created some turbulence between them, and it whipped her coat and hair in different directions. Under the portico the wind came sideways, hard. She pulled her coat around herself. Dirt, accompanied by pieces of paper and Styrofoam raced across the asphalt. She could see a fence to her left at the end of the parking lot where the debris was entangled, cut off indefinitely from some journey. Could a paper cup go all the way from Abilene to Waco? Could it go to the Atlantic? Her car was parked in front of the fence. Pieces of paper and a plastic grocery bag were stuck on the fence. Little criss-cross lines etched into their surfaces. The wind thrashed them against the wires. They buzzed, screaming to get free. She walked over and picked one off the fence. Then let it loose. It shot across a ditch, got caught in a whirlwind and then stuck again in a dead bush. Others were stuck there too. Never meant to make it anywhere. Staying in Abilene.

She opened her car door. The wind yanked the door out of her hand. She reached to keep it from hitting the car parked next to hers.

As Leslie drove across Abilene she could feel the wind lash against her car in the intervals between buildings, on overpasses, and as she passed other vehicles. Dirt darted across the highways, bringing ancient debris with it. She passed strip shopping centers, old and new, then hotels, small neighborhoods and gas stations. Texas was for the most part, unzoned, and there might be a gas station or a strip shopping center or a Wal-Mart right next to a neighborhood. It was sometimes unsightly, but there was beauty in opportunity. In Kansas, she could drive for miles and see only factories, or see only homes. There was beauty in that too.

She turned into an upper end neighborhood, and following Terryl's directions, arrived at the ranch-style home of Dr. and Mrs. Hawley. It was smaller than she had expected. Creamy light glowed from inside. Inviting. Open. Paintings, upholstered chairs and lamps were visible from the street. She guessed this was a forty-year-old neighborhood. There were larger trees here than she had seen in the rest of Abilene. Most likely planted when the area was developed. Somebody was thinking back then. The neighborhood was quiet, dark and the streets were wide. The trees blocked the wind where she was but up in the tree tops she could see its frantic struggle.

The doorbell was answered by barking dogs. Through the leaded glass windows inside the door she could see labs. Eager yellow dogs with thick pipe-like tails wagging their hindquarters from side to side. It looked like they couldn't wait to jump up on her so she was prepared for it when the door was opened.

"Jake, Booker, sit," a soft but stern voice called to them. Instantly the two sat down while keeping their anxious brown eyes fixed on Leslie. Pipe tails still twitching back and forth, storing energy. She reached down with one hand to pet them and the other to shake her hostess's hand.

"Hi, Leslie Cohen. Beautiful dogs. I had labs when I was a kid."

"These are our kids now that Hal junior is grown. And they're a little easier to take care of than he was. I'm Brenda. It's so nice to meet you. We're so glad you were able to come here and take over big Hal's practice for a while."

"Well, the agency just pointed me in the right direction and here I am." It wasn't that clever but Brenda chuckled diplomatically anyway.

"The boys like you but just let me know if they're bothering you." Then to the dogs, "Jake, Booker, settle down." Leslie didn't know if dogs understood "settle down" but they could understand a firm voice. They quieted and trotted alongside of her, watching her every move. Waiting for an opportunity to get a paw up, lick, sniff or better yet, get a petting out of her. She obliged them.

"Come on in the kitchen. You can help me get things finished in here while we wait for Hal. He's running late in surgery. I'm sure you know what that's all about."

"Sounds like things have been really busy. Terryl kind of filled me in this morning." Leslie paused and reached down to pet the dogs again. She continued looking down. "I understand Doctor Hawley is to have surgery in Lubbock on Monday."

"That's right. Everything's going to be just fine. He's just going to need some help until he gets his energy back. Sweetie, everyone calls him Doc. You know, it's just always been that way. If you said Doctor Hawley, well, some people might not even know who you were talking about. Just Doc." Brenda got busy with the food. Leslie was going to have to get used to saying Doc.

There was nothing pretentious about her home, or the lady, for that matter. Brenda was trim. Leslie guessed she was in her early fifties. Short grey hair, pretty grey, no yellow. She looked like she might have been athletic. Maybe still is. Her skin was tanned, a little leathery. Tennis player or something. Might be hard to find the time if she's really managing his practice full time. Some wives just hang out at the office a lot, but don't really manage it. Maybe get in the way a little. One of her former partner's wives did that. Very annoying. Chased off two or three receptionists before she wore out her welcome.

"So Mr. Wells tells me you run the office." She decided to jump right in and get to the meat. A few questions about coding or medical records and she'd be able to tell just how involved Brenda was.

Brenda proceeded to tell Leslie all about the office, how it ran, employees, pension plan, Privacy Act stuff, and before long it was apparent that she was in fact the office manager. Not just sniffing around.

Leslie decided to jump in a little further. "So you've been working for Doc since the start?"

"Well, in a manner of speaking, yes. See, Doc hired me as a nurse when he first started. I did everything basically. Schedule patients, bring them back to the exam rooms, put casts on, *etcetera*. I learned all the insurance and coding stuff as it developed and pretty soon I was just running the office. On the job training. I think I got too expensive so Hal had to marry me instead of paying me the big salary I was worth. Sometimes I think I should have stuck with a pay raise!"

Leslie thought about that romance. Working with someone closely, respecting their knowledge and devotion. The respect turning into admiration and love. One thing leads to another and pretty soon you're doing it on an exam table after hours. She remembered meeting Chris at the hospital. Corporate Vice President for the hospital chain. In and out of town on a scheduled basis, but soon in more than out and one thing leading to another.

"Dr. Cohen, dear, you okay?"

She nodded.

"It just looked like you were off somewhere else for a minute there. I hope it wasn't something I said?"

"Brenda, this is a little difficult, so I'm just going to say something right now, to you, because it's easier that way rather than in front of everyone at the dinner table."

"What is it sweetheart? This sounds serious." Her voice was so kind and concerned. Leslie almost wanted to be held by her. She could be her mom. The southern accent was soothing.

"Well, see, my husband passed away last year. It's why I'm here. It's why I'm not married." Leslie pressed on, not pausing to give Brenda the opportunity to give the usual condolences. "Casual conversation always comes around to 'Why's a nice girl like you not married?' or people try to set me up with someone they know. It's just easier for me to try to control those conversations by bringing it up on my terms."

Brenda stopped what she was doing and came around the island in the middle of the kitchen. The dogs got up and followed her, wagging their tails, oblivious to the moment. She took Leslie's hands in hers and squeezed them, held them there for a moment.

"Sweetheart, I don't know what to say. I'm so sorry. This is so unexpected. I don't even know you and yet my heart is just plain broken for you." Her eyes glistened. They understood each other, because Brenda was going there too someday. Only thing was, Leslie knew she had just told the first lie and kept the first secret. The one no one could understand.

"Now Leslie, where's your momma and daddy? A girl needs her

momma after this kind of thing." It was a simple question, but Leslie had never been asked that one before. She did need her mom after that kind of thing.

"My parents were older when they had me. They died a while ago. Chris was my only family." There, done, seal off any ideas about the possibility of children.

Just then the doorbell rang. Brenda reluctantly headed for the front door. The dogs stayed with Leslie. There was opportunity here and they knew it. She let them jump up on her thighs, one at a time. Jake jumped while Booker glanced out the door toward the foyer. Assigned to be a lookout. He came back for a leg up and a chin scratch. Leslie grabbed a couple of scraps of meat off the counter top and popped one in each gaping mouth. She could hear Brenda talking to Terryl and Selma. Then, "Jake, Booker, you're not bothering Leslie, are you?" They glanced at Leslie, turned and trotted out the kitchen door, barking at the newcomers. "Jake, Booker, sit."

"Selma, this is Doctor Leslie Cohen. Doctor Cohen, my wife, Selma." Selma was a handsome, Hispanic woman in her forties. She had a very slight accent.

Leslie shook her hand and asked her to call her "Leslie."

"Pleased to meet you, Leslie."

"Same here."

Leslie and Terryl sat down in the living room at Brenda's request while she and Selma went into the kitchen. They came out with some hors d'oeuvres. Iced tea, Coke or water was offered. No alcohol. Was Abilene in a dry county? No alcohol except on the outskirts of town, sold in seedy little strip shopping centers. In New York, one rarely went to a party where there was no hard liquor offered. Gin and tonic, 7&7, scotch on the rocks. In the south it was usually beer and wine. But sometimes no alcohol was served. She was driving. She didn't care one way or another. Leslie never went out and drinking alone wouldn't have occurred to her.

They made small talk for a while. The sound of a diesel engine coming down the street put the dogs into a frenzy, barking and running back and forth into the kitchen, where there was a back door leading to the garage. The engine idled in the driveway and Leslie remembered that, of course, it wasn't using any extra fuel. The dogs were literally howling when the door opened and Doc Hawley greeted them like they were his kids. "Booker, Jake, howyuboys doin'?" Silence from the dogs, but she could hear their collars being jangled around by their tail-wagging bodies. Brenda got up and headed toward the kitchen.

"Hal, long day huh? Honey, you'd better go get changed. I'll take care of your things." And then "Jake, Booker, you leave dad alone." Husbands and wives start to call each other mom and dad sometime after their children start talking and understanding. Chris used to call her "mommy." The title sticks.

"Lemme just say 'hi' real quick." Leslie heard them kiss each other. Terryl stood up and took a few steps toward the kitchen. Selma stayed seated. Leslie decided to stand. Better to meet people at their level. Not seated. It puts you in a submissive position. She heard steps across the kitchen. Where Leslie was expecting the elegantly graying, seersucker-suit-wearing doctor, there came a short burly man who looked more like the guy on TV who builds motorcycles with his sons. Greying, yes, but not elegantly. Wearing scrubs. Smiling. Clearly happy to see everyone.

"Terryl, what a day! They had me working out of two rooms over there, and still, what?" He looked at his watch. "Still didn't finish up until six. You need to give those folks a raise. They worked their asses off!"

He looked over Terryl's shoulder, "Selma." He greeted her with a nod.

"Hi, Doc."

Then he turned directly to Leslie and walked over to her. "And you must be my replacement!" He extended his big hand and gave hers a big squeeze. "Hey, do they charge extra for pretty ones, Brenda?" He laughed at his own joke. Brenda just rolled her eyes.

She squeezed hard and returned the shake. Leslie hated weak handshakes. Women usually gave weak handshakes. The problem with weak handshakes is that if you're shaking someone's hand who gives a strong one, it rolls the metacarpal bones of the fourth and fifth fingers together and squishes the muscles and nerves in between. It hurts like hell, but if you give it right back it sort of protects you. She had learned to sense the intensity of the grip quickly and squeeze in a commensurate fashion. You lower your shoulder and bring the forearm directly forward, keeping the wrist in line with the arm. None of this dropping the wrist like the hand is to be held or turning it sideways and handing it to the gripper like a dead carp. She knew Doc could hand it to her better than she could so she prepared for the metacarpal roll. She could have expected what came next.

"Man, I like a gal with a strong handshake. I can tell you're gonna fit right in. Don't you think so, Brenda?"

"Of course she is." Brenda gave her a wink.

"Leslie Cohen, Doc. Pleased to meet you too."

"Same here."

Brenda reminded him to go get out of his scrubs, but he was having none of it. "If y'all don't care then neither do I." He didn't wait for a confirmation. "Brenda, how 'bout some tea." Brenda disappeared into the kitchen, returning with a tray of big glasses and what looked like some little bird breasts, stuffed with jalapeño peppers and wrapped up with a piece of bacon.

Now everyone was smiling, Leslie included. They were all looking at Doc Hawley, Leslie included. There was something about him. He swallowed the glass of tea in about two big gulps, made a big exhale through pursed lips and sat back in his chair. Then he reached over and gave her a gentle swat on the arm.

"Terryl here tells me you had a big wreck last night with ol' Regan Wakeman. I'm gonna have to wring that boy's neck. So tell us about it." He yelled to Brenda, who had gone out to the kitchen to continue getting things ready for dinner. "Honey, leave that stuff alone and come hear this. Doc here had a wreck last night with Regan Wakeman. She's lucky to be alive from what I hear."

Leslie thought about being lucky to be alive and the meaning of lucky. But only for an instant. Brenda came into the living room and sat down on the couch next to Doc. Now they were all looking at Leslie, waiting for the story. She told all the details as best she could remember. They were horrified.

"My goodness, Leslie, you are lucky to be sitting here," Brenda said, "and you're doubly lucky, because you didn't have to get added on to the end of Doc's schedule today!"

Everyone laughed, like they just wanted to laugh. Leslie did too. And the idea of it was funny because patients are always worried about being on the end of the surgery schedule on a busy day. It's natural to feel that way because most people are tired at the end of a long day of work. Not doctors. They can't be. It would be crazy if patients who got done early in the day statistically did better than patients at the end of the day. Like a crack surgeon at seven AM but at six PM, watch out. Doctor from hell.

Some patients are also worried about being the first case in the morning. Right. Doctors suck until they've had two cups of coffee and a warm up case. Do the important cases at 9:30. Do homeless people and suckers at 7:00 and attorneys the last case of the day. No way. Doctors are on twenty-four-seven if that's what it takes. They have to be one hundred percent or as close to it as is humanly possible. Coffee or no. She used to tease her patients who had the guts to question her wakefulness at seven in the morning. "I might just fall out in the middle of your case..." Leslie and Doc looked at each other and shared a fraternal moment, the knowledge of working with full intensity until the job was done. He winked at her. She smiled back.

"Leslie, I think if I had to nail your femur tonight at the end of my schedule, I would've just fallen asleep in the middle of the damn case." He laughed and Brenda scolded him.

"Hal, quit that, you would not." Hal reached over and put his thick hand on Brenda's knee.

"Leslie, you ever had any of these?" He reached over and picked up one of the little bird breast things.

"Can't say that I have."

"Well, you gotta try one. They're good enough to make a bull dog hug a hound." Then he cracked up. "Brenda takes the seeds out of the peppers so they don't kill ya. Here try one." He picked one up with his hand and gave it to her. "Go on, you're gonna love 'em. By the time you leave Texas, you're going to be addicted to hot sauce and jalapeños. Man, I'm starving. What's for dinner, mom?"

"Your favorite. Santa Maria barbecued sirloin. Pintos. Slaw. Y'all excuse me while I go get things ready." She got up to go to the kitchen and Leslie decided to follow her.

"Leslie, you stay put. I've got it."

"I want to check out this Santa Maria sirloin." She disobeyed and wandered into the kitchen with Brenda. Selma came too. Brenda shared her recipes for the meat, beans and slaw, just for conversation. The food smelled delicious. It appeared they were going to eat buffet style. Dishes were set out on the counter top. Everyone would just help themselves.

Conversation started to drift toward family issues and Leslie knew eventually she would be queried. She must have looked distracted because when she looked up, Brenda gave her a knowing look and then diverted the conversation back to the food.

"This beef is going to melt in your mouth. Leslie, I hope you brought an appetite with you. Hal! Terryl!" she yelled. "Come on. Everything's ready."

They lined up, grabbed plates, filled them up and sat down to eat in the kitchen.

"Brenda slow cooks this sirloin all day on the barbeque pit. What do you think, Leslie? Ever had a piece of meat this tender?" Leslie shook her head. No need for an answer, they were all scarfing down the food.

There are some women who can just cook and love to do it. Leslie wasn't one of them. Chris didn't care and the two of them either ate out, brought food home or made simple dishes, big salads and stuff like that. The kids didn't really care either and never reached the age where they understood the consuming nature of her work and why she didn't cook like their friends' moms. Once Vivi announced that when she grew up she was going to be a "stay-at-home mom like Lynn." Lynn was Vivi's best friend's mom and Vivi adored her. Leslie did too for that matter and often thought it would be wonderful to be married to Lynn. Vivi was a little envious of Casey's time with her mom. As the kids got a little older they knew their mom did something important and would say, "My mommy works." But she knew they wished she were home with them. Leslie didn't think that her kids ever really knew what her work meant to her or to them, or to anyone for that matter. But Vivi never reached the age when all girls make the decision, even if temporary, to work outside the home.

She appreciated good cooks like Brenda and Lynn. She wondered what Lynn was doing. When Leslie left New Paltz she never looked back. She never called anyone. Not even Lynn, who took Vivi's death as though it had been her own daughter's. But it hadn't been and in a strange way, Leslie resented her for it. Resented her for the life of her own daughter, for the years she had been able to stay home with her and for the future years she would be able to be with Casey. She could never bring herself around to calling Lynn and strangely Lynn never tried to reach her despite their close friendship. But then Leslie didn't make that possible. She changed cell phone numbers, left no forwarding address. For Lynn to reach her would almost have required a private detective. During the first few months after the accident, people brought her food, tried to stay with her, and invited her out. They called her everyday. But Leslie had entered another world. It wasn't their world. Their world was alive, progressive, optimistic, loved. Her world was not. They had nothing in common anymore. She was on the red planet and they were bound to Earth. They spoke different languages now. Pretty soon, she just stopped returning calls.

Lynn and Casey had come over to say goodbye. They had been crying and their noses were red. Mother and daughter twin red noses and swollen eyes. The similarities so apparent even through the tears. They said they would write, email, call, but Leslie knew she had already changed her cell phone number. They stood in her driveway and waved. Leslie watched them in her rear view mirror until she turned on to the main street out of her neighborhood.

"So, Doc, what d'ya think about going round with me tomorrow to see the folks in the house? Terryl here can give you that tour of the hospital and then we'll go over to the office in the afternoon. I've got about twenty-five patients to see and Brenda can show you around the office too. You're going to have to get a crash course before I leave for Lubbock Sunday night."

"I'd like that. I was planning on it anyway." She was. She had absolutely no other plans and was ready to get to work. Even having a meal, friendly conversation, social interaction, was causing her to think too much of the past. Seeing patients would occupy her mind. Twenty-five patients. It was a lot. That worked for her. The evening wound down and there was no talk about her past, not even about medical school or residency. They all probably knew. She was suspicious because everyone focused on the practice, the hospital and Doc. Maybe she was self-centered. Why should they talk about her? Doc Hawley was undergoing an important change in his life, in their life. Everything could change. Maybe he couldn't even return to his practice. She could see he and his wife were devoted to each other. What would happen if he got really sick, which was a possibility? Why should they talk about her?

They treated Leslie like an old friend. Not like a guest. There were no moments of uncomfortable silence. They reached across her to get the salt or pepper. Doc didn't hold back on being politically incorrect if he wanted and Brenda didn't scold him if he did. They questioned her openly about being a female orthopedic surgeon and how they hadn't ever known one personally, even though they had heard of them. By the time she got into her car to drive home, she was happy she had not begged out on the evening.

"Welcome home, doctor. Will you be needing a call to wake up in the morning?"

She thought about it for a second. Her internal clock was off this morning, and she had eaten a large meal, late. Better not take a chance.

"Yes, please. How about six."

"Six o'clock, it is. Goodnight."

6

*T*he evening had been strange for Leslie and she felt guilty. She had actually enjoyed herself, enjoyed the company, even the food. This was the problem with commitments, long term work, as opposed to the usual short term obligation. Doc and Brenda cared about her relationship with their patients. On shorter term jobs, it wasn't so important. She could do very little harm in a short period of time in terms of getting along with patients. If she just did her job medically, everyone was happy. This was going to be a longer commitment and her temporary employers wanted to make sure she could take care of things on a larger scale. They wanted to get to know her. Chalk that one down to experience. No more jobs longer than a week.

Leslie made sure she carried the torch. It was necessary. She felt it deep inside. It wasn't work for her to do it. It just happened. Three years had passed and she wasn't ready to let go. Rather than try to sleep tonight, she tried to remember. She tried to remember their faces. Chris, tall, thin, marathon runner. That part was easy. His face was almost a blank now. She couldn't remember the shape of the scar on his chin that he got from a bicycle accident when he was six. She memorized the verbal description of his features but couldn't see them anymore. When had that happened? The same with the twins. Both fair. Blonde, curly hair. Couldn't appreciate the curls on Vic because they kept his hair short. In a few years he would probably have started letting it grow because that was the style for teenage boys. Vivian had curls and she had started to hate them, just like her mom did. They had lazy soft eyes, like Chris. Full lips like hers. But she couldn't picture their eyes or their lips anymore. They were obviously brother and sister. The same age. Totally different personalities. Leslie smiled, thinking about them. It was so hard to imagine that she would never ever see them again, except in her mind's eye, and that was slowly fading. She thought about the photos in the storage room back home. Why had she kept them if it wasn't to look at them again someday? She got undressed and went to bed.

The six o'clock wake up call was unnecessary. Leslie was already up. She lifted the receiver and hung it up. She showered, got dressed and drove to the hospital. She ran into Doc in the hall on the way to the cafeteria, where they had agreed to meet.

"Morning Doc," he said to her. Was this to be her title as well?

"Morning. Hey, thanks again for dinner last night. Really enjoyed it."

"Well good. Same here. I think we're all going to get along just fine. You ready for some coffee?"

"You bet. Can't get started without it." They got in line and Doc put his hand out for her to go first.

She got coffee and some bacon and eggs. Doc got a couple of breakfast tacos. "Best tacos in town and at a hospital cafeteria no less."

"I know...make a bull dog hug a hound."

"Doc, you're all right."

They sat down at a table away from everyone else. They talked about the practice, the hours, how he liked to do things. He gave her the lowdown on personalities in the operating room and his office. He poured salsa on his tacos and talked in between bites, leaning over his tray as if the taco might try to escape. He licked his fingers when he was done, then got up to go get a refill on the coffee.

"Can I get you some more coffee?"

"Sure." She handed him her cup. Doc returned carrying a fistful of creamers in addition to her coffee.

"So, what d'ya think? Can you handle it?"

"I think so. It's been a while since I did the whole practice deal, but it sounds like I'm going to have a lot of help."

"You'll do great." Doc wiped his mouth with a paper napkin while pushing his chair back from the table. "What do you say we go and round? I've got about nine or ten folks in the house. Shouldn't take too long." They got up and set their dishes on the kitchen conveyor belt, then walked down the hall to the elevators. Doc pushed the fourth floor button.

"Most ortho patients are on four. Occasionally they go to the fifth floor when they have medical problems or need telemetry."

On the fourth floor, they stepped out, discarded their coffee cups and went to the nurses' station. "These gals can make or break you. They really know their stuff when it comes to orthopedic problem solving. None of that calling you at three in the morning, asking for a sleeping pill for a patient who can't sleep. It's a general hospital, but this floor is run like it's a specialty hospital. Everyone's happy, knows their job."

"Sounds too good to be true, Doc."

"Here we go." As he walked into the station, several nurses greeted him. "Morning, Doc." "Good morning Doc Hawley." Smiles and greetings all the way around. From both sides. Doc happy to see everyone. They were happy to see him.

Doc asked, "Mary Ellen around?"

Then from the room in back of the station, "I'm here, just hold your horses. You'd think I had nothing better to do than..." and it trailed off when she saw Leslie in her starched white jacket. "Ooo, sorry, didn't know we had company!" Then she handed Doc Hawley the cup of coffee she had in her hand. "Black with a skosh of honey."

"Mary Ellen, Doc Cohen. Mary Ellen is the head nurse up here on the fourth floor. And the best there is. Runs a tight ship and knows everything there is to know about your patients, the OR, ER, whatever. You need anything, and I mean anything, you can ask her."

"Doc's just blowin' up my skirts to impress you, Doctor Cohen. We're sure glad to have you here to help Doc out. Come on. Let me introduce you to the staff." She took Leslie around the station introducing her to all the nurses, assistants and the ward secretary. Each stood and shook her hand as if she were a visiting dignitary.

"Y'all want to go round now? Doctor Cohen, how about a cup of coffee? It's fresh."

Even after the two earlier cups, Leslie accepted the offer. Mary Ellen turned around and went to the break room for the coffee. "What do you take in your coffee, Doctor Cohen?"

Leslie volunteered to fix her own because it was always impossible to specifically define a ton of creamer, and then on top of that a pink, a blue, and a pinch of the real stuff. People were always surprised, and it always embarrassed her. Mary Ellen, giving no indication that she was surprised, said she'd remember that recipe the next time.

Right, Leslie thought to herself, and pigs will fly.

She often simplified the position of physicians in her world in terms of a personal experience she had while she was a pre-med student in college. She had been employed during the summer between her freshman and sophomore year as a ward secretary on the surgical floor of the local hospital. She was required to wear a blue and white pin-striped, drop-waisted dress, of an unfashionable mid-knee length. It had a little rounded collar. She wore Keds and bobby socks, which were equally unfashionable at the time. She was introduced to the head nurse who was totally competent, totally in-charge and striking in her tiny starched white, belted dress, with her white cap and school pin in place. Her silky white stockings with lace-up white oxford shoes completed the picture perfect nurse. Leslie couldn't even remember her name now, but in her mind, this woman epitomized what would always be her idea of what a head nurse should be. She ran the department. Saw to the care of all the patients. Knew all the patients. Knew what each doctor on the floor wanted for their patients and in their coffee. She gave Leslie her job description, the must-do list, the next-must-do list and the don't-do list.

But the thing that Leslie remembered most clearly was her instruction on what to do when the doctors arrived on the floor. "You must get up and offer the doctors your seat because they have important work to do."

Eventually an attending surgeon and his entourage of students and residents came on to the floor. This nurse immediately got up to let the surgeon sit down. She then brought him a cup of coffee and asked if he was prepared to go around and see patients. When he replied to the affirmative, she went over to a rack of metal backed charts which she and Leslie had previously prepared with updated hand written lab slips, extra progress report sheets and doctor's order sheets. She wheeled the rack around the hall with the group of physicians and reported on every single patient on the floor.

During her training, Leslie often thought of the day when she would be assisted in this fashion, on some unknown hospital floor, by some unknown head nurse like this one.

When pigs fly.

Thirteen years later, on her first day when she rounded at her first hospital, there was no one to greet her. Forget about that cup of coffee. She tried to identify a nurse. Any nurse. By then nurses no longer wore uniforms. They wore various forms of scrubs and sometimes on Fridays they wore jeans. This made it hard to tell who was a nurse, a therapist, a doctor or a visitor. She went around on her own, to see all two of her patients and then sat down to write in the progress notes. There were none in the chart and so she went to the area in front of the nurse's station to ask where they might be. She was pointed in the direction of some shelves by someone she later found out was the I.T. guy, up working on the computers. She grabbed a couple of progress notes, stamped them herself and returned to her seat where she was promptly approached by a large woman wearing Hawaiian printed scrubs, who said indignantly, "Excuse me. You're sitting in my seat. I was charting there and went to check a patient's vitals." This happened to be the nurse taking care of her two patients.

Leslie, Mary Ellen and Doc then, set off to round on all of his patients. It took an hour and a half. Mary Ellen had the lab results on every patient filed in the charts. In Leslie's experience up until now, most lab values had to be tracked down, either on the computer, a file box at the nurse's station or stuck somewhere in the chart. Mary Ellen knew about any ongoing problems, both medical and social. In Leslie's current experience, she usually had to rely on patients and their families to tell her if dad had a problem today. Only the nurse taking care of the patient had any knowledge of the situation and if they were down the hall or on break, there was no other way to get current information. It could be read in the chart if it was charted. Nurses were overwhelmed and Leslie understood why. They needed help and help was too expensive for the hospitals to afford. The nurses were not to blame. It was a complex problem for everyone involved.

Of course, she never forgot the nurse who asked her to give up her seat, thereby ruining and at the same time cementing her concept of what it would be like to be a contemporary doctor.

Mary Ellen and Doc interacted with patients as if they were

neighbors, Doc taking a seat on the window ledge, sometimes helping himself to candy sitting on the rolling bedside table.

"Take more, Doc!" The patients eagerly encouraged him.

"Oh, no, I'm watching my figger."

Patients were as interested in Doc as he was in them. He introduced her to everyone. "Doc Cohen, my replacement." Patients then calling her "Doc" too. There was something about Doc's easy going, good ol' boy affability that struck a little envy in Leslie. Some guys just have it, and there's just no point in trying to fake it.

They saw four patients who had just had total knee and hip replacements. There were two elderly ladies with broken hips, one waiting to have surgery today. There was a guy who had a herniated disc removed from between his fifth lumbar and his first sacral vertebrae. They said hello to a patient who had her rotator cuff repaired yesterday and had to stay overnight because she didn't have any help at home. Her daughter was arriving from Chicago today to take care of her. There was a guy with a broken tibia and an Abilene Christian College coed with a broken ankle which Doc had fixed. Leslie was surprised to see the two trauma cases because she figured Doc wouldn't be seeing emergencies this close to his leave.

"The fellow with the broken leg is the son-in-law of one of my best friends and Christy is one of the medical floor nurse's daughters." He looked at her kind of stupidly and shrugged his shoulders. "When the agency said you could come and you could stay for a while, I figured, what the hell." Leslie figured the same. Mary Ellen just looked at her, smiled and shrugged too, like, "What're ya gonna do?"

Rounds were done and for once Leslie didn't feel like ripping her hair out. Maybe she had died and gone to heaven. Would Chris and the kids come walking around the corner? Mary Ellen would suddenly have angel wings and Doc would be wearing a robe, hold his hand out to her and say, "Even though you stopped believing, you were a good girl and we're inviting you in anyway." Then pigs would start flying all around her.

"You wanna give me a hand with a couple of cases after you get your credential forms signed? Let's see what a lady doctor can do!" Mary Ellen looked at him with stern eyes and tight lips, like a mother getting ready to scold him. Leslie was totally unoffended because there was no malice in his voice. He was innocent of prejudice when it came to her, she felt certain of it. He was just a good ol' boy and he could have been talking about cattle or surgery, either one. She knew the sound of malice when it came to women in a man's world and she wasn't hearing it now.

They headed to the administrative wing of the hospital and met up with Terryl. He introduced her around the office and she was once again struck with the fact that it seemed she was treated more like a permanent fixture rather than the transient *locum tenens.*

She remembered her arrival at the county hospital in New Paltz. Just having finished her residency and joining the local group of orthopedic surgeons, she was treated nicely by everyone at the hospital. They were desperate for a warm body and she filled at least that job description. The three senior partners were totally beat up, having taken every third night call for the past ten years. No new blood for ten years! They put her to work instantly taking every other night call and the major holidays. The senior partner went into semi-retirement. At Christmas all three took off for a skiing vacation, leaving her alone to run the ship. Of course she didn't think twice about it. That was standard in the industry. It was pretty rare to just walk into a group and get handed an equal call sharing arrangement.

The people at Taylor County Regional Hospital were treating her very nicely and she began to feel good about it. After completing the vast amount of paperwork that would allow her legally to start cutting in Abilene, Texas, she and Doc took off for the operating room. He directed her to the women's dressing room where she got dressed with the female nurses and scrub techs. Male doctors always had their own dressing rooms. Only the newest and largest hospitals had designated female physician dressing rooms. It was only an observation because she didn't really mind getting dressed with the staff. That way she got to know people. Girl chat while getting ready to work. It could be fun most of the time. She could also get the lowdown on some of the surgeons that way.

She slipped on a pair of grey green scrubs, booties, poofy blue paper hat, and was ready to go. She met Doc out in the sterile corridor and he again introduced her around. She thought she might be the only female surgeon they had ever had around there, never mind being an orthopedic surgeon. There were probably some female Ob-Gyns, but they mostly hung out in labor and delivery. Very rarely did they operate in the main OR. Again, everyone clearly having great respect and affection for Doc Hawley, from which she in turn benefited.

Eula Parsons was ready for surgery. She had an empty stomach, a signed permit for a right hip hemiarthroplasty, and a bag of IV antibiotics hanging. She was prepared for her operation. They stopped by the holding area to talk with her a little, then headed down the hall to the sinks outside the operating rooms where Doc did most of his cases. They scrubbed their hands with a sweet smelling pink soap, held their hands up in the air and went into the operating room. Lots of friendly talking with the patient while everyone was getting ready. The anesthesiologist began to administer the Fentanyl through a syringe in one hand while he rubbed the patient's eyebrow softly with his thumb. Very nice. The patient went off to sleep quietly, easily.

Then everyone got very busy with intubation, gowning and prepping. She heard a little benign ribbing between Doc Hawley and the scrub tech. Introductions were made again. How would she memorize everyone's name? At each previous job she didn't have time and it really wasn't expected. These people were important in the day-to-day operations but had become nameless and faceless within days of leaving the town.

The charge nurse in the operating room was a guy. He seemed friendly enough and was knowledgeable and efficient. He tied up the back of their gowns and helped them bring their belts around to tie in front. He then took another look at the permit, reminded and confirmed the right hip with Dr. Hawley. The patient had a big red "YES' written on her right hip exactly where the incision would be. Eula was then gently turned onto her left side with her right side up. Positioning devices were utilized to hold her in place. Her right hip was prepped with gooey Betadine liquid and covered with about a dozen sterile drapes.

Doc stepped up to the table followed by Leslie on the opposite side. He made a curved incision across the side of Eula's hip and cut straight through to the fat underneath. The bleeders were cauterized. Some were squirting blood and it was harder to stop them. He cut quickly through the large flat tendon that goes all the way from the pelvis to just below the knee and exposed the big bone on the side of the upper end of the thigh. He took some leg measurements now so he could make sure the legs were the same length at the end of the case. He then divided the muscles that rotate the hip outward from their attachment to bone. Blood and joint fluid oozed out from the hip joint and had to be sucked out so he could see. Leslie worked quickly to this end. She took just as much pride in being a good assistant as being the primary surgeon.

A giant screw was stuck down into the broken head of the hip, twisted home and the broken head was pulled out of the acetabulum, holding on for dear life until it gave up with a loud sucking sound. It was a brutal maneuver, without a doubt, but there was something satisfying about pulling out that dead, broken head of the hip bone. It had failed its owner and now was useless, because in the process of breaking it had also lost its blood supply and so could not be counted on to heal. Better to remove and replace it than to try to repair it in a patient this age. They made some extra cuts in the bone and then replaced the dead broken head with a brand new shiny metal hip replacement. It was measured to fit the cup, and the leg length was checked. Leslie then took the leg, pulled firmly and rotated it to the point where it went easily home with a soft sucking sound. Eula would be able to get out of bed the next day, and then start walking when she regained her energy. Her overall feeble condition and not the hip would be the limiting factor.

Leslie thought of her own grandmother, who had died of a blood clot which went to her lungs after a long period of bed rest following a hip fracture. Leslie had been in grade school and only vaguely remembered the circumstances. An orthopedic surgeon had fixed the hip but the fixation methods then were not thought stable enough to allow early mobilization. She was placed at bed rest for an extended period of time and it didn't take long before she had bed sores and contractures of her already weakened extremities. When she was finally deemed ready to rehabilitate she got up out of bed, became short of breath and died of the pulmonary embolism that had broken off from the clots which had been growing up the deep veins of her legs for weeks. At that time the majority of people who sustained hip fractures were dead within a year of their fracture, victims of those blood clots and other medical complications. Those statistics had improved remarkably in the past quarter of a century. Still, blood clots were a dark potential.

Doc and Leslie started to close the wound. They got into a rhythm, both of them experienced with this operation. The critical part was done and now the closing of each specific layer. The two got their timing down and the closing became sort of an assembly line of throwing stitches, tying knots and cutting them. Doc threw the suture with the needle driver and Leslie pulled the suture from the needle then quickly tied a single hand knot. Bam, bam, bam. Doc looked up over his mask and gave her a nod. They sailed through all the layers of muscles, fat and skin like they had done this together a thousand times. Doc grabbed all the sutures upwards in his big fist and Leslie cut them very carefully, turning the scissors "just so" in order to keep from cutting the knots.

When she was a resident or medical student and cut a knot, she'd get her ass chewed out in front of everyone. And everyone loved to see it happen. Nothing like seeing a student doctor get humiliated. That might also be an opportunity for an attending surgeon to ask some questions to which she might not know the answer, like naming all the stages in the blood clotting pathway, or something. And everyone loves to see that happen too.

Leslie was confident she would never cut a knot, but she did. Doc looked up at her again, this time with a raised eyebrow. She went over the stages of blood clotting in her mind, thinking, once a student, always a student, and Doc said, "Shit, I knew it. You're a no-suture-cuttin' fool, is what you are." Everyone laughed, Leslie included and Doc said, "Now, I'm gonna have to ask you all the branches of the sacral plexus!"

"But I can recite the blood coagulation pathway."

"Well, that just won't do." Again, chuckles in the OR. "Seriously, Doc, that went great." He put his fist across the table over the patient's hip, to receive her fist in the manner of the "hood." They winked at each other and Leslie was smiling under her mask. It really had gone well...for them and the patient.

They helped the nurse apply dressings, then turned the patient on her back. Doc wrote orders while Leslie looked over his shoulder to check them out. They discussed their opinions on deep vein thrombosis prophylaxis and both were basically in agreement on the protocol for that.

In the surgery waiting room they found Eula's family. Doc introduced Leslie. He told them the operation went great. Talked about the expectations for the next few days, rehab, and the things the family could do to help her progress. Leslie realized she would be taking over the care of their mom and seeing her in the office too. It was strange thinking that Doc would be in Lubbock having his surgery in a few days. She wondered how he was feeling about it. They all shook hands. Doc and Leslie headed off to the doctor's lounge for lunch.

Leslie drove Doc to the office where they were greeted by Brenda who introduced her to the staff. "So Hal, did you take Doctor Cohen to the floor to see patients?"

"Course I did and they all loved her. They can't wait to get rid of me."

"Hal, don't be silly." Then to Leslie in a coquettish tone of voice, "Did Doc introduce you to Mary Ellen?"

"Yes, he did."

"What do you think, girl to girl? Do I have competition up there?" She had a little mischief in her eyes.

"Brenda, leave Doctor Cohen alone. That's not a professional question, and you've always been jealous of that old battleaxe."

"Battleaxe, my ass. Hal used to date Mary Ellen, but she didn't know anything about office management. Basically he needed an office manager more than a nurse. I was cheaper too."

"I think I'll just go check out the clinic layout here..." and Leslie pointed down the hall.

"Brenda, see what you've gone and done, gotten Doc Cohen's nose outta joint."

"Don't be silly, she knows I'm just teasing. Did they treat you good over there, sweetie?"

"It was really nice, for a first day and all. Everybody's very helpful. From what I can tell, things are run very well. Best I've seen in a long time."

"Doc and I operated on old J.T. Cullen's mother-in-law. Remember, she used to be a school teacher. I had her once. Didn't like her at all. She sent me to the principal's office more than once. I thought about making her leg short."

"Well...you did." Leslie said it really seriously. Brenda and Doc both looked at her, eyes wide, and she smiled.

"I can see you're going to have to be on your toes with this one, Hal."

"Tell me something I don't know."

"You'd better come with me. I'll show you around the office. Then we've got over twenty patients this afternoon. You going to stay?"

"Of course."

"Good. You'll see how Doc does things with the paperwork and stuff. I don't know what you're used to, but my staff and I do all the coding so you don't have to worry about that. If there's diagnosis codes you use that we don't know, we'll just ask you, that's all."

That was pretty sweet as far as Leslie was concerned. Coding was a pain in the ass and had absolutely nothing to do with patient care. It was just something used to try to help doctors get paid, but half the time it didn't help and some of the time it had the opposite effect. Plus, she was always paranoid that if her codes didn't match up perfectly, some guys in black coats would come marching through her front doors accusing her of fraud. Ridiculous. Let doctors practice medicine and nurses take care of patients. It's what they do.

They saw the twenty patients together and it was one of the strangest experiences she had ever had in a clinic. Again patients were treated almost like family, and some of them were. People talking in the hall, comparing notes. The staff showing patients off to other patients. A nice incision, a good range of motion. Doc, bustling in and out of rooms telling patients what they needed to do. There wasn't a whole lot of privacy, but no one seemed to care. If there were delicate situations, then those patients were put in a room and the door closed. People were chatting with each other in the waiting room and didn't seem to mind if they had to wait. No one complained anyway.

Today patients were more concerned about Doc. He had a pile of gifts people had brought with them. There were flowers, plants, homemade jelly, a teddy bear, chocolates of every sort, and a number of gag gifts. The whoopee cushion was her favorite. Doc went into a couple of kid's rooms and intentionally sat on it. Then that prompted the kids to start making their own variety of fart noises. Some were adept at doing it with their armpits.

What is it about gas and kids? She remembered having some great whoopee cushion fun with Victor and Vivian. They blew it up and squished it over and over until the thing wore out and Leslie's cheeks were sore from laughing so hard with them. Everyone who came over that week got directed to the seat with the hidden pink balloon. Each time it went off, they all got off, laughing like they had never heard it before.

Later on, after clinic was over, they went into Doc's office where he put the whoopee cushion under one of his consultation chair cushions. Then he called Brenda in and asked her to sit down, because they needed to go over some things. There was ever so slight a change in his voice so she knew he was up to something.

"Now what?" She looked at them suspiciously as she sat down, and out came the bleeeep, riiiip, braaaaap. She jumped up.

"Oh, you. You are just acting like a little kid. I should have known. Look at the two of you."

Her voice was full of indignation. And the two of them just laughing, a knee slapping, gut laugh. It was an irresistible situation, infectious, and pretty soon Brenda was laughing too. And just like that, Leslie felt the tears welling up in her eyes unexpectedly, as she thought of Vic, Vivi and their whoopee cushion. Did she throw it away? To her astonishment, Doc and Brenda saw it too and stopped laughing, kind of fizzled out. She was embarrassed, but Brenda stood up and came over to her.

"This reminded you of something, didn't it sweetheart? Let's quick think of something else. Hal, go get us some Diet Cokes, will you?" And he was already up, moving as fast as he could to get out of that room.

"I am so sorry," Leslie said. "I can't believe that happened. You probably think I'm some kind of baby, crying all the time or something. I don't know what came over me."

"It's okay, Leslie. Don't even think about it here. We understand, and we're like your family while you're here. You've brightened up Hal's day, in some way. I can see it in his eyes. Maybe, in our way, we can return the favor." Brenda put her hand on top of Leslie's and patted it. "I just knew you two were up to no good when I came into the room."

She stood up. The moment gone. All better. Leslie smiled at her.

Doc yelled from down the hall, "Two Diet Cokes, coming up!"

Leslie felt exhausted when she left Doc's office. They made plans to meet again the next day. She gave him her cell phone number, just in case something came in during the night and he needed help. Of course she knew he didn't need help, but she felt ready to get to work, day or night. Work had the ability to exhaust her mentally and physically. It made it easier to get to sleep at night and easier to get through each day. Some of the doctors doing *locum tenens* work wanted low key, easy jobs, but as far as she was concerned, the busier the better. Most jobs were set up to be like babysitting. The surgeon would shut down his practice, farm out the follow-ups to other guys in town or to their family physicians. She would be there only for emergencies. There would be nothing else to do. She could sight see, but a lot of times there was nothing to see. It was excruciating. She would try to read, watch TV, exercise, but always her mind went back to her family.

Already she could tell this job was going to be different. On the one hand the inevitable questions into her background would come. It was simply the way nice people behaved. It would be difficult to keep from telling the truth. On the other hand, Doc seemed to be making no attempt to lighten her load, and was apparently ready to turn everything over to her. This would make the month or so she was there fly by.

It was a cool evening with a soft breeze and a clean smell in the air. A little dust devil stirred in the front of the hotel under the portico. The wind defined west Texas. There was very little to stop its progress. Dust devils were always at play in areas that diverted its course. It was as if the wind was trying to get even for standing in its way. Doors would stay open indefinitely if one didn't turn to make sure they were shut. There were annoying little triangles of dust in the corners of windowsills where the wind constantly tried to penetrate. Grasses and small trees were permanently bent to its will. The little dust devil swirled and swirled unimpeded until she stepped into the view of the automatic eye opening the sliding doors to the hotel. The miniature tornado played out, dropping its contents on the ground at her feet.

"Ah, Doctor Cohen. Good evening! You had a long day. Would you like some coffee? I have some fresh in the dining area over there?"

"You know, I think I will have a cup. Do you have decaf?"

"Of course, of course, if that pleases you. I have just to make it, but it will take no time at all. Please wait, I will fix it. It will take no time. Please come. Sit here." He pointed to a chair near the coffee maker.

"Well, thanks, but I do hate to put you to this trouble. No one else will drink this coffee, I'm sure."

"Do not even worry. It is no problem, I assure you." The decaffeinated coffee was already brewing. Soon the smell wafted over to her. She loved the smell of coffee even more than the taste. She was looking forward to the brew. They had little half-and-halfs sitting out. They would be room temperature instead of cold, which is the best because it doesn't cool off the coffee. She fixed it the usual way. Raghu gave no indication that her manner of fixing the coffee was at all out of the ordinary. She thanked him profusely for his trouble and he again reassured her that it was no trouble at all.

"Wake up call for six again, Doctor."

"Yes, please Raghu. Goodnight." She went up to her room. It was later than she thought and she was very tired. Looking forward to a good night sleep. She took a warm bath and got into bed.

She had not forgotten about them during the day, and they were there with her thoughts now. Some vision, some day in that past life. Tonight it was a birthday. Birthdays were special for twins simply because there were two of them. Things were always special because there were two of them. They looked so much alike, acted so differently, but were connected beyond the usual sibling bonds. Their cake was half pink and half blue. They stood on their respective sides and each blew out four candles. Vic was laughing and sort of spat on his side of the cake while blowing. They cut pieces from the pink side.

Sometime in the middle of the party Leslie went to sleep and appeared to dream. Her eyes darted back and forth under closed lids. She occasionally gritted her teeth and the corners of her mouth wiggled into a half smile. She was in the middle of REM sleep when her cell phone rang.

The phone was across the room. She really hadn't expected any callers so had forgotten to put it at her bedside. She flew out of bed, cleared her throat so she could sound awake and poked at the CALL button.

"Hey, Doc, Hal Hawley here. You awake?" She looked across the room at the clock and could see it was almost two in the morning. It would be admitting sleeplessness to say yes.

"I am now."

"Well, listen, there's a fella in the ER, and I thought we might take care of him. I'm not on call or anything but he's asking for me. I mean, I can say no and they'll get the guy on call to take care of him."

"Say no more, Doc. What's his problem?"

"Horses are his problem. These guys compete out here at the event center until all hours of the night. Anyway, he got tangled up with some rank horse and got his femur broken. Midshaft. We'll need to nail it. You in?"

"Of course. Of course. But listen, why don't you get some rest and let me take care of it."

"Well, I didn't even think of that option. Well, why not? I mean you're taking over here in a few days anyway. I mean I didn't call to get you to do it. Thought we might do it together. But to be honest with you, I'd just as soon flat back it, if you think you can handle it."

"Go back to sleep. I've got it covered. I'll see you in the morning and we can check out the X-rays."

"Sounds good. Let me know if you have any problems." He gave her numbers for the ER and OR. She called the ER to let them know she was coming. Then the OR to put them on standby. She'd have to call them with the details once she saw the X-rays. Then she would decide exactly how she would fix it.

She showered quickly to wake herself up and got dressed, picked up her white coat, her overcoat too, then went downstairs. Raghu was surprised to see her.

"I got a call to go to the emergency room. I guess I should have had that regular coffee after all."

"I'll have some fresh in the morning. You will need it."

It was about 2:20 when she stepped outside. There was dewy moisture in the air. A couple of trucks passed on I-20 going opposite directions. It's always lonely going to the emergency room in the middle of the night. For some reason it doesn't feel like coming home from a party in the middle of the night. Everyone is fast asleep, or it feels that way. They're warm, tucked in. Her bed, when Chris was in it, was warm, hard to leave. She could hear the sound of her children breathing, even out in the hall at home. The night is quiet, moist, dew starting to form, always the same.

There is a patient waiting for her. They're in pain. She thinks about what she could encounter in the ER and makes tentative plans. They may be altered depending on the X-rays. She wonders what the patient will be like. A lot of times, at 2:00 in the morning, they are drunk. Sometimes patients are angry, hostile, especially if they've had to wait a while or felt hassled in the emergency room. Sometimes the patients are grateful. Anxious. Ignorant. There's a different challenge. But they're always in pain. That part is the same.

Cal Wimberly was in pain. He was not drunk. He was clever, agreeable and willing to do whatever it took to "get this thing fixed."

She introduced herself, and explained why she was there instead of Doc Hawley.

"Hey, if Doc Hawley says you're okay, then you're okay with me. Where do I sign up?"

Leslie had reviewed the X-rays. He had a broken femur at about the point where the top third and the middle third met. She decided on the operation to be performed and called the OR. Ante-grade femoral nail. She'd need a C-arm and a fracture table. They started getting ready for her.

She talked about the surgery and went over the X-rays with Cal. Then, her most unfavorite part. Discussing potential risks and complications of surgery. Now most patients know that there is a potential for things to go wrong. But when she starts to lay it out for them it gets scary. It's a lot easier on her and the patient just to tell them she's going to take good care of them and everything's going to be all right. But she had to explain the part about bleeding, infection and blood clots. It had to be done, for the patient, for their family, and for the attorneys. Really, it doesn't matter how many ways she tells a patient they can have a complication, when they get one they're still unhappy about it and if they're angry about it and get a lawyer, sometimes it doesn't matter what they signed.

Cal cut her off in mid-sentence, around the part where she said he could die. "Doc, listen, I'm laying here with my leg half twisted off. I'm gonna die if you don't operate on me. You got a pen?"

She signed him up. In a little while the OR staff came down and they rolled him to surgery. Cal's wife, Jenn walked with them and kissed him goodbye just before they entered the OR.

In OR 3 the anesthesiologist introduced himself. He put Cal to sleep on his ER stretcher and they moved him to the fracture table, turning him on his side at the same time. As they turned him, she could feel the sickening crunch of the two ends of the broken femur rubbing against each other. Leslie strapped Cal's legs into the contraption so she could put traction on the leg. She donned the heavy lead apron which would shield her from the radiation penetrating everything in the room while she X-rayed the femur. She applied traction and used the C-arm fluoroscopy machine to check the position of the fracture.

"X-ray," she loudly announced. Everyone who had lead aprons on turned to face the machine so they had the benefit of the lead protection. Everyone else ran for cover, out in the hall or behind someone with lead. Leslie faced the leg and the X-ray machine. On the computer screen she could see the fracture was not aligned properly yet. A little short and a little angulated. She distracted the leg a little more with a turnbuckle-like apparatus and yelled "X-ray" again. Still angulated. She grabbed the thigh above and below the fracture with her hands and pushed in opposite directions, calling for an X-ray at the same time. The C-arm started beeping, indicating that radiation was spewing forth. On the monitor she could see the bones of her own hands wrapped around Cal's thigh. The beeping and radiation would continue until she indicated otherwise, every beep announcing the radiation going into her hands as well as Cal's leg. There was no getting around it. She could putz around all day with the traction, trying to get it right. Too much trouble. Just grab the thigh, put it where you want it and shoot. Once figuring out the kind of push or pull necessary to put the fracture straight, she could put a crutch or something under the thigh to hold it while operating, and that's exactly what she did.

The leg was prepped with Betadine and Leslie made a short curved incision over Cal's left hip. She cut through the same big tendon she and Doc had cut through earlier that day on Eula Parsons. It was actually yesterday, she reminded herself. She pushed her finger through the muscles connecting the hip to the pelvis, bluntly dividing them, separating rather than cutting the muscle fibers. She felt the tip of the bone and the recess that lies along side of it. The surgical tech handed her the next instrument she requested.

"Awl." Then teasing, but someone eventually almost always says, "Give me your awl," to chuckles. Dumb play on words in an operating room.

The awl. A large sharp curved metal spear used to gouge a hole into the top of the femur so she could then stick a long stout wire down inside the marrow cavity of the bone, aligning the pieces of bone on it like a shish kabob. She made sure with X-ray that the wire was in the bone. Then she threaded the long stiff guide wire down the canal. Once getting to the fracture, she had someone in the room who was not scrubbed and gowned, stick a crutch up under the thigh as she had previously planned. She pushed a little with her fist against the side of the thigh and fished the guide wire across the fracture. Sometimes this one part took thirty minutes, but this time, much to her relief, it went right across. Accomplishing it quickly makes people think the surgeon is really good at what he or she does. She's golden, thumbs up, hey, she's really smart. But just fumble around with this very difficult part of the case and then she sucks. People looking at each other with rolling eyes while they think she's not watching, but she is.

Tonight? Golden. Wait 'til next time. Maybe not so lucky.

She threaded the wire down to the end, just above the knee and then began the process called reaming. Using progressively larger and larger sized reamers, like flexible drills, she ground out the inside of Cal's femur until the bone started chattering around the instrument indicating that she had reached the hard bone of the thigh. She took measurements and called for the desired nail, which was basically a long, hollow, titanium tube. She removed the reamer and left the guide wire in place. Leslie received the nail assembled on a driver. The tech handed her a heavy mallet and she pounded that nail down the inside of the femur, across the fracture and all the way to the end of the thigh bone, just above the knee, using the wire to guide it down.

In order to keep the nail in place and to keep the bone from rotating around on the nail, also like a shish kabob, she had to put screws across the bone, then through the nail, at the top and bottom of the femur. This was a difficult task that had to be done under continuous X-ray vision. Again, there was no other way to do it. The X-rays just blasted away at her hands as she drilled and ran the screws across the bone and nail. Sometimes, she imagined she could feel her hand tingling after the procedure.

They cleaned his leg. There was blood all over the leg, drapes, X-ray machine and the floor. This was always a pretty bloody operation because of the reaming. After applying the dressings they took him out of traction and turned him over. The leg moved normally, solidly. It felt good. A broken femur feels awful. The normally powerful thigh muscles pulling against nothing, the two bones sliding past each other with each contraction of the muscles, the thigh sagging with the weight of useless muscles and bone. Then, suddenly, a titanium rod, applied with some elbow grease, and the thigh is functioning, the muscles have their advantage again. Cal was put back together.

Leslie thanked everyone and went out to talk to Jenn Wimberly. Members of the family. Someone to talk to. Someone to care if the operation went well, to help him recover, rehabilitate. Leslie would someday be one of the rare patients who had no one to wait and inquire about them. A group of people who included the homeless, the alcoholics, drug addicts, people jumping trains, and very old people whose entire families had died before them or had abandoned them for some reason no one would ever know.

She had a long talk with Jenn. They talked about activities, returning to work and mostly horseback riding. Jenn said that Cal would be wanting to ride just as soon as possible. With the use of internal fixation of femur fractures, people could get back to normal pretty quick. As soon as they weren't sore, for that matter, they could get back to walking, doing a desk job, and even pleasure horseback riding. No roping until she gave the go ahead.

"Well, just so you tell him, because he won't listen to me." This was a common request, and Leslie often found herself acting as mother as well as surgeon.

She told Jenn goodbye and went to the recovery room to check one last time on Cal. She checked his dressings, had him wiggle his foot up and down to make sure everything was working. She told him everything went fine. Then he asked the expected question. "Doc, am I going to be able to ride a horse again?"

She had been tricked on that one before, and responded with a question. "Could you ride one before?"

Now, she looked at the clock on the wall. It was 5:07 AM. There was time to go to her room and get a little sleep. She got in her car and noticed the fine mist on the windshield despite the relative absence of moisture in the air. The air smelled fresh. Even though she hated being out at this time of the morning, there was still something special about it.

There was not a single wind current to greet her around the portico. Raghu was there to greet her though. No offer of coffee yet and she didn't want any. There was still potential for sleep.

"Raghu, can you change that wake up call to seven-thirty?"

"You bet."

She laid her clothes out for the next morning and got everything ready for a speedy preparation. Thank goodness she didn't wear makeup. Brushed her teeth, washed her face. Can't forget to put on lotion in this dry climate. Her head hit the pillow and she fell asleep almost instantly. She never reached REM sleep. Her eyes remained still. The sun rose, framing the plastic lined curtains with a shiny square halo.

7

*L*eslie's internal alarm went off at six. She became aware, but did not open her eyes. She turned on her side, dragging the pillows over her head. That was good for about thirty extra minutes. Then she started to feel that little urge to pee. She turned again, and couldn't suppress it.

"Damn." She flung back the sheets and blanket, crawled out of bed and satisfied the urge. She flushed the toilet without hesitation. The habit of not flushing at hotels in order not to wake her husband was one of the first to go. No need to tippy toe back to the bed, and slide quietly in between the sheets. Even when she used to extend that courtesy, she could tell by the change in Chris' breathing, he was awake. Sometimes when she heard that telltale sound, she would stop, face the bed, and leap over on the mattress, causing a startled, slightly put out expression from her husband, who himself was probably trying to ignore the coming of morning.

She sighed as she fell into bed and tried to curl up in the cooling sheets. Just thirty more minutes. Eyes wide open. Thinking about the case. Thinking about mornings with Chris. Time to get up. At least she could get dressed a little more leisurely. Take a long shower. Put anti-frizz product in her hair for a few minutes rather than rinse immediately. Her hair dried fast in the arid Abilene climate so there was a lot less frizz. This was good. She got dressed. "Now, I'll take that cup of coffee."

Doc caught her on her cell phone en route to the hospital. "Well, how'd it go?"

"Slam dunker. No problems. Everything went great. Staff was great."

"Hey, good work. Did Cal mind that I wasn't there?"

"He asked me if I was going to do the surgery. But a lot of people ask me that."

Even when she was in private practice, sometimes when she recommended surgery, the patients asked if she would be the one doing the operation. Depending on whether the cup was half full or half empty, she could interpret the question as their making sure no other fool was going to do the case while they were under anesthesia, or in the case of the half empty cup, they were checking to see if there was a qualified male surgeon who would step in when needed. She never asked. Just answered, "Of course, I am."

"Well, of course you were." They arranged to meet in radiology to check out the X-rays.

She found the films herself. After almost twenty years of having to look for her own films, it didn't take long in any radiology department to dig up some rays. Of course, they were never in the alphabetical files labeled IN HOUSE. That would be too easy. There were always some miscellaneous bins somewhere and sure enough, there was a SURGERY file. The big metal nail stood out on the film, right down the middle of the femur, locked in place up top and down below by the screws.

"Impressive work, Doc. Lucky patient. Lucky me, to have someone like you to cover my practice. I think I'm gonna like having a lady doc around."

"You're just saying that. Beggars can't be choosers."

"Listen, your agency recommended you highly. They said all your previous employers were very complimentary. Some even asked you to stay. I'm real glad you didn't and that you're here."

They left the radiology department and went down the hall. It was busy this time of the morning. Lots of hospital personnel and family members were walking up and down the halls. Leslie and Doc were quiet but she could tell he wanted to say something. And in a few moments, he did.

"Listen, I just wanna say, well," he hesitated, uncomfortable, "well, I know about your husband. And it's not real easy talking about that stuff with a colleague and all, but I'm real sorry for your loss. Well, I hope this work and being in Abilene can help take your mind off things for a little bit. That's what you need. Some time. You remember from medical school Psychiatry. It just takes some time."

"Thanks, Doc. I'm working on it. And, I hope after that little episode over the whoopee cushion last night, you don't think it will affect my ability to take care of your people. I mean, I just want to..."

"Hey, don't even say it. I wouldn't give that a second thought. I just hope to hell no patients fart in front of you, that's all."

The schedule that day was similar to the previous day. They started out in surgery. Doc had a couple of knee arthroscopies, followed by a shoulder rotator cuff repair. There was a carpal tunnel release and last, he took some plates and screws out of a kid's arm. The boy wanted to play football and the prominence of the hardware was painful when he hit another player.

They were running a little late so Leslie offered to round on the patients while Doc went on to the office. She would join him there when she was done. Eula was first on the list. She was doing fine. Progress was pretty slow with her ambulation and so she would make plans to send Eula to a rehabilitation facility where she could get a little more intensive therapy than was offered in the hospital.

The total joint patients would be ready to go tomorrow. None of the patients seemed surprised or disappointed to see her instead of Doc.

Now she was ready to go see Cal, but first she wanted to get his X-rays. There were certain kinds of patients who always wanted to see their X-rays. Cal was one. Usually it was active guys, young or old. Women usually didn't care or were squeamish over them. But the guys, they liked to see hardware in their bones. Like trophies.

She went down to the radiology department and checked out the films, took another look at her handiwork and went back upstairs. In the hall outside Cal's room, she pulled his chart from the "nurse server" shelves. While checking his blood pressure, temperature and lab results, she noticed a lot of noise coming from his room. There were clearly a bunch of visitors, male voices, and they were carrying on with her patient. She couldn't specifically hear the words, but they were teasing and laughing.

Leslie prided herself on her bedside manner. She made it a point to try her best to communicate with her patients and their families on their level. Sometimes this could be difficult, but most of the time it was easy for her. Nevertheless, she found that walking into a room full of people was somewhat intimidating. At the least, it was distracting to the patient. But sometimes it could be distracting to her as well. Family members and friends could be a positive influence on the patient, but frequently in a crowd of more than two, there could be negative influences and even hostility. There were a lot of people out there who were frankly hostile toward doctors and the medical environment. If they were there, she could feel their silent attention to detail.

In a room with more than two or three people there was frequently someone who was self-centered. They wanted to talk about themselves, their problems, their experiences. Someone always had an orthopedic problem and they thought this was a good time for a free consult. They might try to minimize the patient's problem and compare it to their own. It would take every ounce of patience on her part to keep from asking them to please shut up.

Sometimes, in a room of more than two or three there would be someone with whom she might have something in common. It's just human nature to want to talk about something like kids, school, where you were born or hobbies. Then she would feel guilty for diverting attention from the patient. Hospital visits were a time to focus on the patient, and distractions were in general, unwanted.

It sounded like this was a room full of laughing, joking, good ol' boys. She would have to shake everyone's hand. She was sure she would have to be part of some joke at her patient's expense. She would have to ask them to leave while she looked at Cal's leg and checked his bandages.

Oh, well, she thought, here goes. She walked into the room. She looked directly at Cal and decided to take cues from him regarding how he wanted to deal with his friends.

"Oh, oh, boys, we're in trouble now. Here's my doctor."

There was silence for a moment or two, and then, "Figures you'd get lucky enough to get a lady doctor, and not ol' Doc Hawley." Laughter for the joker, followed by general chatting and agreement.

"Doctor Cohen, I'd introduce you to these guys, but I know you must have better things to do. They were all there when I busted my leg. I was beating them, hands down, so they're here to cheer me up. Then they're going to go celebrate, I'm sure."

"Well, don't celebrate too long, you guys. He'll be back sooner than you think." This was followed by comments about her northern expression, "you guys."

The articulation of the plural form of "you" distinguished people as being from the south or the north as much as any other word, phrase or accent. In her travels around the country she had contemplated the use of both and had actually come to the conclusion that "y'all" was much more efficient and pleasing to the ear than "you guys."

At this point she was feeling a little more at ease. Nothing negative or self-centered going on here. She started to look around and make eye contact with the people in the room while she pulled out Cal's X-rays. They all appeared to be cowboys or wearing cowboy clothes anyway. A couple of them had been wearing cowboy hats and had removed them when she came in the room. They had hat hair and little indentations where the hat brim had been. When she looked at each one they gave her kind of a head dip of greeting or acknowledgement and she reciprocated.

"Hey, Doc's got my pictures. Let's check it out." She had to get up alongside his bed and turn around to put the film up toward the light on the ceiling. It was then that she was able to see the man who had been standing off to the side. He was smiling at her and the other guys instantly caught on to the fact that there was some recognition.

"Regan!" She couldn't suppress the surprise in her voice.

"Leslie." A statement of fact. "Now you're one person I didn't expect to see here."

"I take it you two know each other?"

"This is the lady I was telling you about. The one from the wreck." He looked at Leslie. "You didn't tell me you were a doctor."

"What a small world. I can't believe it."

"Man, you tried to kill the lady who was supposed to fix my leg. That's really strange."

They all started talking about the wreck, the coincidence, and Leslie began to feel as if she was party to the situation which took attention away from the patient. She put up the X-ray again and everyone swung around behind her more or less, to take a look. She showed the before and after films.

"This is your bone when it was broken. That's the hip, up top.

Your knee is not on this X-ray, but it would be down here." She pointed in the opposite direction. Someone asked if the bone was broken or was it fractured. She'd had that question asked many times before. A lot of people thought there was a difference between broken bones and fractured bones.

"Both. They both mean the same thing."

They all looked at the guy who asked like he was a dumbass.

"Now here's the after film," she said, to some "wows" and "whoas." This is the titanium nail that is down inside your femur bone, kind of like a shish kabob. The screws up top and down below keep the bone from twisting or shortening."

"I'd like to see that. Cal, with one leg short and turned out."

"Maybe he'd ride better."

"Doc promised me that after this operation I would ride even better than I already do."

"And I'm charging him double for it too." They all started laughing. Leslie noticed that Regan had moved over to the other side of the bed right across from her. She could look at him fairly easily without being obvious. He had dark brown hair with a little grey. It was probably curly, but he wore it short. It was getting a little thin on the temporal area but was otherwise thick. He was in his late thirties or early forties. Her age. He looked at her. They smiled. Cal was watching them, observant.

She talked about plans for the next couple of days. She was starting him on blood thinners, shots, which he would have to give to himself once he went home. His buddies all had a lot to say about that. They talked about physical therapy, how much weight he could put on his leg and when he could go back to work. She needed to look at his dressings and his leg. His friends began to excuse themselves.

"Doctor Cohen. It was good to see you again."

"Hey, same here." She felt funny letting him call her "doctor" but it would be too complicated right now to offer otherwise. She said goodbye to everyone and turned back to Cal.

His bandages were dry. The leg was swollen as expected, but he was able to move it already. Everything looked good.

"Doc and I will check on you tomorrow, okay?"

"See you tomorrow, Doctor Cohen. Thanks again for taking care of me last night."

"You're welcome. See you tomorrow."

She walked out in the hallway and wrote her progress note. She dropped the films off at the nurse's station so they could send them back to radiology, then walked toward the elevator lobby.

Regan was waiting for her down the hall. He was leaning against the wall, arms crossed in front. He shoved off with his shoulders when he saw her coming.

Leslie said, "Hey, you, I'm glad you waited around. That was too much of a coincidence. So weird seeing you here."

"What's really weird is that you're Cal's doctor. You're an orthopedic surgeon?"

"Uh huh. So how do you know Cal?"

"Cal and I have ridden horses together for years. We work together too. Do you ride?"

"Well, not in a very long time. Used to ride when I was a kid. Just rode around mostly. Took some English lessons, did a little jumping. Also did some play day kind of stuff, you know, barrels, pole bending."

"Ever work any cattle?"

"On foot, but not horseback. My dad had some cattle when I was growing up." Now the conversation was starting to get personal and she knew she'd better divert it. Shift it to him.

"So, did I hear Cal say you were all at a show together when he got hurt?"

"Yeah, roping. There was a big show at the Expo center." He paused. Fidgeted a little. Turned his ball cap in between his fingers along its rim. "Are you doing okay? I mean, after the accident. You know, your ankle and all."

"Sure, I'm fine. The ankle's still a little sore and I feel a little achy. How about you? Did you get up the next day a little stiff?"

"Not too much."

They made small talk about the accident, insurance, the weather. When they got to the elevator lobby he asked if she was going down. He pushed the elevator button. When they got on she felt strangely nervous. He was definitely attractive and she felt uncomfortable having considered it. They forgot to push the ground floor button. The elevator started making the obnoxious buzzing noise. They both jumped for the button at the same time and touched each other's hand. She felt a nervous sensation again. He looked at her directly. Searching for a sign where he shouldn't be. As far as he was concerned, she was Mrs. Cohen. Mrs. Dr. Cohen.

"So are you Doc Hawley's new partner or something?" He was searching. Think fast. The elevator arrived on the ground floor and they got off.

"Well, not really. I'm covering his practice while he's out for a while."

"Oh, really. Like for how long do you do that?"

"I think for about a month or so, depending on how long he needs me. It's called *locum tenens*. Doctors who don't have partners sometimes need other doctors to help them out so they can go on vacation or take a break, whatever. So here I am." She tried to sound very matter of fact. "Anyway, I've got to go meet Doc at his office. He's got patients this afternoon. We're seeing them together."

"Well, I'm glad he's here to help you out. Looks like you're handling things just fine."

"Oh, thanks." Leslie looked at her feet, and then at Regan, "Well, I better get going. Good to see you again."

"You too. Hey, Doc. Drive carefully." He gave her a knowing kind of smile, eyebrow raised. She waved and turned toward the Taurus. He headed over to an older looking truck. The white one with the brush guard would be in the body shop.

Leslie took a deep breath. That didn't just happen to her. She felt good about the fact that she kept her distance and was sure he wouldn't have gotten any vibes from her. Still, she must have given him a sign, because there was something.

It was about 3:30. There would still be a lot of patients to see at Doc's office. She was looking forward to it. She was confused by her emotions and seeing patients was just the thing to get her back on track.

Doc was dictating. Feet hiked up on his desk. Stayed in that position when she walked into his office and took the consultation chair opposite him. He asked how things went. How did the patients handle it? How was the femur? He used the familiar, though not disrespectful way of referring to patients by their injured body part.

She assured him that everything checked out just fine. Patients were all tucked in for the evening and the "femur" was fine. She told him about running into Regan. Doc was intrigued.

"He's a good boy." She was struck by the reference to Regan as a boy. "Knew his daddy well. They left him pretty well set up, but he's a hard worker and has built that construction business up on his own. Regan's had his own disappointments, if you wanna know the truth. Nothing like yours, don't get me wrong, but he's had his problems."

"Like what?" Leslie didn't want to appear too interested. Next thing she'd know Doc and Brenda would be trying to set her up with every eligible bachelor in town. She'd seen it before. Widows and widowers are always prime matchmaker material. They got along with the deceased spouse, chances are they'll do well in a second marriage. It was different for her and even though she didn't respond to Doc's disclaimer about the level of severity of her problems over Regan's, she was pretty sure it didn't compare.

"Regan married his high school sweetheart, you know, they went together for years and just finally made it legal. They had the little girl per-itty quick after that. Anyway, his daddy died shortly thereafter and Regan had to get busy dividing the estate with his sister and basically taking care of her. She took her daddy's death pretty hard. Then he got real busy with his work. I guess it was too much for the wife. One day she up and left him for another guy. Took the kid with her. From what I heard he just wasn't the same after that. I think he felt a little guilty because he didn't fight her for custody when they moved off to California. The baby was pretty young and I doubt she would even know Regan. People around here aren't even sure the kid was his. I guess it was the best thing looking back. Maybe she would have left him sooner or later. Now, I don't know him that well or anything. People just talk. I guess he stays busy with work and his roping."

"So he never remarried."

"Nope. Don't know why not. Like I say, from what you hear in general, he's a good boy. No drinking problem like some of those cowboys he hangs with. Good worker. You name it. Pretty eligible in my book." He put his feet down, leaned forward in his big cordovan leather chair. "Well, not our problem, right?"

"Right." Her voice trailing off. Distracted a little.

"That's a real coincidence, you taking care of Cal and all. I guess he had to try to send you to your maker first and then when you passed muster, you could fix up his buddy!" Doc, laughing at his own comment. Leslie had to chuckle at his chuckling.

Brenda stuck her head in. "All right, you two. We do have patients here today. Or should we send them home, y'all have so much to talk about."

"Listen to this, hon. Doc here ran into Regan Wakeman again. No pun intended. Up at the hospital."

"What a coincidence. How's he doing?"

"He seemed fine. We didn't really talk that much. I was seeing his friend. It's the guy I operated on last night."

"Speaking of, Leslie, that was so nice of you to take care of that patient last night. Hal just rolled right over and went back to sleep. Now, get to work you two. Patients are waiting."

The surgeons shuffled out of the break room, scolded school children. Doc introduced Leslie to patients she would be taking over and discharged others, to come back only if they had problems. More presents were handed over though none so compelling as the whoopee cushion. They were a reminder of Doc's status with his patients. Leslie had never seen anything like it in her private practice. There were always some presents at Christmas time. Some patients brought tokens of their appreciation for a job well done, but nothing like this. It looked as if there had been a wedding or baby shower at the office. His patients were really devoted. Leslie hoped she could give them what they wanted and needed while Doc was out. But she was already wondering when he would actually be back. After clinic tonight, they were going to sit down and go over all the last minute details and she would question Doc about his surgery a little. That way she could get an idea. They finished up and Brenda ordered some pizzas to be delivered.

They went over forms, designated stacks of papers, things that needed to be reviewed and signed regularly. There were a lot of tedious things the staff just couldn't do. A lot of ink on paper. Signatures. This was no different than any other office, but she was taking on a fully operational office, not one partially shut down while a doctor was out for a short time. In a practice this busy there would be somewhere in the neighborhood of twenty to thirty forms, notes, or dictations that had to be signed every day. Nursing home and physical therapy notes had to have her signature in order for those companies to get paid. It was really an outrage, but no one could do anything about it. Charts, prescriptions, return to work forms, wheelchair approvals, handicap parking permits. All had to be signed. There were baskets for urgent, semi-urgent and not-so-urgent papers to sign.

The pizzas arrived and the three of them took a break. Leslie decided now would be a good time to get the lowdown on Doc's situation. She would just get to the point. That's one of the good things about being a doctor. She could just ask, even if it's a colon.

"So, Doc. Tell me about your surgery. What's going on?"

"Leslie, here's the deal. Basically, I've got colon cancer. I'm getting a colectomy of some sort. Anyway you look at it, I'm lookin' at my shit in a bag. Right here." He pointed to his stomach." He looked over at Brenda, who was giving him the tight-lipped-angry-eye-look. "What? She's a doctor. She knows what I'm talking about."

"Well, you don't have to put it like that. In those words, I mean."

"Hey, there's no need to beat around the bush here, right, Doc? You gotta stand behind me now. It's you and me against Mother Teresa over there." Brenda was rolling her eyes.

"Look Doc, I'm not taking sides here. While you're out, there's the hand that feeds me."

"Now there's a good girl. You may just have to stay home and lick your wounds by yourself, you old bear."

Leslie wanted to know more. "Seriously now, is this pretty certain? Is there much potential for problems? Chemo? You know. Do you know what to expect?"

"Doctor Calvert and the oncologist at Texas Tech, what's his name, Jimenez?"

"Jimeno."

"That's right, Jimeno. They think it's pretty routine stuff. Nothing out of the ordinary. They're good guys up there in Lubbock. I didn't want to have this kind of surgery here. Can you imagine having to face those nurses and folks in the OR after that kind of a case? No way. Never get any respect after that. Barring any complications, I should be back within a week. And it's not a big deal to go up and down eighty-four to Lubbock for follow-up. If it was an emergency, that would be different."

"Hey, I'm with you on that one, Doc. I wouldn't want to have any kind of personal type surgery in my own town. Plastic surgery, breast surgery, that kind of stuff. An ankle or a knee, a brain. That's different."

"There's a little convenience factor though, Leslie, and that's because I won't be around to help you out here that first week while Hal's at the medical center. It shouldn't be too bad. The staff is as prepared as they can be. I'll be only a phone call away if there are any problems. But, I need to be up there to help Hal with his little bags." She looked at Hal innocently and made little silly hand gestures like she was holding little bags. Leslie looked at Doc. He was in a little denial. Trying to act casual about this serious stuff. There could be complications and at best it wasn't going to be easy.

Tomorrow was Friday, and Doc's last day at work for a while. Saturday he would start his prep for surgery. Sunday they were heading for Lubbock and would stay overnight in a hotel in order to avoid driving early in the morning. Surgery was scheduled for Monday morning. Any other treatment would be based on what they found in surgery.

They stayed at the office for a long time. Brenda continued to show her where things were. Doc wanted to talk shop. Leslie hadn't really thought about it much until then, but one of the things she missed, and she was sure Doc missed, was orthopedic shop talk. It's all good stuff. Rich stuff. Orthopedic talk itself has got to be the best medical talk, she was sure of it. Hardware and drills, putting stuff together, whether it's athletes or grandmothers is just good story telling. What do urologists or gynecologists talk about? There are no screws and plates, high speed drills there. Nobody wants to hear about uteri or bladders. Nope. She loved shop talk. So did Doc. Maybe the only ones who don't like shop talk are spouses.

She remembered a party during her training, when she and the other residents were talking business. After a while, she went to find Chris. She had abandoned him for the shop talk. She found him, asleep, sitting in a chair in the middle of all the resident's wives. They were having their own form of shop talk, just ignoring her poor sleeping husband, whose head was dropped and lower jaw hanging open. She tried from that point on, to be more cognizant of leaving Chris out of the shop talk. He knew something about lag screws and drill bits. But sometimes she couldn't help it. She didn't have to worry anymore.

Brenda didn't seem to mind. In fact, it looked like she was enjoying the talk too. She hung in there for a while. Doc questioned Leslie about how she liked to do things. What brand of equipment did she use? They went back and forth for a few hours. Brenda started to nod off. They decided to call it quits for the night, made plans to meet in the morning. There were no scheduled cases. Doc wanted to round, then go back to the office to do his last clinic. He looked tired.

"Goodnight Leslie. We're glad you're here."

"See you in the morning, Doc."

During the night a kid with a broken wrist came into the ER. They called her directly. She and Doc had decided to list her as the covering doctor from this point on. Doc had taken care of this kid and his siblings before, so they considered him to be their personal orthopedic surgeon. She wondered if Doc got called every night. Tough life. Surely he gives them up to the guy on orthopedic call sometimes. She went in, set the fracture, and came back to the hotel.

A cold front was coming. The black sky was strangely crystal clear and the stars were brilliant. They seemed low and close. The moon was dazzling and full. There was a halo around it. To the north she could see a wall of clouds. The front. The moonlight reflected off its leading edge, shining against gun metal grey. The reflections were repeated on the undersurface of the clouds, like light and dark grey cotton balls. The news warned people to bring in their pets, throw sheets over their plants. They recited brief instructions on how to keep water lines from freezing. These people didn't know what a cold front was. Try a cold front in the Shawangunk Mountains.

Shoveling snow. The weight of snow and ice bending the tree branches over their street. Snow piled high enough that they built tunnels in it. Snow men too. The kids bundled up so thick she could only see their little noses, pink, running. Twin smoke breath clouds. They let her buy blue and pink or red matching outfits until they were about seven, when they developed their own childish sense of fashion.

She remembered a winter when they had blue and red down snow suits. One piece. They could hardly move. They waddled. The moisture collected around their nostrils and froze there. Little crystal webs. They could suck the air through their noses and make their nostrils stick together. She did it too, but she had to squeeze hers together with her fingers. As they got older, and the cartilage in their noses got firm, they had to use their fingers to push them together too, but like the matching snow suits, it didn't interest them so much anymore.

Leslie loved cold weather. Winter was her favorite time of year. She didn't want to think of their favorite winter. But she did.

They had just moved into the new house. Winter was an inconvenient time to move but that's when her favorite house in New Paltz had unexpectedly gone up for sale. She had always wanted that house. It was old. Large enough. Red brick, white trim, black shutters. Snow covered the house. The inside was bright with reflected sunlight through the curtainless windows. Sounds were amplified and echoed off the bare wooden floors. Vivi and Vic ran around the house looking for all its secrets. And there were plenty. There were a couple of attics. Some old sealed boxes were left behind. They had to find where the doors were and had to access them through closets. A basement with an obsolete boiler was very scary. There were closets under stairwells, nooks and crannies. Little windows in strange places where there had been old renovations on top of old renovations. Even a dumbwaiter! There was an old servant's staircase, steep, dark and narrow. It was a magical place and they loved it. In the backyard there was a short hill. They found an old round aluminum toboggan, buried in the snow on its side so that just the edge was peeking through. The kids spent the rest of the winter climbing up and down that hill taking turns on the toboggan. She could watch them through the kitchen window when she was home. Chris and their nanny got to watch them the most. Chris could do quite a bit of work out of the house, when he wasn't traveling.

In any place where the winter is severe and long, there comes a day, a sunny day, when the snow starts to melt. It's not going to snow again. Things that have been stuck in the ice and snow can be gradually pried loose. Water drips from icicles on the roof and erodes little caves in the snow and ice on the ground under them. It was just such a day when Vivi saw a dot of bright color six inches down in one of those little water caves. She ran in to get a gardening shovel which Leslie found in a box in the garage. They went outside to dig up the crusted snow and ice. They found a marble. A single tiger eye marble. It was beautiful. Leslie had not seen marbles in years. Of course she hadn't been trying to see marbles but they simply didn't have the appeal now that they did when she was a kid. This was a find. The kids started digging up the ice under the dripping icicles trying to find more. They found a red marble and a clear one. Then a marble painted to look like the Earth. They found a large bubble gum sized multi-colored one. And then no more. The rest of the snow in the back yard was still way too deep to excavate. They had to wait. As the weeks went by the edges of the snow began to recede, and more little dots of color were exposed. Sometimes they could scout the bright ones through several inches of snow and they would dig them up. By the time the snow melted they had found close to one hundred marbles. There were some very old ones. Some newer ones. Some looked like they had been cracked by pouring boiling water on top of frozen marbles like she had done as a child to make jewelry. It was a treasure. The kids were mesmerized by them and the nature of their discovery.

The one tiger eye was the coveted prize and they decided to draw straws to see who picked first when they divided them up. Leslie provided each with one of her green felt draw string shoe bags. She took two toothpicks and broke one short. They picked, and Vivian picked the short one, instantly throwing herself backward on the bed in agony. She knew Vic would pick the tiger eye. But he didn't. He took the big multi-colored one, leaving the tiger eye for Vivian. Then they took turns picking marbles one after another and putting them in their bags. They lay in front of the fireplace all day looking at those marbles. Looking deep into their little internal structures.

"How do they make marbles, Mommy?" She didn't know the answer. She promised someday she would look it up.

The stranger question was how did they get there? The people who owned the house before did not have any young children. The marbles were spread throughout the yard, not in one place as if they had been accidentally dropped there. She could have found out the history of the marbles easily enough by calling the previous owner, but chose not to.

The magic surrounding them was a beautiful thing, not to be spoiled by reality.

After the accident she had an estate sale and then sold the house in late November. The family who bought the house wasn't moving in until after the first of the year. A cold front came through in mid-December. That night she gathered the two felt bags from under Vic and Vivi's beds. She stood on their back porch for the last time. The night sky was clear, sharply cold. The moon reflected off the gathering frontal clouds which would dump over a foot and a half of snow on upstate New York. Leslie untied the little knots and opened the bags. She searched for the tiger eye but couldn't find it. Then she flung the contents of the bags out over their yard.

The next morning the only thing that interrupted the blanket of white was the top edge of the toboggan leaning against the garage.

8

*A*lthough the West Texas front didn't bring snow, it brought plenty of cold. Cold she wasn't prepared for. Cold that blew right through her black wool coat and chilled her to the bone, whatever that meant. Her bones were probably 98.6 degrees warm, but she was freezing. The wind blew constantly. It made a humming noise wherever it met resistance. She had to lean into it in some places to keep from falling over. She couldn't recall ever being up against that kind of wind. The cold pressure against her face gave her a headache.

All hospitals now have automatic doors. Handicap accessibility. The problem with automatic doors is that they stay open a little longer than they would if a person opened them on their own. The benefit is that if you're using crutches or if you're weak because you've just had chemotherapy or a heart attack, there is no need to worry about opening doors.

Still, every time the automatic doors open, even the sequenced automatic doors, there is a tremendous blast of wind that keeps the lobby breezy and cold. Patients in the lobby waiting to see an emergency room physician look at the people coming in like they are barbarians. Once you're in, you become part of the civilized masses and then the next ones through the door...Visigoths. And so entered Leslie, leaning backward against the wind, hair and coat whipping around her. Patients and families gave her loathing looks until she joined them.

It was about six in the evening and she volunteered to come over and round on the only remaining patient in the hospital, Cal Wimberly. She felt as if he was her patient anyway, so there wasn't any point in having Doc go. Everyone else had been sent home or to a rehabilitation facility for more therapy. Barring any complications, Cal would probably be ready to go home tomorrow. After rounding, she had been invited to eat with Doc and Brenda, the last supper, before he had to start his bowel prep and wouldn't be fit to live with. Brenda was fixing Doc's favorite, King Ranch chicken.

Cal was afebrile, his hemoglobin and hematocrit acceptable. The therapist's notes said he was independent on the crutches, but couldn't do stairs yet. His wife was with him today. Leslie removed his bandages. His incisions looked good. She told him to call the office tomorrow and make an appointment next week to get the stitches out. She gave him the office phone number.

"So Doc, are you joining Doc Hawley or something?"

"No, I'm just taking over his practice for a few weeks while Doc is out."

"Like how long?"

"Probably a month."

"That's some vacation."

"Well, it's really not a vacation. Doc's taking off to have some medical care."

"Hm, sounds serious. Well, I hope everything goes all right."

Jenn asked if Leslie was going to stay the whole time.

"Yes, I'll be here until Doc is ready to start working full time and we're guessing it will be almost a month before he's fully recovered."

"So where are you from?" Jenn asked.

"That's a little hard to answer. I was in Louisiana before I came here."

"Is that where your family's from? I mean, how do you stay away for such a long time? Regan said you were married."

"Well, I guess, in a way, he's right. My husband passed away a while back. So I really don't..."

"Jenn." Cal interrupted her. "Sorry Doc. I mean, we had no idea. I'm sorry to hear that. I mean, we didn't mean to pry into your personal business and all." She saw Cal look at Jenn and roll his eyes, shook his head.

"Hey, don't worry about it. Really. Look, you're doing great. And if you stay without a fever and tomorrow you're able to conquer the stairs, you can go home."

Jenn asked, "What time do you think he can go?"

"I should be up here maybe around ten in the morning. That'll give you time to do your physical therapy. After that you can leave any time."

Jenn looked a little concerned and Cal told her not to worry. He could get someone to take him home. "Jenn's got some function to go to with the kids tomorrow."

"Well, there's no rule about checkout time. I mean, what are they going to do, arrest you for staying late? Jenn, are you going to be able to give Cal his blood thinner shots?"

Unless people were nurses or diabetics used to giving injections, most patients and family members were pretty squeamish about giving shots. Leslie asked Jenn to hang around today so the nurses could show her how to give the little shot under the skin on the tummy. She couldn't recall anyone who, once instructed, was still unwilling to do the dirty deed. She assumed that would be the case with Jenn.

"I'm going to write prescriptions for the blood thinner and his pain pills. That way you can go ahead and get them filled today so you'll have them when Cal gets home."

They talked a little longer about Cal's expected recovery schedule. Leslie told them goodnight.

She then drove over to Doc's place. She didn't know what King Ranch chicken was, but something smelled wonderful. Brenda had made her own salsa. They had frozen margaritas. Leslie had only one, reminding them that she was driving. They had some little tamale *hors d'oeuvres* and tortilla chips. Then the King Ranch chicken. That was some special stuff. Basically it was boiled chicken, cheddar cheese, jalapeños and tortillas all mixed together in a casserole. Totally scrumptious. For desert they were going to have Key lime pie.

"Leslie, I know this meal is sinful, but Hal ordered all his favorite things."

"Doc, you gotta look at it this way. This is the last stuff my ass is ever gonna see and so what am I gonna have here, salmon and steamed asparagus? Look, I should have been eating this kind of stuff all along. I don't think the baby spinach salads and Brussels sprouts did me a damn bit of good, do you?"

"I don't know Doc, but I don't have any complaints here."

"Brenda, pass the jalapeños, please."

"Oh, Hal..."

Leslie helped Brenda clean up. Brenda was quiet. Leslie guessed she was contemplating her husband's future, the unknowns of cancer. Leslie also guessed that Brenda was thinking about their connection. The difference between dead and facing death.

"Leslie," she said after a while, "there is life after death you know." Leslie looked up from the pan she was drying. "I don't necessarily mean in a religious sense, but you can take it however you want to. I mean for you, there is life. Your husband. I know he would have wanted that for you. You didn't have a chance to talk to him about it because he died unexpectedly...and young. Hal and I have had a chance to talk about it, and it's because you came here that we did. I can't imagine my life without Hal, and I can't imagine my life alone. Neither can he. Well, it's silly because I'm an old lady, but you're young. I know I can't put myself in your shoes really, but, I just wanted to tell you how I feel. And now I've probably said too much, but I've said it anyway. And I don't expect you to have anything to say about it either. And you can just tell me to mind my own business if you want."

Leslie didn't know what to say in response to Brenda's statement. She thought Brenda was right, but it wasn't that easy. She and Chris had in fact talked about it once before, in passing. She couldn't remember why. Maybe a patient died, or maybe it was after her dad died. In any case, they had talked, and they had given each other permission to find someone else if the other were to die. Of course she told him the new wife couldn't use her dining room table, silver or china, the antique mirror over the sinks, or her custom shoe cabinets. And he said fine, that her new husband couldn't have sex with her. That led to play fighting, tickling. They made love. Leslie was smiling, remembering that.

Brenda reached out and touched Leslie's hand. "Let's have dessert."

9

*L*eslie woke up early as usual. She didn't want to go up to the hospital until after the physical therapists had worked with Cal on the stairs. The hotel had a gym, so she walked on the treadmill and lifted some weights. Before going up to her room she had breakfast and coffee. On the way to the hospital she stopped at Wal-Mart to get some additional winter clothes.

As she was walking toward the hospital entrance, she heard someone yell, "Dr. Cohen, wait up!" She turned to see Regan Wakeman running toward her from the parking lot. His truck behind him was fixed like new.

"Hi Regan." She stopped and waited for him. It was freezing, and she fought the urge to rush inside where it would be warm. "Looks like you got your truck fixed. Everything okay?"

"Yeah, just fine. Really, just got the bumper and the tailgate. No big deal. Could've been worse."

"No kidding. Are you coming to see Cal?"

Regan nodded with a smile.

"I'm pretty sure he's going home today."

"That's what he said. Had to get cleared by the therapist first. I'm actually here to take him home if you let him go."

Regan had on his black cowboy hat. She had never really thought about it before, but cowboy hats were somewhat attractive. It looked pretty good on Regan anyway. He took it off when they got inside. He wore the same gold canvas jacket he had on the night they had the accident. Starched jeans and his boots.

"So tell me again, besides horseback riding, how do you know Cal?"

"He works for me. Project manager. Construction. Basically, he's my right hand man." They walked down one hall in silence. "I guess he's going to be okay, right. I mean able to get back to work and all."

"Sure. He'll need to rest for a while. He needs to focus on getting his leg back in shape. Does he do office work or is he out in the field?"

"Both, but I can keep him in the office for as long as he needs. He can even work from home if he needs to. Do the books and stuff."

"That'll be good. He ought to stay home for at least a week or two."

When they got to Cal's room, Regan went in while Leslie stayed out in the hall to look at his chart. She could hear him tell Cal that she was there. Then some silence. Were they whispering?

She knocked out of habit and consideration. They did look like the cats that ate the canary. They stopped talking instantly and looked at her. She got busy with doctoring, but felt silly. Trying to act professional and not get distracted by their antics was hard.

After going over his instructions again, she confirmed he had made a follow-up appointment, his wife had picked up his prescriptions, and someone could give him his shots.

"My wife's sister-in-law's a nurse and she's going to come over every day to give them to me."

He was ready to go, anxious to go. The nurses had all his paperwork done. They needed someone to transport him downstairs. Regan would go pull up the truck. Leslie told Cal she'd see him next week, said goodbye and walked out the door. She was writing a note when Regan came out. Her heart was beating a little fast and she felt a knot in her stomach. This was crazy.

"You going down, Doc?"

"Look, you can call me Leslie, okay."

He smiled, "You going down...Leslie?"

She nodded and they proceeded down the hall to the elevator. She pushed the first floor button.

She started to say something but she didn't really know what she was going to say, like, I'm not interested in starting up any relationships here, or something like that.

Regan didn't waste any time. "Thanks for taking care of Cal. Look, I don't know how they do things where you come from, but in

Abilene, if you operate on someone's buddy, then...you usually have to go to lunch with them. It's tradition." He took a step toward her. "Really."

"Really." She was not prepared for this tactic.

"Yeah, and we usually have lunch before the stitches come out."

"Really."

"Uh huh."

The elevator doors opened.

"How about Monday I come pick you up and take you to the best barbeque place in town. Just sandwiches, no big deal."

"Well, I'm not sure about my schedule on Monday."

"I figure you've got to eat. Why don't I call you sometime in the morning when you'll have a better idea about your schedule? Is that fair?"

"Sure." She gave in.

He put on his hat once they stepped outside and stuffed his hands into his pockets. The wind swirled around them as the automatic doors kept opening and closing, the motion detector catching them as they stood there. People glared at them from the lobby. He took her gently by the elbow, pulling her away from the motion detector so the doors would close. He grabbed his hat and pressed it down further on his head. Her curls danced around her head in the wind. She reached up to push her hair back from her face. It was only seconds but she realized he still held on to her elbow.

"I'll see you Monday," he said.

10

*L*eslie was the "on call" orthopedic surgeon for the emergency room on Friday night. Things were busy and she had to go into the hospital three times during the night. She set a wrist fracture in the emergency room. She admitted an elderly gentleman with a hip fracture, putting him on the schedule for surgery the next morning. He would be evaluated by the internists so she could be sure he was stable enough to get through the operation. And at about two in the morning a couple of drunken teenagers came in by EMS with multiple injuries from a head-on collision. The main problems involved their bellies so the general surgeons went to work on them. She would have to fix a femur and an ankle fracture on one of the kids. The other had both bones of the forearm broken. She would fix that in the morning after she worked on the broken hip.

The patient with the femur fracture had to go to the operating room that night so the surgeons could find the source of blood in his abdomen. She went ahead and fixed his femur at the same time. The ankle fracture could be fixed at a later date. It would require some plates and screws and the trauma surgeons didn't want to keep him in the OR any longer than was necessary.

His femur was broken about six inches above the knee, so she fixed it with a nail that went in through the knee joint instead of up by the hip, like Cal's. It was a much easier approach and she didn't need to put the patient in traction, which also worked very well for the general surgeons. Once again the floppy, bent thigh went to firm and straight in about forty-five minutes. After applying dressings to his knee, Leslie put a new splint on the ankle.

Rumor around the operating room was that the people in the other car, the ones who weren't drunk, didn't make it. It happened all too often with victims of drunk drivers. She was amazed at how many drunks were out on the roads late at night, making driving a hazard. A common notion among orthopedists and general surgeons taking care of trauma patients was that the only people out driving after two AM were the drunks and the doctors coming in to take care of them.

She got everyone settled in for the night, then made plans with the operating room charge nurse to start her cases at nine in the morning. At the hotel she chatted briefly with Raghu, then went to bed. There had been no time to think about her encounter with Regan and his invite for Monday lunch. Would she make her excuses or take him up on the best barbeque sandwich in Abilene? She would worry about that on Monday.

She operated on Raul Escobedo's hip the next morning, followed by the now sober Jamie Edward's forearm. She noted to herself that she couldn't remember a time in her career when a drunken patient had inquired about the status of the ones he or she had injured. To the contrary, they were usually demanding, self-centered, whining about their pain. When she was on call, she would frequently end up taking care of both the perpetrators and the victims. Ethically she had to maintain impartiality with regard to care of the patients. Certainly can't take sides, or drunks who caused injury to others would never get fixed. There is no room for being judgmental. But deep down she couldn't help but wonder about the lack of remorse.

This day was no different. Jamie and his parents complained bitterly about everything. The hospital, the nurses, his pain, whatever. No one ever asked about the two dead people. Soon there might be two homemade crosses going up on the side of the highway where the victims had met their premature end. Who were they? Did Jamie wonder? Did his family wonder what they had been doing? Were they husband and wife, lovers, someone's children?

Three crosses had gone up on the side of the highway beside the place where her husband's car had come to rest. She didn't know who put them there. Some locals or maybe Lynn and Casey. There were blue plastic flowers on two of them and pink ones on the other. She felt compelled to drive by the site one last time before leaving New York and it was then that she saw the little crosses. Highway 299, on the way to Mohonk Mountain House. She pulled over to the side of the road and walked back to stand in front of them. She tried to feel something.

Surely that site would surrender some connection to her most precious possessions. Surely if Chris, Vivian and Victor were spirits somewhere out there they would have come to this site and combined their powers to give her a sign. There would be a breeze, or a bird. A leaf would fall. But there was nothing, not a single whisper other than her most earthly feeling of despair. People slowed to stare at her as they drove by.

11

*A*fter fixing the hip and the forearm, she scheduled the ankle tentatively for Monday. Once her patient was stable she could bring him back to the OR and fix it. No rush for now. She was grateful to be busy. No sooner had she discharged Cal, then she had three patients in the hospital and plenty to do. The guys from the other group in town were on call today and Sunday. The only calls she would get from that point on would be patients requesting Doc Hawley.

On Sunday she rose at the usual time and got ready to go to work. She rounded on everyone. Her patients were doing well. She called Doc and Brenda to see how the bowel prep was going and to thank them again for dinner. Doc told her everything was coming out fine. She told him about her evening, the cases. They planned to call her Sunday night after they got to Lubbock. They gave her the medical center and Brenda's cell phone numbers.

Leslie proceeded with what would become a routine on weekend mornings when she didn't have cases scheduled. She worked out again in the hotel gym. If the weather was nice she would try to find a place to jog, but otherwise walking on the treadmill would do. Up until this point she had been fairly busy and there wasn't a lot of idle time. Today would be different. She would have to make busy work for herself. There would be time to get on the internet. She could do some continuing medical education stuff. Sometimes she would return to the hospital for a second visit to the patients. Anything to keep busy. Anything to keep her from dwelling on the past, and now from dwelling on the future and her lunch arrangement with Regan. She still couldn't decide whether or not to make an excuse. Doctors can always plead emergencies. It's a fringe benefit.

She thought about Doc at midnight on Sunday. He could have no food beyond that time and there would be a sign on his door reminding the nurses not to give him anything to eat or drink. She had spoken with them earlier and the trip to Lubbock was uneventful. Doc was ready. He sounded positive. She wished him good luck. It's a natural expression for people to say when someone is having surgery, but in reality she didn't like to think that any of it was luck at all. Hopefully, it's all skill and planning, no luck. No coin flipping. No finger crossing. She wished it for him anyway.

Monday morning the consideration of whether or not she looked okay skated across her mind so quickly that she almost didn't recognize it. And she preferred not to. She left the hotel after coffee and some cantaloupe. Kala was there with one of her children, not school aged yet. Leslie went to the hospital to round.

Her patients were doing as well as could be expected under the circumstances. The two MVA patients were complaining of a lot of pain and their families were wandering around the nurse's station demanding that something be done for them. Everything that could be done was being done. There were no problems, just human beings wanting sympathy...and pain relief. There was pain relief, but no sympathy for drunk drivers. Nurses and doctors all felt the same about that issue. It was never spoken, but always felt.

The ankle surgery was rescheduled for Wednesday. There was still a lot of swelling and Leslie wanted to give it more time to go down. The patient had an elevated temperature as well. She would rather wait for that to resolve before putting him under anesthesia again.

Raul Escobedo was still out of it. He had a big family. They were all there to take care of him, and to hang out with each other. He just lay there, dosing, sleeping. When the nurses asked if he had pain, someone had to shake his shoulder, at which time he would wake up and moan, "*Si.*" Then, he would go back to sleep.

"Doctor Cohen," she heard someone calling from down the hall. It was Mary Ellen and she was carrying a cup of coffee. "Sorry I've missed you this past weekend. I had some time off. Someone's been busy! How'd everything go?"

"Just great. No problems at all."

"How 'bout a cup of coffee. Got it fixed just how you like it...

just a little coffee and a lot of fixin's!" Even though she had already had plenty this morning, once again she couldn't refuse this totally unexpected offer. "Surprised? You know we don't do this for everyone. Just Doc...and you if you want."

"Remind me to tell you a story sometime, Mary Ellen. Thanks for the coffee." She took a sip. "It's perfect. I'm just finishing up with rounds and I've got to get over to the office." She held up her cup in a toast to Mary Ellen.

"Your folks all look pretty good. General surgery will probably sign off on the two MVA's tomorrow, provided they're doing okay. Your little guy in four twenty would be just fine if his extended family would give him a chance to rest."

"No kidding."

"Listen, I don't want you to think you've got to do things like Doc around here. I don't know what you're used to, so I'll take my cues from you. If you want me to round with you in the mornings, I would be happy to do so. Some of the docs want to be left alone, others not. Now Doc, he's just spoiled. Spolt, as we say in this part of the country."

"I'm beginning to see that. I'll tell you what. Let's play it by ear. If I get busy and it gets hard to keep track of everybody, I'll call on you. But if it's light, like today, I'll just go around on my own. I appreciate your offer, but I know how busy you are. Now, I'll probably take you up on the coffee part. This is perfect. I think you must have put in a little something extra, some of those little round hazelnut creamers maybe?"

"It's a secret. Thanks. You let me know when you need help."

Leslie gave her thumbs up and started down the hall. The rounds and chat with Mary Ellen had distracted her from what just now popped into her mind. Her lunch appointment with Regan. Her heart skipped a beat and she got a flood of sensation in her stomach, like just before a speech or a competition. She felt apprehension and excitement. She was looking forward to it even though it didn't feel right. It was just lunch for crying out loud.

In the next instant she was looking forward to clinic, to see how things were going to go now that she was on her own. She needed the distraction.

The office staff was ready for her and eager to please. Things went smoothly. She saw mostly patients she didn't know, but there were a few from last week. All the patients wanted to talk about Doc. Fortunately the schedule was light. They had done this intentionally so she could get acclimated. Brenda knew the patients would want to chat about Doc. It was natural.

Notes were dictated after each patient was seen. She went ahead and filled out a lot of her own codes, but was reminded by the people in billing that they could do it for her. All the paperwork was signed when she had breaks in between patients. At around eleven o'clock one of the secretaries came in and told her that she had a phone call. "Regan Wakeman. Do you want me to take a message?"

"No, that's okay, I'll get it." Was she paranoid or did the secretary look at her curiously. She decided she was paranoid and admitted to herself that she felt a little guilty. Here she had only been in Abilene a week and was going on a lunch date. Even if she had been looking for dates, that would have been a jump start.

"Hello."

"Hey..." and she detected a slight hesitation before "Leslie." People have a hard time referring to someone in the familiar name when they have already called them "doctor." "It's Regan. How're you doing?"

"Fine. How are you?"

"I'm doing fine. What's your schedule like today? You going to be able to take a lunch break?"

"Yeah, I think so. I should be finishing up in the next twenty to thirty minutes."

"What time do you need to be back?"

She called out to Casey at the front desk to ask what time her patients were scheduled in the afternoon, and was told one-thirty.

"One-thirty."

"That's great. The line at JJ's is sometimes pretty long. How 'bout I pick you up a little after noon?"

"Sounds good. Do you know where the office is?"

"Yes, I do. Doc's taken care of me before."

"Really."

"No big deal. Football, horseback riding stuff."

"Sure I don't need to check you out, take an X-ray or something?"

"Pretty sure."

"All right. Well, I'll see you in a little bit"

They said goodbye and she hung up the phone. Her heart was beating away. This was a bad sign. Or was it a good sign? She wasn't going to judge it right now. He might have terrible table manners and talk with his mouth full. Barbeque...damn.

Casey came in and asked if she was going to want lunch. They were going out to get something and could bring some back for her. Leslie told her she had plans for lunch.

"Are you going to lunch with Regan?"

"Yes, I am. Why do you ask?"

"Oh, nothing." Leslie could tell there was something.

"What?" She probed.

"Well, it's just that...well, he just doesn't date all that much. My older sister went out with him for a while. She thinks he's still hung up on his ex."

"His ex?" She pretended not to know. Now she felt like a common gossip. Oh well. A girl's got to be in the know.

"Oh yeah. He got divorced about ten years ago or something. His wife was really pretty. They knew each other since they were kids. Anyway, my sister really liked him, but it just didn't work out. How do you know 'im?"

"Well, Casey, he's the gentleman I had the accident with when I was driving to Abilene."

"Wow, you're kidding. That's pretty interesting."

"I guess you could say that."

"Well, I hope y'all have a good time." Time said with a little catty musical inflection in Casey's very southern accent.

"Thanks. Can you let me know when he gets here?"

She finished seeing patients. From the lobby she heard Casey say, "Hi, Regan. I'll go let Doctor Cohen know you're here." She heard Casey coming down the hall and tried to act occupied, opening a journal. That was really juvenile. But what was she going to do, bounce around off the walls and fan herself. She felt like doing just that. She hadn't had this feeling since she met Chris, but it was different because she also felt guilt, where there had been no guilt with Chris.

"Tell him I'll be right out." This had to be really strange for the staff. They have a lady doctor for the first time in this office, a single lady doctor. And she is receiving gentlemen. She figured this kind of stuff didn't happen too often when ol' Doc Hawley was around.

She checked her hair. Don't fix it up. Just make sure there's nothing goofy going on. With curly hair there's always a potential for something goofy. She walked out to the lobby. Regan was sitting on a chair and he stood as soon as she came out. This had to be one of the more uncomfortable moments she could recall, in her social life anyway. Casey and Delia were standing behind the counter just looking at them. They weren't trying at all to be discreet.

She greeted Regan with a handshake. Introducing Regan to Casey and Delia was somewhat awkward because they all knew each other. Still the girls giggled and acted dumb, accepting the introduction as if they didn't know him. Regan said flatly, "Yeah, Doc, I know these gals. I'll have her back by one-thirty."

Regan was wearing what seemed to be the standard garb for people running construction crews. Beige shirt, blue jeans and boots. It was cold out so he had on a jacket. In the north the boots are usually a plain lace up or slip-on steel toed boot. The shirt is usually a pocketed button-down traditional style shirt. In the south, the boots are of the cowboy variety and the shirt has a western style about it. It's strange, that this outfit is so universal and yet she was certain they didn't get together on the phone to plan it. *Hey, what're you wearing today? Oh, my beige shirt and blue jeans. The taupe cowboy boots, since I'm in Houston. How about you?*

Well, I'm wearing the same but I've got on my Red Wings since I'm up here in Minnesota.

It was similar in orthopedic surgery. At meetings sometimes it seemed like she was sitting in a sea of navy blue blazers and khaki pants. She even wore that type of outfit when the more masculine traditional clothes were in style for women back in the eighties. She had a navy blazer, light blue button down shirt, and a khaki skirt. She loved that look while it was popular. Made her feel like one of "the boys."

Regan got the door for her. He helped her up into the seat of his truck. Been here before. Being here a second time would have been the furthest thing from her mind. He went around the front and got in.

"Well, does this seem familiar? It's really strange being in here with you again. What a small world."

"I was just thinking the same thing."

"You hungry?"

"Sure."

"Well, let me tell you about this place. First of all, don't be put off by the outward appearance. It's in a pretty beat up part of town. A lot of these buildings are abandoned because Abilene's growth has taken business out of the old downtown area. This restaurant is owned by these two old black guys. I don't know how they started or anything, but my dad used to take me to this place when I was a kid. The menu's pretty simple. You can order a sliced beef sandwich or a chopped beef sandwich. Most everyone orders chopped beef. I don't know why, other than to see these two fellas chop it up."

She laughed. "So that's it? The difference between sliced beef and chopped is just the chopping?"

"Sounds pretty obvious, but you're right. There's no special sauce or anything. So just order chopped, because you've gotta see these guys chop the beef. It's worth the trip just to see that."

They turned onto a seemingly deserted street in an old downtown area just as Regan had described. Everything was either empty or seedy. X-Rated movie rentals, check cashing places, pawn shops and cheap furniture stores. And there, in about half a store front area was the very busy JJ's. There was a line of customers extending halfway down the block and it was bitterly cold outside. The bridge of her nose began to ache as she took her place in line. Along with construction workers and bankers there was now a contractor and an orthopedic surgeon. They moved up quickly.

Once getting inside she could smell the barbeque. It smelled wonderful, but barbeque always does. Old marbled green Naugahyde booths with speckled Formica tables were on the left side of the shop. Waist-high yellowed Formica wainscoting covered the perimeter of the entire shop. Above the booth and wainscoting there was a long mirror, hung by little plastic florets with brass screws in their centers. Years of grime and Windex darkened the spaces between their petals. The line of people waited right along side of the booths so there was absolutely no privacy. If anyone sneezed it would be noticed. Conversations were to be ignored.

The line kept moving. Regan and Leslie leaned up against the wall. The mirror made her self-conscious, but it was compelling and in a little while she looked up at it. She looked at Regan in the mirror and he was looking at her. He smiled at her reflection in the mirror, she back at him. She quickly looked down and turned toward the front of the line, very much aware of him behind her.

Now she started to pay attention to the system, because there was definitely a system. Those who were familiar with the system got served systematically. Those who didn't, in other words, those who asked a lot of questions or requested something not sliced or chopped might detect some aggravation or catch a rolled eye. Nothing hostile, just not systematic. Clearly recognized as a novice. Leslie hated to be perceived as a novice.

She began committing the system to memory. When one got to the front there was an old wrinkled white lady who, without altering the position of her lowered head, looked up at the customers over reading glasses. She said nothing, but this was the customer's cue to say, "chopped or sliced, Coke, Sprite or Tea, and what kind of chips: potato, Fritos or Doritos, or none." She then repeated the order to the two very old black men fixing the food. It was simple. "Chopped, Coke, potato," or, "sliced, tea, Fritos." That was the cue for those two guys wearing old folded paper army-like caps to go to work on the order. One of them proceeded to make the sandwiches while the other got the sodas and chips and then bagged everything along with a paper towel. They talked in a familiar way with customers they knew. Every once in a while he told someone that the fixings were on the table in the front. This was not random and she figured it was likely that these old geezers recognized the newcomers regardless of their knowledge of the system. She would test her hypothesis on the limited study of her and Regan.

Leslie, being the consummate student, began to get concerned that she would screw up, get the rolled eyes or something like that, and then be embarrassed in front of Regan. She came through in flying colors with a "chopped, tea, no chips." This was repeated, setting in motion the assembly of her lunch. One of the Js pulled out a bun, sliced off several pieces of beef from a brisket and chopped it up in about ten seconds, his hands moving rapidly in four directions, holding the cleaver with both. Magically, in a blink of the eye, the slices of beef became a little mound of chopped beef. His wooden chopping block was about three by three by two feet square and had deep stained grooves in all four corners where sliced beef had met its ignominious end for decades. The currently used area was not as deep as the others and she wondered what would happen when this area deepened to the point where the cleaver no longer had its advantage. Would they close down or buy a new block?

When the sandwich was assembled it was wrapped in butcher paper and a toothpick shoved through it. The sandwich was handed to the second J who placed it gently in a paper bag. He handed it to her.

"Fixin's are up front."

Just about this time Regan's order came down the line, "chopped, Coke, potato," setting the entire process in motion again. She noted that the first J had already started chopping, even before the order was called and there was no reminder of the location of the condiments. Case proven.

Regan recommended the barbecue sauce. They fixed their sandwiches. There were no available tables. She wondered if he would suggest his truck or that they return to the office. She didn't have to concern herself with this because in a few moments a group of men got up from one of the booths. Regan snatched it. They sat down and spread out the paper around their sandwiches. Now how was she going to handle this sandwich? It would just have to get messy. She dug in. It was delicious and there was just something about its preparation combined with the atmosphere of the diner that added to its flavor.

"You were right, this sandwich is great."

"I told you. Best barbecue in Abilene. The shame is that it doesn't look like anyone is learning to take over the business. Everyone comes in here. Over at that table are a couple of guys from the mayor's office. Behind us is the minister of the Methodist church and his son."

Regan looked up at two men coming through the door and nodded his head in recognition.

"Regan."

"Jimmy. Carl. What're y'all up to?"

"Getting barbecue. You?" The older one of the two came over to the table and Regan introduced him to Leslie.

"Jimmy heads up our electrical contractors on the project."

"Pleasure to meet you ma'am. Regan, I'll see you back out at the site. We've got to get some of these legal issues cleared up before we can continue to dig."

He got back in line and started talking to the other guy, who looked over at Leslie and nodded his head in greeting.

"So exactly what is it you do?"

"I'm a general contractor. It's my business actually, Wakeman Industries. How's that for originality?"

"I like the name."

"Anyway, we do industrial buildings. Started out small buildings, but now it's pretty much large scale projects. We've been on this one for almost two years and it looks like it'll probably take another four months to finish."

"What are you working on?"

"We're building a new football stadium for the school district. It's a big project. The stadium is huge, state of the art, you know, Jumbotron screen in the end zone, newest generation of artificial turf, top-of-the-line field house facilities for the teams, the works. It's really pretty amazing to see something like this go up in Abilene. But this kind of facility is becoming standard for five-A football in this state."

"For high school? That is amazing. So what is your part in all of this?"

"Well, as the general contractor, I hire all the sub-contractors to do the work. Like electricians, plumbers, bricklayers, cement, just about anything you can imagine. So basically I put the whole thing together. Sometimes I make sure the porta-pots get emptied."

Leslie laughed. Taking care of business. A stadium or a hospital. Sometimes it all comes down to the privy.

"It's starting to take shape now. You can tell it's going to be a football stadium. You ought to come out and see it sometime. We can trade. I'll come watch you do an operation."

"I don't know about the surgery, but I'd like to see the stadium. In my next life I think I'd like to be an architect. Buildings fascinate me."

She had finished her sandwich and Regan was eating the last of his chips. It was after one o'clock and people were still waiting for seats.

"You ready to go? We probably need to get you back. What did they say, patients at one-thirty?"

"Yeah, I guess there's no time to go see the stadium now."

"Well, I wouldn't really want to take you there right now anyway. It's fairly busy. A lot of heavy equipment moving around. A little dangerous. Why don't you meet me over there after work? Things start to slow down around three-thirty or four. When are you done?"

They left the diner and walked toward his truck. "I don't know what time I'm done. I'll have to see. I don't know if..."

He interrupted her. "I know. Look, if you want to come out, I'd love to show you around and I think it will appeal to the side of you that wanted to be an architect. If you can't make it, you can't. You can have a rain check. It'll be there."

Regan was frank and confident. It was making her nervous. She wanted to go to the stadium, but she had a hard time making a commitment to meet him, knowing it would lead to some other invite. As they walked toward the truck, the wind was blowing through the streets and alleys, striking them with a blast of cold air each time they crossed an open space.

"Do you ever get tired of the wind out here?"

"Not really. I guess if you're from here, you just get used to it. It keeps drifters away, some Yankees," he nudged her with his elbow, "and folks who don't really want to be here. People who stay in Abilene or any place in West Texas for that matter, just want to be here." They stopped beside his truck. "You get used to it. When the wind stops, you worry about tornados. Look, here's my card. When you're done, give me a call if you want to come out. That way I can let the gate know you're coming."

She thanked him for lunch and took his card.

Regan got her back to the office at 1:20. Casey and Delia looked at her expectantly, wanting to know the details about lunch but she didn't say anything. It was really none of their business. The information would be worked and worked into idle gossip. She saw patients. All of them were Doc's. She thought about her own follow-ups and when she was expecting them in the office. The kid with the wrist in a few days. Cal in about a week. In her previous *locum* obligations she rarely stayed long enough to see one of her own surgeries back. This was getting interesting.

During a break between patients she took Regan's card out of her pocket. Appealing red and black logo, "WI" with Wakeman Industries printed below. His name, address and various contact numbers off to the side. She hadn't made up her mind about calling him after clinic. If she didn't call, it would be done. She was certain of that. She tucked the card into the right pocket of her lab coat and went to see the next patient, quickly forgetting about the potential plans.

Things started to wind down around 3:30. There was one more patient scheduled at 4:15 and at about 4:00 someone showed up claiming they had an appointment but was not on the schedule. Delia came in to tell her about it and seemed uneasy about burdening her with this oversight, a walk-in patient. Leslie told her not to worry. Unless there was some emergency requiring her to leave the office immediately, she would always be happy to see walk-ins. From Leslie's standpoint, she was here to work and not turn away Doc's patients. He would probably lose a few anyway, just because he was not here. She certainly didn't want to be the cause of any additional attrition. Delia smiled and was relieved at not having to turn a patient away.

Leslie saw Gordon Maler at 4:00. He brought an MRI scan of his knee with him, showing a torn cartilage. Before she was done for the day, she had scheduled the grateful patient for a knee arthroscopy. He admitted that he didn't have an appointment and had just come by on the chance that Doc would see him. He was in a lot of pain.

She felt good at the end of her clinic. Sitting at Doc's desk, she made two phone calls. The first was to Brenda. Doc's surgery had gone fine. He was in his room and in only a moderate amount of pain. They had to do the colostomy, as expected. The surgeon felt sure he had gotten everything. Brenda sounded relieved.

Leslie gave a brief report of the day's clinic. Brenda had already heard from the girls. They told her everything was fine and also mentioned that Leslie was out for lunch. No gossip, but Leslie wasn't there when she called so...

"Call him Leslie. Oh, listen to me getting into your personal business. It's just that..."

"I know what you're trying to say. Well, listen, tell Doc I send my best. Y'all," which she said very deliberately, "take care of yourselves, you hear."

She made the second call.

12

*L*eslie followed the brief directions Regan had given her. Once she got out of town on 83, he said she couldn't miss it. She didn't doubt him because it's hard to miss anything in this part of the world. The land is flat, hardly any trees. There was an overpass about a half mile ahead. Over the top she saw some kind of a metal lattice work. It looked at first like some old billboard without the signage, just an iron skeleton on the side of the highway. As she came over the bridge, she realized it was the stadium but it was still a couple of miles away. The sun was coming down on the horizon and the grounds surrounding the construction site were dusty and orange.

Work was still in progress. Maintainers and bulldozers were moving earth, and rising above the dust was a structure that looked more like an Aztec temple than a place where high school boys would one day play football. The billboard iron was actually a huge, three-story press box. It was suspended out over a four-story concrete edifice which would seat the spectators for the home team. The concrete was orange red with reflected sunset light. It looked like a giant cement stairway, intersected in four places by the transverse stairwells for people to go up to second level seating.

On the future visitor's side there was standard metal seating supported by huge concrete pylons. There were upscale snack bars and a tremendous flagstone building which would eventually include the athletic training facilities and field house.

The entire complex reminded her of a trip to Teotihuacán when she was in high school. That all modern stadiums are somehow reminiscent of those Central American pyramids seemed so apparent to her now. She remembered the stair-stepped pyramids of the Sun and Moon, rising up out of the plains south of Mexico City. She felt silly comparing a football stadium to those amazing ancient feats of architecture, but this structure was incredible. Incredible in its scale, incredible in its dominance of the local landscape and incredible as a symbol of Texas high school football. She was impressed.

There was a large billboard-like sign at the entrance. Project of the Taylor County Independent School District, Future Site of the Anson Jones Sports Complex. And below it: Wakeman Industries General Contractor, Regan Wakeman. She thought of how good it felt to finish a difficult case and have it turn out just right. She wondered how it must feel to drive up to this amazing structure every day, if you were Regan Wakeman.

She never really considered the effect of any particular building on a landscape. Buildings were buildings, to be appreciated in and of themselves. But this one completely transformed the area. It could be seen for miles. It could be seen from the windows of hundreds of homes and offices. Imagine it from the air. There were probably a lot of people who wouldn't want to be able to see this from their homes. But its stark immensity was striking. What would it be like to live behind Teotihuacán?

The guardhouse was empty so she pulled in and drove to the area where other cars and trucks were parked. She got out and walked toward the stadium and some portable offices. Regan's logo was on one of them. In a moment the door opened and he came out wearing a hard hat. She smiled, remembering one of her favorite chick flicks of all time, *Flashdance*, where the romantic interest took Jennifer Beal up to some building at a construction site to put the move on her. They wore hard hats. No sex under the bleachers here, that's for sure. If he asks her to put on a hard hat, she'd have to give him a karate chop.

"Hey, have any trouble finding the place?"

"Right. So hard to see it. This is amazing, Regan!"

The heavy maintainers were moving around them, so he had to yell. "I've got something I need to check on. Then I can show you around." He paused. "Why don't you come with me? Let me grab you a hard hat." He chuckled when she rolled her eyes. "That way we'll both have hat hair when we're done."

He returned with a yellow hard hat and handed it to her. "I'm glad you have on practical shoes out here." He said it as if she might have had on a pair of Manolo Blahniks at the office, but took them off for the construction site tour in favor of the Josef Seibels. She smiled. She wondered if you could even get Manolo Blahniks in Abilene. He waved for her to follow him and they headed off toward the bleachers.

By the entry to the bleachers there was a bulldozer-like piece of machinery. Attached to its front end was a giant drill. The bit was about three feet or more in diameter. Basically it was a giant post hole digger. They were digging holes for the huge pylons that would be used to support the stadium light posts. Some of the pylons were already made, the rebar skeletons of others lined up for later use, and the huge galvanized steel posts were stacked on the ground.

"We hit a water main with this drill today. Had to turn off all the water to the site. Pretty much shut things down, until we got it fixed." They looked down into one of the dry holes. It was huge. The next one was eroded and looked as if a tremendous amount of water had spewed out from the large drill hole, but the dry earth had happily sucked up every bit of it. The ground surrounding the area was only damp. Regan talked with a man who was checking out the situation.

Regan took Leslie's arm as they left the area. "You need to watch your step around here. There's a lot of loose gravel and debris." He signaled her to follow him. "Come on over here. I want you to see something." Walking toward the home team side, Leslie could visualize future little Abilene Dust Devils or whatever they were, helmet to helmet, fans screaming, lights blazing out into the Abilene horizon. They walked into the lower part of the stadium, went up some inner stairs until they were out on the first level landing of the temple. She followed him almost to the middle of the stadium and then up one of the transverse staircases leading to the upper level stadium bleachers. They ascended until they reached the unfinished press boxes.

At this point she turned to survey the site. Simply incredible. She was out of breath and the pause helped her catch it. As he beckoned she could see he was going to take her up to the press box area which was open to the atmosphere. The floor and stairwells were finished and there were retaining structures all around the sides so it appeared to be safe. The wind was blowing strong and consistently. Regan suggested that they remove their hard hats to keep them from blowing off.

"Don't worry, it's safe, even though you probably feel a little exposed." Regan read her mind but exposed was an understatement.

They went all the way to the top. The wind was blowing hard. It was cold and loud. It was stunning. The austerity of the landscape was imposing. For as far as the eye could see, it was flat, brown, backed by the golden western sunset and sweeping nimbus cloud formations.

She was out of breath and trying to imagine coaches, athletic directors, and superintendents climbing these stairs. There would be elevators. She was quietly trying to catch her breath and hoped he would not ask any questions that required more than a "uh-huh" or an "uh-uh" for an answer or she would be found out. Regan did not appear to be laboring to catch his breath.

"Have you ever seen anything like this?"

In fact she had. The view of the Shawangunk Mountains from the tower at the Mohonk Mountain House, outside of New Paltz. Despite the absence of trees and mountains, this scene in its magnitude reminded her of it.

But she said, "Uh-uh."

"This is the biggest and definitely tallest project I have ever done and every time I come up here, I am inspired or something. I don't know what."

They stood in silence, looking out over Abilene. In a little while a jet plane took off from the Abilene Regional Airport. The sound was delayed for a few seconds as the jet rose noiselessly. At first it flew straight, but a few seconds after takeoff it began to bank to the left and soon was headed toward the stadium, accompanied by its roar. They were so close she thought she could see the lights in the windows. Could the passengers see them? Tiny lights were sparkling all around the city.

At that moment, someone appeared on the first landing of the stadium.

"Regan, I'm cutting out. You got the generator?"

"I'll get it. See you tomorrow!"

Eventually the lone vehicle cruised out of the parking lot and onto the road, a thick trail of dust blowing off behind it. Regan turned and looked at Leslie. She looked at him, but nervously turned away, afraid of what was coming next.

"Now that I've got your undivided attention..."

"Yes," she said, "you do." She looked down at the stadium below.

"I want to see you again. Not that we've really been out or anything, but that's what I mean."

"You know about..."

"I know about your husband, Mrs. Cohen. I don't want to do anything you're not ready to do, but I think this is okay." He reached over and looped a strand of her hair around his finger. Pulled it back so he could see her face. She looked at him. "I don't want you to feel guilty, or to forget, but I don't think we'd be here if it wasn't okay."

"It's okay." They stood quiet again. The wind wouldn't let up. Nothing to stand in its way. She wondered about spirits, spirituality. What was it? Were the spirits of her family here in any way? Could a molecule of carbon, hydrogen or oxygen from them be here? She would have to think about that one. She blinked a couple of times and felt the tiniest sting in her nose. Then her pager went off.

"Saved by the bell," he said. She patted her coat pockets and realized she had left her cell phone in the car. He handed her his phone. She answered the call. It was a patient requesting medications. She called in the prescription. From up here the reception was clear as a bell.

Now it was dark. Hard to see. The iron was black against the sky.

"I think we better get going before it gets too dark. I could get in trouble. Get fired."

"Somehow, I doubt that."

When they arrived at the top level of the stadium, she was again reminded of the great Aztec civilization. They used to sacrifice live victims, people they had conquered, at the top of the pyramids by cutting out their hearts. According to the few historical records, there were times when the blood ran in rivers down the stairs of the pyramids and into the streets. What would people say about these pyramids a thousand years from now?

Regan walked her to her car and asked if she would go to dinner with him Friday night. She would. Before he turned to go back to the trailer, he said, "By the way, next time you come out here maybe there'll be an elevator to the top." He winked.

From her rear view mirror she could see him walk back to the office. In a few moments every single light in the construction site went out. It was pitch black. She could barely see the silhouette of the stadium against the sky. The headlights on Regan's truck came on and she saw them turn in the opposite direction.

13

*T*he rest of the week would be a good representation of what she could expect out of this assignment. There was elective surgery scheduled on Tuesday and Thursday afternoons and Friday morning. Wednesday and Thursday morning were spent in the office. Friday afternoon Doc usually took off early, depending on how busy he was. Right now the clinics were light, but people were calling in regularly and scheduling appointments regardless of the fact that Doc was out. One patient had actually requested the new "lady doctor." Her surgery schedule was light. This week, the only elective case she had on the books was the knee arthroscopy she had scheduled on Monday. The ankle surgery was on the schedule book too. She would adjust things as she got busier, eventually settling into a pace as she had done in New Paltz.

During the week a couple of emergency cases came in, one while she was on emergency room call and the other a specific request for Dr. Hawley. By the end of the week, only Raul Escobedo was left in the hospital. He was not progressing well in physical therapy. The family was having a hard time deciding who would take Raul home with them. He would require full time care, so they had to figure out who could be with him on a rotating schedule. He needed a hospital bed, a walker, an elevated toilet seat and some other pieces of equipment. These arrangements were not made by Friday, so he would have to stay in the hospital over the weekend.

Leslie continued to work out every day at the hotel. She also found a local park for walking or jogging when the weather was good. Wind, not temperature, was often the limiting factor.

Cal Wimberly came in for his post-op appointment on Thursday. Since his incision was healed, one of the assistants in the office removed the staples. His X-rays looked good. They were taken to make sure everything was still aligned. It would be too early to see healing. Cal had driven himself to the office, and she quizzed him about it. He assured her he was no longer taking pain pills, which was pretty good for a femur fracture. Just one of those patients with a high tolerance for pain. This difference between one patient and another with regard to narcotic use was hard to understand. Some people could take a dozen pain pills in one day, while others needed none for the same injury or operation.

Cal was doing fine. They went over some exercises he could do on his own. To Leslie's surprise, he had already tried to go back to work a little and she cautioned him about doing too much too early. He could expect more swelling and soreness if he was up walking a lot. She doubted he would stay off of it.

She looked for signs of mutual knowledge from Cal. Did he know she and his boss were going on a date Friday night? She felt silly. The details of her private life were something she really didn't like sharing with her patients. It didn't seem right. However, living in a smaller town makes it hard to keep intimate information secret. It's just part of it. Part of being a country doctor. Cal didn't say anything. Didn't give her a knowing look. She had him make another appointment in a month.

Regan called her Thursday night at the hotel.

"Hey, how're you doing?"

"Okay. Heard you saw my boy today."

"He's doing really well. Good patient. I think holding him back is going to be the main problem."

"You'd tell me if he shouldn't be at work, wouldn't you?"

"Sure. But honestly, I'm okay with it unless he starts to have a lot of swelling."

"Good. So, we still on for tomorrow night?"

"Of course. I guess there could always be an emergency, but hopefully things will be quiet. I'm actually on call for the ER on Saturday. What time, and what are we doing?"

"I figure we can go to dinner around seven. There's not a lot to choose from in Abilene. There's a pretty good steak place we can check out. Afterwards, if you feel like it, there's a horse show going on over at the Expo Center which is right down the road. You might like that. It's a nice facility. I'm not sure what the schedule is but it's an American Quarter Horse show so there could be anything: trail riding, cow horse, western pleasure. I know they're not roping or cutting, because I'm doing that on Saturday morning. But the others are fun to watch. We can play it by ear, depending on when we get done with dinner and whether or not you get called in for any emergencies."

"That sounds like a plan."

"How do I know you won't just pretend to get called into the ER?"

"You won't. One of the benefits of membership. But, I'll tell you what. You'll be driving. You can drop me off at the ER, and at least you'll have the satisfaction of knowing that I'll have to walk back to the hotel if I'm lying."

"Oh, that makes me feel better."

They chatted for a few minutes and Leslie was feeling like a high school student. Regan was easy to talk to. Honest. No games. This was good. After they hung up she got into bed and allowed herself to think about her first phone call from Chris when he pretended he needed information about the orthopedic services in the OR. She thought he really wanted to know and gave him an ear full. She didn't find out until after they had been going out that it was just a common ploy to get her to meet with him for lunch the next day. Funny, Regan had done the same, and even though it was more of a tease, it got her there just the same.

14

*T*erryl called on Tuesday asking if she would like to get together for lunch after surgery. In the doctor's lounge they were enjoying a reasonable meal for this venue when another doctor came in and sat down at their table. Terryl introduced him as Frank Long, one of Doc Hawley's orthopedic colleagues in town. They shook hands. He asked her how things were going and offered to help her out if she needed a break. She didn't take him up on it at this time, but tucked the offer in the back of her head. She extended the same to him. In Abilene there were two other groups of three orthopods each, besides Doc Hawley. Even under ideal circumstances, every third night call for them would probably get old. As a *locums*, she had sometimes been asked to help out the competition.

They got to talking and she discovered that Frank was a runner and golfer. Sounded like he was pretty good at both. He looked like a natural athlete. Maybe a wide receiver in high school who over the years had trimmed down in terms of muscle mass but maintained his athleticism. She decided to test her position recognition skills. If she worked the conversation enough, she could get any guy to talk about his high school football days, if he played. Sure enough, he had been a wide receiver and punt returner at Abilene High in the sixties. Chris would have been proud of her.

He mentioned that he was currently the chairman of the orthopedic department and had just finished signing off on her files. She would officially have full provisional privileges next week when her appointment went to the Medical Executive Committee. It was kind of a moot point in view of the fact that she had already been cutting for almost two weeks with her provisional privileges. Operating with provisional privileges was standard in the *locum tenens* business. She thanked him for the update.

That evening after work she went to the park and jogged three miles. She timed herself, making a plan to increase the distance and the speed over the next few weeks. Leslie liked running only because it was a fast, cheap way to exercise and one way to keep her mind off the personal stuff. Otherwise she thought running, or any high impact exercise for that matter, was bad for the weight bearing joints. Most people were not biomechanically sound to run for long distances, and it eventually caused problems for them. Walking was difficult for her because she could think while she walked. While she was running it was hard to concentrate on anything else.

She nearly froze while she was out and again had to go look for more cold weather clothes. While shopping Leslie began to contemplate what she might wear on her date. In the past three years she had purchased only the bare necessities, including several pair of practical pants, several shirts or sweaters, and a couple of pair of practical shoes, as Regan had so studiously observed. She frankly had not had the mental energy to go look for clothes, to coordinate bottoms and tops, and then to lug them around from city to city. She did not want to attract attention with her clothes for the same reason she didn't own or rent a vehicle that made her stand out. These were things that led people to think they understood who she was and gave them an interest in finding out more about her.

She felt different today and found a little upscale clothing boutique near the hospital.

On Friday morning, Leslie saw patients and signed lots of pieces of paper. She called Doc in Lubbock. He sounded good. He was coming home Saturday or Sunday barring any complications. He still wouldn't be coming to work for a while because the surgeon wanted him to take it easy. Brenda was determined to make sure he followed the doctor's orders.

She ran on Friday afternoon, and then went back to the hotel trying her damnedest to stay occupied up until the last minute. She felt unfaithful but knew that Chris would never have wanted that, especially not three years into it. He couldn't speak for the kids though. She made up her mind that she was going to go with what felt right. Hell, she was only going to be here for a few weeks, tops. She already had another assignment.

After speaking with Doc, Leslie sensed he was doing well physically and spiritually. She contacted her agency. They had a couple of guys in Evansville, Indiana who desperately wanted to take their families on a vacation together. They did their residencies together. Decided to hang up their shingles together as well. The problem was, now the best friends could never do anything together because they were on call every other night. *Locum tenens* to the rescue. She agreed to do it without hesitating. Doc would be back in the office sooner than expected and would have time to get acclimated to the schedule. She would take a week off and if he still needed her, there would be some leeway.

This was her *M.O.* and the consistent ability of the agency to move her, made her feel secure. She would never have to get involved in a relationship if she kept on moving. She wanted to stay committed to the memory of her family as they were committed to her for eternity.

After a shower Leslie got dressed. She hoped her off-the-shelf jeans didn't look like they had just come off the shelf. She made sure all of the tags were pulled off. Her black high-heeled above-ankle boots were to die for but she felt a little strange in them after not wearing heels for so long. An olive green turtle neck sweater topped off the outfit. She took Regan's call from the lobby with confidence, feeling relaxed with her new assignment in mind. She decided she would tell Regan about Evansville as soon as the opportunity presented itself. Throwing her new camel pea coat over her arm, Leslie went down to the lobby to meet him.

Regan was making friendly conversation with Raghu when she arrived. A lot of her confidence went out the door when she saw him standing there. Men are so at ease with themselves. She was envious of that. They don't have to do much to look good. Maybe that was just a woman's perception. Perhaps he considered her the same way, because he definitely looked at her like "you don't have to do much to make yourself look great." He had never looked at her like that before. Just blatantly looked at her. He didn't try to hide it. She felt thrilled, got a little knotted sensation deep in her tummy.

Even Raghu saw it. He was beaming like he was a dad or something.

"You two have a good evening please."

"Thank you, Raghu." She said it with a touch of sarcasm, but he missed it.

"Good to meet you, Mister Wakeman."

"Night, Raghu, same here."

Regan took her arm and led her through the first sliding door. The temperature difference was abrupt and from experience she knew the next door would bring a blast of freezing air. Regan stopped.

"Let's get your coat on. It's really cold out there." He took her coat from her and helped her into it, one arm, then the other. He then gently turned her by the shoulders, straightened the collar and buttoned it up! Her tummy knotted up again. This couldn't go on all night. She was going to have to do something. She was just going to tell him that she was going to Indiana in a few weeks. That's what she was going to do. When they got in the truck.

The truck was parked under the portico. Engine running. After opening the door for her, he jogged around to get in. He turned to her. "You look great."

I'm going to Indiana in a few weeks. The words never came out.

What did come out was, "Thanks, you do too." *Oh, that was rich,* she thought to herself.

"Well, we've got a mutual admiration club goin' here. Off to a good start."

They went across town to the restaurant. It was crowded. She saw nothing but trucks in the parking lot and most of the people inside were wearing distinctly western clothes, down to the spurs. Regan told her it was the crowd from the horse show, which would be going on until two or three in the morning. People just took a break for dinner and came directly over to this restaurant since it was close by. A lot of them would go back to the Expo center after dinner to warm up their horses or to compete. Regan knew a number of the people and introduced her. She asked him to introduce her as Leslie, not Doctor.

He ordered a beer. Leslie declined. She would allow herself a glass of wine with dinner, but that would be it. Regan was just beginning to understand the fact that while she was here in Abilene, she was basically on call one hundred percent of the time. She had her pager with her and this time didn't leave the cell phone behind. Tonight she wasn't on ER call but had to be available for patient phone calls and any emergency room patients requesting Doc Hawley.

They ordered steaks and baked potatoes. From what she could see it was the restaurant's most popular fare. They had a glass of red wine. Regan toasted, "To Doc Hawley. If it wasn't for him, you wouldn't be here."

"To Doc."

15

*D*inner was pretty good, for Abilene, Texas. There probably weren't a lot of great restaurants in this city, but so far, she had enjoyed pretty good, even if not sophisticated, food.

She was surprised at how easy it was to talk to Regan. They had a lot in common, jogging, books, politics. They both had interesting jobs. She was intrigued with his work and they talked about his career up to the point of doing the stadium. He dabbled in home building for a few years, but preferred office and industrial type jobs. Eventually he got into a niche. He just bid on the stadium site and got it. It was definitely the highlight of his career so far.

"Well, we've spent the entire evening talking about me," he said when the check arrived. "You're going to have to go to dinner with me again so we can talk about you."

It was just as well from her standpoint that they didn't get too far into her career because so much was tied to her family. It would be hard to lie to him. She didn't want to do it, but knew sooner or later she would have to. She also remembered that sometimes clever people who know enough about dates, life, careers, can put two and two together and figure out that something's missing. This was the problem with getting to know people.

Once she was talking to someone about a concert she had gone to just prior to her husband's accident. For some reason he queried her regarding the specific date of the accident and she told him her usual "year ago" story. Strangely and coincidentally, he recalled that the concert she was talking about had occurred two years prior. She found herself having to bullshit her way out of it. She thought she could read into his voice that he didn't quite buy it. Maybe she was just being paranoid. Nevertheless, lying was just hard to do.

"Do you feel up to going over to the horse show?"

"Sure. I can't believe it's going on this late."

"Well, believe it, because they almost always do. Sometimes we're roping at two in the morning. Like I said earlier, I don't know what's going on tonight, but whatever it is, it'll probably be interesting. Even though I don't do it, my favorites to watch are the reined cow horses. I know they're not going in the morning because the ropers are. Those poor cow horse fools always get stuck at the end of the day or first thing in the morning."

Regan paid the bill. She felt funny about not paying her part but figured he probably wouldn't let her pay for her own dinner, so she didn't bother to offer. She wondered how much money he made, and then remembered Brenda or Doc telling her that there was also some inheritance. She didn't feel so bad after all. They left the restaurant and drove to the Taylor County Expo Center.

Sure enough, there was a lot of activity there, even at nine at night. And it was cold. That would be hard to tolerate, riding late at night when it's this cold. They walked around the barn first. It was warm in there and smelled like horses and hay. It brought back memories of her childhood. They walked up and down some of the aisles and he pointed out the different body types of the quarter horses, depending on the event for which they were bred. There were huge, gaunt, sixteen to seventeen hand horses. They didn't even look like quarter horses. These were bred for western pleasure and English riding events. There were horses that looked like thoroughbreds, used in the hunter jumper events. Then there were the very typical quarter horse conformations; large hind ends, shorter stature and big chests, bred for performance horse events like cutting, reining and cow horse.

Regan said that his "granddaddy" had a quarter horse that could run the quarter mile, work a cow and then compete in the halter division, which is basically a conformation competition. Today horses are bred specifically for halter. They're like body builders. They're not ridden and perform no particular function other than competing in a class that theoretically defines the appearance of the ideal quarter horse. He told Leslie that one time he was asked to put one of his roping horses in a halter class in order to fill the class so the winner could earn more points. His mare, whom he thought was perfectly formed for a quarter horse, looked like an old nag compared to those specimens.

They walked slowly up and down the aisles, stopping occasionally at a stall to look at a horse. Some were curious and came up to the side of the slatted pens for attention. She loved to pet their soft noses and feel them breathing on her fingers. It seemed as if they seduced her to put her hand in the stall, and then they would try to give it a nip. Some horses totally ignored them, while others put their ears back, defying Leslie to come near. They would swing their heads at them, aggressive but probably harmless. Regan spoke of the horses just like her dad had. They're marginally intelligent, so they can learn some tricks in order to eat. But Leslie could swear those big soft eyes could see straight into her soul. What is it about horses? Why had she stopped riding? Too many other things to do.

Regan found out that indeed, there was a cow horse event going on in an outdoor covered arena and suggested they drive down there to check it out. Several horses were tied up to the fence and the contestants were riding horses around in circles, trying to stay warmed up. They got out of the truck and walked up into the middle of the bleachers.

Just as they sat down a horse and rider entered the empty arena and stopped in the middle, facing the bleachers. The horse looked up as if suddenly surprised by his surroundings. But other than ears twitching back and forth, he stayed perfectly still. In a little bit the rider gently cued him to step off into a big circle to the right. She recalled the leads from her riding experience and noted that this was a right lead, the horse basically pulling with his right front leg. When he came around to the middle he did a flying lead change to the left and ran around the circle twice. Then he switched leads again in the middle. Leslie was amazed at the apparent ease of this maneuver for the horse and rider. She remembered having to slow down to a trot sometimes, and she always had to do a lot of holding with the reins as well as hard pushing with her legs to get her horse to change leads. Sometimes her horse would leap out of the lead change and take off running. These lead changes were barely detectable. Regan was talking her through most of this, but she remembered some from her childhood lessons.

The horse went around the corner but instead of riding in a circle, he straightened out and began to gather speed until he was galloping fast down the middle toward the other end of the arena. The sound of his hooves beating the ground could be heard above the wind and country western music on the loudspeakers. What happened next was totally unexpected. The rider, without changing positions or pulling on the reins, said "whoa" to the horse, cueing him to stop. But because he was going so fast, he couldn't just stop. He had to slide to stop his forward progression. She was sure the rider had to hunker down to keep from being hurled over the front of the saddle. The horse's front legs kept pulling while the hind legs remained flexed and dragging through the sand. He left two tracks in the sand that she guessed were at least twenty to thirty feet long. This was amazing. She looked at Regan and he gave her an approving look and a thumbs up sign for the horse and rider.

The next maneuver even surpassed the stop because she could never recall seeing a horse doing this. He spun on his hind legs with his front legs pulling him around in a couple of twirls. He ended up facing the other way and ran down to the other end of the arena to do another stop, followed by another set of spins in the opposite direction. Then he went only halfway down the arena, stopped and backed up. End of event. Simply amazing.

"That part of this event is called reining, which is now part of the Olympics. It's the first western horse event ever to be in the Olympics."

Now that's impressive, she thought. When most people think of western events, they think of bronc riding, barrel racing, calf roping. Things you wouldn't see in the summer Olympics. But this clearly required a lot of skill on the part of the horse and rider. She equated it to dressage, but in a western fashion. She wondered what made some equine sports appealing to the Olympic committee and others not. The other western riding events required skill on the part of rider and horse as well. At least as much skill as the luge. But she couldn't envision cows in the Olympics.

Regan nudged her arm. "Now watch this." At that point the horse and rider turned toward the far end of the arena, where a small herd of cattle was penned up. The rider gave someone in the pens a nod, the gate was opened and out came a calf. The horse stepped up. The calf appeared somewhat agitated, as if wanting to get out of the arena. The rider then began to work the calf from one side of the pen to the other. The movements were somewhat like cutting but the rider moved the horse with his rein and legs to a greater extent. She recalled cutting horses that appeared to work the cow on their own once the rider put the hand holding the reins on the horse's neck, signaling to the horse that it was time to do his thing. Of course the cutter uses his legs but not so it's obvious. This rider openly used his legs to move the horse and correct its body position. After doing a little of this cutting-like action, which Regan called "boxing," the horse then brought the cow around to the long side of the arena and essentially chased it down the fence, heading it off before it got to the other end. The horse and cow were running at a high rate of speed and when the horse moved ahead of the cow, the cow stopped sharply and the horse turned it. It seemed as if it would be natural for the rider to just keep going in the original direction rather than hanging on for dear life and turning with the horse and cow. Of course this impressive maneuver was followed by a huge cheer from the crowd. Rider, horse and cow then went the opposite direction and repeated the step to more cheers.

When the cow popped out into the middle of the arena, the horse went after it and circled it to the right and then to the left. Suddenly while circling to the left, the horse lost its footing. It looked to Leslie like he was going to go down, and everyone gasped. The rider lifted up on the reins, the horse looked like it scrambled a bit, then regained his footing to go on and finish the turn. Everyone cheered, Leslie included.

"I really want to do that," Regan said.

"Well, why don't you? You know how to ride cutting horses and rope."

"It's more difficult than that. The reining is really a challenge. You'd have to learn an entire new deal. Get a reining horse. They're expensive. I'd have to get hooked up with a trainer. It's a lot more complicated than it looks."

"It's exciting, no doubt." Leslie was cold and shivering.

"You're freezing. I'm sorry. Why don't we go back to the barn?"

"I'm a little cold, but I'd like to see a couple more of these horses, really. It's just my hands. I should have brought gloves." She held her hands together and rubbed them. Regan reached over and took her hands in his. She stiffened up a little and started to pull them back, but he held on. His hands were warm. She remembered the slight roughness she felt when they shook hands on the night of the accident.

"That feel better?"

She nodded. One way or another it did. Another horse was already riding but they weren't paying attention. Regan opened her hands and rubbed her fingers. She became self conscious because her hands were dry and she had a couple of deep hangnails. Her hands were forty years old but were aging a little faster than the rest of her because of repeated scrubbing with harsh antibacterial soaps. When her hands were dry she had a bad habit of picking at the cuticles. She silently scolded herself for not having trimmed them earlier.

"Don't look at my hands. They're so dry."

"I like your hands. I like to imagine what they do. Look at mine, if you want to see dry hands." He held his out in front of her. He had neat trimmed nails but he was right, they were dry. His hands too were victims of the work he did. He took her hands again, and very deliberately put the palm of his right hand to the palm of her left. He left it there for a moment, and then flexed his fingers down in between hers. She wanted to keep looking at their hands, or at the horses, but couldn't resist the urge to look at him. She folded her fingers against his. Her heart was beating madly. Could he feel it? He put his left arm around her and pulled her to him. She was warm now.

They sat in silence and watched the next three horses compete. When a tractor came out to fix up the dirt in the arena, Regan suggested they go on back to the barn. They walked out to his truck, drove over to the main barn and walked the aisles again.

"Hey, here's one of my roping buddy's horses." There was a stout grey horse in the stall. He was almost white. He came right over to the gate and put his nose up to it. Regan opened the door to the stall and pushed the horse back out of his way a bit while softly clucking to him. The horse quickly obliged him. Leslie moved toward the horse. He jerked his head up and down causing her to have to step back.

"Whoa, Bullet," he said softly. The horse put his head down and stood still.

"Bullet? Whatever happened to Blue or Whitey?"

"I think it has to do with beer, like silver bullet. Get it?"

"Bullet, that's not a very cute name." She said it in a tone of voice as if speaking to a child. She put her hands on his soft nose and rubbed. Bullet breathed with short warm puffs and smelled her hand. Then, suddenly, he curled up his right nostril, and snorted out of his left one. Horse buggers went all over her.

"Gross!"

Regan was laughing. "I thought you grew up around horses. That's what you get for loving on him."

She looked down. There were little brown snotty spots all over her new coat. She looked up at Regan, who just shrugged.

"You knew he was going to do that, didn't you?" She reached out to play punch him in the stomach. Instantly, he grabbed her hand and pulled her around, pinning her hands in front, her back to him. He bent his head around the side of hers and then, down to her ear.

"Oh, oh. You're in trouble now." In a frank tone of voice. Serious.

"Regan," she whined, "no fair."

He turned her around and looked down at her. "Is too." He kissed her on the forehead and let her go. Bullet lightly snorted, letting them know he was still there.

They stepped out of the stall and Regan closed the door. He slid the latch into its slot and then reinforced it with the horse's halter, buckled around both the door and the side of the stall.

"Let's go. It's getting late. You've probably got to work tomorrow and I've got to get up here early to warm up my horses."

"So, what time do you ride?"

"That's a good question. The show starts at eight o'clock. I won't specifically know when I ride until I see what my draw is. It could be any time after eight depending on how many contestants there are. I'll probably get here around six in the morning."

"You're kidding?"

"No. I've got to haul the horses in from my place. When I compete in Abilene I usually leave them at home to avoid paying stall fees."

"So are you roping or cutting tomorrow?"

"Roping. You can come up here tomorrow if you want. You know, if you get done with your work and all. We'll be here all day. You've got my cell phone number. Just call me and I can tell you where we are on the schedule. Then you won't have to wait around the whole time."

"Well, maybe I can. It depends on what's going on at the hospital. I'm on call at the ER tomorrow."

"Sure. Well, just call me, okay."

They walked to his truck. Frost was crystallizing on his windshield. He ran the engine so the frost could thaw and he could use his wipers to get it off. He turned on the radio. Country music was playing.

"You know, when you drive a truck, it's a rule, you've got to listen to country music. It's got to at least be on three of your buttons."

"Really."

"Yep. Really."

"There are a lot of strange rules around this place, if you ask me."

"Who's asking? You don't seem like a country western kind of girl."

"Honestly, I don't listen to a lot of music. It kind of reminds me of things. I like classic rock, alternative rock, whatever. I'm not really picky."

"I know what you mean. I like rock music too, but nobody I know, except you now, likes it, so I don't keep it on the radio."

"That's weird, a cowboy who likes rock music."

They were quiet until they pulled up to the hotel. Leslie was thinking about how easy she was with their silence. When people really connect, they're comfortable with any level of conversation, even the silence. Even stupid stuff is fair game, silence is just silence. No need to say things like, "penny for your thoughts" or "what are you thinking?" That's for people who are anxious with each other and with the silence. It was easy with Chris too. And now with Regan. No need to make up small talk. No need to talk about the weather.

Leslie started getting nervous about the goodnight kiss she knew would come. The juvenile expression "Yikes" came to mind. This was totally strange. They're grown ups! No need to sweat it over a kiss. What if he does? What if he doesn't? For that matter, why does he have to control it? She wondered if he was worrying about the same thing. Should he kiss her, or not? She doubted any guy ever worried about that.

She started getting that maddening little cramping sensation down low in her belly. He pulled up to the portico, turned towards her and shifted his weight in the leather seat.

"I had a really good time."

"Me too. Thanks."

"You're gonna call me tomorrow, right." He turned and pulled the door handle, opened his door and started to get out. She did the same. He met her coming around the front of the truck. The turbulent air in the portico was blowing all around them. The engine was running and gave off warmth and noise. Regan stepped toward her taking hold of her arms and rubbed them up and down, waited for an instant, then smiled. He tilted his head slightly, still looking at her eye to eye. Leslie thought she might pass out. Then slowly he bent his head to her and their lips met. At first closed, soft. He kissed her once. She returned it the same. Then his lips parted and took her upper lip with his, lightly, for only a second. Leslie had to take a deep breath. His skin smelled good. She leaned into him. He pulled his lips from hers, touched them to her forehead and held her for a moment. Then backed away. Putting his hands in his pockets, he did the little hopping thing which she now found quite endearing.

"I'll see you tomorrow," he said. She headed toward the hotel doors, then turned and waved. Regan drove away. She could still hear the engine even after both doors slid closed.

She found Raghu working in the dining room. He had some decaf coffee brewed, and offered it to her. "Ah, Doctor, you're home. Did you have a good evening?"

"Yes, Raghu, I did."

"The young man seems very nice."

"Yes, I think so too."

16

*S*he knew there would be hell to pay when she got up to her room. If there were spirits of her family actually waiting up there for her she could not have felt worse. Would they question her? Would Chris be angry or jealous? Would the kids be curious, never having had a chance to experience their own sexuality? Somewhere between the lobby and her room, Leslie's subconscious mind began to manipulate the emotions to work in her favor. In the way she currently wanted them to work.

She was interested in Regan. She felt good with Regan. Not feeling like crying tonight made her feel guilty. Her guilt was quickly replaced by anger. She sat down on the bed, stewing about it. It's been long enough. She convinced herself that she'd worn black long enough.

The next thought was not anticipated. The two little silver boxes in the bedside table drawer. They are always there no matter where she goes. This is where she always puts them. They sit quietly in the night stand, in the dark. She doesn't routinely take them out to look at them. But a lot of times, when she goes into one of her crying spells, she goes ahead and pulls them out to open them and feel the little loops of hair, or smell them. Why not? She convinced herself that it wasn't morbid. At those times she was already as morbid as she could get. Why not add insult to injury? She can only cry so much.

And now, in the middle of trying to justify her newfound feelings, the boxes beckoned. She lay back in the bed and reached for the drawer, opened it and pulled out the two silver boxes. They were antiques, some kind of stamp boxes. The two curled segments of hair were tucked in there, one tied with pink, the other a blue ribbon. She remembered when they got those first haircuts like it was yesterday.

For some reason Victor did not want to get his hair cut. Vivian didn't mind. He struggled in the seat, and the minute the hairdresser brought the scissors up to his head he screamed and twisted around. She finally just hacked around a little bit and gave up. Vivian sat quietly for hers and afterward demanded the reward Leslie had promised to give. A trip to the local ice cream parlor.

Like Pavlov's dogs, she began to tear up once she held those boxes and strands of hair in her hand. The direct connection to her babies was too much to bear. This was their hair. Hair she had washed, combed, smelled and kissed. Invisible to her eyes but there nonetheless, deep within each hair fiber, was the genetic code for the twins. And for her husband. If the genetic codes were there in her hand, in some strange way, were they not there too? Leslie looked up at the ceiling, found her patterns, and finally went to sleep.

17

*I*n the morning she woke up thinking about the kids. She must have dreamed about them. She suddenly remembered thinking about the genetic code held within every cell of the body. Brain, heart, hair, it didn't matter. The entire code for making them was there. With cloning, entire individuals could be replicated. But people weren't sheep and no one could do it with humans. Yet the frightening potential was there. If they could clone a horse, then why not a child? At first scientists would use it for an honorable cause: transplant organs, bone marrow, things like that. But eventually someone with enough money would want their dead child, parent or spouse replicated.

She wondered what she would do if her children and Chris could be cloned. Well, she would do it in a second. But then she would have Chris and the kids all as infants. That would make a good Twilight Zone. The greatest fear of all would be losing them again. Nothing could prevent that. Nothing could prevent losing anyone again. Losing Regan.

There would be risk in getting too close. And it was one she didn't think she could take again. People expect to lose their parents and perhaps even to lose a spouse, but no one could possibly be prepared to lose a child. To lose two children. To lose all of them at once. No way to prepare.

The cell phone rang.

"Doctor Cohen?"

"Speaking."

"This is the medical exchange. We tried to page you, but there was no response. I hope you don't mind if we reach you on your cell phone."

"Not at all. What can I do for you?"

"There is a call for you from the Regional Hospital ER. A Doctor Hackett."

"Thanks, I'll give them a call."

She hung up, dialed the ER and was immediately connected to Dr. Hackett. He told her they were expecting an air ambulance transfer to the ER. A couple of transients were jumping trains early that morning. Somehow both fell off or were pushed from the train and had sustained serious injuries. He didn't know exactly what was injured or whether or not there were fractures. He just wanted to give her the heads up, because they were anticipating orthopedic injuries.

Of course, she thought. When trains come in contact with frail human bodies, bones get busted up. Their ETA was approximately thirty minutes. Leslie told him she was on her way.

She arrived at the emergency room just as the helicopter landed. The landing dock was ready with stretchers. She went inside to get the report from Hackett. He would have been in contact with the people on the scene of the accident and with the helicopter. She found him talking to one of the general surgeons on call for the trauma team. She listened to his report. The trauma surgeons were usually the ones who managed all patients who had at least two different body system injuries. It could be ortho or urologic, neuro, pulmonary. These patients had to be observed closely by someone who could manage all their problems and get help from specialists as needed. The only time she would admit trauma patients was if there were only orthopedic problems involved. Just a broken leg. Or even a leg and an arm. If there were a lot of fractures, fractures of the pelvis or spine, then again the trauma surgeons were involved. They were the ones best trained to manage these patients in a general sense. A train injury victim was just that kind of patient.

Now train injuries could almost without exception be considered serious. It was rare that she took care of train wreck victims or unsuccessful train jumpers who weren't seriously injured. Pretty rare to have an isolated fracture.

Even though the train company frequently was blamed, and therefore sued by the victims, usually the most obvious thing was that these folks were doing something they shouldn't have been. Like jumping a train, or trying to beat a train at a crossing, or sleeping on a train track. From what she had heard, people slept on the tracks because they were waiting for the train and figured the sound or vibration would wake them up. Most of them don't make it to the ER. They usually get run over or wake up and sit straight up when they hear the train just as it rolls over them.

The two people coming in tonight were no exception. The Darwin Awards came to mind. The two had jumped a train outside of Abilene just before it started to pick up speed. They had pulled themselves up the ladder on the side of the train. One stayed on the ladder while the other slid in between the two trains and perched on the coupling device. Somehow, the one perched on the coupling device got his pants leg caught in it. He didn't know it until the pants leg began to get twisted up in the coupler. As it twisted it became tight like a tourniquet. When he finally realized what was happening, he called for help.

His buddy tried to reach him but lost his footing and fell from the train. He landed on the track and his arm was run over just below the elbow. He was able to get up and find help. He spoke only Spanish so it took a while for someone to understand what he was trying to say. He'd lost a lot of blood but was stable and had an isolated orthopedic problem. Leslie would take over his case.

The other guy had not yet arrived. He was picked up a little further out. Someone eventually got word to the engineer, and the train was stopped. She remembered hearing that it takes almost a mile of track for a fully loaded train to come to a complete stop. The engineer got out and ran back, checking around every car as he went. He finally found the guy between the twenty-first and twenty-second train. He was still attached to the coupling device.

As his twisted pants leg became tighter and tighter it began cutting through his skin and muscle. As he tried to free himself, a lot of the skin and muscle were gradually stripped away. By the time the engineer arrived the guy was in a state of shock, but had managed to stay perched on the coupler. His leg looked like raw flesh from just above the knee down to about six inches below. Most of the ligaments of his knee had been torn in the process as well. The veins in his leg were clotted because of the tourniquet effect of the twisted material. This gave the lower part of the leg a swollen liverish appearance. It took a while for them to get a pulse because the large artery behind the knee was in spasm. He was taken for an arteriogram to make sure none of the vessels were transected or clotted. Wet gauzes were packed over the raw, exposed muscle and blood vessels. This patient was admitted to the trauma surgeon for coordination of his care. Leslie would be responsible for his knee. A plastic surgeon would be needed for skin grafting.

This type of degloving injury was basically like a deep burn. There would be a lot of tissue fluid lost and the patient would also be at risk for development of renal failure because of the accumulation of substances in the dead tissues which are toxic to the kidneys. The surgeon would get consultations from specialists as needed.

His friend would need some type of definitive amputation. Even though the stump of the arm had been recovered it was not reimplantable because the train had run over it a couple of times, crushing the bones and soft tissues.

Leslie's initial job was to clean up all the wounds on both patients. Assisting her on the leg was one of the local plastic surgeons. While under anesthesia she examined Jesús Camacho's knee so she could make plans for the ligament reconstructions she would have to do later. She cleaned up his large open wound and looked for a possible communication between the contaminated site and the knee joint itself. A joint that was breached by the wound could definitely complicate his condition because of the potential for an infection to develop.

Kelly Briggs was a pleasant, fortyish plastic surgeon who lived outside of Breckenridge, Texas, about halfway between Abilene and Fort Worth. He worked in both cities but was probably trying to build his practice in Fort Worth. A lot of guys worked in smaller communities surrounding larger cities in order to develop a referral base and divert some of the referrals from the busier established guys in town.

He had some good ideas for treatment of the huge skin defect on Jesús' leg and Leslie was glad to have his help. Despite having done a lot of skin grafting and wound care in her training, it was not her wish to start doing it now.

It took a couple of hours to get the knee cleaned up and prepared for a return to the operating room the next week for definitive treatment. She and Briggs had a cup of coffee in the doctor's lounge before he left to drive home and she went back to the OR to clean up the arm amputation. It had been severed just below the elbow. A blessing for him, it was his non-dominant arm. He might try to wear a prosthesis. She wondered what would eventually happen to Emilio Torres. He would return to Mexico where the expense of a prosthesis might be prohibitive. He would likely live his life without one. There would be no option to work as a manual laborer. There would be no organizations to fund his training to use a computer or do telephone soliciting.

The same would be true for his buddy. In Mexico, he would probably have received an above-the-knee amputation right off the bat. Knee ligament reconstruction and skin grafting would not be an option for this impoverished patient. Theoretically, citizens in Mexico all have access to medical care but complex care such as this is just not available to the average citizen. They can receive basic medical care but there is no guarantee regarding the quality or amount of that care. Wealthy patients pay cash for their treatment and in many cases come to the United States to get it.

She remembered a young waiter she had met on a vacation in Mexico. He had learned she was an orthopedic surgeon and asked if he could talk to her about his knee. He had sustained what sounded like a meniscus cartilage tear during a soccer game two or three years prior. The doctor had told him all he needed was to have the knee drained regularly. He went in every week for the doctor to put a "trocaro" into the knee. The waiter had described a pointed sharp metal tube, like a giant, thick needle, which the doctor would stick into his knee to drain the fluid. In time a permanent hole developed and the knee became infected. From the tone of his voice, Leslie could tell that the young man accepted this treatment and outcome as if it were expected.

From that point on he had a continuously draining hole in the side of his knee. He had to wear a bandage all the time to absorb the cloudy fluid that oozed out. He pulled up his pants leg to show her. He was wondering if there was anything else he could do because he still had the pain on the inner side of his knee, just like after the original injury.

That wasn't a surprise to Leslie. He still had the torn meniscus as well as a deeply infected knee. By this time he probably had infected bone as well. In time his knee would deteriorate to the point where he would have to have an amputation. There would be no other choice for him. She told the young man, there was not much he could do, because there wasn't. This boy did not have the option to come to the United States. He did not have the money to be cared for properly in Mexico. He would lose his leg. He was a handsome kid and she felt sad for him and amazed by his innocence.

Her current patients might not remain so innocent. Lawyers and local friends, if they had any, would advise them to consider suing Union Pacific. The attorneys would try to convince them that the easy access to the train was clearly negligent. Union Pacific would eventually find it cheaper to settle rather than to go to court and take their chances with a jury, perhaps sympathetic to these injured young men. Emilio and Jesús might return to Mexico with some money. Of course their attorneys would get most of it.

Regardless of their future situation, while in the Taylor County Regional Hospital, her patients would receive the best medical care available. She, Briggs, and everyone involved would make sure of that.

She finished up with both patients and rounded on the one patient she still had in the hospital around one o'clock in the afternoon. Doc and Brenda called to let her know they were home. Doc was doing fine. He was in good spirits but still feeling a little weak. According to Brenda, he was not coming into the office next week. Leslie could hear him complaining to her in the background. Brenda spoke a little more quietly and told Leslie he would be starting chemotherapy. The pathology results demonstrated a high grade type of tumor that had penetrated the wall of the colon, and the doctors recommended chemo. Doc was going for his follow-up appointment next week and they would know more then.

She heard Doc yell, "Quit whispering in there." In a scolding voice, Brenda told him she wasn't whispering and to mind his own business.

Leslie talked about her patients, and about how things were going at the office. She didn't mention Regan. Didn't need to mention Regan, because she had made her plans.

18

*W*hen she got back to the hotel, she called Regan on his cell phone. The phone rang once, twice. "Hello."

"Hello, Regan?"

"This is Regan Wakeman. Sorry I can't answer your call. Please leave a message after the tone."

The sound of his soft Texas accent on a recording surprised and at the same time, disappointed her. She hung up. She would wait until later and try again. Or should she call back and leave a message. Suddenly her phone rang. The caller ID said R WAKEMAN and a phone number. She pressed the talk button immediately then subconsciously admonished herself for not letting it ring a couple of times.

"Leslie? Hey, it's me, Regan. What are you doing?"

"Just calling you."

"Sorry, I had my phone on silent mode because we're in the middle of riding over here. I didn't feel it in time to answer. You coming over?"

"Well, I just got done in the OR."

"Really. Wow. Are you tired?"

"Not really. Just a little worried that something else might come in, since I am on call over here."

"Yeah, I can understand that. It would probably be a hassle for you to come over here. It would probably be kind of boring too. You'd just be sitting around watching me sit around on my horse. And every once in a while I go rope a cow. How's that for spending your afternoon?"

"I doubt if it would be boring. Just worried about the ER. That's all. I don't know why, but if I get really busy first thing in the morning I get paranoid that the rest of the day is going to be like that. It doesn't make any sense statistically. It's just a feeling."

"Well, I guess as a patient, I would feel good if I knew there was a doc like you ready to take care of me if I got in trouble."

"I guess so."

There was silence on the phone from both ends.

"Leslie, I want to see you. On your terms. Whatever. You tell me."

"I want to talk to you too."

"Oh, oh, sounds serious."

"What time do you think you'll get done today?"

"It's hard to say. Maybe four or five. Why don't I call you when I'm done and we'll get some dinner? We can just go to that place outside your hotel. It's pretty good."

She laughed.

"What?"

"Oh, nothing. It's just that restaurant. Everybody who mentions it says it's pretty good."

"Well, have you eaten there?"

"Yes."

"And?"

"It's pretty good."

"Well, there you have it. I'll call you later. We can have your talk. How's that?"

"Sounds good. See you later."

She felt relief. This was going to work just fine. She was setting him up so he'd be prepared. Like a good boy scout. Always be prepared. He's a guy. He'll handle it.

She did get called back to the hospital around four-thirty. Another kid with a broken arm. She set it in the emergency room. The break was right through the growth area of the six-year-old's wrist. She sedated the girl and then popped it back in perfect position with one properly placed push. She applied a splint and while her hands were deep in plaster, her cell phone began to ring. She was anxious to answer it, but couldn't and in a moment it stopped ringing. She finished up the splint, trying not to act distracted. Didn't return the call right away just to prove to herself that she was in control of this situation. She gave the family her card, their instructions for care of the splint, problems to watch for and a prescription for some pain pills.

Then she called Regan back.

"We're just playing phone tag today, aren't we?"

"Looks like it. I was in the middle of setting a kid's broken wrist."

"Well, shouldn't you just drop everything to take my call?"

"Next time. So what's your status?"

"My status? Now that's one I've never been asked. Must be a medical thing."

"You know, I never thought about it before, but I guess it is. It is kind of strange, really. Let me start over. Are you done riding?"

"Yeah, I'm just putting the horses in their stalls."

"I thought you usually take them home when you're riding in Abilene."

"Not tonight. Changed my mind. Too tired to deal with it."

"How did you do?"

"We came in third. Hope I can make it up tomorrow. Maybe win a prize."

"Like what, a ribbon?"

"No, baby. This ain't no run-around-a-pole-play-day operation. We're going for buckles and cash here. Welcome to Texas."

Now that was all so precious, coming out of his mouth. She didn't know what to say.

He continued. "Well, all right. Why don't I call you when I'm on my way over there and we can just meet at the pretty good restaurant in front of your hotel? Sound good?"

"Sure. I'll talk to you in a little while."

"Bye." She noticed the pronunciation of "bye" like "bah." Air pushed through the mouth along with the sound of "b" and "ah."

"Bye."

19

*A*s Leslie pulled up to the restaurant she saw Regan's truck was already parked in front. When she walked inside he stood up from his table. No one paid much attention as she walked over to the corner table by a window. It was empty around them. She wondered if he had asked for this lonely table knowing they might have a serious discussion.

"Hope you don't mind my attire. I've been riding all day and couldn't change." He was wearing a red plaid shirt, his starched jeans and very dirty boots. She had noted them when he was standing by the table as she came in. He also had on his black hat. He didn't take it off. The brim cast a shadow over his eyes.

"You're fine."

The waitress offered a menu and asked what they wanted to drink. They both ordered iced tea. They made small talk. The show, her cases, and even the weather.

"Hey, now we're talking about the weather. So what's on your mind? I know you wanted to talk to me. What's up?"

She didn't expect this sort of affront. It got her a little more nervous than she already was, but she quickly recovered.

"Listen, Regan, I really like you a lot. You're a very nice person." Regan leaned forward and looking straight at her, raised one eyebrow. Tightened his lips. He knew what was coming.

The waitress returned with their tea and asked if they were ready to order. Regan noticed Leslie had not looked at her menu and asked for a little more time "for the lady to decide."

Leslie said, "I know you're going to think this is crazy, but I'm craving breakfast stuff, like eggs, you know. I'm just in the mood for that right now. Is that weird, or what?"

"Sweetheart, you get whatever your heart desires. I'm up for a good old fashioned hamburger."

When the waitress returned they ordered.

Regan waited a moment before he spoke. "Listen, Leslie. I think I have an idea about what you want to say. And I've got to be honest with you and say that I don't want to hear it. I don't want to hear it because: A, I like you, and B, I hate to see you waste your life like that." He counted A and B with his fingers as though they were numbers. "Not that I'm going to change any of that and keep you from wasting your life or anything. But there might be someone out there who could."

"Regan, I just don't think you understand. How could you?"

"You're absolutely right. I can't put myself in your shoes. No way. Can't pretend to feel what you feel. That's not to say that I haven't had my share of problems. I was married too. It's been a while."

Leslie made no sign that she already knew that.

"Anyway, she left me, and those details aren't critical to know right now. Just that she's gone. And took our daughter with her. It's strange for me. Knowing I have a child out there who thinks some other guy's her daddy. So maybe my wife and kid aren't dead, but it's like they're dead to me. So I think I can understand part of how you're feeling."

"I'm sorry about that Regan, and I don't mean to imply that I'm some kind of special case."

"Well, I didn't tell you that to get sympathy, just like I don't think you want sympathy. And maybe you just want to be left alone."

"Regan, it's hard for me to know what I want right now."

"Listen, I think I can simplify this for us. You're only here for what, three more weeks or something like that?"

"More or less."

"I figure, other than your work, there's not a lot going on. And frankly, the same goes for me. I have to be truthful and say that I like your company, whatever way it comes. Like I said before. On your terms. We're both grown ups here. No games. I'd like to count you as a friend. You know, everybody needs a good orthopedic friend."

She laughed at that idea, because it was true. She was always pretty handy for her friends. They always needed orthopedic advice, and she was always willing to give it. She loved to give it. Felt honored that they would ask for it.

"And I feel the same about you. I mean, not the orthopedic part. Being a friend and all."

"Hey, there's our mutual admiration society again. We're back to square one."

She wondered if, in fact, they were. Back to square one. Dinner came. The eggs hit the spot.

When they had finished he said, "There's still an open invitation to come out to the Expo center and watch some roping. Maybe you'll bring me good luck. You can meet Cinco and Gomez."

"Cinco and Gomez?"

"My horses. You can help me warm them up. You said you used to ride."

"Well, yes, but it's been a long time."

"It's like riding a bicycle. You haven't forgotten how. Besides, you'll just trot or lope them around."

"Well, I'll see how things go tomorrow. Maybe I'll see you out there."

"If you come out, go to that outdoor barn. The one where we saw the cow horses the other night. Remember?"

Did he give her a knowing look or was she imagining it? Because she did remember. She nodded and offered to pay the bill, but he grabbed it from her playfully. She protested and he said she could buy dinner tomorrow night when they were done riding.

"Come on out tomorrow. Just something to do." He shrugged his shoulders and turned his hands out, palms up.

"We'll see. A lot depends on the ER."

They started for the hotel. She remembered last night and for the millionth time got that squeezy feeling deep inside. She knew where. She stopped when they were in line with his truck and turned to him.

"Thanks for dinner again."

"You owe me one." He reached out, winked, and gently poked her shoulder.

20

*L*eslie woke up early on Sunday thinking about the horseshow. Looking forward to seeing Regan on their new, mutually established terms.

At the hospital she ran into Briggs and Long talking in the hall. They were headed to the lounge and asked if she wanted to come along. It became apparent that the two of them had been talking about the cases from last night. Long said, "Hey, sounds like you got a train wreck in last night. No pun intended." The reality of her cases last night gave credence to that expression.

They sat down to have coffee and each of them proceeded to tell their best and worst train wreck stories. In general, train wreck stories are profoundly upsetting because they're so preventable. Leslie remembered her worst one but she didn't share it.

A woman had driven over a railroad crossing, thinking the train was way down the track. It is generally thought that people assume trains are farther away than they really are because the light sits up so high, creating an optical illusion. She'd crossed the tracks right in front of the train and her car was hit. Maybe a better term would be pummeled. One of her children got his legs cut off. The others had serious injuries, broken bones mainly. The police found her in a state of hysteria. Sitting next to her car she seemed to be trying to comfort the dead child while one of the other children watched helplessly, since both of her legs were broken. The third child had been thrown across the road and was lying in the path of oncoming traffic. Someone pulled the boy to safety.

Leslie had almost forgotten that family, until her own accident. Remembering that woman and her situation gave Leslie someone to identify with when she thought she was the only one on the red planet.

They were now all sitting around telling gross medical stories. It is something doctors do. The human body and its diseases are a rich source of tragedy and folklore. Doctors have a wonderful advantage over everyone else in the world. If they think their situation is bad, they can always think of someone else's whose is worse.

Leslie enjoyed the conversation with Briggs and Long. They were easy going, pretty funny. Didn't act like she was an outsider. They questioned her about Doc's progress and whether or not he would be coming back to work. How long would she be there? Where did she come from? Where did she do her training? That was always a topic of conversation among younger doctors.

When she told them where she had done her residency, Long appeared surprised. It seemed one of his best buddies had done his training there as well. When they compared dates and names, Leslie found that she had crossed paths with his friend. She didn't tell him that she actually knew him fairly well. Long hadn't talked to him in ages. That was good. A number of her fellow residents, by then out in private practice like herself, had come to the funeral. That kind of word got out quickly. The circumstances of the accident also got around quickly.

The funeral was devastating. Her husband's family was as distraught as she. Chris was their only child. They were Vic and Vivi's only living grandparents, and they doted on them. They questioned her over and over regarding the accident details, as if there could be some mistake, a glitch that could bring back their son and grandbabies or somehow reconcile the tragedy. Just as she was envious of Casey's life, and Lynn's possession of her daughter, she was certain Mitch and April were envious of her life. Why not her instead of Chris? She would have traded it in an instant. It's easier for the ones who are gone. Mitch and April left the reception early. They didn't even say goodbye.

"I gotta get in touch with Peterman. I haven't talked to him in ages. We had some crazy times in medical school." He changed his voice to a high pitched nasal tone. "There was this one time, in anatomy lab..."

They all laughed, recognizing the play on "there was this one time, at band camp," from *American Pie*.

Leslie hadn't talked to Peterman since the funeral. He and his wife came. They didn't bring their children.

They finished up their coffee and ran out of train wreck stories. Long took off. She and Briggs talked a little about their mutual patient, coordinating plans for surgery the next week. He would have to take the patient back to the OR a couple of times to clean the wound and then finally do the grafting. Leslie would get a shot at his knee once that was all healed. No sense operating on an open, unstable wound. The knee could get infected. The guy could end up losing his leg anyway if the muscle and knee couldn't get covered with skin. He told her he would give her a call once he felt she could go to work on him. She wasn't looking forward to this case. Maybe she would be in Indiana by then. Now that would be a bad case to dump on Doc.

Leslie then went to see her three patients, the one from last week and the other two from the train. Her amputee was doing as well as possible. He was experiencing "phantom pain." Again, she was reminded of the fascinating brain. Even when an extremity has been completely severed, whether traumatically or surgically, the brain continues to perceive its presence. Sometimes it is painful, other times, it's just there. It takes a while for the brain to get used to the fact that there's no more leg or arm.

Leslie knew some Spanish. Discussing phantom pain was a little beyond her capabilities. She tried to work through it, but ultimately had to find someone to translate. The young man seemed stoic. Asked about his friend. She told him he could go see for himself, visit Jesús, since he was able to walk. She gave Emilio his buddy's room number.

Jesús was not so stoic. It had been necessary to sedate him all night. What he had experienced must have been terrible. The slow, progressive strangulation of his leg, knowing what would happen in time and being helpless to do anything about it. She tried to imagine the train picking up speed, the cold air, the helplessness and the loneliness once his friend had fallen off. She put her hand on Jesús' shoulder. He quieted down a little and in a moment asked about Emilio. She told him he would be coming to visit in a little while.

Emilio and Jesús were both very dark, and tiny. She guessed five feet, two inches at the most. They looked like children, but they were in their twenties. Their hands and feet were calloused and filthy, with the exception of Jesús' injured leg which had been repeatedly scrubbed for surgery. Their clothes had been cut off in the ER and were in such bad shape that they had been thrown away. Some volunteer organization would provide them with new clothes. For now, it was the humiliating white and blue hospital gown with the backside open.

She talked to Emilio a little about his problem and what she and Dr. Briggs planned to do. He asked no questions. The situation was beyond his scope of understanding, and he would passively allow himself to be cared for with little regard for the outcome. She had seen his type before.

After rounding she returned to the hotel and tried to decide whether or not to go to the arena. It was only twelve-thirty and she couldn't imagine sitting around for the rest of the day thinking about it. She decided to go, but didn't call Regan to let him know she was coming. That way, if she wanted to, she could back out.

The Expo center was a lot busier today than it had been two nights ago. There were horses walking across the parking lot, warming up in outdoor arenas and tied up to trailers. Cowboys and cowgirls were everywhere. Almost everyone wore a black felt cowboy hat. She walked down to the open arena.

Leslie observed the differences in horses and riders depending on the event. There were guys and gals on the very tall slender horses Regan had pointed out Friday night. They were dressed in very fancy western wear, the girls wearing sparkles and leather. Beautiful clothes even if they weren't really to her taste. Black jackets and chaps. Sequined vests. An elegant look. The men wore more traditional garb, and some had small scarves tied around their necks. There was a ton of silver on the saddles. It was a very beautiful picture even though she found it far from the trappings of a traditional cowboy.

The horses were all slick. She remembered her furry horses in the winter. These horses had no fur. Their fetlocks were shaved. Up close she noted that even their faces were shaved. How would they protect themselves from dirt, cold and rain? Probably didn't need to. They lived in a protected environment.

She noticed some women running circles in a smaller outdoor pen. They were wearing jeans, no chaps. Some of their jeans were brightly colored and the blouses didn't match perfectly. Some had on shirts with fringes, no sequins. Their hat brims were large and more flattened and they had stampede straps around their chins. A few were letting the hats flop behind their shoulders, hanging by the stampede strap. They rode in loose, fast circles, leaning into the curve. They appeared agile and comfortable in their fast riding. Remembering play days as a child she figured these were barrel racers or pole benders.

As she came closer to the outdoor arena, she noted still another altogether different look about horse and rider. The horses were large, some slick, some with winter coats. None were shaved. The bridles had single reins attached to them. The horses' heads were held down by something like a martingale and there were large strips of black rubber wrapped around the saddle horns, for dallying the rope when the calf was secured. All of the riders had ropes, either tied on the side of their saddles or in their hands. If they were carrying the rope, they were twirling them about their heads or off to the side of the horse. Ropers sit their saddle differently than anyone else she had seen. Basically they don't sit. They push their feet deep into the stirrups and stand up, leaning slightly forward. Out in the parking lot they were trotting all around, keeping themselves and the horses warm. Most were lined up together, talking, messing with their ropes.

"Doctor Cohen?"

"Hey, Cal. I didn't expect to see you here. And I especially didn't expect to see you on a horse."

"Well, I can't say the same. Regan said you might be coming over. He's up there with that group of fellas."

Leslie glanced over toward the group of about a half a dozen cowboys. It was hard to tell which one was Regan. There were a couple of skinny guys and a couple of really big guys. The rest were just guys in black hats and heavy coats.

"Anyway, you didn't tell me I couldn't ride. I'm just sitting on Regan's horse anyway, so don't worry. I'm not roping."

"I wasn't worrying. I guess you're doing okay."

"Yep, you do good work, Doc." He turned his head away and yelled to the group of cowboys, "Hey, Regan, look who came to see me!"

Instantly, the third one from the end with a navy blue plaid shirt and a black down vest turned his head. He waved, and in the next instant all the rest of the cowboys turned their heads. Regan backed his horse out of the line and headed over. Why did that picture look so good? What is it about horses, and the guys on them? No fancy silver, no shaved horses, no scarf. Just a cowboy, his horse and a rope. Cute. Regan was trotting, and assumed the roper position, half standing in his stirrups. Cal was grinning from ear to ear.

"Hey, Regan, what do you think about docs that make arena calls? Now that's service." Then to Leslie, "You gonna charge me extra, Doc?"

"Probably double." She looked at Regan. "These your horses?"

"Yeah. Leslie, meet Gomez and Cinco."

Both horses were of a grey variety, but very different. Leslie couldn't remember her horse colors. One was light grey with a reddish-black mane, tail and legs. The other was almost white, like Bullet. He was covered with little brown spots, like freckles. They were both pretty hairy. Muscled, heavy horses. Cold air vapor was coming out of all of their noses, including hers, Cal's and Regan's. It blew across their faces and out into the atmosphere where it trailed off and disappeared.

Regan got down and when his feet hit the ground she heard the jingle of spurs. They stuck out from under his heavily starched jeans. She remembered the night she had met him, when his starched jeans were all wet and bunched up around his boots. Not today. The starch made them fold and wrinkle fairly high up onto his calves. She looked up his legs to his waist, where he wore a tooled belt and one of those huge belt buckles. How long she was looking from his feet up to his waist she didn't know. It could only have been a second, but when she got to his face he was already looking at her with his mouth in that half grin. Mutual admiration society.

"I was wondering if you were going to make it."

"Well, I had a lot to do this morning and I just got done."

"I'm glad you're here."

"Have you ridden yet?"

"Once, but I'm on another team in the next set."

"How did you do?"

"Missed my throw."

"Sorry."

"No big deal. Come on over here and meet some of my buddies. I'm really glad you came. I thought after our talk yesterday, you might just blow it off."

They walked. Cal trotted off ahead of them. When he pulled up to the group of cowboys, they all looked over at him. He said something to them and they all turned around to look toward Regan and Leslie, then went back to talking. Some of them bent their heads down into their jackets to keep their faces out of the wind.

Regan walked slowly. Spurs clinked with each step. The horse seemed anxious and started trotting, lifting its legs up high. Like a high step. He looked like a small washed out Lipizzaner.

"Whoa, Gomez, come on." Regan gently pulled on the reins bringing Gomez' head down. The horse resumed the walk and with each step there was a hollow clopping sound on the asphalt. The wind was broken by the horse. The two sounds, spurs and shod hooves interrupting their comfortable silence.

As they approached the group she could hear their boisterous conversation. Regan introduced her. There were polite, "ma'ams" and "pleased to meet yous." Hats being tipped. She recognized a few from Cal's hospital room, and there were smiles and words of recognition. Conversation quieted while she was there and she felt somewhat out of place. Hell, she was out of place. What did she expect?

She looked at Regan, and he was looking at her, smiling. Proudly? She smiled back.

He said, "Let's go. I'll show you where you can sit to see things the best. In a little while they'll call my number and I'll have to ride down to the other end of the arena." He took her arm just as the wind caught his hat and almost whipped it off. He caught it and pressed it down, then bent his head to the wind. He put his arm around her and pulled her close, shielding her from the wind with his hat. Gomez was behind him, and pushed with his head, making Regan stumble toward Leslie. Her head bumped into his, but not before hitting the edge of his tipped hat and flipping it up. They started laughing and Regan put his hand in the middle of Gomez' flat forehead, pushing him away.

At that moment there was an announcement over the loudspeaker. "That's me," Regan said. "Gotta go. You know where we sat the other night?" She nodded. "Well, go down a little further. For roping you need to be at the other end. Not in the middle. If I get down that far, I'm not doing any good anyway. Wish me luck."

"Well then, good luck." She did a little bow as she said it and turned to go toward the bleachers. She then turned back around, hoping to watch him walking off, but he was still watching her. He climbed up on Gomez and trotted off. The other guys joined him and as soon as they reached the inside of the gate they took off galloping and twirling their ropes in the air. Leslie found her way to the far end of the arena, close to the area where all the calves were held in working pens.

The announcer called two numbers over the loudspeaker. Two riders came quickly over, swinging their ropes. They went into small piped in areas on the sides of the chute. They were open to the arena. They backed their horses into the corners, paused and got ready. The horses were excited with anticipation, their muscles quivering, their legs all moving simultaneously, trotting in place, while they held position, rumps pressed against the pipe. Twin pipes of steam shot out from their nostrils into the frigid air. Their ears, pinned back for the most part, alternately tweaked forward and backward, ready for action. The rider on Leslie's side of the chute nodded his head and the gate sprung open loudly, releasing a smallish horned calf with a leather cap-like object around his head and horns.

The two riders took off at almost the same instant, the one on the left leaning forward, twirling his rope aggressively. Within seconds he threw his rope and it found its way around the calf's horns. The cowboy began to wrap the end of the rope around the saddle horn and when the calf came to the hard end of the rope, the horse pulled to the left, abruptly swinging the calf around. The second rider roped the back legs of the calf, dallied the rope and jerked his hand up in the air, as if the rope was hot. Done. The buzzer went off and everyone cheered. The time clock above the arena read 5.6.

The announcer called it, along with the qualifier, "and this is our new leader, with a combined time of twelve point three," to more cheers from the crowd.

Two more teams went, and then she heard Regan's number called. Her heart began to beat rapidly. Regan began the ritual of twirling his rope like the others. He looked for her and nodded when he caught her eye. Then went around to the pen and backed in. Gomez was prancing in place and wouldn't stand still. Regan spurred him forward, away from the thick pipe, reined him around in a circle, and then backed up again. He looked over his shoulder until he saw Gomez' rump touch the pipe. His partner was already in position when Regan nodded and the chute clanged open.

A brown calf lunged out, tail in the air, head down. Regan charged after it, rope circling over his head, standing in his stirrups. His rope was in the air within moments, and it caught the calf. Regan dallied and swung to his left, allowing his partner to catch both legs with the rope. The calf plunged to the ground as Gomez continued pulling, feet backing up continuously. Leslie looked up at the clock. 5.6 seconds! The crowd cheered as they were announced as the new leaders with a combined score of 11.7.

The remaining teams finished and no one had bettered the 11.7 score. When it was over Leslie went to meet Regan. He quickly dismounted and before she could congratulate him, he hugged her. She couldn't help but hug back. He kept his arm around her while some of his competitors came over and shook his hand.

"See, you're good luck. I knew it. Now you're just going to have to come with me every time. Just quit your day job and go with me to all my ropings."

"Sure, no problem," she said with a laugh. "So, did you win the buckle?"

"Yeah."

"Way to go!"

"I'm going to go load these guys up in the trailer. Then we'll go pick it up at the show office."

The trailer was just like new. Shiny white and bright silver aluminum. She thought of the night they had met. What an amazing turn of events.

He unsaddled the horses. She felt like she ought to help but remembered that if you're not familiar with how to saddle and unsaddle, it's better to just stay out of the way. People who ride have their own system of organizing their gear. Regan went about his business efficiently. He didn't act as if he needed or expected any help whatsoever.

The horses were loaded into the trailer. Loading horses was something that always made her nervous when she was young. Horses can be flighty in a trailer, and she thought about one of her dad's friends who had been trampled when a horse spooked while loading up.

Gomez walked up to the edge of the trailer door, peered in and put one foot up on the ledge. The other three legs quickly followed. Cinco, on the other hand, looked like he was having none of it. He stopped in the doorway, looked in, and despite the fact that Gomez was already in he would not move. He just sniffed at the pine shavings on the ground and then tried to back up.

"You just have to be patient with Cinco. He probably had some bad loading experience before I got him. We'll just work on this very slowly." Regan stepped into the trailer, firmly pulled on the lead rope and clucked to Cinco. The horse started to move his front legs and after about two minutes, slightly reared up on his hind legs then lightly came down on the ledge with both hooves. He stayed like that for a few seconds and then hopped up. After giving Cinco a loud pat on his thick neck, Regan tied him up in his slanted stall.

Just as the gates closed, both horses raised their tails and relieved themselves. Leslie and Regan looked at each other and shook their heads. One of the most dangerous and difficult parts of transporting horses almost always ends with this ignoble act.

"Let's go get your buckle."

The presentation of the buckle was unceremonious. The first place buckle was just handed to him by an indifferent woman behind a counter. Cash prizes would be mailed to him. Leslie was impressed by the buckle's beauty. It was squoval, a term she used to use to describe the way she liked to file her fingernails, squared off but with rounded corners. It was mostly silver, but also had copper and gold colored metal as well. There were tiny flowers around the perimeter and across the top were the words, Palo Blanco Ranch Winter Circuit, then below, Roping Circuit Champion. There was a lot of scrollwork in the lettering so it was hard to read. In the middle was a carved picture of two cowboys roping a calf. For such a masculine sport, and one where clearly the majority of riders were guys, the highly sought-after buckle had a distinctly feminine appeal.

"I want you to have this buckle," Regan said. "You brought me the good luck."

"Regan, I couldn't possibly take this. You earned it."

"I have a million of them. I want you to remember me when you look at it. As a matter of fact, let's go get a belt for it." And with that

Regan led the way to an area where there were vendors selling anything from candlesticks and cards with cowboy themes, to reins, bits, boots and of course, belts. He looked around until he found a black tooled belt with tiny acorns and leaves.

"Let's try this one." He guessed at a couple of different sizes and once finding the right one, attached the buckle and placed the belt around Leslie's waist. "Perfect."

He paid the vendor and they headed for the trailer.

Leslie felt strange in the buckle, but it was pretty, and she felt some sense of pride and...belonging...wearing it. She realized that it was the first real gift she had been given since the accident three years ago. She hadn't received a single thing, not for her birthday, not for Christmas. Had she even thought of her birthday since then? The Christmas holiday was agonizing because patients would be trying to get out of the hospital on Christmas Eve so they could be home with their families. The hospital cafeteria would serve Christmas dinner. Chubby men in cheap Santa costumes would come to visit the children left in the house. Leslie would go to her hotel room and rent movies.

Other than her two little silver boxes, she had no sentimental possessions. Until now.

"Hey, hey, sweetheart, what's going through that head of yours?"

"I don't know, just thinking I guess."

He put his arms around her and held her to him. Put his face in her hair. "Uh huh. Well quit it. This has nothing to do with anything, just you brought me good luck. That's all."

"Regan." She tried to step back a little but he held her tight. "What?"

"What about our talk yesterday, you know about us?"

"What about us?"

"You know. Our agreement. To keep it friendly."

"Baby, that's where you made your mistake. We didn't shake on it. You know. We didn't even agree to agree. And if we did, then I'm afraid I've gotta take it back because I've really got nothing to lose here."

He leaned down and gently kissed her. He placed both hands around her face. He kissed her lips again, then her eyelids, one by one. When he returned to her mouth she returned the kiss, hard. He tilted his head sideways to take full advantage of her willingness to kiss him.

The hat was in the way and he removed it, pressed his hand with the hat in it to her back and held her tight. Then they stood there, holding each other. Regan slowly rocked from one leg to the other as he held her and Leslie relaxed against him.

"Regan...Oh, hey, sorry. Uh..."

Regan turned around to find his roping partner staring at them. "Hey, don't worry about it. What's going on?"

"A bunch of us were going over to Allen's, have a beer, celebrate. Winner buys. You game?"

"Y'all go on and I'll catch up with you in a little while."

"Sure, see ya over there." He looked over at Leslie. "Doc, you're welcome to join us. Regan's buying."

She smiled. "I've actually got some work to do tonight so I may need to take a rain check on that."

"Suit yourself. Regan?"

"Be there in a minute."

"You really have to go?" Regan asked after his partner left.

"I haven't seen Doc since he got back and I was planning on dropping by there tonight."

"Listen, Leslie, the timing on this deal is a little unfortunate, but I'm leaving in the morning to go out of town for the week."

"Really."

She didn't know whether she was disappointed or relieved, but she thought at least sixty percent disappointment. "Where are you going?" Trying not to sound disappointed.

"Down to Beaumont to check on the shipping of the light banks we've ordered. Then to Illinois to finalize the details on our bleachers and stadium seating. I won't be back until late Friday night."

"Wow. Well. I guess I'm surprised to hear it."

"Bad timing. But it's good for the project. We're ahead of schedule so this trip got moved up."

"Well, that's good for you Regan."

"Yeah, I guess so. But look, I'm going to call you every night to make sure you're not starting to think on your terms again. Okay? Leave your cell phone on?"

"It's always on."

21

*L*eslie was expected and Brenda had sandwich fixings for the three of them. From her surgical internship days she was trying to remember how long it was before colostomies could start eating regular food. How long before Doc could start eating King Ranch Chicken?

Doc looked good and they were both glad to see her. The same went for Leslie. Damn, she thought to herself, more memories and sentiment.

Doc was more quiet than usual. Probably listening for his colostomy. She recalled that some patients did become quite attached to their colostomies and much more aware of the intestinal percolations than those of the original equipment.

"You know, somehow, it's not very glamorous having sick bed visitors for a dang colostomy. I mean, what are we gonna talk about? How's my shit lookin' from here?" Leslie laughed out loud but quickly stifled it when Brenda scolded him for talking like that in front her.

Doc nibbled on a ham and cheese sandwich while Brenda and Leslie ate some spicier varieties. Nothing like a good old fashioned sandwich. They talked about her week and she told them about the train accident. Of course Doc had his own train stories to tell. Even Brenda couldn't resist the appeal of a good train wreck story.

Leslie thought about trains a lot. There was something about them. She had worked on an H scale train set for the kids to which she added cars every Christmas. Once they had moved into the big house there were enough rooms so they could leave the train set assembled year round in one of them. They had villages, hills, bridges, even two train tracks crossing each other. She had become a regular at the local hobby shop, collecting for the kids, or was it for herself?

She had vowed at one time to start collecting the German LGB trains. That was about as close to the real thing as she could get. LGB had begun manufacturing American style trains. They made some modern American diesel engines like Santa Fe, and her favorite, Union Pacific. Computerized sound chips she could mount on the tracks mimicked the sound of the diesel engines and the air horns.

The trains represented some of the greatness of the United States to her. The meeting of east and west, the expansion of the 1800s. Leslie loved the sound of the engines. Sometimes in her various hotel rooms she could hear their whistles blasting across the landscape. It could be 1901 or it could be tonight. She wished she could be an engineer for a day. Bring a 19,000 ton coal train going 9-0 to a dead stop. See another train coming at her on the adjacent track, a headlight meet. Run out over a gorge on an open bridge. See the light at the end of a tunnel. These were things she would never see. Do train engineers want to see the inside of a knee?

Brenda and Doc were pleased with the way she had been running things and apparently the staff had nothing but good things to say about her bedside manner. They also had something to say about Regan.

"By golly, who'd a thunk it." Doc was looking down at his lap and shaking his head.

There was something about that scene that was funny. Both Leslie and Brenda started laughing. That was the end of it. No questions asked.

Brenda had rented a movie and they asked if she wanted to stay. She did, so they watched *The Wind and the Lion*. Candace Bergen and Sean Connery never kissed once in that movie, yet Leslie thought it was one of the most romantic movies she had ever seen. She suddenly remembered kissing Regan, and her heart started beating fast for an instant.

After the movie, Leslie reminded Doc that she felt she had everything under control and he shouldn't worry about coming to the office too soon. Actually looking forward to having him around, Leslie had to remind herself that she was there to give him time to recover.

The weekend's cloud cover dissipated by the time the sun went down and now, at ten thirty, the sky was clear, the waning moon was a sliver less than full, and bright. Stars flickered across the sky. As she drove across an overpass she could see the moonlight reflecting off light colored structures. From here she could appreciate the flatness and openness of the plains. She could see other highways. Headlights shot across the landscape like flying saucers. Giant concrete silos were lined up like stalwart soldiers in vacant fields. Somewhere out there in the blackness, the draws brought water down from the Llano Estacado on its way to the Brazos River.

There was strange beauty in this land.

22

*O*n the way to the office Monday morning, Leslie thought about Regan's flights to Houston and Chicago. She tried to picture him in an airport. Somehow it just didn't fit. Did he wear his boots and jeans? A suit? Did he rent a truck? Or a Taurus. Would he call her tonight and every night like he said he would? Leslie hadn't thought about these kind of trivialities for almost twenty years. She felt silly and yet the thought of them was irresistible.

Brenda was at the office as if she had never left. Patients were asking about Doc and many had brought get well cards and more offerings. Both the morning and afternoon clinics were almost booked, fifteen in the morning and sixteen in the afternoon. Brenda advised her that there might also be work-ins. Over the lunch break she dictated and filled out forms. She squeezed in some journal reading for continuing medical education. Wednesday she would do the questionnaire and submit her answers so she could get her credit hours. Someone brought in lunch, sandwiches from a local deli. She was thinking about JJ's when they called her to come see her first afternoon patient.

This patient had carpal tunnel syndrome. He was complaining of numbness in both hands, especially at night. Doc had given him some splints to wear at night and they helped a little, but didn't get rid of the numbness he experienced during the day when he typed on a computer. Some nerve tests had shown that the median nerve was compressed at the wrist. The patient was frustrated with his pain and numbness. He wanted to go ahead and have surgery. He had already been talking to Doc about it. Leslie felt it would be okay for him to go ahead and schedule surgery when Doc got back but the patient wanted to do it as soon as possible, right hand first. She felt somewhat guilty scheduling the kind of case that could certainly wait for Doc, but the patient insisted. She scheduled him for Friday morning, knowing she could at least see him back for his first post-op appointment to remove his sutures. Doc would get to do his left hand. She had already seen a couple of Doc's carpal tunnel releases return to the office for follow-up and knew that she and Doc made basically the same type of incision in the palm.

That afternoon, as expected, a couple of additional walk-in patients arrived. One of them was Regan and Cal's friend, Steven Ware. She remembered this one from the horse show. He was a welder, and had dropped an acetylene tank on his foot, breaking a toe. The injury itself wasn't too bad, but the foot was very swollen. He was insisting on returning to work and needed a release. She advised him to get a larger steel toed boot to protect the toe and accommodate the swelling.

"Doc, are you gonna be out at Regan's this weekend?"

Leslie gave him a questioning look.

"Maybe I spoke out of turn. You know, Regan has his annual pig roast. It's kind of a tradition with all his friends and family. You know, just an outdoor barbecue. I'm sure he'll get you out there. If he doesn't, it will probably be the last time I ever get invited."

Leslie laughed. "Listen, keep this foot elevated as much as you can. It's going to stay swollen for months. Actually, it will probably be bigger than the other side forever. That's just the way toes and fingers heal. They always get a little big. It's just the scar tissue."

"Well, that's good to know, Doc."

"I probably don't need to see you again, unless you have problems with it." She went over all of his instructions and gave him his release to go back to work. He didn't want any pain pills.

"See you this weekend, Doc."

"Sure."

After clinic was finished, she and Brenda sat down to chat over a cup of coffee. Brenda told her that Doc was thinking about coming up to the office for half a day on Wednesday. Brenda didn't like the idea, but she thought she wouldn't be able to keep him from it. Doc felt the need to start getting acclimated.

Leslie assured Brenda that she didn't think there would be a problem with a few hours Wednesday, Thursday, and Friday if he wanted. It would probably be good for him to move around a little anyway. Brenda seemed relieved to have her opinion on this matter and Leslie was relieved to know there would be nothing to keep her from the assignment in Evansville if Doc could start getting back into his routine.

They talked about Leslie's plans to go to Indiana right after she completed her agreed upon commitment to Doc Hawley. Leslie asked if that was going to work out for them.

"Of course it will, dear. It's just that, I guess we've just grown attached to you is all. It would be nice to think of you around here in a way. Well, here I go, just making plans for Doc to have a new partner or something. Imagine that, Doc with a lady partner from New York! Seriously, Leslie, I was just enjoying having you around. Wish you didn't have to leave. But you've got your work ahead of you."

"I do. But Doc'll be just fine. It's not like I'm leaving tomorrow or anything. We'll get him used to being up here, and if he doesn't have any complications from surgery or chemo, everything will be just fine."

"Oh, I know it. There's just no holding him back."

"I do think you'll need to keep his schedule light early on, though."

"The girls will take care of that." She hesitated and then looked up at Leslie with a naughty smile on her face. "So. Let's just you and me talk about Mister Regan Wakeman. Now, tell me the truth, Leslie. Are you going out with him?" She didn't give Leslie and chance to answer. "You're just going to have to think of me as your surrogate mother, since she can't be here herself to keep you out of trouble."

"Brenda, you're too much. I don't know what people around here have been telling you but, like, we went to lunch once and then out on one date if you want to know the truth. I can't be starting something serious with a guy here. I'm leaving in a couple of weeks."

"Hmm. Well, I guess I was just hoping there was something besides this brown dirt and mesquite to hold you here in Abilene. And to get you thinking about something besides the past."

"That would be a tall order to fill." One of her dad's phrases. It certainly wasn't one of hers, and she couldn't recall ever having said it before. She could remember her dad saying it though. Out on their front porch, when she was a kid. He'd been working outside. Sweat running down his face. He had on a V-necked T-shirt. Old, worn out.

Was he wearing old beat up khaki's? He pulled out a handkerchief from his pocket and wiped his face. He always had a handkerchief. Mom ironed a clean one for him every day. "Now that would be a tall order to fill," he said while wiping his face. What had she said? Why did the memory stop there?

Dad, I wanna go to college, make straight As, get into medical school and become an orthopedic surgeon.

Dad, I wanna learn to drive, always obey the two second rule and never run into the back of any car.

Brenda was saying something about having some fun while she was here. Leslie nodded and figured she would probably end up doing just that.

23

*T*hat afternoon Leslie went to run, making three miles at a pretty good pace. The wind was blowing hard the whole time and she felt exhausted afterward. Her face felt gritty from blowing dirt. She was getting a natural skin peel. She walked for another mile after that. Her mind was full of Regan. Somehow they had connected. It was strange to have happened that way. What did the accident have to do with it? Would he have asked her to lunch if they hadn't had the accident? She thought not. She tried not to think about where this could all lead. She tried not to think about Chris and the kids, or the boxes. She reached up and touched the two rings hanging from their chain under her sweat shirt.

She got in her car and drove, not to the hotel, but the opposite direction. She spotted the press box first. It was still open and now there was scaffolding for the elevators. The pylons for the stadium lights were up. What massive structure could be depended on to hold up lights like that? Top heavy, they would create a tremendous lever arm. She would love to be around to see them when they went on for the first time.

There was a new sign in front. Someone making claim to the stadium. Big block letters. FUTURE HOME OF THE CHISHOLM TRAIL WRANGLERS. She thought, Go Wranglers.

A lot had been accomplished in a week. Some metallic structures had been added to the stadium. They would probably anchor the home and visitor seating to the Aztec temple. Dirt had been moved around the perimeter making things appear tidy. Additional parking lot areas were now covered with asphalt. Blue metal roofs had been added to the snack bars and athletic facilities. She felt proud of Regan.

She looked up at the press boxes. There was more structure to it. She would never see it finished. That was so simple. She would not see it finished. Maybe she would look it up on a website someday. Anson

Jones Stadium. Chisholm Trail High School.

She stepped out of her car. Everything was silent except for the wind, and the clanking of a piece of metal somewhere. She looked all around the stadium. Couldn't tell where it was coming from. It would eventually find its place, along with the seating and the lights.

Beyond the parking lots there was just brown dirt and mesquite. Her heart was full, of the good and the bad. Regan versus her memories. Her thoughts were interrupted by a deep rumbling and she looked in its direction. A jet airplane was taking off from the airport across town. As it rose it looked as if it was going away from her, but shortly it began to bank and she knew its direction. The broad silver belly began to disappear as its wing bent deep and it came around the stadium, not over it. Darkish clouds of jet exhaust, barely visible in the dusk, streamed from its engines. Moving in slow motion, it pushed against the earth to rise and head...where? Where she was going.

Raghu was checking people in when she arrived at the hotel. He greeted her and reminded her of the fresh coffee. She took a cup of decaf and said goodnight.

"The usual wakeup call, Doctor?" This felt uncomfortable. Her privacy. The other clients turned to look at the person who woke up at the same time every day and was staying here long enough to have the hotel clerk know the time by heart. Oh well. She couldn't blame Raghu. He was just trying to be helpful. She wouldn't have to call him later to remind him of the wakeup call. That was service.

"Yes Raghu. Thanks."

While drying off after her shower, her cell phone rang. She fastened the towel around herself and, soaking wet, jumped across the king-sized bed and grabbed the phone.

"Hey."

"Hey." They were on a no-need-for-introduction basis now. She would not expect anyone else to casually greet her and he would count on her to recognize his voice. They got past the "what are you doings?" and the "nothings." It struck her as funny, that no matter what their age and the significance of their work, they were still doing "nothing" until they relaxed and got into the long distance phone call.

She told him about her day at work. Seeing patients, scheduling surgery. Told him about her patients from the train accident. The train accident fascinated him like it did everyone. The coupling mechanism, the amputation, mechanically how that could happen. The work she had to do on them. They talked about it for a long time.

Regan was in Beaumont inspecting his lights before they were shipped. They would be shipped to Abilene first thing in the morning on three eighteen-wheelers. Two light banks on each. Wide loads. It was hard to imagine a set of lights that would hang over the sides of a flat bed. It would take all day for the trucks to get to the stadium. The next morning Cal would supervise the unloading. The lights would be connected to the steel poles on the ground. The entire assembly would then be raised into place with cranes and the poles bolted to the pylons.

She told him she had seen the pylons. That she had gone out to the site. She didn't know why she did, because once it was out, she knew that he would know he had her.

"You were out there? Was anyone there?"

"No."

"You were just looking at the stadium."

"Uh, huh."

There was silence on the other end as he contemplated this unexpected turn. I've got you now. You know it and I know it. And if she didn't want him to know it, she probably wouldn't have told him.

The rest of the conversation was small talk, or no talk. She asked him what he wore to Beaumont, what kind of car he rented. "Jeans, boots. What else would I wear?" Someone from the plant picked him up at Hobby airport. They would take him back in the morning and he would be off to Illinois.

With a little silliness in his voice he said, "I've got a pair of khaki's, some kind of blue shirt, loafers and a mid-sized rental for the Illinois leg of the trip."

"Oh, thanks. I was just curious. I'd like to see you in khaki's."

"I bet you would you ol' Yankee."

"No, it's not that."

"Hey, I can take a hint. You just don't like cowboys." Acting hurt.

They teased back and forth for a while. The cell phone began to get hot against her cheek.

"Hey, before I forget, do you have any plans Saturday? You know, are you on call or anything?"

"I don't think so but let me check my social calendar." She said it sarcastically.

"Hey, I wouldn't just assume that you'd be sitting around waiting on me. Besides, you are on call sometimes."

"Well, seriously, I know that I'm not on ortho trauma call this Saturday. I'm only on for Doc's patients."

"Okay, I have this party, or barbecue thing going on Saturday evening, like starting around five. It's something I've had the third Saturday of this month for, I don't know, six or seven years."

"That sounds like fun."

"It's a lot of fun. We have a pig roast. I have to put this pig in a pit in the ground and it cooks all day. Almost as good as that barbecue sandwich from JJ's. Everybody brings stuff. Got music, friends, family, you know, just a good time. It's a tradition now."

"So, I guess you're inviting me."

"Right. I was thinking you could come out early, maybe help me get set up. You can cut up the pig." He was laughing.

"How far out do you live?"

"About fifteen miles or so. Why? Are there rules about how far from the hospital you can be?"

"Well, yes, if I'm on at the ER, then thirty minutes is the rule. In fact it's the law. Anyway, even if I were on call I could still go out there since it's not more than thirty minutes away."

"Good. That would be important to know." Did she read more into that than was there? "So we're on?"

"Sure. One of the local orthopods offered to cover for me sometime if I needed it. Maybe I'll get him to cover me for the whole evening. Then I wouldn't have to carry my pager. Doc may even be willing to take calls for me. He's getting anxious to get back to work anyway. Maybe this would be a good way to ease back in."

The reminder of the completion of her assignment in Abilene struck them both at the same time, dampening the mood. In a few minutes Regan teased that his phone was overheating. He would call her tomorrow night. She could call him too if she wanted.

They said goodbye, leaving the call on a slightly down note.

Leslie fondly remembered the phone calls she and Chris had once she realized she loved him and felt sure he loved her. She wouldn't, couldn't, say the "I love you" words first even though they were on the tip of her tongue. The easiest place to say them would most certainly be on the phone, the little washed out "luv you." It would be a slight cop out, but that would break the ice for the real thing. They waited for the real thing. Neither ever uttered the watered down version. They went to Cuernavaca, Mexico for a long weekend. Stayed at Las Mañanitas. She couldn't remember when it was. When did she have the time for a long weekend? After walking all over the city they had bags full of trinkets and souvenirs wrapped up in newspaper. Everything was piled on the floor under their table. They drank real margaritas. Room temperature. Fresh lime juice, tequila and Triple Sec. Their heads were swimming. Solid alcohol, which they hardly ever drank. He said it first, and she knew he would. She could see it in his eyes. And the look in her eyes gave him the courage to say it. She would have said it that afternoon even if he didn't. So much angst and energy in three little words. "I love you." He was the first and only person she had ever loved. That way. Once they said it, then it was easy. And "luv you" no longer seemed watered down. It was just an abbreviated form. Like "y'all." Two syllables rather than three.

24

*T*uesday. Surgery all day. Briggs took Jesús Camacho back to the OR to clean up his wounds and start the process of grafting the huge skin defect. More skin around the edges of the wound had died so there was an even larger area to be grafted. An island of skin remained on the front of the knee overlying the kneecap. Briggs was able to get plenty of graft material from Jesús' thighs. By scoring it diagonally he could stretch it to cover more area. Fortunately there was no bone exposed. He applied the compression bolsters, dressings and splints. Leslie assisted him so they could cut down the operative time. Once the grafts were stable she could get in there to examine the joint and reconstruct the two ligaments.

She had a couple of other cases to do. Patients she had seen in the office. There was a bad ankle fracture and a patient with a meniscus tear. Leslie operated on both of these patients after helping Briggs. Finished by noon, she went up to the floor to round.

Emilio was better. He was accepting the phantom pain and moving his elbow very well. In Spanish Leslie complimented his progress. The social workers had already been up to talk to him about funding and a charity organization in town had volunteered to help get a prosthesis. Leslie felt a combination of pride and relief. She would have hated sending him home without one. The therapists could start wrapping the stump to get the swelling down. Once that was accomplished they could fit him with his arm. Then Emilio would have to learn how to use it.

She went back to the office. Brenda and Doc were in, despite there being no patients to see. Just visiting. Doc had lost weight. He looked good though and she was sure she'd see him up at the office on Wednesday. She decided that now would be as good a time as any to talk to him about Saturday. They were sitting in the break room.

"Doc, I got a favor to ask you and please feel free to say no if you don't feel up to it."

"What can I do for ya?"

"Saturday night..."

"I'll be damned if you don't have a date." He yelled to Brenda. "Hey, mom, get in here. Doc's bailin' out on me for another guy."

"Wait a minute, Doc. That's not a fair statement."

Brenda walked in, arms on her hips. "What's going on now?"

"I was just getting ready to ask Doc if he could maybe cover phone calls for me on Saturday for a little while. I've been invited to a picnic."

"Picnic my ass. You're going on a date."

"Hal, shush. Leslie, where're you going?"

"Well, if you want to know the truth again..."

"Of course we do dear. Where you're going, what time you'll be home and a phone number where you can be reached."

"Okay, mom and dad. I'm going to a barbecue Regan has out at his place every year."

"Sounds like fun. Of course Hal will cover you."

"You go have some fun, girl. And just so you could have a beer or two if you want, I'll cover you through Sunday. How's that sound?"

"What if patients show up in the ER and ask for you?"

"If they need to be admitted, I'll do it over the phone and you can see them on Sunday morning. If they need surgery right away, we can get one of the other guys to do it. They're on call anyway. You might give whichever one of them is on call Saturday a heads up. You've been on call every day twenty-four-seven for the past two and a half weeks. You can use the break."

"Thanks Doc. I'll owe you one."

"Sure thing." He rolled his eyes.

Leslie finished a couple of things around the office then checked the internet to see what kind of weather they were expecting in Abilene this weekend. Possibility of showers, but warmer temperatures.

She thought about getting something new to wear. Besides her work clothes, the only things she had to wear were the jeans, turtle neck and boots from the other night and this probably wouldn't work if it was warm. She stopped at the boutique where she purchased her jeans and found a flowered tank top and a blue jean skirt. They had a vintage sweater that could go with the tank. Just in case it got cool in the evening. Dillard's had plenty of adorable sandals to pick from.

Regan called at about eight-thirty. She told him about getting Doc to cover for her. Told him she had bought something to wear. He told her about the stadium seating. Shipping out Thursday by truck. They would be in Abilene by early next week. The seats were blue. Chisholm Trail Wrangler colors were red and blue. She remembered the blue metal roofs on the snack bar and athletic facilities. The blue accents complimented the white flagstone trim around the stadium and buildings.

The last big item to be shipped was the Sony Jumbotron. That was supposed to be completed and ready to ship in May. She couldn't believe a high school stadium would have one.

"You have no idea. This is a twenty by twenty-five foot screen supported and surrounded by a seventy foot structure that includes an LED scoreboard and advertisements for sponsors. The ads will cover the cost of the whole board. It's state-of-the-art for any stadium worth its salt nowadays. Still to us old timers it's amazing for a high school. It's even got its own elevator."

"What else?"

"Are you sure this stuff isn't boring you? You're just asking to be nice because we talked about your gory train wreck last night."

"Of course it's not boring me. Are you putting in grass or Astroturf?"

"Well, we don't really call it Astroturf anymore. There's a couple of companies that make the newest state-of-the-art artificial turf. Sprinturf and Fieldturf. It's a lot more like real grass than the old stuff. Theoretically there are fewer injuries with it. It even looks like grass. The blades are individual and there's sand or rubber grains down inside of it so it behaves more like dirt. High schools prefer artificial turf because there's a lot more activity on a high school field than on, say, a college or pro field. You know, you've got freshmen, JV and varsity all playing on separate nights. You've usually got track events on another night. Then there's band practice. All that activity makes it hard to keep a grass field in shape. So they want artificial turf."

"Things have changed in high school football since I was there. I don't even remember if we had lights. When is it going to be done?"

"It's scheduled for completion in early August. I want to have it all ready for final inspection by mid-July." She liked the fact that he wanted to beat the deadline.

They chatted a little more about the stadium. Then about nothing, and everything. They said goodnight and that they missed each other. "Miss you" and "miss you too."

After the call she couldn't sleep so she went down to the workout room. CNN was on the television suspended from the wall and she stared at it absently while walking on the treadmill. Headline stories included political races, health issues, securities fraud and abuse, and the war in Iraq. She rarely watched the news. It was depressing. And not much affected her now. She was just moving through the world on a course unaffected by what might happen in education or a senatorial race or the stock market. She had no dependents. The issues in education, like standardized testing for students and teachers, didn't matter to her. These kinds of things used to consume her and she would carefully research the candidates in local school board races, finally giving time, money and her vote to the ones she felt represented her interests.

The politics of medicine didn't faze her anymore. She and Chris used to agonize over the factions chewing off bits and pieces of their income earning potential. They were involved in the activities of the local medical society. They had the future of their children and their retirement to worry about. Now she was flying solo. No dependents. No college tuitions to worry about.

Her money was tied up in various funds but she didn't worry about what was going on with them. Even if the stock market completely crashed and she lost every cent, she could set fractures for food. She could do some kind of volunteer work. There would always be a roof over her head. It just didn't matter. There was no need to watch the news.

But here was CNN. It's easier to walk on a treadmill while listening to the news. After about forty-five minutes it seemed that the prevalent message was that people were dying all over the world. If it wasn't from disease, it was from a bullet. If not from a war, then a holdup. People were dying. And she wondered how similar her situation was to theirs. How many out there had lost more than one at a time? People in places like Iraq, places where there is war, or places where the death rates are high, don't think about life the way Americans do.

Even recalling the difference between infant mortality in Africa compared to the United States or Japan for that matter, where infant mortality is the lowest in the world, she wondered if the perspective or the expectation for survival was different than hers. Because her children were expected to survive. Her husband was expected to join her in retirement. As she watched pictures of shopping centers blown up by car bombs she knew this was a self-centered way of thinking. Whole families would, of course, be blown away. An American soldier standing outside would come home in a flag-bearing casket. But the expectation that an American soldier would return from war was probably greater than the expectation that an Iraqi would ever return home from shopping. And people's lives would change forever, the same as hers had.

She grabbed the remote and switched to the food channel where some guy was basting a chicken on a rotisserie. Her mind jumped quickly to the roasted pig and then to Saturday.

25

*T*he next day she ran into Terryl at the hospital. He reminded her that she had a few charts to sign in Medical Records and offered to show her where it was. They talked about her plans while walking down the hall and Leslie advised him of her commitment in Indiana. Terryl told her they had really enjoyed having her around, and he knew Doc appreciated her work.

He introduced her to the people in Medical Records. After a secretary brought out her stack of charts she sat down in a cubicle to complete them. It had taken Leslie about a year and a half to get used to referring to Medical Records as Health Information Management. Every time she called the hospital operator asking to be connected to Medical Records they would reply, "I'll be happy to connect you to Health Information Management." The older operators knew that the two were one and the same. Sometimes operators with youthful sounding voices would hesitate, not even recognizing Medical Records as an office.

She remembered when she finally said the words, "Health Information Management," without thinking Medical Records. Like when she finally spoke Spanish without thinking first in English and then translating. The operator had hesitated and then said, "I'll be happy to connect you to Medical Records."

Medical Records. To Leslie the medical record was the physical embodiment of the problems with medicine. The cost of maintaining the detailed medical record. The impossibility of creating the perfect medical record. The administrative push for it and the manpower behind that push was mind-boggling. The medical record was the intellectual and physical report card of each patient's body and, usually, illness. She couldn't think of any medical record that would not represent an illness. In some woman's mind, even small breasts or wrinkles under the eyes would be considered an illness. It was somewhat useful for rounding purposes, somewhat useful for review, almost never useful for extensive analysis except by lawyers and federal agents. It was like the picture of Dorian Grey. The papers were all neat and categorized. Each admission resulted in a swarm of secretaries, clerks and administrators descending on it to check for mistakes, look for deficiencies and evaluate the care of the patient. When everything was said and done, the record appeared neat and was suitable for billing purposes. Underneath, the real picture was pock marked and scarified, silently filed in numerical order, waiting someday to be pulled and the pox and scars transferred to the doctor.

Leslie worked diligently on her records. First of all, she wasn't that busy so she had plenty of time. Secondly, there were only a few charts. Her admission notes and her operative notes were read word for word. She reviewed all the lab work, not just those values that applied to her part of the care of that particular patient. Her notes were signed legibly, not the usual scribbled signature that perhaps only contained two of the eleven letters that comprised her name. An 'L' and half a 'C' that looked more like another small 'L.' She printed neatly on the demographics sheets used by the billing office for completing the billing statements. She wouldn't be back to make any corrections. It would be hard to find her for questions. Now these records might be close to perfect.

After rounding on Jesús and Emilio she went to the office. Patients were scheduled to come in at nine o'clock. Doc usually started at eight, but she wasn't scheduled that heavily, so nine worked out fine. She got there around eight forty-five and Doc had already seen the first scheduled patient. He looked proud of himself and she felt like a mom must feel when her kid finishes his first week away at college. He's ready and everything's going to be okay. It would be hard to leave Abilene if Doc wasn't ready. She had mixed emotions, probably just like that mom would. She would soon be unnecessary. And, of course, that was the plan.

Leslie scheduled a couple of cases, people who wanted surgery just before spring break so they could take advantage of the holiday to recover. There was a woman who had a wrist fracture pinned several years ago and the pin was starting to back out causing a painful red spot over the tip of it. That needed to come out before it wore a hole through the skin. She put that case on for Friday, to follow the carpal tunnel release. She and Doc planned to schedule some cases together during her last week. She would assist Doc and then he would be following the patients. Just the opposite of the way they started.

Again, at the end of clinic they sat down and talked about the day and the plans. Doc would have to have chemotherapy. 5-FU. Not too toxic. He should be able to keep working. Might not lose his hair. Having it on Friday would give him a chance to rest over the weekend. He had already arranged with the other guys in town not to take any ER call on weekends.

In fact, he was thinking about not taking anymore ER call, period. The other orthopedic surgeons in town were not overworked in the ER and would likely be willing for him to get off the schedule. The hospital by-laws allowed him to stop ER call once he had been practicing there for fifteen years. He had already exceeded this. Leslie had done *locum tenens* work in some communities where there were not enough orthopods to cover weekend calls. So many surgeons were dropping off the schedules because of the high risk cases that came in through the ER and also because some of the hospitals were just frankly difficult to work in. Those hospitals had to change their by-laws to require that any doctor who practiced in the hospital had to take ER call in order to continue to work there. It didn't matter how many years they had already volunteered. It was now a requirement. But even with those changes, some hospitals still had to hire orthopedic surgeons or pay doctors to cover the ER. Sometimes that still wasn't enough and they had to pay top dollar to get people like Leslie to come work for them. In the worse case scenario, when there was no orthopedic coverage, and this was becoming more and more commonplace, they would have to divert patients with broken bones to other hospitals that had coverage. There was a serious problem developing and the public wasn't aware of it.

In her opinion, it really did come down to the doctor's desire to work in certain hospitals. Instead of seeing the forest for the trees, and making the hospital just a little more physician friendly, the hospital paid money to get other docs to work there. Eventually, the hired hands would see the same problems and move on. Back to square one. Maybe the message was that the hospital just couldn't change. Too many restrictions, too many expenses. Easier and maybe cheaper to pay some hired gun a half a million dollars than to make a few philosophical changes. Of course, hospitals had their hands tied, to a certain extent, by the government. Medicare and Medicaid.

At this time and in this place, it probably wouldn't matter. Doc had done his time, and now he was ready to slow down a little. He could still see his own patients when they requested him. It was an enviable position for any physician of any currently practicing generation. Reach the point where the practice is stable and a physician can stop seeing no-preference emergency room patients. It's also a somewhat sad time in a career. The doctor is on the path to retirement. In Doc's case, and probably with most physicians, a tremendous amount of energy had been put into developing each individual relationship with each patient and each referring doc until the point at which referrals begin to increase exponentially. Reach the pinnacle, hang there for a while and then slide to retirement. Because so much time has been devoted to this endeavor, it is hard for many physicians to let go. She wondered if it was the same in other professions. She thought that medicine was different for many reasons, not the least of which was the thirteen years of education it took just to hang up the shingle.

Her situation was completely different by choice. She would not have to maintain long standing referral sources. When she became less useful or started having pain in her hands from arthritis, she could simply stop. There would be no retirement parties, no winding down the practice, no sending letters to referring docs and devoted patients. It would be easier for her than for her colleagues. As for Doc, he would go into retirement kicking and screaming. She admired him for his hard work.

Doc planned to come to clinic tomorrow and Friday. He might even come to the OR with her on Friday, if she didn't mind. Of course, she didn't. Her evening passed in the usual fashion. Jogging, working out. When she came out of the hotel gym, there was a delicious smell of curry coming from the kitchen. It was an odd smell in a Holiday Inn Express, because there was no restaurant. Walking down the hallway to the dining area she found Raghu and his family fixing dinner. It was the first time she had ever seen them all together.

"Ah, Doctor Cohen. You have met my family, have you not?"

"Yes, Raghu, I've met your wife and two of the children, but I don't think I've met your oldest."

"Yes, certainly. Remember this is my wife, Kala. My oldest daughter, Vijaya. The oldest son, Mohan, and the younger daughter, Usha."

"Pleased to meet you all. I'm Doctor Cohen." She used her formal name because she was certain that culturally this would be expected. She remembered the moms and dads of her children's friends introducing her as "Mrs." Or even by her first name. She was rarely introduced as "doctor" to acquaintances in their social circles. She didn't expect it. She knew that even if she introduced herself informally to Raghu's family, he would insist they refer to her as "doctor."

"Doctor Cohen, would you care to join us for dinner?" Kala asked. We have plenty of good homemade curry. Please sit." She indicated one of the tables with an extended hand. Leslie didn't want to refuse and frankly couldn't. She could detect excitement on the part of the children at the prospect of a guest and the curry smelled wonderful.

Dinner was served on paper plates. There was a yellowish rice dish, which had a lemony flavor, a chicken curry, and a very spicy vegetable dish of spinach, carrots and chickpeas, called "kora." There was bread that reminded her of the Italian bread, *foccacio*. It was dense and chewy. They offered and she took a second helping of rice and curry.

After dinner the kids asked her questions about being a doctor and they wanted to show her what they were doing in school. She slipped easily into the interested-adult mode as she had done with her own. Talking in a slightly higher tone of voice, slightly elevated, totally interested. While the older two were getting her attention, the youngest came over and leaned on her, touched her arm. She carried a small drawing in her hand which she placed on the table in front of Leslie, waiting until she looked at it. Usha had drawn a portrait of Leslie. There was yellow curly hair, black pants. There was no shirt but she didn't need one because up top she was only a stick figure. Leslie was touched. It had been a long time since a child had made one for her. Somewhere in a climate controlled storage unit in upstate New York there were curly headed stick figure drawings.

The grownups drank coffee, talked about India. Raghu and his family had come from Pondicherry, a moderately large city in southern India. There were educational opportunities in Abilene and they ended up staying. Leslie sipped her coffee, talking for quite a while, grateful for the company and the distraction. The children soon finished their homework and Kala started packing everything up. When they were ready to leave, the children all gave her a hug. How long since she had held a child. Her only contact with children was to push on a broken bone. They were soft, small shouldered, like her own.

By the time Regan called she had already showered and was in bed watching TV. She picked it up after the first ring. She was excited to hear his voice. They started out with the usual review of the day's activities. He was just about done with his business in Illinois.

Somehow they gravitated to the circumstances of their meeting. It is natural for lovers to have this kind of conversation, because the connection between two people is chance. They might never have met if not for the wreck. Would he have considered asking her out if it hadn't been for that? Would he have followed her out into the hallway? Would he have come to the hospital to pick up Cal? No, no and no. He was certain he would not have had the guts to ask out some orthopedic surgeon who had just nailed his buddy. They laughed at the double meaning.

And he would never have suggested to his friend's doctor that silly thing about going to lunch. Regan teased her about the "rule" and suggested she had been duped. Finally, he wouldn't have gone out of his way to come up to the hospital to pick up Cal. That was way out of his way and a total pain in the ass. He and Cal had contrived that one all the way, just on the chance that she would be there. He almost missed her coming into the parking lot. Jenn had thought it was disrespectful and assuming.

"I told them I wasn't assuming anything. You were going to lunch with me."

"Regan, that was awfully presumptuous."

"Not really, I just felt something when we saw each other in Cal's room and when Jenn and Cal told me you were a widow, I knew it was there. Leslie, I had to do something. I knew you wouldn't, because of your husband. I knew you wouldn't do it. So you tell me. When did you know it?"

"I guess in the elevator the first time..."

"Right, when we hit the button at the same time. I was like, if this gal is married, then it's not right."

"Would you have asked me out if you knew I was married?"

"No, I wouldn't bring that kind of trouble on myself." There was uncomfortable silence at both ends for a moment. The chance meeting and their awkward touch on the elevator making the difference between goodbye and a lunch date.

"So, when are you getting in on Friday?"

"It'll be really late. There just aren't that many flights going in and out of Abilene. I think we'll just have to wait to see each other on Saturday. Why don't I plan to pick you up around one or two o'clock. That way, you can be there when everyone else starts to arrive. I can show you around the place. It's old. Been in my family for ages. There's some interesting stuff out there and the house is registered. But to tell you the truth, I want to see you before I have to start paying attention to my guests."

"Me too."

26

Speaking in Spanish, Leslie told Jesús about his surgery next week. Her plan was to reconstruct his two torn ligaments using tendons from a person who had died and donated his tissues and organs to other patients. An allograft. This wasn't easy for some patients to understand, even in English. But in Spanish it was even harder to explain. Mexican nationals had very little understanding of transplantation and tissue grafting. At least in the United States most people had heard of transplants: kidneys, hearts, corneas. They often had a fear of rejection or of diseases, such as HIV. It was rare for an American, even a Hispanic American, to refuse an allograft. With the Mexican nationals, it was both a lack of knowledge as well as a cultural fear of that which comes from the dead. She once had a patient accept the graft, as long as it wasn't from someone who had killed another person. That was a pretty hard one to work through. And it made her think of a potential movie theme. TRANSPLANT. She could go just about anywhere with that thought. Maybe someday she would. She also remembered a patient who asked her if she could get a graft from a black athlete.

Jesús really had no choice, except to refuse the surgery altogether. All the tissues generally used for ligament reconstruction were exposed and damaged when the skin was sheered off his knee. She told him that the tissues were from a person whose family had agreed to donate his or her parts, like the kidneys, heart, liver and tendons so that others could live or have a better life after an injury or illness. She told him that if it were her knee or the knee of her child, she would do exactly what she was recommending. This always seemed to give patients confidence and she truly believed it. When contemplating surgery, she could always ask that question of herself and get the answer for her patients. *If it were my knee or my child's knee, what would I do?*

Jesús agreed to the operation and signed his Spanish permit for surgery on Tuesday. His skin grafts were healing. She and Briggs felt he was ready.

Emilio was still in the hospital, mainly for social reasons. He had no place to go. Social workers were still trying to get him an arm. A prosthetist had been consulted and the stump shrinking sock applied to the arm had reduced the swelling for a better fit. As soon as he got his arm the hospital would work with Immigration to send Emilio back to Mexico by bus. Jesús would stay for a while longer, then return in a similar fashion.

Leslie did the carpal tunnel release, knee arthroscopy and the hardware removal. They were quick cases and she was done by eleven o'clock. Doc met her at the hospital but decided not to scrub with her today. Instead, he went down to the doctor's lounge and ran into Frank Long.

"Hey, Frank. You're just the fellow I've been looking for."

"Hal! You doing okay? Everything come out okay?"

"Yeah," he chuckled, "in a manner of speaking. It looks like I'm gonna live. Now, when I'm changing this goddamn bag you'd think I wasn't."

"Shit. Thanks for letting me know. So, what can I do ya for?"

"Well, I'm thinking about cutting back a little, maybe giving up the no-preference ER call. Just wondering if you and the other guys can handle it."

"Hey, no problem there. Do you want us to just go ahead and take your name off the schedule? I know your gal has got a couple of days scheduled on ER call before she takes off. Do you want us to take those?"

"No, she'll want to cover them. She's a hand now. Done a good job for me and my patients."

"You know I'm covering for her this Saturday. She said you were taking her phone calls. That okay?"

"Oh yeah, we already talked about it. Thanks for that. I think there's a fellow she's seeing."

"Really? No kidding." Long shook his head. "Man, it's a shame about her family."

"Oh, you mean her husband. Yep. It is a shame. Well, it's been a year. Maybe it's time for her to get out some. It's too bad she's leaving in a week. I wouldn't mind having her around."

"A year? I thought it was three." Doc gave him a questioning look and he went on. "I got a buddy from medical school who did his residency training with her. Anyway, I gave him a call last week after meeting her because it reminded me of the fact that I hadn't kept in touch. Peterman, Michael Peterman. Anyway, he tells me that three years ago he went to a funeral for her husband and two kids."

"Jesus, Frank, you're kidding me. She told us her husband died in a car accident a year ago. She never had kids."

"I don't know, Hal. I mean, this guy seemed like he knew her pretty well. They trained together and all. Kept in touch, you know, kids the same age and everything. I can't see why he would lie about it. And here's the bad part."

"You mean it gets worse?"

"My buddy tells me it was one of the most depressing funerals he's ever been to. Apparently the wreck was somehow Cohen's fault. I mean, not intentionally or anything. It was an accident. He didn't know the details. No one was talking. She wasn't talking."

"You're goddamn kidding me, Frank." Hal Hawley felt like someone had just gut punched him.

"Hey, that's just what my buddy says. Now, he lives about an hour away from where she lived, New, New...something, New York. Like upstate New York."

"New Paltz."

"Yeah, that's it. Anyway, he lives a couple of hours away. And about a year after the funeral he gets a call from her best friend who says Cohen's totally disappeared off the face of the earth. Sold her home. Everything. Poof. Disconnected her cell phone number. This friend of hers had been trying to track down people Leslie might have known to see if she could reach her and it had taken her that long to finally get to Mike. Well, he knew absolutely nothing, that is, until I called him last week."

"Small world."

"No kidding."

Doc left the lounge and headed back to his office. He kept the information about Leslie to himself. Didn't know what to do with it. Had to figure it out for himself right now. He felt sick. Felt old. He felt so damn lucky.

"Hal? You okay?" Brenda asked as she came into his office.

"I'm fine, sweetheart. Just tired."

"See, I told you that you were going to work too hard and have a setback. We're going home right now. Leslie can handle things this afternoon."

"You're right about that." Brenda came around the desk to help him get up. He hugged her when he stood up. "Did I ever tell you I love you?"

"Every once in a while, Hal," she said, "and I love you too."

27

*B*y the time Leslie got to the office Doc and Brenda had already left. After finishing up she didn't feel like running so she went to the park for a walk. It was hard to think while jogging. Tonight she wanted to think. Most of the trees were still bare although a few were starting to bud. Teased into blooming by the variable Texas weather. All their branches permanently driven in a single direction by the prevailing wind. It was strange to see a city where all the tree branches were bent one way, like flames. Maybe someday she would investigate the source of that wind.

Leslie was excited about this weekend but she was nervous. She felt buoyed by the constant tension in her belly. It was a wonderful feeling. She would have denied even the potential for it a month ago. She had mixed emotions and knew that within the next twenty-four hours she would have to reckon with them. As she walked around the park she tried her usual methods to help her make decisions. She made lists of pros and cons. She tried to look at it through the eyes of a third person. She took philosophical and logical approaches to the question: to make love to Regan or not. It was that simple. It wasn't to have a relationship with Regan or not. It was much more basic. Or was it?

No third party was available for advice. She could have asked Lynn. Her mom? The decision and its consequences were hers to make and hers to live with. Regan had to live with them too. She hadn't really been fair to him because she had not told him the truth about the accident. She would wrestle with that one later.

Leslie walked for an hour or more, not paying attention to the time. The sun started going down. The horizon was pink and gold sateen. Geese created long V lines over the lake as they paddled across and she realized she had never seen this water so still. The wind always caused a slight turbulence on the surface. The Vs spread and spread until they reached the shore where they melded into the pebbles and mud or met each other in a herring bone formation.

She wasn't sure how long she'd been walking when her cell phone rang. When she saw R WAKEMAN on her caller ID, the answer to her question was obvious. She couldn't wait to hear his voice.

"Hey." She quickly thought of how caller ID had changed the nature of the telephone greeting. A "hey," or a "hello," or a "yes," depending on who was on the other end. The one she wants to talk to. The one she can't wait to talk to, a "hey." Said in her best I-couldn't-wait-to-talk-to-you, "hey" voice.

And responded to in his best I-couldn't-wait-to-talk-to-you-either, "Hey. What're you up to?" So much in a voice. She had to find somewhere to sit down. There was a swing up ahead. One of those black rubber ones hanging from two chains. She couldn't walk and talk to him at the same time. The sun had almost set. Just a glow on the horizon and a reflection off the underside of some clouds.

"Talking to you."

"Are you outside? It sounds windy."

"I'm at the park, walking. Just didn't feel like jogging today."

"But baby, it's getting dark."

Was he trying to take care of her from a thousand miles away?

"It's okay, there's other people jogging here still. Where are you anyway?"

"Airport. DFW."

"You're kidding. Plane's delayed?"

"Yep. Weather here in Dallas. I sure hope it's not coming to Abilene."

"What happens to your pig roast if it rains?"

"Oh, we have it rain or shine. It's tradition. Or didn't I tell you that already?"

"I think you might have mentioned it."

"Yeah, I've got a couple of barns out there and we'll just get wet, if we need to. A little rain doesn't keep us from having a good time."

She had planted her feet on the ground under her and was rotating around them on the swing. Occasionally, she would pull around too fast and lose her balance, push off and swing around again. She did this absent-mindedly over and over again, absorbed in the conversation.

"Are you going home pretty soon, or am I going to have to come get you on my way home from the airport?"

"You're funny. I tell you what. If it will make you feel better, I'm walking to my car right now."

"Good. That makes me feel better."

"You know, I was thinking, why don't I just drive myself out there? I'm sure you're going to have your hands full, getting everything ready. Especially since you've been out of town."

"Well, that'd be kind of..."

"No, I insist. Really. It's no big deal. You just need to give me directions."

"Okay, but if you have anything to drink then I'll have to take you home. And after midnight, there won't be any designated drivers. Just to warn you."

"Then I am forewarned." Her heart was racing. The intended meaning of that simple interchange.

There was brief silence on both ends. She could hear the weird echo of the wind coming through her phone. A strange hollow sound. Regan gave her directions. She opened her car door and grabbed a pen and paper, quickly jotting them down. It would take about ten to fifteen minutes to get there.

She started just to say goodbye and then thought of Regan in an airplane, and bad weather. "Regan, have a safe trip, okay. I'll see you tomorrow."

Before Leslie went back to the hotel, she drove to Dillard's and bought perfume. She had thrown all of her perfume away three years ago. Coco. That was one she had never used before. She had loved Chanel No. 5, but it was nothing like Coco. Nail polish, for her toes. Not her fingernails. New underwear.

She wondered how she was going to get to sleep tonight. She thought about the pig roast. There would be tension, drawn out. What time would everyone leave? Would she be the last to go? Would he invite her to stay? Would she stay? Would it just happen that way? It would happen. She thought. Her belly tensed with the idea of it.

And while she was again wondering how she could coax herself to sleep, her cell phone rang. TAY CTY REG HOSP and a phone number she recognized as the ER.

"Doctor Cohen?"

"Speaking."

"Hi. Royce Kennard here. ER. Sorry to bother you but I've got an ankle here I need to talk to you about. You're not on call but apparently Doc Hawley takes care of this gal's mom and they're requesting you. I mean Doc Hawley. I told her someone else was covering for him and she said that would be fine. I can call the guy on call if you..."

"No, no, that's fine. What do you guys have down there?"

"It's a bad bimalleolar fracture. Displaced. The ankle mortise is widened. Pretty swollen, but not too bad yet. Do you want me to splint it and send it to the office?"

"Nope, that's okay. I'll come in and see it. Let's get an IV started. I may decide to operate on it tonight. Once it gets really swollen, I won't be able to touch it for a week. Don't let her eat."

"Sounds good, Doc. Do you want to give any orders to the nurse?"

"No. Just keep her in the ER. I'm on my way."

Bad ankle fractures don't take long to swell to the point where they can't be operated on for a while. If she hears about the fractures early from the ER, she can take care of them quickly, so the swelling can be prevented. The bones bleed from the raw edges. Putting them back in place slows down the bleeding and swelling.

Once again she felt as if she had been saved by the bell. When she was in private practice she really didn't look forward to going to the hospital in the middle of the night. Now, night time calls shielded her from her demons. She would take care of this tonight. There was the added bonus of not having it hanging over her head tomorrow.

After the hour and a half it took to actually get the patient to the operating room and the hour and a half of operating with a twenty pound lead apron hanging off her shoulders, she was exhausted.

Leslie fell asleep the moment her head hit the pillow, demons bouncing ineffectively off the walls and Styrofoam particles on the ceiling ignored.

28

Saturday morning Leslie slept as late as possible. It was seven o'clock. She put on some scrubs to go round. Threw her lab coat on over them. When she stepped outside she felt a little warmth in the air. And the wind. Big cumulus clouds zoomed by overhead dragging shadow and sunlight patches with them. As she drove to the hospital she could see slanted columns of rain on the horizon. It was an amazing sight. Bright morning sun shining like a floodlight down on earth, shining on someone's home, or a fallow field, or a 7-11. Splotches of cloud cover where, in this part of the world, someone was praying for rain. The rain their neighbor was getting, and only their neighbor. The droplets would recede before satisfying the prayer. By the time she got to the hospital, she had the opportunity to get a panoramic view of the city and saw four of the rain columns holding up the sky.

The ankle was doing great and her patient complained more of the inability to get any rest in the hospital than of the pain. She wanted to go home once P.T. confirmed she was independent on crutches.

Jesús was *status quo*.

On her way back to the hotel, she noticed that there were still four columns of rain but they had moved around. Were any of them heading south, toward Regan's place? She didn't have her directional bearings. What difference did it make? He said he was ready, rain or shine. The smoking pig came to mind.

From her hotel phone she checked out to Doc and Frank Long. Both seemed really eager to help her. She was covered until Sunday. Doc was taking calls from patients. Frank, the ER calls. She could just check in with them on Sunday. "Have a good time."

After hanging up the phone, her heart began to race and her tummy tightened. Now all that was left was to get ready to go see Regan. Leslie turned on the shower and undressed. The mirror steamed up.

She stepped into the shower and began washing her face, then her hair. The ritual she performed every day of her life but this time different. She remembered another shower, another time, the same ritual, but with Herbal Essence green apple shampoo rather than the high dollar stuff she now used. French writing under English. The shower she took almost twenty years ago before she and Chris were having dinner in Manhattan. Both were coincidentally at trade meetings in the city. She was on a medical student budget, he on an expense account and they went back to his hotel room afterwards. It could have been yesterday, the memory was so clear.

Leslie picked up her razor, lifted her right leg to the edge of the tub. She bent forward to reach down and shave her leg, starting above the ankle. The gold chain and rings swung away from her chest and dangled like a plumb line in front of her chin. She reached up with her free hand to hold them in her fist. She quieted them. The water was warm as it ran down her hair and onto her face. And from her eyes, water of a different temperature ran and mixed with the shower water. The tears ran down her face and into her mouth, tasting salty even diluted. She brought the two rings to her lips and held them there for a moment, then pulled the chain over her head and set it on the fiberglass ledge of the shower where the water couldn't reach it.

29

*L*eslie went south on 36 about fifteen miles to Ranch Road 605. About a mile down 605 the asphalt ended, merging into dusty caliche. On the left hand side of the road barbed wire turned into finished black pipe fence and she knew this to be the northeastern boundary of Regan's family homestead. Beyond it foothills formed a backdrop to the ranch. She followed the fence for half a mile to a large black pipe gate, two large uprights with another welded across the top, slightly overhanging the two poles. Clear Fork Creek. Black metal letters were welded to the horizontal pipe. She drove across a cattle guard. There was a slight upward grade to the property. Regan told her to continue on the caliche road to a stand of oak trees, the big oak trees she could see in the distance. There were deliberate patches of old oaks all across his property and in this rain cloud light they were shady green mounds. About ten miles south of Abilene, oak trees suddenly sprouted out of the prevailing mesquite underbrush. She could now see his home and at least a couple of barns.

The black pipe fence surrounded the aged, yellow limestone house. Two stories with full frontal balconies up and down. Four massive Doric columns supported the porches. Fans hung on the balconies and the porch ceilings were painted powder blue. Three doors lead out to the balcony upstairs and over each was a transom. In between the doors were large rectangular windows surrounded by shutters. Real shutters, with hinges and hooks, just like her home in New Paltz.

The double front doors had beveled glass panes three-quarters of the way down. Three windows on each side of the door matched the symmetry of the doors and windows upstairs. All were set deep into over a foot of stone. There were chimneys on both ends and a galvanized steel roof. Temporary scaffolding was erected around the chimney on the left side of the house.

Drizzling rain had followed her as she drove from Abilene. She parked her car and walked quickly up to the front porch, protected from the drizzle by dense tree cover. As she got to the porch she heard a rushing sound and the rain broke out.

A round metal plaque beside the door verified the house's historical registration. Leslie knocked. Heard nothing. She looked in through the leaded glass and could see dark, wide planked, wooden floors. Wide doors with transoms overhead led to rooms on both sides of the hall. A stairwell to the left rose to a balconied second floor, all doors looking out over the entry hall. Straight back she couldn't see much but it was probably the kitchen. When no one answered her knock she walked to the edge of the front porch. It was raining hard now. She could just see one of the barns off to the right. It was made of the same old limestone on bottom, but had been restored up top with steel, painted deep creamy yellow and white. The paint picked up color from the limestone. There were shutters on the barn windows. It was far enough away that she would have to get in her car to avoid getting soaked.

She made a run for it and when she got to her car the cell phone was ringing.

"Hey, darlin', thought I heard you pull up. I'm down at the barn. I had to start getting things set up in here when it looked like rain. Do you want to wait up there?"

"Are you kidding? Where are you?"

"You're probably looking at the old barn, if you're at the house. I'm down at the horse barn. It's behind the house. Just drive down the road and you'll come to it." He was almost yelling, because the rain was pounding against the barn's metal roof.

She passed the old barn on the right and kept going. Beyond the big oaks, out in the open, was a large metal barn, the same yellowish color, with horse stalls on one side and a porch and office on the other. There was a big sliding barn door in between. It was open and Regan was standing there waving to her. He had on jeans and a T-shirt. A ball cap.

Water was pouring off the sides of the barn, overflowing the gutters and running down the drive. Regan was shaking his head because he knew she was getting ready to get soaked. It wasn't how she pictured this happening. She took off her adorable sandals and set them on the floorboard and hung her precious little vintage sweater over the back of the passenger seat. She counted to three, swung open the door, got drenched with water immediately and made a run for it in her bare feet. Regan grabbed her the moment she was inside the barn and hugged her tight, laughing. He knew she had to be pissed. Knew she had made an effort to look good. He lifted her slightly off the ground and swung her around a quarter of a turn, then gently put her down.

"Look at you. Soaking wet."

He hugged her again, pulled back, and smiled.

"What?"

"You look beautiful. Even wet."

No makeup is great for rain, crying and waking up in the morning. She had nothing to say. He kissed her. She kissed him back. He ran his hand through her wet hair pulling it off her face, back off her neck, cradling it gently up into his hand as he tilted her head back and up toward him.

He tilted his head and kissed her hard. Pressed her to him. Their tongues met. He took off his baseball cap and threw it somewhere. She reached up and ran her fingers through his hair. She wanted to touch his hair. What was it like? Thick, wiry, persistent in its direction. He kissed her lightly on the cheek, the ear.

"I missed you," he whispered.

"Me too." Leslie looked away. "I guess we can't just stand here all day. You've probably got things to do to get ready. Do you think it'll keep raining?"

"I doubt it. I think it's going to clear up in the next hour or so and we'll be fine. The water soaks right up in this ground. The pig's the only problem and he'll be okay as long as the rain stops pretty soon."

"So, exactly where is this pig?"

"Right out there." He pointed to an open area where the ground was freshly dug up and some cinder blocks were sticking up above the ground.

"I'm looking forward to seeing this."

"Me too."

When she turned to look at him, he was looking at her, not out at the barbecue pit. No more playing. He looked at her eye to eye, didn't stop when she looked away for an instant. He turned her face back to his and kissed her softly. The cramping in her belly squeezed tight and she felt something give, down below. He saw it in her eyes before they shut for a moment. Her mouth felt dry. She opened her eyes and knew what was going to happen. It would happen here, in the open barn, in the daylight. Not in his house, on his bed, in the dark.

He wrapped his hands firmly around her back and pulled her toward him. He moved them around and down the sides of her chest, his thumbs just barely brushing the sides of her breasts. Her heart pounding, she made the second half-hearted attempt to control the situation.

"Regan, won't someone see us?"

He put one hand up and touched his index and middle fingers to her lips. He was smiling. He turned her face out toward the wide open barn door and then pressed her head to his chest. It was pouring down rain. As far as she could see through the rain there was not a single building, house or movement that wasn't his. Black pipe fencing stretched out across the pasture until it disappeared into grayness.

Now, not smiling, he kissed her, at the same time running his hand down her hip to the bottom of her short skirt. Leslie felt the need to stretch, like a reflex. The muscles of her legs and everything tightened up. He pulled up her skirt, turning her halfway around at the same time and reaching inside her cotton panties, then his finger inside to see if she was ready. She was embarrassingly ready. She could feel him pressed against her hip, ready too. She took a deep breath, out loud, and swallowed.

"Come on." He guided her over to a huge stack of square hay bales. The lower ones were covered with tarps so people could sit on them. He eased her down on the tarps and reached down to take off her panties. When they were down far enough, she pulled up her knees to help get out of them more quickly. He pushed her back on the hay and kissed her again. She reached down to undo his jeans and he was helping her, both fumbling around. He pulled down his pants. Moved up to her. On the way he grabbed her right leg in the crook of his left arm and hiked it all the way up so her knee was up to her side. Her other leg folded around him and she pulled him to her, guiding him into her. There he paused for a moment. Looked at her as if to ask if it was okay.

"*Come on.*" Did she say it out loud? He started to move against her. She pulled him to her again with her leg and her arms. Now, moving again, faster and harder. And she felt that cramping sensation down deep inside. The answer to the tightness in her belly. The rain so loud against the metal roof she could hardly hear him cry out. Or herself, for that matter. He came hard inside of her and stopped, burying his face in the crook of her neck. They lay there. Still.

They stayed like that, joined for a while. He let go of her leg. She set her foot on the ground. She rubbed her hand across the smooth slope of skin below his waist. He messed with her hair. The rain began to slow and instead of the roar it had been making on the roof, Leslie began to hear the pitter patter of individual raindrops. Regan moved inside her, and she felt a light gasp come from deep in her throat, then that extraordinary desire to stretch again. As he slid off the hay he pulled her skirt down over the top of her thighs. She would have done that herself. Her left knee was bent and resting against the side of a bale of hay. He kissed the inside of it as he moved down. He pulled up his shorts and pants. Buttoned them up. There was a soft strip of dark hair going down from his belly. She wanted to follow it up to his chest even as much as she wanted to see the rest. He still had on his T-shirt. The ball cap was across the barn on the floor. He reached his hand down and pulled her up in front of him.

"That wasn't how you thought this would happen, was it?"

"Now, why would you say that?"

They both laughed. Half out of the surprising intensity of the moment and half nervousness.

"I had everything all ready at the house and I was going to get you up there. Couldn't wait until after the party. Then the damn rain and I had to get some things into the barn. Let's go up to the house." He took her hand. "It's still ready."

They ran in the rain to his house and went in through the back door. She was still barefooted. She wiped her feet on a rug. He took off his boots and socks. He had nice feet and she would notice that.

"You only get the cook's tour right now." He indicated with a sweeping gesture that this was the kitchen. Then he took her hand and led her down the hall she had seen from the front door. "The hall." He took both her hands and pulled her up the stairs.

"This is the stairwell."

At the top he went to the left and down the balconied hallway. She wasn't sure if he was playing with her or what, but when they got straight to what she was sure was his bedroom, she knew he wasn't teasing.

There was a high four poster bed covered with an ivory colored down comforter. He pulled her toward the bed and pulled off his T-shirt. The strip of dark hair thinned out below his belly button. He had a small area of dark hair on his chest. She moved toward him intentionally to lessen the distance and keep him from openly looking at her. He stopped her and put his hands around her waist. Then he lifted her tank top over her head and tossed it on a chair. She had on her new beige colored bra...and her blue jean skirt. He undid his jeans and pulled them down. Threw them on the chair. He had on navy blue boxers with a cute western print. Like little boys have on pajamas. Bucking broncs and horseshoes or something like that. He wore them low on his hips. She smiled at his shorts and he gave her a look she had seen before, with his right eyebrow raised slightly. A crooked grin on his lips.

He reached for the buttons on her skirt. He began unbuttoning them one by one, but the skirt still rested on her hips. She didn't know if she could just stand there and let him pull her skirt off. He still had his shorts on. In an instant he pulled her to him as he pushed her skirt down and it dropped to the floor. He started laughing and they jumped into the bed, pulling the comforter around them. He reached around her back, undid her bra and tossed it somewhere. She pulled off his shorts and he found her again. They made love twice more before showering and returning to the barn to greet his guests.

People started arriving around five o'clock. She recognized a lot of them from the hospital and the horse show. Cal and Jenn were two of the first to get there. It was nice to know someone else besides Regan. He would be busy putting everything together. Cal was walking without crutches and proud of it. Right away, he wanted to show her his knee range of motion since that was one of the things she told him would be most difficult to achieve. She had to admit, he was doing very well. Now, if Regan wasn't around to introduce her as his friend, Cal would be there to introduce her as his doctor. The one who fixed up his leg. It was like she was there as his guest. His doctor. Some people had to wonder what the hell Cal's doctor was doing there.

For the most part, however, Regan was at her side. He really didn't have to do much because everyone seemed to have an assignment. Cal and a couple of other guys were the ones in charge of the pig, and they settled in around the homemade roasting pit until it was done. They had prepared the pig while Regan was out of town. There was a lot of beer drinking associated with the pig roasting. A lot of down time. She spotted Steven Ware and he raised his beer can to her. He touched his index finger to his lips. "Shhh." His premature invitation, their secret.

Most people brought food with them and soon there was an entire buffet of sides, breads and desserts assembled in the barn next to the hay bales. Leslie felt flushed when she thought about someone sitting down there to eat dinner.

Country music was playing over a loudspeaker system. Galvanized steel troughs outside were filled with ice and cans of beer and soda. She hadn't even noticed them when she drove up. But then, why would she? It had been pouring and Regan was standing in the doorway of the barn. *And I Only Have Eyes For You.* A song her mother used to play on the piano. It suddenly came to mind.

Leslie Cohen was at a good old-fashioned country redneck barbecue. It was a beautiful thing. People were having a great time. Some had been there for every pig roast since the beginning. Veterans with old pig roast stories. Failures. Successes. There were more recent invitees, hoping to become part of the Annual Clear Fork Creek Ranch Pig Roast folklore. There were couples and singles. Old and young. Even children.

Regan's sister and her husband came. According to Regan, this was the first time they had come to the roast, and Leslie gathered there were still issues. Regan didn't fuss over his sister and she blended into the crowd. This was not the time to get involved. She remembered Doc telling her that the sister had taken the death of the parents hard, and perhaps it was as simple as avoiding the memories. That was easy. Don't go home. In order to put that line of thinking out of her mind, she wandered over to the pig roast team.

These guys were into it. They told her how they had built the pit with cinder blocks. They got the idea off the internet. Came up with their own modifications, which changed every time some fiasco occurred. Like the time they incinerated the pig. They were proud of their record. Regan was usually part of the team. They implied that they were disappointed tonight because he was otherwise occupied. The team made much issue of the "dis." There was a lot of teasing going on.

According to history the pig would be ready around seven or so. This was not an exact science. Leslie moved on, and grabbed a beer. It was something she usually didn't care for, but she was influenced by her peers and the freedom of no call at this point.

She found Regan. She didn't want to tie him up all night, but he wanted to be with her. He put his arm around her and they walked around the barns. Cinco and Gomez were running around in one of the paddocks. They stopped and came over to Regan and Leslie while they were standing by the new barn. They did and didn't want attention. They would put their big heads over the pipe fence but when she or Regan would reach for them they would pin their ears at them or each other and run off. It looked like they would repeat this endlessly. Regan and Leslie moved on.

"They just want food. Remember."

They walked over toward the old barn, beyond which was the seemingly endless pasture Leslie had been asked to check out earlier as proof of their privacy. As the sun was going down, there was a golden glow across the foothills and a moist haze hung in the air. The barn, isolated trees and a windmill made long shadows across the winter rye grass which created an unexpected carpet of deep green. Rust colored cows with white faces walked slowly across the patch, heads bent, eating, ruminating. How had the word for the processing of a thought come to be called by the same word that describes the cow's act of eating, with their strange digestive system? The dark silhouettes moved slowly across the pasture, cows staying together for protection. Better grass and procreation were the prime movers. The two lovers stood quietly and watched the cattle forms disappear into the night to the point where they could only be heard; an occasional loud hollow breath or a lone bellow was answered by another. A signal. Position. Danger. The procreator.

There was coolness in the air now, and Leslie wished for her sweater. It hung over the back of the passenger seat in her rent car. Regan had delivered her sandals earlier, but forgot the sweater. There was no need for it then. Now she didn't want to leave his side. Didn't need it bad enough. He put his arm around her and pulled her to him. Leslie locked her arms around his waist. She could hear the country music coming from the other barn. Some sad sounding song, strawberry wine in the words, or something like that. She'd heard it before. The waning moon peeked weakly in and out of huge dark clouds that glided across the night sky like tanks in formation. Above those clouds a thin layer of wispy clouds moved at another speed in what seemed like another direction. Leslie and Regan held each other tightly.

Interrupting the moment, there was a big commotion behind them. The pig was being excavated.

"Are you hungry?"

"Absolutely. I've worked hard today."

"Yes you have." He kissed her on the forehead. They walked over to where the team was lifting heavy aluminum off the top of the pit. A delicious smell of barbecued pork rose up from the thick smoke. At this the crowd began to chant.

"Mojo, mojo, mojo!" Four of the men reached down in the pit and pulled up some metal frames with chain link fence wired to them. And sandwiched in between was the pig, all splayed out.

"Mojo, mojo, mojo!" They raised the apparatus above their heads and marched the pig from the pit to a huge tray on a table alongside the pit. She thought about *"The Lord of the Flies."*

The air was filled with a delicious aroma and the sound of the chanting pig roast team. Beer was going down easy into empty stomachs and things were livening up. Children ran around screaming "Mojo, mojo," imitating the natives.

"What's with the 'mojo'? Is that part of the tradition?"

"Yeah. About four or five years ago, we were looking for some tips on building a better pit and we found these guys on the internet who had a description of their pit and cooking techniques. They also had a marinade for the pig. We tried it and it was great. Well, these guys from Miami called the marinade Mojo. In Texas, we think the term mojo had its origins from a football team in Odessa who used to be the perennial state champions and their chant was mojo, mojo, mojo. Across Texas anyway, mojo came to be an accepted chant anytime you needed, you know, some mojo. Motivation. Inspiration. Whatever."

"I see."

"Do ya now?"

"I think it means we've had tons of beer and now it's time to eat." They followed the chanting pack over to the table where the mighty pig would be cut up into bite-sized morsels.

"What's in the Mojo anyway?"

"Oh, I don't know if I can tell you." He turned to the crowd. "Hey! Can I tell Leslie what's in Mojo?"

She heard someone yell, "Yeah, but then we'll have to kill her." Followed by an even more enthusiastic, "mojo, mojo, mojo!"

Everyone was having a good time. The pig, getting carved up. Music playing. Kids running around. More food.

"Mojo's got stuff like garlic, orange juice, oregano and olive oil in it. Good stuff."

"So now are you going to have to kill me?"

"No, but I'll have to lock you away so you can never get out to tell the secret to people in Minnesota or something."

The thought of going somewhere else struck Leslie wrong right now. A downer in the middle of so much fun.

Regan caught the feeling. "Hey, baby, not so serious." He took her hand and turned toward the barn. "Let's go get something to eat."

People were lined up at long tables in the barn, piling food on their plates. There were tables, chairs and hay bales set up all over. Leslie and Regan sat outside with Cal, Jenn, and some other guys from work. Regan went over to get another beer and signaled to Leslie, "Want another one?" Yes she did.

Now, orthopedic surgeons are pretty good company for the most part. Leslie had seen it many times. No matter what group of people she is with, no matter how much or how little she may have in common with them, no matter what age or country of origin, everyone has something to say to an orthopedic surgeon and everyone wants to hear something from an orthopedic surgeon. She really couldn't think of any other profession, except maybe a plumber, that would have so much in common with so many. If she went to a party or a meeting or function, she never needed to be nervous about not knowing what to talk about because people and her job always provided her with the material. Tonight was no exception. Besides the fact that Cal was bragging on her all night, people enjoyed curbside consults and free medical advice. She was always glad to give it. She loved her business and never minded talking about it.

People wanted to tell her gross bone stories. Like when uncle so-and-so got a mesquite thorn stuck in his tibia bone. Or when their next door neighbor got her hair caught in a tractor power-take-off, nearly getting scalped. When she grabbed for her hair, the sleeve of her shirt got caught in the PTO, nearly cutting her whole arm off. All of them fascinating stories. She could contribute to them, of course, but she started feeling like this was the Leslie Cohen show.

She went for seconds on some delicious carrot dish called "Copper Pennies." There was another carrot dish next to it that brought back some scary junior high memories. Carrot and raisin salad! She stayed clear of that one and she wasn't the only one. There weren't many takers.

The dessert table was a killer. Anything she had ever associated with a southern-style barbecue was there. Banana pudding, cobbler, and homemade ice cream. She was already pretty full, but had a little room for a skosh of cobbler, with only a touch of fruit, just the way she liked it. No Adkin's diet options here.

In every crowd there are always a group of people, usually women, who linger around to clean up. They're not assigned, they just do it. Leslie hung around to help. It wasn't too hard. Most everything was in disposable containers, even the cooked stuff. That was a good idea. The dishes were paper and plastic. In about forty-five minutes everything was picked up and thrown into giant plastic bags.

Then the children started dancing to the country music. They danced with each other, and then tried to drag their parents into the middle of the barn. Lights were turned down. Someone had CDs and was picking out songs. The kids were uninhibited. Particularly the girls. The boys held back a little and no parents, or any adult for that matter, wanted to be the first on the floor for everyone to watch.

One of the girls came over to Regan and asked him to dance. He pretended to be shy and tried to turn her down, but everyone egged him on so he obliged her and stepped out onto the makeshift dance floor. These little girls knew how to dance and play the role of follower like pros. She looked like she might have been Vivi's age, and at that age Vivi would never have asked an adult male, with the exception of her dad, to dance. She took his hand and he guided her around the floor with ease, her steps just barely awkward. Shortly, the music ended. He bowed to her, she curtsied to him and went running off to her buddies. Her parents were laughing and teasing Regan. He looked over to Leslie. She worried for a moment that he might ask her to dance out in front of everyone. She pretended to read her beer label.

Someone put on a song which got everyone up and onto the floor, starting to form lines. Some kind of a polka. Dadl a da di da boom, dadl a da di da boom. Not giving her a chance to refuse, Regan came over and grabbed Leslie. People got in lines and put their arms around each other. There were varying levels of expertise with this dance, as with all line dances in which she had ever taken part. It was pretty simple though, and within about two full stanzas, she had it down. But then the tempo started picking up. The drunks were hanging on people, making those lines falter and bump into other lines. The serious dancers switched lanes and moved on. Regan held tight onto Leslie so she wouldn't get left behind or knocked over. By the time the song ended, she was laughing so hard her cheeks were cramping. All the stand-offers were now out on the floor. It took just this to get them there and now folks were staying where they wanted to be, primed to dance. Regan and Leslie included.

Everyone waited to see what song would come on next. It was a slow song and Regan stepped up to Leslie without taking his eyes from hers. She had never really two-stepped to country western music, but she knew ballroom dancing and felt comfortable with her ability to follow as long as Regan could lead. At first he held her away from him and she noted that a lot of the people danced that way. But once they got comfortable with the tempo and the steps, he pulled her closer and they stayed like that. She could feel her heart beating just below her ribs. Was it her aorta? Or was it his? Pairs of dancers moved past them. They moved past very few. They turned. They paid attention to no one. Or at least she didn't. Regan kept her from bumping into other couples. He must have seen them in his peripheral vision because the song ended and they stepped apart, never having taken their eyes off each other. She wasn't sure if she had even blinked.

The next was a country swing type song, and she wasn't sure she'd be able to handle that one. She signaled him to sit out with a sideways jerk of her head, but he denied her with a twist of his in the negative.

"Just follow me. You'll be fine." He took her left hand in his right and put his left hand firmly around her waist. Even though in the same position as they were for the two-step, his hold was firm, braced. Regan took a step forward, Leslie back. At first he guided her in relatively large loops around the floor. Sometimes they moved straight ahead to get out of the way of those who were plodding along. It was easy to move with him. He held her up and his grip on her waist and arm tightened. The beers she had made it easier in a way, to let go. She couldn't resist the urge to look where they were going or to look down to the floor. He nudged her and she looked back at him.

"Quit looking down. Just follow me. Look at me." And in just a few turns they were totally in sync. He stepped up the pace by decreasing the radius of their turns and soon they were essentially spinning. His right leg in between hers and her left leg to the outside. They were gliding, floating, like tops. She was starting to sweat. It was physical, but not hard to keep up and stay locked in that position. She leaned back slightly as they fell into the centrifugal momentum. Leslie closed her eyes. She remembered as a little girl dancing on her daddy's feet and feeling like that. It was all daddy. All she had to do was stay on top of his feet. She was dizzy and simply allowed herself to be pulled around and around as long as he could pull her. When the music stopped Regan spun her around a few more times then pulled her tight to his chest. They slowly stepped around, and stopped. Regan put his lips to her forehead and kept them there. It was quiet. No one else was on the dance floor.

Everyone who has ever been in love remembers when they first knew it. The first time they looked into each others' eyes with equality in that emotion. And like recognizing the sound of an old favorite song, or the taste of a favorite dessert, it can be forgotten, but always remembered again when tasted or heard in that form. And once lost, it is always desired again. So it was tonight, when everyone there who knew what it was, saw it, tasted it and desired it again. One by one, the children started running back on the dance floor.

Soon everyone packed up what they had brought, and said good bye to both of them. They told her they were happy to meet her, and she thought at least four of the guests told her they were going to have to make an appointment to see her next week. Next week was her last week in Abilene. She didn't want reminders.

"You can stay?" A question. A statement. She could stay. It had been a magic evening. It was just a barbecue, but it had been perfect. The people, their children, the way everyone worked together to make it happen, the way country barbecues had been happening since people came out here two hundred years ago.

30

*L*eslie woke up early the next morning. She assumed Regan was still asleep. She couldn't see his face because morning light had not yet broken through the shutters. She moved a little and listened. Regular breathing. Asleep.

When Leslie was married to Chris, and a long time after they had become comfortable with each other's nudity and daily natural functions, she had joked with him about going to the bathroom with him around. She had vowed that in her next relationship, sometime after she was widowed at eighty-five, she would never again be so silly about having to pee.

Leslie would turn on the fart fan. She would try to let it out slow. She would scoot to the edge of the toilet so it would hit the sides and silently flow into the bowl. But despite all of her contortions, it would never fail to make noise. Of course Chris just went in and let it loose. He didn't seem to care if she was disillusioned by the sound of his stream. She tried to picture him aiming for the side of the commode to keep it silent. She couldn't remember how long it was before she didn't care anymore.

Her bladder was full. Right now. The master bathroom was attached to his room. There was no fan. The house was old. People didn't worry about that stuff a hundred and fifty years ago. Had to worry about eating or staying alive. She had already scoped it out and had used the toilet, but they were running around, getting dressed, trying to get ready for company. No time for him to listen to her pee.

If there was going to be an opportunity, it would have to be now. She could look around for another bathroom. She sat up slowly. Stood up silently. Took a step.

"Where're you going this early in the morning?" Regan's sleepy voice.

Shit. "This is just when I get up."

"Me too. That's cool. I was trying to be quiet in case you were still asleep."

"Really."

"Yep. Okay. You go to the bathroom first and I'm going to wait right here."

"Regan! That's not right!"

"Hey look, I remember my ex talking about it after we got married. What all she did to keep me from hearing her. You go baby. Hurry and get back, cuz I wanna make love to you first thing this morning. Make up for falling asleep last night."

She could just barely see him as her eyes got used to the dark. He had propped himself up on the pillows. She walked reluctantly to his bathroom and closed the door.

"Hey, don't forget. You're a doctor. We've all gotta do this stuff."

She rolled her eyes to no audience. And peed.

Regan was standing up waiting, when she came out. He hugged her. He was morning warm. He was ready. To pee anyway. She knew that much. He made a soft groaning sound, and kissed her.

"See, that wasn't so bad. Now go get in bed. And don't listen."

It was warm where they had been. It had their smell in it. Her perfume, his cologne or shampoo. Their skin. Their sweat. Regan climbed into bed next to her, wound his legs through hers. Softness next to softness.

31

*L*ater Regan made coffee. While it was brewing he showed her around the house. Big refurbished rooms, high ceilings, transoms over all the doors. Deeply stained doors framing etched glass led into the living and dining rooms, the two rooms she had seen from the front door yesterday. The furniture was a combination of old stuff belonging to his family and newer things. All of the bedrooms were upstairs. The beds and wardrobes were old. There were no closets in the two extra bedrooms. He had built a closet and added to the master bath out of a fourth room.

She was surprised his sister had not wanted any of the old furniture. "It's here for her if she ever wants it. Moms always want their daughters to have the dining room table and the dishes and stuff. It's been ages since I've had a meal in this room." All the dishes were neatly arranged in a hutch. "I just eat out or in the kitchen."

They returned to the kitchen. It had been completely renovated but the walls were of the original stone. New, stainless appliances gave a functional look to the room. There was a breakfast nook in a large bay window, but the focus of attention and the place where they would eat breakfast this morning was around a big stone island in the middle. Against the back wall was a large stainless steel gas range surrounded by granite countertops.

"I restored my grandmother's old stove over there, but it's really too hard to use. It would take all day to cook a meal on that thing. No wonder women back then couldn't be surgeons and contractors. Just keeping people fed was a full time job."

"No kidding. Feeding my ki..." And she hesitated for a split second. "...husband and me was hard enough." Regan caught the hesitation and looked up, quizzical look in his eye. Leslie pretended to ignore it. It was easy enough to make into a truth, but she had been thinking about the kids, not just her husband. Her heart was beating fast.

"Yeah. It seems like you guys would've just eaten out or made something simple. With your busy schedule and all." He went on about food or something, but she was distracted and couldn't focus on it.

When he stopped talking she said "Right," and hoped that her subconscious mind had kept up with Regan while she was distracted.

"Hey, but I can cook bacon and eggs. How's that sound?"

"Sounds delicious. What can I do?"

"Just fix your coffee and sit right there so I can look at you. Then you can tell me what you've got going on this week. I want to see you as much as I can before you have to go."

She relaxed a little. She skated on that one. She was paranoid, more sensitive to the lies than he would be. She hoped it just blew by him. Leslie fixed her coffee. Of course there was no Sweet n' Low or the blue stuff. Just sugar. She loaded it on. After years of using all that imitation stuff, it took a lot of sugar to sweeten coffee to her taste. Regan was watching her. His coffee was black. He was looking at her like she was pouring rat poison into her cup.

Now he started to do a little gyration with his pelvis. He had on some other pair of western print boxers.

"Hey, baby, pour..some..sugar..on..it," to the Def Lepard tune, singing it. With the spatula in his hand like a guitar. "Don't you know that shit's bad for you? I mean I'm no doctor or anything..."

"Regan, you're about to get on my bad side."

"Uh huh. I didn't know you had one of those." That look again.

She made like she was going to dump the coffee on him. He gently took it from her, set it down on the island, and popped her on her rear end with the spatula.

"Ow." She said it like a cat, pretending to be hurt.

Regan pointed with the spatula to a stool at the counter. "Go sit down like a good girl, before you get in trouble." She grabbed her coffee and did as she was told. Now she could just watch him, while he cooked. Unobstructed view. There was a little light colored mole on his right shoulder blade.

"So what's your schedule like?"

"I've got clinic all day Monday. Not sure how busy it will be. Doc's probably back in the office almost full time."

"So he's doing okay from his surgery and all?"

"Oh, yeah. He's ready to take over."

"Too bad. For me I mean. Good for him. So what else?"

"Tuesday, I have one big case. Maybe one small one, I can't remember."

"That's good. I'd hate to be that second guy you can't remember."

"Regan," she scolded, "it's all on the schedule and I'll check it on Monday."

"I'm just kidding you. So what's your big case?"

"It's that guy I was telling you about. You know the train accident. I've got to reconstruct his knee ligaments. That'll take me a few hours at least."

"So what are you doing with his ligaments?" When he moved the heavy, cast iron pan around on the flame, his scapula elevated slightly against his chest wall. There were a few freckles on his shoulders.

"I'm going to rebuild the ligament with a tendon from a dead person, an allograft. I'm going to scope his knee."

"You mean like arthroscopy."

"Exactly. I always forget to use the term most people know because scope is just so commonly used by all hospital people."

"Hey, I may have been born at night, but it wasn't last night."

"Okay, I get the point, mister...mister...sensitivity, read-it-on-the-internet-last-night-because-I'm-trying-to-make-it-with-an-orthopedic-surgeon."

"You got that right, princess."

He kept cooking, standing with his legs slightly apart and she remembered that stance when he was talking to the police officer in front of his truck, in the rain. Never in her wildest dreams could she have imagined that a month later she would be standing in his kitchen looking at those legs with nothing but bucking bronco boxer shorts on them. She smiled at the thought of it. They could have saved a lot of time if they had just known it then.

"And you were saying...about the surgery. Knee arthroscopy."

"Oh, right. Okay. So I'll reconstruct the ligaments."

"You already did that part."

"Right. So inside his knee I'll look for torn cartilages and other damage. And whatever is wrong with it, I'll take care of it through the scope. I'll open it with an incision only if I have to."

"But you were saying the other day that he didn't have any skin left over his knee."

"Right. It was all just stripped off like a banana peel. Somehow, and I really can't picture it, the coupling mechanism of the train just slowly put the twist on his pants and then his leg. Then the skin got pulled into it. Well, it's got a skin graft now, but it won't be the same. There won't be any fat there."

"That's so weird. I can't believe you can do stuff like that. It doesn't make you sick?"

"Not really. But I'm always amazed at the fragility of human bodies. It just doesn't take much to toss us around and mess us up. Any horrible thing you can imagine, it can happen."

"Yeah, but sometimes the really amazing thing is how we can come out okay. Not get hurt, or bounce back after getting hurt. You know, like Cal."

"Well, Cal is lucky. Lucky to live in a time when we have an operation to take care of his leg. People used to have to be in traction for six weeks and then a body cast for a fracture like his. But you're right. Some people just recover easily. They do their exercises. Stop taking pain pills. They move on. Others let these things consume them. In that regard, the difference between one person and another is really remarkable."

"Yeah." There was something pensive that she read in his voice. She ignored it. "It'd be cool to be you for a day."

"Speaking of being cool to be someone for a day. I'd like to be there when you put up those lights. When are you doing that?"

"As a matter of fact, we're doing it Monday and Tuesday, hopefully. Everything's here. The lights are parked outside the stadium. Electricians are set up to connect. Pylons are up. You probably saw them the other day. It's a go. If you come out there Monday or Tuesday, even if it's late, you'll probably catch one going up. How do you like your eggs?"

"Over easy. So how do you get them up there?"

"We've rented a crane. A big crane."

"Like what's a big crane?"

"Like a two hundred ton hydraulic truck crane. Talk about a toy. Truck's got sixteen wheels, five axles. It's just basically a big hydraulic boom. We'll have attached the light banks to those galvanized steel poles you saw out in the parking lot. The boom will just lift it into position so we can set them. There's six of them and we figure it will take all day to do three. The cool thing is, once they're set right and connected, then we've got light. Guys can start working out there overtime and, barring weather delays, I get my project done ahead of schedule. We still have a lot to do indoors."

"What do you mean?"

"Oh, you know, under the bleachers, in the field house. Things like that. Still, bad weather keeps the crews from continuing to work. It hurts the bottom line for everyone when things get off schedule."

"Just gotta pray for good weather then. I'm going to try to come out. Maybe Tuesday afternoon."

"So what else you got going on?" He served up her bacon and eggs, then his. He sat down. "Salt and pepper?"

She nodded and he jumped up to get some. He didn't have a six pack or anything, but she could see the line that divided the erector muscles of his abdomen, the *linea alba*. He had a small umbilicus, with a little strip of skin that delicately stretched across the top of it. Guys were lucky to be so easy with nudity, especially their upper bodies. Bathing suits, underwear. That was all.

She rolled up the sleeves of his bathrobe and they ate breakfast while she told him about the rest of her week. And her scheduled flight. Six twenty-three, Friday night.

"I can't figure out why they make flights at those odd times. Why not six-thirty? It won't take off before then anyway. I know. Whenever I'm out late at the stadium, I see it. Never before six-thirty. What's your connection? Dallas?"

"Yeah. Then to Evansville Regional Airport."

Regan looked down at his plate. "Leslie, I want you to know now, that I wish you weren't going." He reached across and put his hand on top of hers, squeezed it. "I don't know what to do with you. Or with me for that matter. I'm really going to miss you. You don't have to say anything right now. I just wanted to say it." He squeezed her hand again. Like enough said. She didn't say anything. Took a sip of cold sweet coffee.

"Hey, look at the time. Daylight's burning and we've got things to do." Leslie looked at the clock and saw that it was only eight.

"What do we have to do?" She was glad for the change of subject. She would clean stalls for that change of subject.

"Well, first of all. Let me not just assume anything. Do you need to go see patients today? Or can you hang out here?"

"I do need to call Doc and make sure everything went okay last night. Probably need to see my patient in the hospital. There's just the guy I was telling you about for surgery on Tuesday. Then, I'm all yours. Why? What's going on?"

"I've gotta go feed horses. Then, I'll take you into town to get a change of clothes, you know like jeans or something. We can come back out here and I'll show you around the place. We can even ride horses around the property if you want to. If you don't want to ride, I've got the next best thing."

"I'm afraid to ask."

"The John Deere Gator. Next best toy if you can't afford a two hundred ton hydraulic crane."

"Sounds pretty interesting. Boys and their toys. Look, I'm going to have to get some boots if we're going to ride."

"Well, can you afford it?"

"It wasn't on the budget, but I'll give up something else."

They cleaned up the kitchen and she got back into her bra, underwear, tank top and blue jean skirt, all of which had been through quite a lot these past sixteen hours or so. He drove her around to her car so she could get her sweater. It was hanging over the seat where she had left it yesterday and her stomach tightened when she thought about that moment. She put it on. When she got in the truck Regan gave her an approving look. They smiled at each other and Regan reached over, put his hand around her neck and they touched forehead to forehead.

"Pretty sweater."

32

*O*n the way into town Leslie called to check in with Doc. Things were quiet. No new admissions during the night and very few phone calls. Doc had her covered. They agreed that if things stayed quiet they would see each other at the office on Monday. Doc seemed almost overly generous but she didn't think much of it. Maybe he was just ready to prove he was back on his feet. She had a childish sense of guilt wondering if he guessed she had spent the night at Regan's.

Regan dropped her off at the hotel, said he'd be back to get her in ten minutes. He was just going down the road to fuel up. Diesel lingo. No gassing up. It's diesel fuel.

Sneaking into the hotel and hoping Raghu wasn't at his post, she felt like a naughty school girl. She heard noise coming from the kitchen. Good timing. Leslie took the world's fastest shower, changed into jeans and a long sleeved cotton tee and grabbed her lab coat. Regan was waiting when she came down. Raghu was standing behind the desk.

"Bye, Raghu," she said casually as she scooted out the door.

"Let's go get you some boots. We can ride a little. It's really the best way to get around the ranch."

At a western wear shop they found a cheap pair of boots for her. They looked a little odd with her bell-bottomed jeans, so she splurged for a pair of western jeans.

"Now you look like a real cowgirl." She had to admit she looked like some of the women she saw at the party last night. And the western jeans were definitely more flattering to a woman's figure than the hip hugger model she had on.

At the hospital she quickly slipped on her lab coat before she went to see Jesús.

"That was fast. How's your boy?" Regan asked when she returned.

"Doing fine. Seems ready for surgery Tuesday."

As they headed back to Regan's place he told her about its history. His great grandparents had moved to Abilene about one hundred and fifty years ago. They came from the east, somewhere in Virginia, and weren't poor, actually had a little nest egg saved up. Noah Wakeman bought ten thousand acres outside of the little town of Abilene and the original ranch was still intact. They raised cattle, grew some crops, and got involved in business deals that panned out. They had a bunch of kids, but like a lot of families back then, most of them died, including his wife. She died in childbirth. Regan seemed saddened by that cold fact.

"Regan, it was pretty common for women to die in childbirth back then. Really, it was common up until modern times. Your great grandmother must have been pretty hardy to have survived having all those kids. Modern medicine and, you know, things like C-sections have saved a lot of our lives, and our babies' lives too."

The only surviving grandson, Carl Wakeman had taken over operations. The original home was made mostly out of wood and it burned down in 1901. That's when his granddad built the existing house and the old barn. The top part of the barn was also wooden. It burned down in 1958. They lost three horses in that fire. His father rebuilt it with wood, but Regan tore the wood down about two years ago and finished it in steel when he built the new barn. He'd been refurbishing the house bit by bit and kept the original mustardy yellow color his granddad bought on sale at the feed store. Someone had ordered it but decided not to take it and the store owner gave him a deal.

The east chimney, his current project, had a bad foundation.

"So tell me about your sister."

"It's a long story but I'll give you the short version. Carla was really close to our mom. For some reason she and my dad never saw eye-to-eye. I think it always bothered her. You know, the fact that they never really got it figured out. I don't ever remember my dad hugging her or anything like that. It wasn't something I ever paid much attention to when I was a kid. Just something I remember. That's all."

Leslie thought about the foot dance with her dad again.

"My mom died first and after that Carla never came back home.

I'm sure she meant to, but in the end, she never made it. When dad died she just couldn't deal with it. We split things up. She didn't want anything to do with the place. It was that simple. She got some of the other assets based on the appraised value of the ranch. She came to dad's funeral and that was it. Until last night she's never been out here. I've been working on her and so has her husband. That's pretty much it in a nutshell. Kids...probably be easier not having them, right?"

Leslie gave a half-hearted shrug. "Maybe."

"Hey, are you hungry?"

They ate some lunch as soon as they got to the ranch, leftovers from last night, and then headed down to the barn. Gomez and Cinco were a mess because of the rain, so they had to be brushed down before being saddled. Leslie took two curry combs and worked on Cinco. When she brushed his back, his ears tweaked back and forth as if he didn't like it. When she brushed the left side of his neck, he arched it and pushed against her hand as if he loved it.

It had been a long time since Leslie had ridden horses, but she felt fairly confident knowing that Cinco and Gomez were ridden regularly and familiar with the property.

The first thing they came to was the family cemetery. There were a lot of graves. The two newer stones on his parents' graves stood out. Very old obelisk-type headstones for the great grandparents. There were lots of small ones for the children. Graves told so much. The evidence of generations of one family, together, in one place. All now equal in death. The great grandmother's grave and one of the baby's graves were dated the same. There were five little graves lined up next to the great grandparents.

"Great grandnana had two other daughters who got married and left town. They never came back. My mom tried to track down those relatives but didn't have much luck. You know, back then people just left home. I figure that those sisters just became part of their husband's families. Travel wasn't easy. Life was hard. I probably have some third cousins or something out there. It's hard to imagine. It's hard to think about losing four kids, then your wife and newborn. My great granddad never remarried. A lot of men would have. You know, marry a young wife and start all over."

The horses were tied up to an old metal fence that surrounded the cemetery. It could have been spooky. Every once in a while she could remember seeing old cemeteries like this out in the middle of nowhere, sometimes by the side of a highway. She guessed someone had sold their property for the highway easement and either it was illegal to move it or there was some historical interest and the highway department just took care of it. They were creepy to her then. Now she had cemeteries of her own and she couldn't help but think of the analogy. Lose five children and a wife. It was an expected part of life back then.

"These are my grandparents." She noted the personification of the graves. His grandparents. "I felt about as close to them as a kid could to any parent. Nana anyway. They built this place as far as I'm concerned. It's their place. They were the generation that had to struggle to keep it. The depression. The fire. They built the house. Planted all the trees." Regan and Leslie stood and read them quietly. Anna Regina Wakeman. April 2, 1886 – January 15, 1977. Ninety-one years old. She calculated that Regan would have been in his teens when she died. He definitely knew his grandmother. But not his granddad. Charles Parker Wakeman. September 13, 1883 – September 10, 1951. He didn't make his sixty-ninth birthday. That was eerie.

"How did your granddad die?"

"Cancer. Everyone hoped he could live until his birthday, but he just couldn't hang on. Even though I never knew him, I feel like I did."

"So she survived him by twenty-five years. That's a long time to live with a memory."

"Leslie, I haven't forgotten about your memories. You're not alone out here." Regan put his arm around her. They stood quietly. The wind blowing across dead grass made a rustling sound. The three o'clock sun pushed their shadows in front of them onto the graves of Regan's ancestors. Leslie wondered where her grave would be. Did she belong in New Paltz with her family? Or some place like Abilene, Texas, where she would take her place in a new family. Like Regan's great aunts. Or some place like Evansville, Indiana, Rolla, Missouri, or Jonesboro, Arkansas. She thought of places she had been and places she would be.

They left the cemetery and walked the horses for a little while, soon coming to the ruins of the original homestead. Only a remnant of the chimney and a stone foundation remained. She could understand why Regan loved this place. Strange how history or coincidence had always left this land to one person. One who would cherish it, add to it and continue the tradition. Surely Regan had to be thinking of who he would leave it to. His estranged daughter? Some future heir?

They got back in their saddles and Cinco loped off, prompting Gomez to follow suit. Soon they came to a patch of oak trees. There were a few cedars with lots of mesquite mixed in. She thought the cedars and mesquite were beautiful; the cedars giving color in the winter. The big grey mesquite trees gnarly and mysterious.

"They're weeds. The cedars grow right next to the oaks. They have deep roots and so they steal the water from the oaks and eventually kill them. The mesquites aren't even native. Their seeds were brought up from Mexico in the bellies of cattle and spread in their manure. Now it's all over the state. I keep the small ones killed off. It's kind of hard to kill off the ones that have become trees in their own right. Someday all of Texas will be covered with giant mesquite and cedar trees. Some other plant will be their scourge and it'll serve them right. Anyway, what I want you to see is in these trees."

They looped the horse's reins over low tree branches and went into the wooded area. Deep inside were three giant rocks that looked like huge logs.

"Petrified wood. It's like a whole tree just fell here and got petrified. I've always wanted to excavate this area to see what I could find but I'd have to cut down the surrounding trees because it would take a bulldozer to get them uncovered. I don't really want to disturb what nature decided to expose for me."

"How'd you find these?"

"When we were kids we would come out here to play hide-n-seek or ally ally oxen free. And one of those times, like magic, there were these logs. I swear we had been through this patch a hundred times before and never seen it. I can remember that day like it was yesterday."

She knelt down to get a closer look. She could see perfect annual growth lines and knots. Smaller pieces were lying around like splinters.

"This area was all under an ocean at one time. I guess the trees came before that and when the water covered the region, all the trees became petrified through some chemical process." Leslie knew the process of petrification, but felt no need to mention it. She was charmed by the place and Regan's simplified explanation.

"I figured you would like this. You're a scientist. Don't get to see this kind of thing every day. You'd think this entire area would be full of petrified trees, but it's not. We did lots of excavating out at the stadium, and never turned up a piece of anything old except a few arrow heads, but I've found many more around here in the dry creek beds."

"You're kidding!"

"Got them up at the house in a box. I'll show 'em to you later."

Back on their horses, they soon reached the outer limits of his property. Barbed wire fencing defined the property line.

Regan pointed to some houses and barns in the distance. "Out here you can see how some of the surrounding land has been sold and subdivided. I worry about it more now than I used to. A lot of pressure can be put on land owners to sell. You can end up with a subdivision, trailer park or even a highway in your back yard. With this amount of acreage I can hide from it to a certain extent. This place used to be totally out in the boonies."

The horses knew where they were going now. Although they didn't speed up they were definitely on autopilot. She relaxed her hold on the reins, but kept her heels deep just in case they spooked at something. A grocery store plastic bag stuck to a fence could be enough to send some horses flying in another direction. Maybe not these guys though. Still, she didn't trust any horse when it came to spooking and herd behavior.

For now Cinco and Gomez seemed totally at ease, lowering their heads as they got into an easy walking rhythm. Leslie and Regan talked about the land, the cattle, crops and whatever the trail ride brought to mind. The horses sporadically interrupted them with a snort. Occasionally some imperceptible action would cause one horse to pin back his ears and swing his head at the other. Occasionally a fly would land on the horse's hide causing him to shake the muscles under the skin to rid himself of the pest. They walked the boundaries of the property like this for a long time.

Leslie had lost her sense of direction but the horses eventually wound up at the barn. They unsaddled, rinsed off the horses, and fed them, then sat in the barn a while and talked about the things that lovers talk about. The commonalities, the coincidences, the shared experiences. Could they have met another time, in another place? Maybe not.

They talked about their first Friday together. They talked about last week and last month. They did not talk about this Friday. Or next week. Or next month.

Regan asked her to stay over, but Leslie needed time to think. "I have a really busy day tomorrow, and I'm on ER call."

He accepted that. Didn't try to make her change her mind. In fact, he cautiously kissed her goodnight knowing that passion would make both of them give in. Leslie turned on her car for the first time in over twenty-four hours and drove back to the Holiday Inn.

Raghu greeted her like business-as-usual. She would have expected no less. Leslie asked for a wakeup call and went up to her room. Signs of her hasty shower remained. Deodorant and perfume out on the counter instead of put away. Her blue jean skirt, tank top, beige bra and panties were tossed carelessly on the floor in the bathroom. She thought about the chaotic weekend that outfit had endured and smiled as she picked them up and threw them in her laundry bag along with her new western jeans and the rest of the clothes she had worn today.

Leslie knew that Regan would ask her to stay tomorrow night and the next and that she would accept. There wasn't much time left. She also knew that Regan would ask her to stay in Abilene or at least to return to Abilene to see how things might work out between them. Given her response to him this weekend it would be hard for him to accept the rejection she would ultimately have to give. If he knew the truth, he would try to convince her of his durability and ask her to give up her vigil.

Leslie opened the nightstand drawer and took out the boxes. She lay down on the bed and set them on her abdomen. Tonight she allowed her mind to drift to the last time she had seen her husband and children alive.

It was a perfect day at the beginning of a long weekend in the spring. Sunny, cloudless, seventy-five degrees. The kind of day that is sorely anticipated by northerners exposed to a long winter. They had decided to spend it at Mohonk Mountain House, the family's favorite vacation spot, despite its being practically in their backyard. The car was packed on Friday night and ready to leave early on Saturday. The initial plans were for all of them to drive up together on Friday and return on Monday night. But Leslie had an unexpected problem with one of her patients and was going to have to come back early to operate on Monday morning. They would have to take both cars so Chris and the kids could stay later on Monday.

Despite all the early preparations and packing, things were chaotic Friday morning, and it took longer to get ready than they had hoped. They stopped at McDonald's to pick up breakfast on the way. The kids were fired up about that, but they knew their mom wouldn't allow eating Egg McMuffins and hash browns in her car. Usually when taking two cars, one would ride with her and the other with Chris. That day, they both went with him. She remembered feeling jealous. It was so easy for them to get along with Chris. It took a little more work with her. They were excited about Egg McMuffins and eating them on the road. Leslie got a cup of coffee. The kids had their breakfast in hand and had run out to the car.

Chris knew what she was thinking. He could read it in her face. Something between aggravation and just plain loneliness. Didn't want to drive there alone. Didn't want the kids to just want to ride with their dad. They didn't even ask to ride with her. They knew better. He reached over and put his hand around the back of her neck. She leaned toward him as they walked to the car, and he kissed her on the cheek.

"Hey, it's just fifteen minutes. Then I'll race you up to the tower." The kids were waiting for him to open the doors. He hit the remote and they climbed in. They waved to her from the open Volvo sunroof as they pulled out of the parking lot. She hadn't kissed them goodbye. She opened her sunroof, blew them a kiss and waved back.

Chris leading, they drove through town and then headed west on 299. There was very little traffic and he started to speed up. Leslie fell in behind, watching them and the road. She could see the kids talking, turning their heads. Every once in a while Chris turned his head to say something to them. She could see it so clearly.

The sun roof was still open and even though the weather was perfect, for some reason the wind was bothering her. Blowing her hair, creating pressure in her ears. She looked up to push the button to close it. Why did she look for the button? The German engineers who designed the car had put it in a place where it could easily be found by feel. But she looked up this time. She pushed it and in that singular instant she heard something and jerked her head down, stomach heaving at the same time, the feeling of needing to go to the bathroom instantly. Smoke was coming out of the back of Chris' car. The red tail-lights were on. She slammed on her brakes, but was too late. She was going to run into them. She tightened her jaw and arms and put every ounce of power in her legs into the brake pedal. BMW anti-lock braking mechanism working full force to protect her. The car stayed true...and slammed into them. Not enough to hurt them, but it was enough to push them out into the east bound lane where they were tipped by another car. And then plowed into by the eighteen wheeler. The car spun, and then flipped. She didn't know whether or not she actually saw them spinning, but for some reason the thought that they were was forever impressed in her mind. Paint in a centrifuge. Souvenir pictures from a carnival.

People were pulling over. She jumped out of her car. Someone yelled that they were calling 911. In a knee-jerk reaction she yelled out, "I'm a doctor, I'm a doctor." And she was running to their car.

Someone was already there. "Doc, I don't know how much you can help here." A lay person told her he didn't know if she could fucking help.

She was screaming, crying, "Help me with the doors please. Help me get them out." She reached for Chris's door. She couldn't see him because of the blood splattered on the broken window. Matching stains were on all their windows. Their seat belts were in place. The front air bag had deployed. But their delicate skulls and necks couldn't hold up to the blows they received.

A guy came running up. "I'm an EMT. What do we have here?"

Leslie didn't answer, she was yelling to Chris, Vic and Vivi. She was pulling hopelessly at the smashed in doors. The back passenger window was completely broken and she ran around to Vic's side. She looked in, yelling their names.

"Jesus Christ, she knows these people."

"It's my husband and my children. Somebody help me!"

She doesn't remember how they got them out. When they got them out. She remembered pulling on the safety glass. Pulling pieces of it out. Vic's head was swollen, bloody, purple against his blonde hair. His chin was resting on his chest. Vivi was lying to her right on the seat, her head touching Vic's thigh. Together in the beginning...and in the end. Chris was pressed up against the head rest by the airbag. There were no sounds. No movement. No labored breathing. Nothing. She could smell Egg McMuffins mixed with the smell of burning rubber and plastic. And blood.

"Doctor, please sit down. Let me take care of this." The EMT was off duty. Just happened to be in the area. He went to work. She heard sirens. The police and ambulances arrived. They quickly and efficiently went to work. Her family was extricated from the car. They were extricated!

Leslie walked numbly over to her babies. A highway patrolman thought about trying to stop her for a second, but let her by. What was the point? She knelt on the ground and lifted the sheets. Their hair was matted down to the sides of their heads. Their little twin faces, different but the same in so many ways, were peaceful, asleep. Opposite head injuries. Opposite but the same in its effect. A loose spring breeze blew through. Their hair floated around their faces where it could. She bent over and kissed them. She smelled their skin.

She had spent almost half her life with the man under the third sheet and she went over to look at him for the last time. The sheet was distorted over his right leg and she could tell it was broken. She thought for a second about how she could have fixed that. There was blood on the left side of the sheet by his head. She pulled the sheet back and saw her children in his relaxed face. She reached out to touch it. To pat it. To make it better.

Her husband's car, the ambulance and the police car formed a loose triangle around her family. The breeze created little eddies that moved about the space lifting the sheets slightly as they moved. The reality mixed with the want and she thought she saw breathing, the wind breathing life. They could be alive...if only.

33

*L*eslie went to sleep thinking about the ifs and what ifs of that day. If they had eaten breakfast at home. If she had obeyed the two-second rule. If they had left the house five minutes earlier or later. If she had kissed them goodbye rather than blown them a kiss. These were the thoughts she had gone over and over for the past three years.

She woke up the next morning thinking about Regan and Doc, Abilene, Texas and Evansville, Indiana. She was thinking about New Paltz and the storage room. For three years she had avoided uncertainty and disorder. She had avoided commitment. And gifts. She steered clear of these things and it had served her well. It had provided her the strength to persevere. Now she felt confused.

But she had been confused before. She would work this out. She had worked out worse things. Many times before. Now she would get out of bed and work through it like she had done before. Get ready for work. It could be that simple.

She showered, dressed and went to the hospital. Only Jesús was left in the house. Emilio was visiting him and he had a prosthesis. He was going to physical therapy in the hospital to learn how to use it. He could pinch with the two hooks. Leslie knew it wouldn't be long before he could use it functionally. She was proud of him and proud of the system that took care of him. Emilio would wait in Abilene until Jesús was ready to go home. Then the bus ride back to some mean border town. She didn't want to think beyond that for them.

She had Jesús to concern herself with now. They discussed his surgery again and she thought he had a fairly good understanding of the operation. Leslie went over the risks and complications so he could sign his permit. Going down the list of potential complications she could tell she had lost him after the basics of bleeding and infection, and injury to nerves and blood vessels. He looked at her like Cal Wimberley had when she had gone over the permit before his operation. Jesús reached for the pen and the clipboard holding the *permiso*. He signed his name and handed it back to Leslie.

"Estoy en sus manos, Doctora." And indeed he would be in her hands. Tomorrow. She shook his hand and told him everything would be fine. Jesús replied, *"Si Dios quiere."* In his mind it all came down to that.

Doc was already at the office when Leslie arrived. She looked forward to seeing Doc and Brenda but realized that they also contributed to her confusion. She felt commitment to them and from them. It was something she didn't really want, but she couldn't say she didn't like it.

In the break room she fixed a cup of coffee and helped herself to a glazed donut. At that moment Doc came in, and she sensed instantly that there was something different in his demeanor. Her mind started asking questions and answering them too. Did Doc have to go into the hospital over the weekend and work without her help? Was he tired? And the obvious question. Did he know? Her mind jumped to Frank Long and his buddy, Peterman. Her buddy, Peterman. It would only be a matter of time.

"Did you have a good time this weekend?" Doc asked with a smile.

"I did. Did you get any calls?"

"Hell, no. Everything was quiet. Just the usual phone calls for pain pills. That's about it. Wha'd'y'all do out at Regan's place? He have some kind of a shindig?"

"He did. They roasted a whole pig! Pretty good eating too, as they say in these parts."

"You know, I think I had heard that he did that. He's built some kind of underground pit to cook it."

"That's right," Leslie replied and then told him all about it. "I had a really good time."

"Glad to hear it. You needed the break."

"Thanks for covering for me." Leslie was anxious to change the subject. "So, do you think you could give me a hand on our fellow from Mexico?"

"Sure. Look forward to it. What time's it scheduled?"

"Seven AM."

"Sounds good. You're reconstructing both his anterior and posterior cruciate ligaments, right?"

"Right. I'm using allografts for both. Went over it with him today. I think he's as ready as he going to be. His buddy's already got his below elbow prosthesis. The hospital did a great job with that one. That's a crack team of social workers over there."

"They get the job done."

Leslie started to feel like they were making small talk. She got a little uncomfortable. Doc had not sat down yet. He was drinking his coffee standing up, so she stood as well. In a little while she asked how many patients they were seeing in clinic today. They heard Brenda coming down the hall with her efficient got-work-to-do step. The three met in the hallway.

"First patient's up."

Doc and Leslie converged on the single patient. Leslie helped Doc get caught up but tried to let him see the patients for the most part. She introduced him to some of the new patients she had treated while he was out. It was a strange day because it didn't seem that long ago that he had been doing the same with her, and it put in perspective the short duration of her stay in Abilene and the even shorter duration of her affair with Regan.

At the end of the day, Doc seemed pleased. He was ready to get back to work. She was happy for him but had a sudden sense of uselessness for herself. Doc saw a patient in the office who had waited for his surgery until he was back. He scheduled that case to follow Jesús on Tuesday. They would be done with surgery by noon. She thought about going out to the stadium Tuesday afternoon. Seeing those lights go up was something she didn't want to miss.

Wednesday would be a full day, but as far as she could tell, there was nothing scheduled for Thursday morning or Friday. She was leaving Friday night so having that morning off would be good. She'd talk to Doc about it.

"Doc, you got a minute?" She approached him in the break room after clinic was over.

"Of course. What's on your mind?" They headed down the hall to his office and sat down on opposite sides of his desk.

"Well, you are really doing well, and I'm thinking you might not need so much of my help. I mean, I'm here if you need me, don't get me wrong."

"I know that."

"I was just looking at our...your schedule and thinking that you're paying me a lot of money for basically half-time work this week."

"Well, you're right, things are slow, but by design. I don't really feel up to working full speed yet. Still..."

"Let's see, tomorrow we have two cases. You'll be helping me on Jesús, but your other guy, well, that's up to you. I can help if you want. If not, I'll just take some time off. Same with Thursday and Friday. I could use Friday morning to pack and all."

"Sounds like you've got things figured out. Got plans with a certain cowboy?" Now he was sounding like dad.

She gave him a school-girl innocent look. "Now you're getting personal."

Doc's facial expression suddenly became somber. Leslie knew what was coming. She had known it all day. He knew. Peterman. Long. Doc. Twenty-one days too long in one place. He reached across the desk and put his hand on top of hers. A hand dry, like hers, only thick, stubby fingers. He patted her hand.

"Doc, now I know something I'm sure you didn't want me to know. It just happened by accident and I promise you I wasn't looking for it." When he looked at her face he knew it was true. "Godamnit, I didn't want it to be true, more than just about anything I didn't want that to be true. But you know, in my heart I knew it was true." Doc looked down at his lap. "It explains a lot. In fact, it explains you."

Leslie stared at their hands through tear glazed eyes. Couldn't focus and couldn't speak. Couldn't speak because since the time she had described the accident over and over to Chris' parents, she had never spoken out loud about the accident to anyone. She didn't want to say the words. *My husband and children are dead. I made a mistake.*

"I don't know what to say, Leslie. I can imagine that you don't want to talk about it. But since I heard it, I haven't been able to get it off my mind."

"Long."

He nodded. "I don't think he knew that it was something you were keeping to yourself."

"No, I know that. He just found out by accident. An old buddy of his from medical school. Doc, it was bound to happen sooner or later. I just usually don't stay anywhere long enough for people to figure me out, that's all. It's been three years and I haven't been any one place for longer than a week."

"Jesus, Leslie, that's just hard to imagine. It's a wasted life. I mean your personal life. It's wasted."

"It's not a life, Doc. It's not that hard to do."

"You can't tell me that, Leslie. You're wrong about that. There's a lot of life in you. I've seen it with me and Brenda, the staff, your patients. I'd be willing to bet on Regan Wakeman too. You're trying to waste a life, but you can't. In time you'll get tired of trying. And you know what?"

Leslie looked up at Doc.

"I hope when you get tired you'll think of Abilene. And I'm serious about that."

Leslie didn't know what to say. She was touched but didn't want to be.

"You don't have to say anything about this at all. It's just one old fart talking to a colleague, okay?"

She nodded as Doc handed her a Kleenex from a box on his desk. He stood up, and she was thankful that he hadn't pressed her for details. Enough said. A man of few words who had just probably said more than he had ever thought of saying before. She appreciated him.

"So about our deal, Doc. Is it on?" Leslie asked as she regained her voice.

"What deal is that?"

"You know, me working half-time."

"Oh, hey, a deal is a deal, and your pay was in the contract. I'm not going to cheat you out of that just because we're not that busy this week. Our original agreement wasn't based on volume. You can take as much time off as you need, but I'm still planning on paying you the same."

"Doc. I don't need the money. And you're ready to work."

"Well, if you're gonna put it that way, maybe we can work it out."

"I'd like that. I have a lot of things I need to get in order."

Later, as Leslie was running in the park, she noticed it was staying lighter a little longer. Lots of people were out walking, jogging, swinging. Not much later Leslie was thinking about Regan and their two-week romance. Two weeks wasn't long in the scheme of things, and there was a scheme. Regan was an unwitting player. She felt bad about that. He would be fine, but for selfish reasons she needed the rest of the week to be with him. She liked being with him. She needed him for the next few days. And she needed to end it, what...honorably? Could there be honor when there was a lie?

Leslie knew she would leave a piece of her heart in Abilene and wondered where that piece would come from.

Her phone rang. R WAKEMAN. "Hey. Are you jogging?"

"More like walking. What are you up to?"

"Lights."

"Are they up?"

"Two of them are. Took longer than we thought. I was hoping for three, but you know I had to save some for you. Are you coming out tomorrow?"

"Wouldn't miss it for the world. I'll be done in surgery around noon or so. I can call you when I'm through."

"Sure. Sooo, what are you doing tonight?"

"For starters, I'm on call for Ortho at the ER. Then I've got an early case tomorrow. We're starting at seven."

"That's right. Your train accident guy from Mexico. You were determined to get him done before you leave, weren't you? Good for you both."

"Yeah. It's good. Doc's going to help. He'll be following him up in the office if he doesn't get deported, so it'll be better if he knows first hand what I did."

"Sounds like a plan. Are you on call any more this week?"

"I'm pretty much done, other than a few half days in clinic, unless some emergencies come in. Doc has one other case tomorrow. I may or may not help him with it. I should be done around noon."

"Why don't I come to town and get you when you're done. We can grab a bite to eat and head out to the site. You're not going to want to miss these lights. For the benefit of your next career."

Leslie walked and jogged until the sun went down. She was exhausted. Her legs felt heavy and stiff. She wanted to fall asleep when her head hit the pillow. Didn't want to think about Regan, Doc or the accident. Either sleep or go set a wrist fracture. She slept. No one got hurt. There were no children jumping from one bed to another tonight. There were no nursing home residents slipping out of wheelchairs tonight. No one stubbed their pinky toe on the edge of a bed. And no one hit anyone head on coming home from a bar. Leslie slept.

34

*J*esús was being given his preoperative dose of antibiotics at about the time Leslie woke up in her hotel bed. They took him down to the surgery holding area where nurses checked all his paperwork three times over and asked him if he had any allergies the same number of times. They asked him to mark the thigh of the leg which was to be operated on with a "YES." He couldn't actually mark the knee because the grafts made his skin rough, like a thick screen, so he had to write just above the area, where the skin was normal. He laughed as he did his best to write on the involved leg because it seemed like it would be obvious that this was the correct leg. The nurses didn't laugh with him. It was like making bomb jokes in an airport.

The stacks of paper in his chart were reviewed again, and for the fourth and last time Jesús was asked, this time by the anesthesiologist, if he had any *alergias*. It was then that Leslie walked in, well rested, followed by Doc. She introduced Jesús to Doc. They shook hands. She asked Jesús if he was ready and he said "yes." She asked if he had any questions and he shook his head. With the purple skin marker she wrote her initials next to the "YES." The nurses took him back to the operating room, Jesús went under anesthesia and Leslie started the case at ten minutes after seven.

First she examined his knee. Without the benefit of the strong muscles of the thigh to guard it, the knee was easy to manipulate. Her exam confirmed the absence of functioning anterior and posterior cruciate ligaments. She would still take a look at the ligaments and make the final determination after actually seeing the problem inside the knee. She had all the equipment and tendon grafts for any potential injury she might find. She was "loaded for bear." A fellow resident, a Texan, had used that term to describe "everything but the kitchen sink." Guns and the things they shot were not generally the stuff of colloquial expressions in New York.

Jesús' leg was cleaned with the gooey Betadine gel. His skin grafts had taken well. She injected the incision sites with local anesthetic and epinephrine to cut down on bleeding, then pumped the joint full of water and put the scope inside through a small incision. Examining all parts of the knee with the small fiber optic camera, she found that Jesús had some minor damage to the surface cartilage of his knee but the meniscal cartilages were okay. Both ligaments were completely torn so she had the nurse thaw two of the tendon grafts. They were removed from Styrofoam containers filled with dry ice.

Doc was gowned by this time, and both went to work on drilling holes where they would insert the grafts, ultimately reproducing the function of the two ligaments. Once these were completed Leslie cleaned out the bone shavings from within the knee. One of the scrub techs prepared the grafts on another table. By the time the knee was prepared they were ready to insert.

She put the graft replacing the posterior cruciate ligament in first because its location was harder to see. Once that graft was screwed into place the tendon for the anterior cruciate was inserted. Proper tightening when two ligaments were torn was a little harder since there was no anatomic reference point as there would be with only one torn ligament. They did their best to put the knee in a neutral position for final tightening of the grafts. This being satisfactory, the last screws were inserted. The stability of both grafts felt good, and they were basically finished. Leslie closed up the small incisions. Doc broke scrub.

"Great case, Doc," he said as he walked out. He thanked everyone for their help. Leslie felt good about the surgery and relieved to have it behind her.

After she was done and Jesús was headed to recovery room, she met up with Doc in the lounge. Over a cup of coffee they talked about the next case, just a basic knee arthroscopy on a patient with a meniscus tear. Doc felt he could do the case himself and Leslie thought that he wanted to do just that. She told him she had medical records to sign and would be in the hospital if he changed his mind. He could just page her overhead.

She finished her dictations and signed all her orders on the charts. She would have the final transcriptions on Jesús' chart tomorrow and hopefully there would be nothing incomplete when she left town. Leslie called up to the operating room and learned that Doc had finished. She swung by the family waiting area, but no one was there. Not even Emilio. Leslie felt some common bond with Jesús. No one to wait on him. No one with whom to share the photos of his knee operation. It also reminded her that no one who knew Jesús would ever appreciate the complexity of the surgery he had on his knee.

At 11:15 she called Regan to tell him she was finished. He would pick her up at noon and then decide about lunch. Regan would try to think of some other gourmet restaurant between now and then. "I wouldn't be disappointed in JJ's or the place out in front of the hotel to be honest with you." Leslie was just looking forward to seeing him.

She took a quick shower since she had bad operating room hat hair. It ranked up there with hard hat hair. Maybe worse because the mask straps cinch it in two places and the poofy OR hat makes it stick up straight in front. Made her hair look like a hay bale or something.

A typical west Texas spring day is powder blue, cloudless, and brings with it a fair amount of wind. She had not appreciated the slight warmth early in the morning when leaving to go to the hospital. When Leslie got to the lobby she could see the truck under the portico. Regan was talking on his cell phone, but he got out of the truck and followed her around to open the door. He tipped the phone upward away from his mouth and kissed her before he let her in. He kept talking as he went back around to get into the truck. He was saying something about the light situation. It sounded like there were problems getting them hooked up for power.

"Listen, Cal, Leslie's here. Gotta go. I'll see ya out there in a little bit. We're going to grab some lunch first."

He hung up and reached over, grabbing her thigh just above the knee and squeezing. Like Chris used to do. Kind of a hurt tickle. Vic had tried to imitate his dad but his hand never got big enough to get any leverage on his mom's knee. It would then be Leslie's turn and she had plenty of leverage on Vic's skinny thigh. Vic would squeal in partial pretend pain ahead of time since he knew he would have to pay for the attempt on his mom. Then he'd go practice on his sister where he might get some reaction if he could catch her off guard. Now Leslie squealed in partial pretend pain. Just a reflex. She grabbed his hand. They kept hold.

"Where do you want to go eat?"

"I don't care really. Over here's fine unless you have some other place in mind."

"Let's see. Too many memories here. This is where you told me you didn't want to get serious. Memories at JJ's too. That's where we had our first date...sort of. Hmm, we're running out of places to eat."

"I can see it's a problem for you."

"I know. There's a greasy spoon down the road. Pretty good food." He headed down the highway a few miles, made a couple of turns and they were there. It was exactly as advertised. A greasy spoon. Red brick walls. Low roof. Windows all around. A few handmade signs painted on the windows, advertised their specials. Chicken Fried Steak Special. $5.99. One big open room with a smoking section designated on the left side so there was a definite smell of cigarettes in the air. It didn't really bother her even though she was getting spoiled since leaving the northeast where most restaurants still allowed smoking. As she went west, more and more places restricted smoking altogether.

"Ever had chicken fried steak?"

"Can't say that I have." She had heard about the evils of chicken fried steak. Adkin's, Pritikin. Name it. Chicken fried steak was on everyone's short list of things that are unequivocally bad. And here was her lover getting ready to order one. Should she say something? Warn him?

"Well, you haven't had southern cooking until you've had a chicken fried steak. Let's split one. They're huge."

There was something suspicious about chicken fried steak. It just didn't sound right, but she gave in and agreed to taste it. Next would probably come a craving for fried pig skins and those little homemade pecan pies she saw in all the southern gas stations.

The waitress came over with menus, but Regan ordered iced tea and the steak before she could put them on the table.

"Ma'am, what do you want for your sides?"

"What do you have?"

In a monotonous tone the waitress began to run down a long list of side dishes. Okra, three bean salad, corn on the cob, creamed corn.

Leslie lost track. She asked Regan what he was having.

"I always get it with mashed potatoes and gravy, and green beans."

"That sounds good. Gravy on the side, please" She looked up at the gum-chewing waitress.

"That's how it comes, ma'am." Regan was smiling at Leslie. "So it's mashed potatoes and gravy, green beans for both of you."

"Yeah and bring an extra plate please. We're going to split the steak."

"There'll be an extra charge for her sides."

"No problem."

"How do you want the steak done?"

Regan looked at Leslie. "I always get it well. Is that okay?"

Anything sounding as strange and evil as a chicken fried steak probably needed to be cooked. A lot. She nodded.

"So, tell me about your case. How'd everything go?"

Leslie gave her best layperson-friendly description of the operation. She tried not to use too many technical terms although a lot of the things she did were familiar to people in the construction fields. People like carpenters, architects, contractors and Regan had little trouble understanding. They had talked a lot about Jesús and he knew she was relieved to be able to fix his knee before she left. He reached over and squeezed her hand. "I'm proud of you."

Now that embarrassed her. She rolled her eyes. "Hey, it's part of the job description."

"Right. You're too much."

"So, what's going on out at the stadium?"

Regan did his best layperson-friendly description of the light situation for Leslie. "We're getting the lights up. Problem is the electrical power. You've got six banks of lights. Each has about a hundred, fifteen hundred watt halide lights on it. That takes some special electrical specs and really, we were prepared for that, but the inspectors came in today and just changed them. Boom. We can go ahead and put up the lights but it will delay getting them turned on by a couple of days. In the scheme of things it's business-as-usual. Over the course of this project, legal and inspection delays probably cost me about thirty days. Frankly, I wanted you to be there when we turned them on."

"Oh, don't worry about me. I just want to see the lights go up. I can see stadium lights anytime." She wanted to make him feel better about not getting the lights on, but somehow it didn't come out like that. "I mean, I can see lights on some other time, you know like on some other stadium...or something." She was chewing on her foot now.

"Sweetheart, I know that. Don't worry about it. It's just one of those things." He squeezed her hand again. It had been there, holding hers the whole time.

"Okay, here we go. I got your chicken fried steak here." The waitress waited a moment and looked down at their hands. The table was small and there were two gigantic platters in her hands, along with a basket full of those thick pieces of bread they call "Texas toast." Regan let go of Leslie's hand and scooted back in his chair a little. He put his hands on the top of his thighs, elbows out to the side a little. Like he was surveying the situation. Leslie thought she might just crack up, because this was too cute. He had probably sat like this for a chicken fried steak a million times before. His granddad probably sat like this for a chicken fried steak. She decided to try it. She backed up in her chair a little. Spread her legs apart a little. Put her hands on her thighs, fingers turned in and leaned forward toward the platter displaying something that looked like a nuked Frisbee. Regan caught her theatrics.

"Well, check it out." They both started laughing. Regan picked up his rolled up fork and knife, undid the napkin and put it on his lap. Then positioned the utensils to cut the slab in two.

"Whoa," Leslie said. She put her hand up. "Maybe just half that much."

"Baby, I'm gonna eat the rest of this in about forty-five seconds and you're gonna wish you had asked for your half. Trust me."

"You trust me. I don't care how delicious it is, I can only eat so much food, period." He cut her a smaller piece and put it on her plate where it sat beside a giant blob of mashed potatoes, with the skins mixed in, and a big fist-full of green beans, onions and bacon. There was a white porcelain cup of cream gravy on the side.

When Leslie's mom was teaching her about manners, she reminded her that if she was ever in doubt about how to eat something, or which utensil to use, she should just watch the host and imitate what they do. She watched Regan take his little cup of gravy and pour it over the entire steak and mashed potatoes. She followed suit. He cut a piece of steak, speared some green beans and swiped it through the potatoes. She did the same. And her taste buds were met with just about the most delicious single medley of food she had ever had in one bite. Maybe the Thanksgiving bite of turkey, dressing and mashed potatoes compared, but that was influenced by the good old fashioned Thanksgiving memories. Maybe this was too. She dug in and about fifteen minutes later they had both cleaned their plates and were sopping up the gravy with the Texas toast.

"Check please."

Regan grabbed a toothpick from one of those little stainless steel roller thingamajigs and put it in his mouth. The lady at the cash register asked for $10.79. The low price, another reminder of the dubious nature of the meal.

"Want one?" He pointed to the little thingamajig and smiled. Walked away from the counter without waiting for an answer.

She started to put her seat belt on in the truck, but Regan stopped her. He leaned over and kissed her full on the mouth, right outside of the restaurant. Then he said, "Scoot over here." Just commanded her to scoot over toward him. He was in a company crew truck and the front seat was a bench, not the leather bucket seats like in his other truck. She looked down at the seat in horror. A forty year old orthopedic surgeon sitting in the middle seat of a truck, legs straddling the hump, with her boyfriend's arm around her, driving down the highway. No way. Next thing she knew, she was scooting over and he put his arm around her as they drove away.

35

*L*eslie scanned the horizon as they crossed the overpass. The three lights completely changed the appearance of the stadium. They now dominated the structure and gave it symmetry. Defined it as a stadium, not an Aztec temple. As they approached the stadium, she saw a lot of activity surrounding the setting of the lights. Besides the lights and the poles, the tremendous mobile crane being used to raise them stood out. LIEBHERR. Black block letters on a huge yellow tank-truck-like body. There were stout hydraulic outriggers on the four corners and the middle of the vehicle lifting the entire apparatus off the ground for stability.

The crane looked like it was fully extended. There was a thick base from which rose progressively smaller extensions, like a periscope. At the very end a weighted cable dangled that she guessed would lift the pole and lights into place.

As they pulled into the construction site, Leslie shifted back over to the passenger side of bench seat. Regan looked at her and winked, then became focused on what was happening on the east side of the stadium.

"Let's get hats." They got out and went over to the trailer. Regan went in and came out wearing his and handed her another. "Hang on just a sec."

He went over to talk to Cal who waved at Leslie. She waved back. They talked for a minute, hands gesturing, pointing up, over, this way and that. Cal wrote down a couple of things on a clipboard, and Regan came back.

"We're going to go up there so we're out of the way, and I can tell you what's going on." There was a lot of noise, and he had to yell. The lights were going up on the visitor's side of the stadium. They hurried into the stadium and up to the far side of the new bleachers. On the other side she could see crews putting in the blue seats for the home team spectators. They matched the color of the tin roofs on the field house and snack bars. The press box building was still open, but Leslie could make out the framing for the elevator and the glass.

They had a great view of the lights going up on the opposite end of the bleachers. "The stadium has about six hundred of these fifteen hundred watt metal halide lights. It's great for television. There's no yellow cast to the lighting."

"How tall are the poles?"

"They're about one hundred thirty-five feet tall including the light banks. We'll leave them the light galvanized steel color so they won't stand out against the sky. The architect, school district and the city decided on poles this tall in order to cut down on the glare you get with lower lighting. That crane can lift something over one hundred and eighty feet in the air."

They watched as the boom swung out over one of the assembled light banks in the parking lot. Several workers were needed to attach the weighted pulley to the top of the rack of lights. Additional cables were assembled along the length of the pole to stabilize it as the crane raised it into the air.

"All the bulbs and luminaries are pre-assembled. That way no one will have to climb up there to work on them. They've been tested and everything. Of course we won't know for sure until we throw the switch."

Someone whistled, the crew stepped away and the crane went to work. Several things happened simultaneously. The entire crane slowly swung around while the various "booms and jibs," as Regan was calling them, began to extend. The light pole left the ground, light bank first, followed by the rest of the pole, until it was hanging straight up and down. Now the crew gathered around the pylon that was to accept the pole. There were about a dozen large bolt-like objects mounted on the pylon and matching holes in the bottom of the galvanized steel poles.

"Now they've got to get it over the post and set it. Once it's in place on the bolts, they'll level it up and fasten it down. Simple. No rocket science here. The part of the crane at the very end is called the lattice. You'll see it kind of unfold and fine tune the position of the pole."

Leslie could hear a lot of yelling, see a lot of hand signaling, inches left or right, up or down. The men were huddled around the base. They brought in power wrench-like machines to put on the bolts and fasten them down. Welding sparks spewed like fireworks. The job of attaching this huge, top heavy structure that would be subjected to decades of West Texas windstorms, maybe even tornados, was done. No rocket science here. Just get it right.

"Well, that's about it. Splice the electrical connections at the bottom of the poles and we're cookin'. What do you think?"

"Your guys made it look easy. That crane is pretty amazing."

"No kidding. Leave it to the Germans. Hey, okay if I leave you up here for a minute?"

"Of course. You go on. I'm fine."

"I'll be back up in a little while. When they get to the pole at this end, why don't you move to the other end of the bleachers?

As Regan started down the bleachers, Leslie called to him. "Regan. I'm really proud of you."

He stopped on one of the benches and turned around. He had to yell to be heard over the engine noise. "Just part of the job description!" Then he took off, jumping from one bench to the next until he got to the stairwell.

The next light went up the same way and finally the last one. It was about 5:30 when they finished. The stadium was totally transformed with all six light poles in place. It had an incredible effect on the landscape, good or bad depending on one's perspective. But as an isolated structure, it was unequalled in its imposing immensity out here on the west Texas plains. She did feel a sense of pride in Regan's achievement.

Suddenly she heard a whistle. Regan was waving to her from the lower level, signaling her to come down. Choosing not to climb down, bleacher to bleacher, as Regan had done, Leslie found the nearest staircase to make her descent.

"There's not a whole lot to do around here on the weekdays," Regan said, and he suggested they go for a jog and then maybe a movie. Leslie was amused that he had his jogging stuff with him. They went back to the hotel and he told her he would wait outside for her after he got changed in the lobby restroom. She thought about inviting him up to her room to change but that would be too personal for her. Her lifestyle was strange and he would see that. Her lack of clothing, just her lack of sentimental things would be apparent to anyone, even a guy. What if he saw her little boxes?

She and Regan had never talked much about where she came from or her past. Did she have a home address? What would he think if he saw what she had with her and knew she had no home where things were stored?

If she had to buy extra items because of unexpected weather, she always left them unless the weather where she was headed was going to be the same. If she saved winter clothes, gloves, boots and things like that she would have to travel with trunks. She bought inexpensive stuff and left it behind. All her possessions fit in two suitcases.

Jogging with Regan was another first for Leslie. She had not run with anyone since Chris. After the twins they bought a Baby Jogger and they were four on the track. Chris could always outpace her even when he was pushing the kids. Regan could too. They stayed together on the trail for a couple of miles. She was running faster than her normal pace and started to get winded. Trying not to act winded made it worse, and pretty soon she couldn't talk. She finally had to slow down and told Regan to go on. She kept jogging but slowed her pace. He went on and lapped her. On the next lap she started to walk. Regan caught up and they walked together.

"Where were you that Friday when I called you from the airport?"

"Out here. I went over and sat on those swings."

"I wanted to be here with you that night. I don't know why I was so disappointed not to be. I knew we'd be together all weekend unless something weird happened."

"Hey, something weird did happen."

"You know what I mean." Regan took her hand. His hand was warm, sweaty. "It was just a strange night. And now here we are."

"It was strange. I felt the same way, but there wasn't anything I could do about it. I thought I would stay out here until you came home. I just knew you were going to drive up to the park any minute. I thought maybe you were in Abilene already."

They walked in silence holding hands. After a couple of turns around the path they went over and sat down on the rubber swings.

They twisted around in them and swung back and forth a little, trying to keep the obvious things on their minds from surfacing.

Regan thought about where Leslie came from and where she was going. He was mystified by the sudden development of their relationship. Thinking also about Friday, coming on like the still before a storm, he was just as powerless to alter its course.

He stood and stepped behind Leslie on the swing. He started pushing her. For a moment the mood lightened. Leslie's grip tightened on the rough chains. She laughed in delight as her swing climbed higher, leaning back on the upswing, then pulling with her arms and legs at the peak of the swing's arc. Even though her hips became uncomfortable in the rubber swing more suited to a child, she wanted to prolong this moment.

Once Leslie had the momentum, Regan climbed into the swing next to hers and started pushing himself. Leslie felt a thrill as she reached that highest point where she briefly hung, suspended in air, before gravity pulled her back. She felt a competitive rush as Regan gained on her. The youthful impulse to swing high, lean back and pump with all their might won out over the need to talk.

The wind whipped across them, increasing the difficulty of staying straight. Leslie relaxed a little and the swing gradually began to decelerate. She had the sudden urge to vault out of the swing as she had done when she was a kid. She looked over at Regan whose swing was also slowing down. He caught her intention immediately.

"Don't even think about it. I won't know the first thing about turning your leg back around."

She chickened out anyway and when the swing was almost stopped she kind of hopped out of it and took a couple of running steps to decelerate. Regan did jump and intentionally stumbled over to her. He grabbed clumsily at her, pretending to catch himself and then challenged her to a race back to his truck.

Behind them the swings were caught in a shortened arc by their remaining momentum. They swung back and forth over bare patches of red dirt. The evening breeze blew perpendicular to their path and picked up the dust loosened by Regan and Leslie's feet.

When they got back in the truck, Regan asked Leslie to come home with him as she knew he would.

36

*J*esús was doing fine the next morning. He was in a lot of pain but was getting plenty of pain medication. He was used to walking with crutches since his first surgery so that wouldn't take much time to relearn. In a couple of days he would probably be ready to leave the hospital. Leslie talked with him about his operation. She also asked about Emilio. Not only was he was still in town but had found a place to stay. Jesús could stay there too but transportation was a problem. He would have to pay someone to bring him to Doc's office. She wrote an order in the chart for the social workers to check on funding for transportation. Jesús would have to find a way to get to the office or Leslie would need to keep him in house until it was time to take out his stitches.

She saw patients with Doc in the morning. Brenda invited Leslie over to dinner that evening. She thought about Regan but then decided she could go out to his place after dinner. He had asked her to stay with him until she left. She had accepted.

That afternoon she saw her own patients with Doc but used some of the time to fill out and fax some forms to Indiana. She made some calls to the agency and to the doctor she was covering. It was going to be *locum tenens* work as usual. Most patients had been rescheduled. She would be checking post-op patients and those who couldn't wait a week to be seen. She would also be available for their emergencies through the ER and for walk-in patients in the office. It would be light work, early hours and a short stay. Back to her usual M.O.

She started to get up from the desk to go see if Doc was getting along when her cell phone rang. She didn't expect anyone to call except Regan and she nearly answered it without glancing at the caller ID. Habit took over her impulses and just before pushing the TALK button she glanced at the caller ID screen and saw a name she had not seen in three years. Prior to three years ago she had seen it everyday, sometimes two or three times a day. L MCCULLEN. And below it, the familiar area code and phone number in New Paltz, New York. Lynn.

Leslie didn't answer. She wasn't prepared to answer. How did Lynn find her? How did she get her phone number? Her heart was pounding in her chest, and it was painful not to answer. She waited for the phone to ring the usual five times before she knew her voice mail would kick in. In a few seconds the light on her screen went dark. There would be a message. She didn't want to hear it. Not now.

With her mind full of questions about the call, Leslie went to see more patients with Doc.

She was expected for dinner at 6:30. She called Regan to let him know and then drove to the hotel. In the privacy of room 225 she pushed her voice mail code and listened.

"Leslie." Her best friend's voice. She had heard her friend cry many times before and she could tell she had been crying. "If this is the number for Leslie Cohen. Leslie, I can't believe maybe I've found you. Please call me when you get this message. Please come home. We miss you. Call me."

Leslie started to push the callback button but hesitated. Touch one button. It wasn't that easy. Where had she been for three years? Where was she living? What was she doing? So much time had elapsed. Any answer would be incomprehensible. She put down the phone. She didn't need those questions right now.

When Brenda opened the door, Leslie could tell she knew the story. She hooked her arm in Leslie's and walked with her to the kitchen table. Leslie suddenly thought about how much she missed her mom and dad. How things would have been different if they had been alive at the time of the accident.

"Hal! Leslie's here!"

And from somewhere down the hall, "I'm comin'."

Brenda was broiling fish and had prepared a salad. "Now she's got me eating healthy," Doc said as he walked into the kitchen.

Leslie asked if she could help, but Brenda told them to sit down. She noticed that Doc was wearing a loose fitting shirt and baggy pants. Covering up the prominence created by the colostomy bag.

Brenda had everything ready to be served up family style again. A simple but delicious meal. The past month had taken its toll on Leslie's figure. She could tell that her pants were fitting a little bit tighter. Nothing out of control, just a little tight. She would get on a diet when she got to Evansville.

Doc went on about some patients, the surgery on Jesús, emergency room call and a couple of other things that weren't that important. Brenda chatted about the office help, billing problems and the difficulties with all of the Privacy Act stuff. Small talk.

They got quiet and Leslie could hear chewing, the second hand on a wall clock, a knife clinking against the plate. She looked over at Booker and Jake. Jake caught the movement. His head popped up and she could see the beginning of a tail wagging. Booker knew better. No chance for food yet. Mom and dad were in there. His head stayed down, eyes closed.

"Leslie, Hal and I were wondering what you were up to." Brenda got to the point. "I mean, we were thinking about after you leave here and all. I guess we were wondering about your home and your family."

"You're wondering about a lot of things, I know, and I'm sorry I wasn't more up front with you from the beginning. I'm going to tell you as much as I can, and as much as I know." She knew she owed them that much.

"Honey, you don't have to tell us a thing if you don't want to. I think we just want to try to understand, or help, or something. I just wish we had met three years ago. You needed someone then. It breaks my heart to think of you out there, alone."

"Now Brenda, Doc here can take care of herself. Don't you doubt it for a minute."

"Hal, you hush for a minute. I know she can earn a living. I'm talking about other things."

Leslie then told Doc and Brenda all about the accident. She left out the part about the kisses and the way Chris' leg was twisted under the sheet. Brenda was openly crying and using her napkin to dry her eyes. Doc got up to get something to drink.

She told them about selling her houses and leaving her practice and putting the keepsakes in a storage room. She left out the part about the marbles and the mausoleum and the three wooden crosses out on 299. Brenda took Leslie's hand and held it.

She told them about the past three years of keeping on the move. Abilene was just another stop, albeit an overextended one.

Doc just shook his head. "I'm amazed that you could do that."

"I've gotten used to it."

"Listen, Leslie, Brenda and I have been talking about some things. You know, this surgery, the cancer and all, have really gotten me to thinking about my practice and really, about my life. Now I feel fine and all, but I'm just getting to where I don't want to work such long hours. I want to take time off, do some traveling. You know that sort of thing."

"Leslie, what Hal is trying to get out is that we surely would love for you to come here and stay in Abilene. You know, work here for good. Join Hal."

"Well, I guess now that they shut off my asshole, the other end's not working either," he said, laughing at Brenda's interruption.

Leslie laughed too, glad for something to break the tension.

"Brenda and I have really enjoyed working with you. The patients like you. Hell, they're even asking about you and that's a first. You know I've had *locum tenens* docs before and most of them aren't fit to live with. There's a reason some of those fellas aren't in a practice, but you're different. You're just different in a lot of ways and both of us felt it when we met you. I'd be honored to have you join me. I need a partner."

"Doc, I don't know what to say," Leslie replied, touched by the offer. "I've really enjoyed working with you too, and I think that if I had my act together I would ask you to show me where to sign up. The problem is, I don't have it together yet. If I did, I'd still be practicing in New Paltz and we might have passed each other in the hall at some orthopedic meeting. For me, there's a problem with falling into a wonderful practice like yours, just like there is a problem with falling in love. I'm afraid to fall. I made a mistake coming here for a month. I got to know you guys. I got to know Regan Wakeman. Now I care about you. The last people I cared about are dead."

"But that's not your fault, Leslie." As she said it her words trailed off ever so slightly as she realized a common expression to give comfort to most, had a different meaning to Leslie.

"I know what you're trying to say. I'm not implying that because I care about someone, they die. I mean I've had my fill of the inevitable. I've developed a formula for peace of mind as I know it. If I keep moving, I don't connect. Doc, you said I was different than others and that's why you liked working with me. I appreciate the thought. I really do. There's a side of me that is grateful for what this time in Abilene has done. It's made me realize that even though my heart still has the capacity to care, my original pathway works and keeps me from loving and caring and getting too confused. It just works. I'm sorry to have to tell you that. Abilene is a wonderful place and if I could, I would stay."

Doc reached over and squeezed Brenda's hand. "Well, we didn't expect you to change your mind this quickly, but we wanted to make the offer." Then he poured himself a glass of tea. "So, your next stop is Indiana."

"Right. Another *locums* position in Evansville, Indiana. It's just a one week shift. That's my usual. One week or less. The two guys in this practice are taking their families on a vacation together."

"Then what?"

"I don't know. I haven't made any plans yet beyond Evansville. To tell you the truth, I'm thinking about going home. If you can call it home now."

"Of course it's your home, Leslie. Your husband and children are there, in their way. They need you to watch over them. You are their guardian. Not some old grounds keeper."

Leslie thought about their space in the mausoleum. Cold. Impersonal. No meaning. Just a rented space. Not like Regan's cemetery. There was history there. There was love and attention, pride. She pictured Chris, Vic and Vivi's graves in the Wakeman cemetery. Vic and Vivi's graves would have the same birth days and the same death day, which would be shared by all three. Someone looking at those gravestones a hundred years from now would be struck by the chilling dates like she was by the graves of Regan's great grandmother and stillborn child. The history of Chris, Vic and Vivi's lives was with her. It ended with her.

"Well, if you ever change your mind about things, and think you could put up with an old fart like me and a dry town like Abilene, the offer's there. Just for the record."

"Thanks Doc. Really, I mean it."

"And I sure hope I could call you again if I ever needed another vacation. Only a week or less, of course."

"Of course you could."

They finished dinner and went to the living room to drink coffee. The dogs followed, Jake yawning with a little half howl, mouth open wide at the sides.

Leslie wasn't coming in on Thursday. They struggled with goodbyes. She went over her plans for Jesús, were she staying. How long to keep him on crutches and in a brace, range of motion restrictions.

She hugged Brenda and shook Doc's hand, firmly. They all wished each other the best and said they hoped they would see each other at a meeting one day. But Leslie never went to meetings.

36

*L*eslie drove out of Doc's neighborhood in the direction of Regan's ranch. She called him on the way to let him know she was coming. His voice so calm, so confident, so Regan and for some reason it reassured her. He would not make it hard on her, and that's what made it hard on her. She had stayed too long. Why didn't she just get on a plane tonight? She was selfish. She wanted to hear his voice, see him, and feel him one more time. What did Regan want? Same thing Doc and Brenda wanted. To keep her. She wasn't anyone's to keep.

As she pulled up to his house Leslie suddenly felt sorry for Regan even though she knew he would never want that from her. She knocked on the door. There was light coming from the kitchen. Warm apricot colored light. There was dim lighting from the living room and from upstairs. Through the window in the front door Leslie had a panoramic view of his house. Regan appeared at the top of the stairs and waved. He had on warm-ups, a T-shirt. No shoes. He hopped down the stairs, very casually, easily. He opened the door and stepped aside for her to enter. She smelled coffee.

There was extraordinary warmth to the house tonight. Like a Christmas house. The wooden floors, the old dark crown molding, the smell of coffee brewing. She felt as if she had never seen it before. Regan closed the door, stepped up behind her and put his arms around her. He kissed her gently on the neck.

"This is my favorite place in the house. You can see more rooms from here than from any other spot. If you're standing right here, in this spot, you don't know if it's now or nineteen hundred, but if you take two steps in any direction, you know exactly when you are here."

Leslie felt like she should turn around and she made a slight move to her left. He held her tight. "Nope. I want you to stay just like this. I don't want to see your face when I say this. I'm only going to say it once and then we go on, I promise. I don't want this night to be hard on you or me." He kissed her again, leaving his face against her hair. "I want you to come back. Tomorrow, in a week, whenever, I don't care. I just want you to stand with me here again." Now he turned her around, but he didn't look her in the eyes when he bent down to kiss her. And with that kiss he asked her to stay again thereby breaking his promise.

Before she could say anything, he pulled away, and the moment was gone. "Now take two steps back. It's two thousand four." He pointed to his right. To the living room. "Do you play?" A box of dominoes rested on a small table.

"As a matter of fact I have. I wouldn't say I do, because I haven't played since I was a kid. My dad and his buddies used to play and every once in a while they would let me in."

"Let's get coffee and see whatch'ya got."

The dominoes were wonderfully ancient. She guessed they were ivory or bone, yellowed, used. The pips were not painted on, but separate inlayed pieces of ebony. About six of the twenty-eight pieces were a slightly different shade of yellow, a lighter patina. Even though the same size, the wear on the edges and the color and size of the pips was different. Replacements for lost dominoes. They took their seats across from each other. Regan turned the dominoes face down and mixed them up with his fingers, the ivories making the familiar soft chinking noise. They did rock, paper, scissors to see who went first. Leslie could never win with that method. Regan went first and won several times until she got the hang of the game again. They played for three hours straight, getting up only to fix more coffee. Leslie was happy with the diversion.

Before long they both started yawning, and Regan sent Leslie up to bed while he cleaned up and turned off the lights. He kissed her tenderly before she went to bed, and she felt like it was a goodnight or maybe a goodbye kiss, but really didn't pay much attention to it. She went upstairs, brushed her teeth and got into bed. She fell asleep, perhaps thinking that Regan would wake her up when he came upstairs.

After finishing the dishes, he absentmindedly wiped down the granite counter tops and then picked up the dominoes and put them in their worn wooden box. Lastly, he turned out the lights to the barns, around the house and the kitchen.

Upstairs Regan heard Leslie's deep, regular breathing. The light in the bathroom was still on and he sat down in a chair beside the bed and looked at his lover. Her eyes moved slightly under her lids and he knew she must have been tired. He wondered how well she slept. Maybe didn't sleep very well at all. She was asleep now. He could see a small gap between her lower and upper lids. The lashes crossed over the space but behind them he could see her irises moving erratically from side to side. The rhythm of her breathing was unchanged. He stood up, bent over slowly and kissed her eyelid, then breathed in the scent of her skin. Perhaps he hoped she would wake up. The movement caused no more than a slight change in the rhythm of her breathing. Regan walked around the foot of the bed, got undressed and climbed in under the sheets.

Leslie heard noises and felt movement around her. She slowly opened her eyes. She saw the strangest thing and wasn't sure what to make of it. In front of her was a desk, like her desk from grade school. There were etchings on the top of it. Little flowers and stars, angles and squares, doodles. One square stood strangely on end, 3-D. They circled the pencil slot carved into the top of the desk.

Chris was sitting at the desk. It was so strange to see him there, but she wasn't surprised. She tried to reach out to him. For some reason she couldn't move her arm. He laughed and she could see the little scar on his lip where he had cut it as a child. It was small but he always kept a moustache because of it. The scar was light and she could only see it when he shaved. She was surprised the first time he shaved after they were married. Surprised to know her husband had a secret scar. When he smiled deep creases appeared on both sides of his mouth. His left front tooth protruded just a bit in front of the one next to it. She could see his face perfectly clear now, even down to the tiny caramel colored birthmark under his right eye. His hair was longish, like when they met, but his face was older, like when...

Noises came from out in the hallway. She could see the front door of the house and she could see all the rooms from the bed. She was confused. Kept her eyes closed tight. Then she could see the hallway.

Victor was standing in the doorway. Just standing there. Looking at Chris. There was no sense in this. Vivian was sitting on a picnic blanket on the floor. An old bedspread they converted to a picnic blanket when it was too beat up to put on a bed any more. She was playing with dominoes, standing them on end, in rows and then tipping them over. The twins' faces were clear at first, but then she couldn't keep them in focus. Chris just sat there and slowly Leslie's conscious mind began to realize that she was dreaming. She tried to squeeze her eyes closed. Victor waved, to her? Or did he wave to Chris. She tried to call them. "Vvv," was all the muscles of her mouth would allow. "Vvv." It was more like air passing between her teeth and lower lips.

"Leslie."

She started to cry, but it wasn't really crying. Just a muffled sob. The strange paralysis of sleep had contorted the muscles of her mouth, tongue and vocal chords.

"Baby. Wake up." She felt a hand on her hip. Chris was reaching. For her, or for the kids. He was gone. There was a chair next to the bed.

Regan turned her over on her back. Tears were welling up in the corners of her eyes. He gathered her in his arms. "Leslie, you were dreaming. You were talking. I couldn't wake you up for a second."

"I don't know what I saw. It was so strange." She was crying now and the tears rolled down the side of her face. "I was here, but Chris was there and the..."

Regan was kissing her. Holding her. He kissed her tears against her face.

"Shhh. It's okay. You're okay."

Leslie kissed him back and tasted her salty tears on his lips. In the next breath the kiss of tenderness and protection became desire. Leslie and Regan made love for the last time. They were sweating when they stopped and the room was cool. The wind was blowing through the open windows. The curtains billowed softly into the room. The sweat on their bodies evaporated quickly, cooling their skin. Regan pulled the blankets over them. Leslie turned on her side and looking out the door of his bedroom could see only a banister.

37

*I*n the morning Regan got up early so he could be at work by six. Leslie made coffee while he showered and got dressed. They had already decided he wouldn't see her off at the airport that evening. Leslie didn't think she could deal with an airport goodbye and he had accepted her decision.

He encouraged her to stay at the ranch for the day and do as she pleased, ride a horse, walk around, go back and look at the petrified wood. He had even made a little map for her. As he left, Regan kissed her and then just a few words. He kept it short, simple. She would call him when she got to Evansville. Then he was gone. She heard his truck drive away, deep reluctant sounding diesel engine, early on a cool morning.

After showering and putting the sheets in the washer, she had another cup of coffee. She walked around the house, even snooped in his medicine cabinet. She smelled his cologne. One of the bedrooms was a study. Even though he had given her the cook's tour already, she wanted more. She looked at the books he read. She wanted, but decided not, to look at a photo album on one of the shelves. The stone absorbed the cool air that flowed through the open windows and circulated through old transoms and open doors, chilling the house.

Outside it was cloudy but didn't feel like rain. Leslie walked to the barn. The bales of hay lay where they were last weekend, the tarp folded up and tucked away on top of them. She could hear Cinco and Gomez snooping around the barn. She walked outside and down the drive leading away from the house. The two horses followed her as far as the end of their pasture. They stood in the corner of the pasture and watched her for a while, then turned to look for a patch of good grass.

The road approached a fence line clearing. A walk around the perimeter of the ranch would take too long. She would cut across the middle when time ran out. In West Texas, springtime doesn't bring forth the abundance of flowering plants seen in other parts of the country. Still, if she looked, there were plenty. Unusual plants had adapted to this dry climate. There were large numbers of dwarfed flowering plants which formed an early ground covering. Many had already bloomed, going into a growth phase after the freeze had been followed by uncommonly warm weather. She remembered that freeze and her first date with Regan.

Cutting across the corner of the property, Leslie found the clearing in the woods with the petrified tree. It was as fascinating as before. One day, maybe millions of years ago, a tree had fallen, or more likely was knocked over by a flood of ocean water, cutting off its oxygen supply. Leslie knelt down to look at the age lines and the knots in the wood. It was perfect. Silica had flawlessly replaced every bit of organic material in the tree. There was no evidence of prehistoric decomposition.

She sat down on one of the logs and convinced herself that she was ready to leave, regardless of her feelings for Regan. She was ready to go to Indiana, but even more than that she felt ready to go home. She would wait until she got to Evansville to return Lynn's call. What would she say? How would she feel when she saw Casey? Casey would remind her of Vivian. They were the same age. That twinge of jealousy was still there.

Suddenly a vision of Vivian sitting on the ground flashed through her mind. Parts of her dream came back to her piecemeal. Chris, Victor. She could see Chris' face so clearly. That which she had almost forgotten. Yearning for a message in the dream, she tried hard to remember but could only see the fragments and nothing that made any sense came to her. The dream was random.

Now she remembered how Regan woke her up, and that they made love. She pulled her knees up and wrapped her arms around her legs. How long would she be able to physically remember that? Within three years she could hardly recall the appearance of her husband's face.

At three o'clock Leslie left Clear Fork Creek Ranch. She left things clean. Clean sheets on the bed. She thought about leaving a note but couldn't think of anything to say that hadn't been said already.

Kala greeted her from the desk. "You will be checking out today, Doctor Cohen?"

"Yes, Kala. Can you put my charges on the credit card?"

She laid out the clothes she would wear on the plane and began to pack. She doubted she would need any of the inexpensive cold weather clothes she had purchased at Wal-Mart. They were tossed on a chair. She left her western jeans and boots too. No need for them where she was going. She decided to exchange one of her older pair of jeans for the more updated version and kept the olive green turtle-neck sweater. She tenderly folded the denim skirt, tank top and sweater around her trophy buckle and placed them in the suitcase. She piled everything else on the chair and wrote a note to the housekeeping staff, "Maybe you can use these." Otherwise, experience told her, they would take it to lost and found and call her repeatedly requesting a mailing address. She avoided the aggravation with this simple note.

She calculated the time she would need to arrive at the airport in time to return her car and pass through security. She left the place that had been her home for the longest period of time since 2001. As the sliding doors closed behind her, she noted the light breeze and the clear sky. It was a good day to fly.

38

*R*egan was locking the utility room underneath the second tier of the home side bleachers. He had been preoccupied thinking about Leslie all day. He had nearly gone home at lunch time and then almost went to the airport. But they had an agreement. Leslie had made him promise. Now it was too late. He looked at his watch. 6:28. He knew this flight and was going to be here when it left. He was alone in the stadium.

Leslie took her assigned seat by the window. Exit row. It gave her more leg room. She fastened her safety belt and blocked out the speech about oxygen masks. As the engines whined, then roared and the plane backed away from the gate, she settled into her seat turning her head toward the little window on her left. The setting sun was so bright she pulled down the shade. Then, closing her eyes, she caught a tear between the lids as she tilted her head back.

The plane moved out on the tarmac. Now the sun moved to the other side of the plane and even through closed eyes she could sense its rays scanning the fuselage. The engines went full throttle, and the cabin began to vibrate. She opened her eyes. Tears blurred her vision as the body of the 737 surged forward.

Regan listened to the jet engine. Its roar came across the city, the sound waves distorted by wind and buildings and silos. From the construction site he had been listening to planes take off from Abilene Regional airport for over a year. He unlocked the utility room.

Leslie felt the pressure as the plane accelerated. It pushed her back into her seat. The front wheels lifted, and it seemed that the plane stayed suspended in this position longer than usual. Her heart raced for a second. In a moment the plane took a small lunge and broke free of the bonds of gravity. Her ears popped, and she swallowed. She heard the familiar whir of the wheels as they withdrew into the body of the plane. The sound was accompanied by the change in resistance to air. Through the windows on the right side of the cabin she saw the wing lift and then felt the tilt.

The pilot came on over the loudspeaker. "Ladies and gentleman, if you are sitting on the left side of the plane you can see the new Anson Jones Stadium, a multi-million dollar project of the Abilene Independent School District, scheduled to open this fall."

Regan pulled open the door of the utility room and threw the switch to all of the stadium lights. There was a loud knock, followed by the collective hum of five hundred halogen lights coming on above the stadium.

A little boy sitting with an elderly woman in front of Leslie said, "Look, Nana, they just turned on the stadium lights for us!" Leslie opened her shade to look out the window.

Regan ran as fast as he could up the second tier of bleachers toward the press box. He saw the jet just start to bank above the horizon. Its shiny body reflected pink from the sunset. He took the stairs to the top, two at a time. As he got there the plane was straightening out, heading directly to his left. He could see the windows and the belly of the plane. The roar was tremendous. He knew everyone would be looking at the stadium. He took off his ball cap and waved.

The air quieted and Regan watched the plane until it became a speck. He blinked and when he opened his eyes it was gone. He walked down the stairs and stood at the top of the concrete structure. The lights were perfect. Not a single bulb was burned out. A few bugs had already found the new beacon in their midst. Somewhere across the stadium he heard a clanging noise he hadn't noticed before. Regan made a note to check it out in the morning.

39

*H*al Hawley had just finished seeing the last patient on a Wednesday evening when Brenda walked into his office and stood by his desk.

"Regan Wakeman is on line one."

"Well, put him through." He punched the button next to the green flashing light. "Regan, Hal Hawley here. What can I do ya for?"

Brenda listened and watched Doc's face.

"Well, that does sound a little strange, son." He got quiet for a moment, then glanced up at Brenda. "Uh huh. Well. Listen, Regan, I think maybe we need to talk."

More silence. Doc leaned back in his chair.

"Anytime's okay with me. You could come here to the office or out to our place."

He sat back up.

"Sure, come on over. See you in a sec."

He hung up.

"Well, what did Regan want?"

"Apparently he's been trying to reach Leslie on her cell phone for almost two weeks and now it's been disconnected. Keeps getting a recording. He wanted to know if I had heard anything."

"Well, have you?"

"I haven't talked to Leslie since we had dinner with her."

"So why would her phone be disconnected?"

"I'm not sure, sweetheart. But you know, there's something about that phone thing that kind of rings true to me. I don't know. It's just a hunch, but do you remember how I told you about my conversation with Frank Long and the story about Leslie and her family?"

"Yes, but what's that got to do with the phone?"

"Well, I just remember that the guy who was Frank's old med

school buddy told him something about Leslie's best friend trying to track her down and it taking three years to do it. You know, I told you how she sold her house and everything."

"Yes, and..."

Well, it's seems like Frank told me she disconnected her phone and that's why her friend couldn't reach her."

"Hal, you don't think she'd do that again do you? Just to keep Regan from finding her?"

"You know, Brenda, I don't know what she'd do. Even if it doesn't make any sense to you or me, it seems pretty clear that Leslie's trying to keep from putting down any roots or having other people to worry about. I guess we'd have to walk in her shoes to be able to think like she thinks."

"So what are you going to tell Regan? Do you think Leslie told him the truth?"

"I don't think she did. But we'll soon find out."

Brenda went up to the front desk to close out the books and make sure everyone was checked out. She then went back to Doc's office and told him that she was going to go home once Regan got there.

"Chickening out on me, eh?"

"No. I just think this would be better coming from you than from the two of us. And I might just start crying anyway. I don't know why, but that Leslie just touched me so. And it kind of breaks my heart to think that she might have touched Regan the same way."

"Well, you go on then. I'll see to him."

They heard the front door open. "Anybody home?"

Brenda hadn't seen Regan in a number of years and had forgotten just how handsome he was. Taller and bigger than Hal, she felt a little intimidated. She reached out to shake his hand at the same time he reached for hers.

"Miss Hawley."

"Regan, it's good to see you. Let's see, I can't even remember the last time I saw you."

"I think it was my dad's funeral."

"Goodness, has it been that long? How's your sister doing?"

"She's fine. Thanks for asking."

"Hal's waiting for you in the back. I'll show you to his office and then I've got some things to look after." Before directing Regan into Doc's office, Brenda turned to face him. "We sure do miss Leslie, Regan."

"Well, you're not the only ones." He smiled, but behind the attractive smile was a certain sadness.

"Hal, Regan's here to see you." They shook hands again. "Regan, let's not be strangers now."

"Regan. Come on in. Sit down, sit down." He indicated the chairs in front of the desk. Regan reached out his rough hand to shake Doc's thick one, both grasping firmly.

"Doc, it's good to see ya."

"Same here. Did I hear you tell Brenda that we haven't seen you since your daddy's funeral?"

"I think that's about right. It's been a while anyway. Doc, you're looking good," he said, taking a chair.

"Yeah, well, you can say it. The cancer word. I'm doing fine. They think they got it all. I'm not ready for them to put me down just yet."

Regan laughed. "Well, that's good news. I appreciate your taking the time to talk to me."

"So, tell me about this business with Leslie's phone."

"Well, I started trying to call Leslie shortly after she left town. Maybe a couple of days later. Anyway, at first I just got her answering service so I didn't think much of it. She's a busy lady. But after about four days, it was hard to think that it was just oversight or business. After about a week I began to feel a little rejected. To be honest with you Doc, I felt pretty serious about Leslie. Asked her to stay or come back."

"Yeah, we did the same. I even asked her to stay and join the practice."

"Really. That's pretty amazing. She didn't say a thing about it."

"It's the truth," Hal said, putting his hand up like he was taking an oath.

"Then this week, the recording changed to one of those 'this number has been disconnected' type of messages. I had reached a dead end. To tell you the truth, I've been pretty frantic about this situation. I don't even know if I really know who she is."

"You may be closer to the truth in that regard than you think." Doc wished immediately that he hadn't said that in such a flippant way.

"Doc, I need to find Leslie. What's going on?"

"Regan, what do you know about Leslie's past?"

"She's an orthopedic surgeon. And she's a widow, of a year more or less."

Doc put both of his hands up. "And that's what we knew as well. About the first fact, you can rest easy. According to our credentialing process, she is a *bona fide* orthopedic surgeon. And a damn good one I might add."

Doc then told Regan everything he knew. He felt a little guilty telling the story without Leslie's permission.

"I knew it. I knew she had kids. She was a mother. God, I can't bear to think about it. There was something about her. That emptiness. It doesn't come from a husband or a wife. It comes from kids. I would have never let her go if I had known."

"Regan, if you had known, she wouldn't have been the gal you..."

"Fell in love with. I told her but I didn't tell her. You know what I mean. What the hell am I gonna do now?"

Regan sat quietly for a minute, looking down at his lap. He tried to remember the signs of her motherhood that he should have picked up on. He cursed himself for not asking. His intuition told him that she had children. Maybe children lost in a divorce. He would never have guessed death. When they were in the kitchen and she started to say something about cooking and eating out. Whatever it was, he could remember it didn't sound right.

Two kids, twins, and her husband in a car accident. All at one time. And maybe her fault. He couldn't even imagine it. If he had known, he would have held her every minute he could. He would have made her a promise. Then he looked up. "I'm gonna go get her, that's what."

"How're you going to do that?"

"Well, she left here and went to Indiana. Then where? Did she give any indication of what she was doing next? Another job?"

"Well, now that you mention it, she said she was thinking about going home." A smile came across Regan's face.

40

*R*egan packed his bags that night after he got a call from Doc Hawley who had tracked down a Dr. Peterman. He had a phone number for Leslie's best friend. Regan would call her when he was close to New Paltz. He wanted to have the advantage of surprise. It would take a couple of days to drive to New York. Sixteen hundred miles plus or minus a hundred, depending on his route.

Cal could take care of things while he was gone.

For now he planned to drive east on I-20, and would decide later when to go north. When he needed to rest he would pull over and check into a motel. Sleep. Get up. Start over. Regan thought about Leslie and the images helped keep him awake. Where would he find her? How would she react? He envisioned their reunion. He couldn't wait.

Regan drove all day, stopping only for lunch and coffee. Staying on I-20 took Regan all the way through Louisiana. As he crossed the state line into Mississippi the sun went down and it started to rain. Regan decided to look for someplace to sleep and went north on the Natchez Trace Parkway heading to Tupelo.

41

*R*egan had to turn his wipers on high to clear the windshield enough to see. They slashed water across his view. He was tired and wished he hadn't pushed himself so far. There was a lot of water on the road, and he hydroplaned a couple of times. He slowed down once but as he got comfortable with the driving conditions he inadvertently accelerated. Signs on the road indicated he didn't have far to go.

Up ahead was another car. He gained on it quickly. Driving slowly, way under the speed limit, on a highway. Some people. He was irritated because the diesel engine was harder to gear up for passing. No lights in the oncoming lane and no double center line. He dropped back a little and then stepped on the gas, giving himself plenty of distance to pass the car before he pulled back over.

Now the car he'd passed was speeding up behind him and parking itself right behind the trailer. He couldn't see it unless he went around a curve. It was really irritating him. People who don't pull trailers have no appreciation for those who do. He was always tense when pulling a trailer.

Regan was determined to leave the car behind, but it was tailgating him. Occasionally he would see its headlight shine into his side view mirror. He felt a drag as his truck hit pooling water on the road, followed by an echo as the trailer did the same. He had driven in rain a lot and was confident in his rig and driving ability. But that damn car was distracting him.

Then, going a little too fast, he hit more water on a curve. He anticipated the echo from the trailer, but there was none. He started hydroplaning. He touched the brake pedal. No response. Then again. Nothing. Regan shoved the brake pedal down now. He felt the rapid fire pumping of his anti-lock brakes, but the rig didn't respond and then, in his driver's side mirror, he saw his brand new four horse trailer sliding out sideways from behind him.

"Shit," Regan said out loud as he felt an impact from behind and his truck lunged forward. He quickly turned his steering wheel to the left. Looked up ahead. Road empty, thank God. He was driving in the oncoming lane. Once he felt the trailer lock in behind him, he gently turned back the other way. Trailer moving. Righting itself. "Now, where's that car?"

As the trailer swung back in place behind him he felt another crash. He couldn't see. Too dark. Too much rain. He just kept pulling forward. Driving.

Then, his heart racing, he pulled over as quickly as he could. Put the truck in park, called 911, and jumped out. It was pouring and he was soaked in an instant. He ran toward the car. It looked like it was totaled. Talking out loud as he ran, "Be okay, be okay."

"Hey, you okay?" The safety glass was broken but firmly intact. He tried the door. It was smashed in and wouldn't budge. He ran back to the truck and got a crowbar out of the tool box.

He pried the door open. There was a woman inside. The airbag was deployed but she didn't have her seat belt fastened. Regan reached in the car and put his hand on her shoulder. "Are you okay?"

She mumbled something. "I think so." She was breathing rapidly. Short catchy breaths. No time for worrying about neck problems. He reached in, pulled her out and placed her on the ground. He took off his jacket and used it to shield her from the rain.

"Talk to me. Where does it hurt?"

"My chest. Can't catch...my breath."

"I've called for help. They're on their way. Just hang on." She was pale. And very pretty. He pushed her curly hair back from the sides. There was blood in her left ear.

"Ma'am, what's your name?"

She tried to answer. Her lips moved. He heard a gurgling noise in her throat or somewhere. He started thinking through the CPR stuff he had learned a long time ago.

"You just stay with me now. You hear me. Just stay with me." There was no conviction in his voice.

She opened her eyes a little and smiled up at him. "I was...too... close. I'm sor..."

"Hey, shh, shhh. Don't talk." Regan heard the last breath. A hollow sound. Her eyes were still open but not looking. Was she still smiling?

"Come on now, don't leave me." He patted her cheeks. Nothing. He felt for a pulse at her wrist. He bent over, tilted her head back slightly, put his lips on hers and blew a deep breath into her mouth. A strange hollow sound came from her chest. He felt for her sternum. Put the heel of his palm there. The other hand on top and pushed. Something felt entirely wrong.

Regan slowly sat down and leaned against the Taurus. He put his head back against the car and looked up at the sky. Rain coming down hard. The strips of water seemed to arc away as they fell to earth. He tasted salt from his own eyes, mixed with the taste of rain. In the distance he could see flashing lights.

42

"You know, I don't know why I bothered to get us packed up last night if we were going to add fifty million things to the suitcases this morning."

"Honey, I don't know why you did it either. You knew the kids would want to add more stuff. It happens every time. Let's not worry about it. We don't have to catch a plane. We'll just get there when we get there."

"I know, but you know how I love to get there early and walk up to the tower before lunch."

"Kids, come on! I'm going to count to two hundred and twenty-three and you'd both better be in the car or no McDonald's! We'll just eat cereal here and you can take your time. One, one thousand, two, one thousand..."

Two blonde, curly headed kids came running down the stairs, arms full of toys. "We're ready. Let's go."

"This time I'm going to beat you to the top."

"Wanna make a bet?"

"Yeah, I'll bet you a dollar that I get to the top before you do."

"Fine. And if I win then I get to use your PlayStation all next week."

"All right kids. Let's not argue about who's getting to the top first because you know your dad and I are going to win."

Vivian eased over and hugged her mother. "How about you and me beating dad and Victor," she said quietly as she looked at Leslie with expectant eyes.

Leslie winked at her. Their secret plan.

Both the Volvo and the BMW were packed up with stuff for the weekend. Way too much stuff. Both kids got into the Volvo without even looking at the BMW. She felt a little pissed because one of them could have at least driven with her to McDonalds. It was only after they got their food that they knew she wouldn't want them to ride in the BMW. Still.

She followed Chris to the neighborhood shopping center and parked next to him. The kids ran in and got in line. Chris followed. She asked him to get her a cup of coffee.

Leslie couldn't control her aggravation with the whole situation. She had spent all of last night packing so they could leave early and now she was odd man out. Having to drive behind Chris and the kids just so they could eat their Egg McMuffins in his car. And so she could drive back early on Monday morning to do surgery on Betty Fergesen.

Chris delivered Leslie's coffee to her. He reached into her car and pulled her gently toward him, kissing her on the side of her head. "Hey, it's just fifteen minutes. Then I'll race you up to the tower." She smiled.

He opened the Volvo doors with his remote. The twins climbed in. Leslie suddenly realized she hadn't kissed them goodbye. She had a little wrenching feeling in her stomach. She reached up to push the button that opened the sunroof. Leslie blew a kiss to the kids and waved through the sunroof. They blew kisses back to her. She followed Chris out of the parking lot. They headed to Mohonk Mountain House on Highway 299.

It was a beautiful day. Cloudless sky. The sun was warm through the sunroof.

Chris watched to make sure that Leslie was behind him when he got on 299. There she was, probably PO'ed. He didn't blame her. He felt bad about how the morning had gone and looked forward to getting to Mohonk.

The car smelled like Egg McMuffins and hash browns. He looked in the rear view mirror again. He could see Leslie close behind him. The distinctive BMW headlights looking at him like an eagle. He thought one of these days he was going to stick an Egg McMuffin under her seat, just to mess with her. He laughed to himself. Looked again. Leslie's curly hair was blowing all around her. She looked so pretty. Like a mermaid.

As they headed out of town, Chris gathered speed. The kids were making a lot of racket in the back. He was thinking about going around a slower car up ahead. He looked in his rear view mirror again. Leslie was right there and he saw her reach up to close her sunroof. Then he heard screeching brakes. The guy in front of him had slammed on his brakes and he was coming up fast. He pushed as hard as he could on the brake pedal. The kids screamed. "Daddy!"

He looked at them for a second and then to Leslie who was right up on top of him. He braced himself, now helpless. "Hold on, kids."

At that moment the car in front pulled away. He had braced himself for the impact from behind, but it didn't come. An eighteen wheeler sped by in the oncoming lane. As it passed, the displaced air hit the Volvo and he felt a shudder. He accelerated and pulled over into the slower traffic lane. Looked behind him. Leslie waved. Blew him a kiss. He saw her pat her dashboard. Good dog. Their sign for a well-behaved car. Chris waved back.

The kids were laughing in the back.

"Look, daddy!"

A whirlpool of air had caught one of the hash brown bags in its current and was spinning it around in an absurd little circle.

Printed in the United States
100488LV00008B/28/A